Journey to Unknown Consequences

A novel

By John H Gray

All characters and events in this book are fictitious. Any similarity to real persons, living or dead, is coincidental and not intended by the author.

.

Other works by the author:

Journey of Betrayals (2017)

ISBN 978-0-9952387-1-8

Acknowledgments

I must thank all those who encouraged me to write the sequel to 'Journey *of Betrayals.*'

To my wife Bobbie I again thank her for all her patience during the process.

The challenge I faced was to write this book for new readers who have not read 'Journey *of Betrayals'* and make it appeal as a new book and avoid confusion with the characters and story, yet make the story continue for previous readers of 'Journey of Betrayals'. In this regard, I thank Michele Thorne again for her thoughtful insight and comments.

I extend a special thank you to Dawn Frobisher who sampled parts of the book and gave an unbiased reaction. For the special assistance I received in Aruba from Beverly Williams-Perez.

Thanks go to the US Coast Guard Office of Public Affairs in Washington, D.C. for providing answers and information to my many questions.

I also thank the Trans National Institute (TNI) in The Netherlands who have special NGO consultative status with UN Ecosoc since 1974, for the information on the smuggling, money laundering, drugs and other crime in the Caribbean during the 1960's

Foreword

"Journey to Unknown Consequences" is the sequel to "Journey of Betrayals" in which the lead character, Jakob Klassen, betrayed and used many friends and accomplices while searching for his ancestral relatives. After some tumultuous times during WWII in Europe, Jakob settles into a relatively calm life on the Caribbean Island of Aruba in the Dutch West Indies.

Following on from his adventures and dramas in the book "Journey of Betrayals", this story follows Jakob's curiosity regarding the consequences of his actions on those he had encountered and betrayed during his European adventures during the years of WWII. His later life in Aruba has been good for Jakob and his family, though not without some heavy drama. In "Journey to Unknown Consequences", new and unsavory forces challenge his family's businesses. Jakob's continued thoughts and reminiscences play on his conscience and torment him as they increase in frequency. Finally he convinces his second wife, Solange, whom he married after his first wife was shot by a Nazi patrol while attempting an escape from Holland, that he needs to settle things in his mind. He is getting older and needs to find some peace.

After seeking out information on the whereabouts of the

people who had helped him in his past, Solange and Jakob set off on the adventure together not knowing what the consequences of Jakob's earlier actions had been and how those he had betrayed would react. Nor do they realize the situation they are leaving behind in Aruba. Jakob's attempts at reconciliation are rejected by some. Others accept that what he had done, and how he had acted, was due to the circumstances of war, desperation and immaturity.

The story has many interesting scenes threaded in and flowing on from the first book, "Journey of Betrayals."

Part 1

A Silent Shadow emerges over Paradise

Chapter 1

Savaneta, Aruba.1960

The Aruban summer was dwindling to a conclusion. It had been a long, dry and blistering hot summer. Many of the locals had sought daily relief on the velvety white sand beaches and relaxed in the turquoise waters with the cool of the steady trade winds.

At a small waterfront Villa in Savaneta, Jakob and his wife Solange had joined with Carlita to celebrate the birthday of her missing husband's cousins, who were twins named Miguel and Alejandro. Carlita's husband, Juan was both loved and respected in the small fishing community. His impact on the community was so strong that the neighbors and friends still talked about him. It was now two years he had been missing.

The guests at the party had left. Jakob sat alone on the beachfront porch relaxing and enjoying the late Sunday afternoon while waiting for the sunset. At this time of year he particularly enjoyed the Aruban sunsets with the golden and pink clouds framing the sun as it dropped into the western ocean.

 Carlita's husband, Juan, had gone missing while fishing. Since then Jakob and Solange had become confidantes and Carlita's closest friends. They would often hold family dinners at Carlita's at which Juan's relatives....Miguel and Alejandro and their families would attend. They had become a tight little group. Jakob and Solange had guided and assisted them in their business ventures involving restaurants and real estate. They had all prospered but each of them missed Juan. He would never be forgotten by any of them for the contribution he had made to each and everyone.

A little earlier, as Jakob was leaving the porch to join the others inside, he had watched as a small boat raced to the shore, its small outboard engine screaming. It had slowed and beached on the sand in the low surf. Two men jumped from the boat and lifted an older man out and up onto the beach. They then raced back to the little inflatable boat and sped back out into the Caribbean. With the sun setting over the horizon and its intense rays bathing the small bay and the Villa, Jakob had squinted to try and identify the man. His heart leapt. For a moment he was sure it was Juan, but then realized that his aging eyesight was playing tricks on him.

Jakob sighed. He opened the door and entered the Villa. Carlita and Solange were fussing around the table placing bread and food on plates at the centre. When they were finished, the three sat to enjoy an early dinner and engage in light conversation.

Carlita passed around a carafe of sweet red table wine from which they each poured a glass. She spooned out a rich sopi into some hand potted bowls. Jakob loved the aroma of the stew. It reminded him of a traditional Mennonite meal that his former wife used to make and of the time they had spent together in Holland. His thoughts drifted back to those days. He was troubled as he thought about how he had abandoned her in Holland and how selfish he had been. It seemed as if now, each day there was something that reminded him of the months he had spent searching for ancestral relatives in Europe while she was left alone. He recalled the many surprises that he had uncovered during that journey.

As he sat quietly at the table, his thoughts drifted back to his parents, his early years and life on the family's farm in Canada. He wondered what it would be like now, after having been away for so many years. He still owned the farm and had leased it to a large Mennonite family who had migrated to Canada and wished to farm. The rent was meager but he didn't mind. His business ventures in Aruba paid him handsomely. He vowed that he would one day return with Solange to show her the beautiful lands that his father, Isaac Senior and mother Inge, had settled and developed.

Conversation drifted back and forth around the table. Carlita was watching Jakob with some concern.

"Jakob, you seem to be somewhere other than here with us. You look troubled."

"While leaving the porch I saw a strange thing happen at the beach. Two men came ashore in a small boat and left an old man on the beach. For a moment I thought it might be Juan. This thought has disturbed me. I should go and see this man and find out if he needs help."

"Please be careful, Jakob" said Solange. "You are not as young and strong as you once were".

Jakob laughed. "And no, I am not yet in the grave either".

Jakob pushed back from the table and went toward the door that lead out to the porch.

As he approached the door, there was a loud crash and it flew open.

An old man, dressed scruffily in torn dirty white cotton pants and a tattered pale blue shirt, crashed through the door and landed on the floor near where Jakob had been seated at the table. There was dried blood on the rear of his shirt. Jakob knelt to turn the man's head in an attempt to identify him. The face was burnt from exposure to the sun and elements. A salt encrusted knotted mess of a long grey beard hid the features of his face.

Jakob placed his hand over the man's heart. The pulse was slow and weak.

"Carlita, bring some water quickly. I think he is suffering from the sun. This man is weak and ill. He has heatstroke. Solange help me to gently turn him onto his back. We will try to give him a small amount of water. We must be careful doing this. Too much will cause him to choke or vomit."

Carlita returned with a small porcelain cup containing cold water. Solange took the cup and raised it to the man's dried and blistered lips. He did not make any attempt to drink. Jakob recalled how, when he had worked at the refinery, he had learned to treat a person with heatstroke. Jakob pushed his finger through the man's lips and into his mouth where he explored for anything that may obstruct getting the water into him. When he was satisfied that there was no problem, Jakob forced the edge of the cup through the man's lips and gently tilted the cup to give him some water.

Jakob asked Carlita to bring more water so they could cool his neck, hair and body.

As they bathed the man with the cool water his eyes flickered and a croaking sound emanated from his mouth. Suddenly his arms started flailing the air and the rasping croak turned into gibberish shouts.

Jakob looked at Solange and Carlita.

"He is delirious. We need to get him help. This person is seriously ill"

Carlita left the Villa and ran to the neighbor's house. She knocked vigorously on the front door. After the door was opened she quickly told them of the situation. The neighbor immediately agreed to drive to the local Doctor.

12

Chapter 2

Recovery for the man was a slow process. Carlita and Solange arranged a bed in the back room of the little Villa. After two days of intense care, he started to show encouraging signs. During the late afternoon of the third day he regained his consciousness and attempted to sit up on his own.

Carlita was startled. She telephoned Solange who was at her office and asked her to come to the Villa. It seemed like hours passed before Jakob and Solange arrived.

Jakob entered and immediately went to the man. The man's eyes darted around nervously. Jakob reassured him. "There is no need for you to be concerned. We will help you. What is your name?"

The man stared blankly at Jakob and spoke in a whisper. Jakob strained to listen. He could not understand the man. Carlita, who had been standing behind Jakob, knelt down beside him.

"Jakob, he is attempting to say something in Spanish. I speak this dialect of Spanish so let me assist."

Jakob nodded. "Please ask him his name. We will not ask too much right now. Let him get a little more strength and then we will find out what this is all about. Offer him some food."

Carlita spoke softly and clearly to the man. As she did so she sensed him relaxing. When she had finished Carlita turned to Jakob and Solange. "His name is Moreno. He is from Colombia. He has asked for a small meal of beans. That is something traditional for the Colombians."

As she spoke the man looked from one to another absorbing the situation. Every now and then he would glance at the door as though plotting an escape. Jakob watched intensely and was becoming concerned.

"Had trouble just arrived in their little paradise?" Jakob wondered.

Moreno turned toward Jakob and spat on the floor while shouting in Spanish.

Carlita looked shocked at the sudden outburst. She threw her hand across her mouth.

"Jakob, he does not trust you. He is using swear words that are some of the worst a Colombian would use."

Jakob walked forward to the man and place a hand on his shoulder. "Carlita, tell him he is safe with us. We will not harm him. Ask him why he is so upset."

Carlita engaged in conversation with Moreno for some time. When she had finished she turned to Jakob. "He is frightened and scared. He asks you do not contact the authorities. He is terrified someone will come looking for him. He refuses to tell me who those people are."

Moreno sat perfectly still and stared at Jakob.

Jakob turned back to Carlita.

"Carlita, I do not think it is safe for you and your children to be here alone with this man. Solange, do you agree that we take him back to our house in Malmok? If those men are planning to return and look for him they will search here in Savaneta, not in Malmok or Arashi. They would probably assume that he would not be able to make it that far up the coast or that he would go to San Nicolaas and try to escape by ship."

Solange stood thinking for a while.

"If you think we will not have trouble then I will agree. Maybe Carlita should join us for a few days to assist with translating the Spanish and helping us to understand his customs."

Carlita was delighted at the invitation and to stay with her best friend.

"Yes of course. Carlita is most welcome to stay. I will return later for her children."

Carlita ran to her room and set about packing some clothing and a few items into a canvas bag.

While Solange and Carlita prepared clothing and other items, Jakob went to assist Moreno up to their car. He opened the door onto the porch that faced the beach. He immediately stopped. The small inflatable boat that had brought Moreno was slowly cruising up the shore. The men on board had rifles slung over their shoulders and were scanning the shore. Jakob went back inside and quickly took Moreno to the rear door and half dragged him up to the car which was not visible from the beach. He ran back to the Villa and shouted for Solange and Carlita to hurry.

The women raced to the car. Solange sat in the front seat alongside Jakob, while Carlita sat in the back, and distanced herself from Moreno.

Jakob turned to Solange. "I am concerned that trouble may be visiting us. Something tells me that there is much more happening here with this person Moreno."

He pointed to the small boat moving slowly along the shore. "Those men are very determined to find him. They are not the same men who left him on the beach. "

Jakob selected low gear and gently eased the car up the narrow dirt packed drive and out onto the unpaved road.

As he did so he glanced at Moreno and observed that he had shrunk himself down from the windows of the car.

 They drove slowly northward crossing over the small bridge at Spaans Lagoon and followed the road as it wound past the water desalination and electricity generating plant at Balashi.

No one spoke. Eventually Solange turned to Carlita.

"Carlita, when we reach Oranjestad I will have Jakob stop. We will visit the market. I need fresh fruits and vegetables. While we shop, Jakob can take Moreno for a beer at one of the open air bars. Maybe that will help to make Moreno relax."

Carlita frowned but nodded her agreement. "What is Solange up to?" she wondered.

They crossed over the small bridge into Oranjestad and Jakob pulled over to the dock area where merchants were selling their produce. Fruit sellers immediately converged around their car. Solange leaned over as if to kiss Jakob's cheek. Instead she whispered quickly in his ear.

After Solange and Carlita exited the car, Jakob beckoned Moreno to join him and pointed to a small bar that was on a small lane that ran off the main street. Moreno smiled and together they walked to the bar.

Chapter 3

Malmok, Noord, Aruba.

The morning had presented Isaac Junior with several unexpected events. Isaac, the son of Jakob, had grown from the small boy who enjoyed childish adventures in the streams and cunucu of Aruba, into an astute and respected young businessman.

He had not expected any visitors to his home this morning nor had he received any advance information regarding the two men walking up to his front door. He did not know who they were or what their business was.

He greeted them at the door but blocked their entrance into his home.

"Yes. Can I assist you? I am Isaac Klassen Junior. I must advise you that I do not conduct business here in my home. If you wish we can schedule a meeting at my office where we can take notes and have access to any necessary information. Who are you and what is it you want to see me about?"

Isaac surveyed them closely. One was of huge stature with an acne pocked face and greased back thick black hair. The other was slim with sandy brown hair and penetrating eyes set deep in their sockets. Both were perspiring heavily in the early morning heat.

As they stood there in silence Isaac tried to assess who they were. He surmised they were neither cops, government representatives nor developers. His instincts told him to be wary. Nothing felt right. Why had they arrived unannounced at his home?

Finally the slim one spoke. "I am Tony Vitto. This is my associate Vincenzio. We have travelled here from Chicago and have a proposal we wish to make with an established business here in Aruba. We have checked out the Klassen operations and believe we can have a mutually beneficial success."

Isaac absorbed the information. "Gentlemen, I do not wish to be rude but if you wish to make a proposal then we must do it at the office where I will have other managers involved."

Tony Vitto spoke. "No. This is business for your ears only. We were told by your friend Hans that you would be most receptive."

The mention of the name Hans put Isaac immediately on edge. What had his half brother gotten the family into this time? Hans, the half brother sired by Jakob in Germany at the start of WWII with a prostitute had previously brought troubles to the family.

"If you wish to meet, those are my terms. If that is acceptable then tell me where I can contact you when the meeting is scheduled."

Tony Vitto spoke. "We are staying at a hotel "Golden Beach on the Water". The room is under my name. I suggest you do not wait too long before arranging this meeting. Things have a way of happening."

They backed away from the door and started down the cactus lined drive to where their large black car was parked. As they were walking away, Jakob and the others arrived and pulled into the driveway. Jakob was confused and studied the two men. He looked up to see Isaac standing in his doorway. Jakob sensed a problem. He had never seen these men on the Island before. Their dress in dark suits and their posture made him both curious and cautious. Recently there had been a number of shady and questionable characters arriving on Aruba from Miami and Venezuela.

Jakob watched as they pulled away. When they were gone he left the car and beckoned to Moreno to join him. Solange and Carlita walked quickly ahead eager to see Isaac's children.

Isaac greeted them and then frowned when he saw the scruffy man with Jakob.

"Who is this person with you, Jakob? Why have you brought him here?"

Jakob explained the strange arrival of Moreno and the subsequent activities of the small boat and the men who were obviously looking for him.

"I did not want to leave him at Carlita's. I feared for her safety from both this man Moreno and men who are presently searching Savaneta for him. I am asking you to help. You are very wise and also you speak and write fluent Spanish. That is what he speaks."

Isaac wanted to refuse but was intrigued by the situation.

"This day is certainly full of surprises."

Chapter 4

Caracas, Venezuela April 1960.

Tomasso (Red Tomato) Rossini looked from the second floor windows of his rented office out at the bustling traffic on the "Avenida Principal". Even at this hour in the day the pollution from the cars and trucks below was choking.

He was amazed at the wealth of the city. Venezuela was celebrating the commencement of the World Fair and some of the most prestigious and formidable companies in the world were participating...IBM, Ford, Eastman Kodak and many others. The Government had funded the construction of aquariums, new pavilions and venues. All around were the signs of extreme wealth that the oil economy had brought. Tomasso had never lived in such an affluent and prosperous country before. He mused to himself that the decision that the boys in Chicago had made was indeed a wise one. With the large Italian population and especially so many from Sicily, "The Sicilian Club" would do well in Venezuela.

He walked from the window across the office to the dark panelled wall and pressed a small white button. A panel slid open revealing a mirrored bar stocked with wines, whiskies and other spirits. Tomasso reached in and removed a bottle of carbonated water. He found that any alcoholic drink during the day caused him extreme tiredness in the hot climate of Venezuela.

He returned to the window and absently watched the action on the streets below. His mind was preoccupied with planning and implementing the mission he had been sent to put in place. The Colombian players had already been recruited and he had sent his Chicago lead man, Tony Vitto, across to that godforsaken barren rock of an island, Aruba. As much as Tomasso despised Aruba, he understood its importance in the plan. He would avoid all travel there unless it was essential. Tomasso was much too immersed in enjoying the excesses that Caracas had to offer with its many clubs, bars, gambling, women and deals. He realized he needed to be careful and keep himself in control or others could become envious and end his unabated pleasures. While the life he enjoyed was filled with excitement, it was not without danger from the local rival gangs. A bad decision could end up being reported to Chicago or worse still, in his demise. Tomasso decided he needed to curtail his nightly activities. He was becoming too well known and now questions were being asked. He swore to keep a lower profile until the plans were executed.

As he stood reflecting on the situation, the cream colored phone on his desk jangled alive. He frowned. Only the Chicago "office" had that number.

He reached over the desk and picked up the receiver. Instead of the crackling reception he normally encountered when answering calls from Chicago, the line was clear.

"Pronto" he muttered into the mouthpiece.

"Tomasso it is Tony. We have made contact with Isaac Klassen Junior here in Aruba. He received us very cool. We will need to play his game. He wants to arrange a meeting with his people. I have given him a little word that he needs to meet us soon. I am concerned that if we push too hard that things will not go well here. He doesn't seem like a guy we can scare too easily. The Klassens have a lot of friends here on the island. Vincenzio and I will be visiting some of our friendly families from the old country and some "executives" here in Aruba who are in the same line of business as us. Better they start considering being part of us."

"Whatcha wanna me to do aboud it? You know the plan. The head office will not go easy on you if you fuck this up. Do I maka myself clear you? Don't come cryin for help you turd."

Tomasso slammed the receiver back into its cradle.

"It is so dammed hard to get good help." He said aloud. "Shit, I will probably need to go to Aruba. How can that idiot convince the bankers and other "friends" to cooperate with our plan? There is too much that can go wrong." He fumed.

Tomasso opened his office door and called to Yulia, the pretty but mentally vacant secretary to join him. If it wasn't for those breasts and her sexual prowess he would have fired her months ago.

She slid back from her desk. Masticating the huge wad of gum in her mouth she responded. "Sure boss. Anything the big boy wants, he gets."

Tomasso was getting tired of her. He watched as she sashayed across the reception area. There was no doubt she was beautiful and her lack of intelligence was equal in proportion to her beauty. The tight knee length skirt had ridden up displaying a fine set of legs and more. She was wearing a tight flamingo pink blouse that was knotted above her midriff. Not exactly the attire that most secretaries would wear at the office.

"Come in. Arrange me a trip to Aruba early in the morning. I will stay a week. I wanna nice place to stay. Not one of those tourist dives. I will be on important business. Get me there real early before it get too stinking hot."

As he sat in his huge overstuffed black leather chair behind his desk, his thoughts wandered. "Why not? It's almost time to leave for the day. A little fun wouldn't hurt anyone."

"Yulia how about a little going away present for the Big Guy?" he chuckled.

Yulia needed no encouragement to abandon what had been a particularly boring afternoon. She untied her blouse and her voluptuous breasts sprang forth like unleashed hounds in pursuit of an escaping rabbit.

Soon they were entwined on the huge chair which creaked and groaned under their acrobatic performance.

Chapter 5

Malmok, Aruba.

Jakob waited outside Isaac's home. The ladies had gone inside looking for the children. He looked around at the beautiful landscaping that Isaac and his wife had personally done. Like Jakob, Isaac Junior was an ardent gardener and tried to grow the most difficult plants to culture. There were Bismarck palms, tall Yucca plants with profuse white blooms, areca palms and a huge swath of bougainvillea plants of orange, white, pink and purple. Jakob marveled at how they had been able to plant and develop such a beautiful garden in the dry desert conditions of Aruba. He strolled through the garden and seated himself on a bench that faced through the garden and out to the Caribbean Sea. He was soon joined by Isaac Junior.

"Who were those two men who left as we arrived?"

"I do not know exactly. They are from Chicago and they stated that they have a business proposal for us. I have told them that I will only meet them at the office with some of our managers present. They did not seem happy with that and as they left they made a strange comment. It was almost a threat that things might happen. They claim to have been talking with Hans and he directed them here.

27

I think we need to get Hans here very soon to explain this."

"I think we will go and visit Hans. Do you have any important business at the office or can you come with me?"

"No. I sense this is important. I received a bad feeling from those men. Let us deal with it now before it can develop into something we cannot control."

"Hans is running his little business from a hut and tent on Palm Beach. We will drive there and afterwards we will go to Oranjestad. There are some things we all need to discuss privately."

Isaac went into the house to fetch keys to his car and tell Solange, Carlita and his wife that he and Jakob were leaving for a lunch in Oranjestad. He did not tell them any details of the plan to meet Hans.

The drive from Malmok down to Palm Beach on the narrow road was leisurely. Jakob looked out at the still turquoise waters of the Caribbean and the few white hulled boats that dotted its surface. As they headed south he watched several locals fishing from the rock shelf at Boca Catalina. Metal buckets rested beside them and on occasion water would splash from one of them as a fish thrashed in an attempt to escape. Jakob was at ease. He loved this life in Aruba. As he reflected on this, the old feeling of guilt and conflict arose in his mind again. It seemed to him that the frequency of these thoughts had increased rapidly over the past few months. He needed to find a solution. He thought back to his youth and the conflict he had experienced in trying to accept the teachings and beliefs of his strict Mennonite upbringing.

They followed a gentle curve in the road and past the salina in which herons and other birds were standing. Isaac turned sharply to the right and followed a small track down to the sand of Palm Beach. There were a few tourists either lying on the beach or sitting in deck chairs. Off to the left was the brightly painted hut advertising diving and boat tours. They spotted Hans talking to an older couple of tourists. As they approached he looked up and waved to them.

Isaac and Jakob stood back and waited. Hans finished his business and hurried across to them

"This is a surprise to see you both here. What is happening? Why are you here?"

Jakob spoke. "Hans we have had a visit we would like to speak with you about. Isaac and I are going into Oranjestad for a lunch. I want you join us. There are a number of things I wish to discuss."

 Hans frowned. Isaac looked perplexed.

"We have a trip scheduled at 2:30 this afternoon to take some wealthy Americans out to dive near the Antilla wreck. It is now 11:20, so yes I can join you. In fact I look forward to that. Please wait and I will put on some better clothing that is more suitable."

Jakob and Isaac waited in silence while Hans went inside the little tent beside the hut to change. Within a few minutes Hans emerged dressed in smart casual shorts and with his hair groomed. The transition was astonishing.

The three of them walked to Isaac's car making small talk on the way. Isaac opened the door and held it open to expel the stifling hot air. They drove off in silence.

In Oranjestad, Isaac turned left and away from the docks and vendor stalls. He drove up Main Street and into a small narrow one way street. He pulled his car up onto the curb. Oranjestad was busy at this time of day with the workers from the stores and offices leaving and going to their homes or favorite places for the 2 hour lunch break or to take a siesta.

Isaac left the car and beckoned them to a restaurant with a chalk board proclaiming that the best fish in Aruba was being served there. The owner saw Isaac approaching and bounded out to meet him.

"Senor, Senor. It is good to see you again. Who are your friends? Will you stay for lunch with us? Today we have the best wahoo and barracuda. We also have a special treat as a shipment of smoked eel from Holland has arrived. To serve with this treat we have some fine new Alsace from France. It is as smooth as the milk from a mother's breast. Come, join us."

Isaac couldn't help but smile at the exuberance of Pedro the owner. He had known him since Pedro and his young wife started the restaurant. He had not told Jakob that he had privately invested some of his own money into the place.

"Yes Pedro, but we only expect the best as this is my father Jakob and a relative Hans."

"Certainly, Senor. I will have the private booth at the back prepared for you. Come. Come. It is too hot and dusty for fine men like you to be standing out here amongst all these people who are rushing everywhere."

Chapter 6

San Nicolaas, Aruba.

The twin brothers, Miguel and Alejandro, watched as the doors of their new restaurant "El Coco Loco" opened and curious new customers ventured in. Miguel greeted many whom he knew from his years working at his other restaurants and bars in San Nicolaas. There had been considerable excitement regarding the opening of this restaurant. The brothers had arranged special foods and live entertainment. Throughout the afternoon the crowd swelled. Miguel was surprised. The lunch diners were soon replaced by refinery workers coming off early shift. They were hungry and thirsty and stayed longer than normal. The noise of their conversations carried out onto the street. Outside men stood with bottles of beer and some with pastechi and other light foods.

The number of patrons seemed to remain constant in size. Miguel and Alejandro were pleased. While happy, Alejandro expressed a concern.

"Miguel in the far corner there are two men who have been here since we opened. They have ordered food and occasionally a drink. I have been watching them. Once in a while I see them staring in our direction. Do you know them?"

"I have never seen them before and I certainly know most of the people here in San Nicolaas who frequent the bars."

"There is some purpose to their watching us. I will find a way to speak to them."

Miguel called out to an old friend, Henry who worked at the nearby San Nicolaas refinery. His friend stopped and Miguel hurriedly crossed through the crowd to join him.

"Let's walk. I have a question for you."

Miguel grabbed two bottles of beer from the bar and they drifted out onto the street. Cigarette smoke hung in the air and mixed with the ever present fumes from the distilling plant at the refinery, producing a heady concoction.

They sauntered off down Main Street until they were alone.

"What is so important that we need to meet like this?"

"San Nicolaas seems to be changing. The girls who work the streets and barrio are scared, the cholers and drug dealers are everywhere yet the polis are staying away. There are new faces here that no one knows. It seems that since the end of the war Aruba, and especially San Nicolaas has a different atmosphere. In the bar right now there are two men who are obviously foreign. They are not Dutch or American. They have been watching Alejandro and me for hours. I am worried that they could be planning something that could damage us. Can you help me to find out more?"

"I will find a way. I ask that you and Alejandro keep an eye on me in case it goes badly."

They swigged down the last of the beer, threw the bottles into an empty oil drum and slowly strolled back into the bar.

Once in the restaurant Miguel's friend took a battered cigarette from his jacket pocket and went through the motions of trying to light it. He wandered by the two men and stood striking a match against the table top. In disgust he threw the match and cigarette to the floor. He spun to the men and asked "Can you give an old working guy like me a fag? Mine get destroyed in that god dammed refinery with all that steam and crap that floats around. "

The heavier and taller of the two reached inside his jacket and withdrew a silver case which he flipped open. He held it forward. In heavily accented English he asked "You from here? Whadaya know about this joint. Whataboud those fellas there running the place. They good? "

Miguel's friend immediately picked up on the question.

"Been here all my life. Went to the school at the refinery. Work at the refinery. Live in one of the houses in the Colony. I guess you could say I am from here and still am."

The tall man continued. "Join us. Whatcha drinking? Wanna beer, whiskey, vodka... what you want. We new here and want to make some friends and get to know the place."

Henry glanced across to see both Miguel and Alejandro casually watching the performance.

"Tell ya what. Me missus hasn't let me have a whiskey in years. Let's do that guys, but only if you join in with me."

The larger of the two stood and pushed his hand forward. "I'm Vincenzio. This here's Tony. I'll go get us some drinks."

At the bar Miguel discreetly smiled as he took in the act. He served Vincenzio the whiskeys and watched as he returned to their table. Soon all three were talking in earnest. Miguel decided to take the bottle and offer a free drink. He wanted to keep them there and talking as long as possible. At the table he poured large repeats.

"Miguel these are my new friends Tony and Vincenzio. Like some of the guys at the refinery they come from Italy. Nice enough guys. Seems like they want to start a business. Tell me that they had a restaurant and bar before. Looking to invest here."

Miguel was suspicious. "Why not come back tomorrow morning and we can talk. It is too busy now but I am very interested."

"We be here at 10:00 tomorrow."

Tony Vitto and Vincenzio stood to leave the bar. Vincenzio removed a roll of American dollars and pealed several off that he then threw on the table. With that, the Italians left the bar.

Chapter 7

Oranjestad, Aruba.

Pedro had found a private booth for the trio. They sat around the table facing each other. Jakob realized the lunch would be awkward for all, so he summoned Pedro and ordered a bottle of 7 year old Angostura Gran Anejo. Pedro quickly scurried into the back room and emerged with the bottle of amber liquid. He placed small glasses in front of each of them and poured a finger full into each glass. He bowed, and after telling them to call him when they wished to order, he retreated to the bar area.

Jakob raised his glass "Salud". Hans and Isaac raised their glasses in unison.

Silence fell. All three of them instinctively knew that the conversation they were about to have would be difficult. For Jakob it would also be emotional.

"Hans this morning two men arrived unannounced at Isaac's home. As you know this is not an acceptable business practice for us. They told Isaac that they had been speaking to you about a business opportunity and that you had advised them to come to us. Who are these men and do you know what they want?"

"I was at the "National Bank of Aruba" last Thursday making the deposits for my business. I was joking and talking with Yipsy who is our manager. As I was about to leave she stopped me and said she had been approached by some foreign investors who were looking to partner with businesses in Aruba, and in particular, they wanted a water sports business. Yipsy knows our business is growing and thought it may be a good opportunity. I told her that they could contact me at the hut on the beach. On Friday afternoon as we were closing I received a visit from the men. I left the closing of the business to one of my boys and we walked up to one of the newly opened bars on the street. The men wasted no time in getting to the business details. They represent a large group of investors and are looking at establishing several businesses in the Caribbean. They are looking at a hotel, a gambling operation and some other tourism related opportunities. As you and Isaac know, I am not an astute businessman and recommended they contact Isaac. I did not send them to Isaac's home. I understand how inappropriate that would have been."

"How did they find where Isaac and his family live?"

"It is no secret on the island where the Klassen residences are located. I am sure they could ask any local and get directions."

"Thank you, Hans. I now understand. Isaac do you have any questions?"

Isaac studied Hans for a moment before answering. "No. It seems innocent to me. Hans, it seems that with your business you have been keeping away from trouble. Jakob and I hope it stays that way."

Hans thought back to the fights, womanizing and the severe beating he had received at Miguel's hands.

"Since coming to the island from Germany I have found a purpose and feel calm here. Growing up in war time Germany and during those horrible post war years was not easy. I needed to prove I was tough and the leader of the gang. I have no interest to do that again. I have a nice little business, a good group of young boys to help me and most of all a steady partner who helps me to see things differently"

Jakob and Isaac were surprised. Neither knew of this partner. Jakob smiled.

"Tell us more about your young lady."

"Her name is Irma. She is Aruban and from a family who have been here for hundreds of years. I was waiting to find the right time to tell you and bring her to meet you all."

Jakob and Isaac were even more shocked.

"That is great news. I am very happy you have found someone to have in your life. I am sure Solange will want to meet her soon. Lets us raise our glasses in a toast."

The talk drifted off to topics of new buildings, rumors about the refinery, politics and nothing in particular. Throughout this, Jakob said little. He was pensive.

Eventually he signaled Pedro who arrived at their table in seconds.

"Today for lunch I recommend the Barracuda. It was caught fresh this morning. It is served as a steak topped with a light lemon sauce and served with fried yucca or plantain, carrots and black beans."

All three ordered the recommended lunch. Jakob ordered a bottle of the Alsace. He sampled the wine when it was delivered to the table. He smiled.

"Yes. This wine is smooth, not too sweet or acidic and has a full crisp taste. This was an excellent choice Pedro."

The food arrived and they ate in relative silence. When they had finished, Pedro offered desserts and coffee which they declined.

After the table was cleared, Jakob looked around at the neighboring tables. They were empty. Finally he looked at Isaac and Hans.

"I have something to say to you both. It was not easy for me to decide to tell you these things, some of which Isaac is aware of. Hans it is time for you to hear some truths."

Isaac and Hans sat back in their chairs with eyes focused on Jakob.

"Hans you should know that Isaac is your brother."

Isaac dropped his wine glass on the table. He was in shock. It was only years earlier that Jakob had sworn him to silence and to maintain the secret when Jakob had revealed to Solange and Isaac the situation he had created by getting Ilsa Wolfe pregnant in Germany and deserting her. What had compelled Jakob to expose this to Hans? What was happening?

Hans appeared to be in a daze.

"Jakob I need to know more. My mother Ilsa never told me this. She said my father was killed in the war."

Jakob looked at both Hans and Isaac Junior for several minutes.

Jakob continued.

"Hans most of what I am about to tell you is already known by Isaac and my wife Solange. I was born into a poor Mennonite farming community in Ontario, Canada. I loved my parents yet could never learn the ancestry of our family. All I knew was that they had migrated to America from Europe with other families in an attempt to start a new and better life. The circumstances in America turned against them. There were several severe and crippling winters coupled with major outbreaks of illnesses that took the lives of many. My father, Isaac Senior convinced a group of fellow Mennonites to mount a party to explore some often rumored lands in Canada. They found some ideal land and formed settling parties to break in the land and establish dairy, sheep and other livestock farms. In

41

addition they planted huge crops and soon became valued merchants at the local farmers market. Amongst the settlers there were skilled craftsmen who built furniture from the trees they harvested and processed in their small mill.

It was an idyllic life but was interrupted by war in Europe. I had started to question the teachings and belief of my religion at that time. I witnessed some terrible things and never understood the teachings that forbid us from fighting back. We were to be pacifists and were forbidden to get involved in these matters. We suffered a personal attack on our farm but could do nothing. My frustrations grew and I became totally disenchanted. I watched as new inventions were made and entered into the life of neighbors who were not Mennonite. None of it made sense. I rebelled. An unfortunate accident took the life of my father. It was after that that I tried to settle down and accept the teaching of the religion. Eventually, I married my neighbor's daughter, Anke whom I loved and had grown up with. Before we married, Anke travelled to be trained as a nurse in a hospital far away from our farm. It was during this period I questioned many things and a member of the community provided me with documents that would forever change my life. These documents included lists of relatives still living in Europe, mainly in Holland. I researched these names and wrote many letters in an attempt to find out more of our ancestral background. Some responded and others did not. As time progressed I became more determined to find these relatives and also challenged the beliefs I had been brought up to adhere to.

Eventually, and against the advice of friends and family, I convinced Anke to undertake a trip with me in search of these relatives. She was reluctant, yet I persisted. We went to Holland and stayed with her uncle and his family.

In Holland I experienced another life. There was music, clubs, drinking and a freedom I had never seen in Canada. I took advantage of the situation and soon started to run into troubles. Anke's uncle and his son arranged jobs for me including one on their farm. It was during this period that I travelled to meet some of the relatives, some of whom spoke openly and others who said nothing or were close guarded in what they said. Finally, I did learn the reason for my parents' departure from Europe to North America. It was a feud between my father and his brother over a girl. That girl became my mother.

It was while I was visiting these relatives in Holland that I received a letter from Germany. In that letter was the revelation that my father had a younger brother and the suggestion that we meet at some future time. I was instructed to stay in Holland and not visit Germany as there were rumblings of war.

I was stupid, ignorant and head strong. I went to Germany in pursuit of the relative. It was then that fate dealt me some blows. While there, war broke out and I was stranded. Other disasters struck and I was truly trapped. In an effort to find a way out of Germany and to earn some money I played the saxophone in some clubs. It was during this period of time that I met your mother Ilsa and got her with child. That child is you, Hans. Scared, without funds and papers, already married and in total conflict with all beliefs, I fled and left her. I had agreed that I would stay and look after her but that was all a lie. I had no intention.

I escaped as a crew member on a German Merchant Marine ship that was headed to the East Coast of America. It was my plan to leave the ship there and send money to bring my Anke back to me. The ship was diverted to the Caribbean. After a stop in Colombia, where again I got into trouble, the ship left and docked in Aruba. It was here with the help of a senior crew member I was able to escape. It took a lot, but I finally established a life here in Aruba.

I did not make any attempt to contact Ilsa. I found out that my wife, Anke had been gunned down during an escape attempt with members of the Dutch Resistance. It was some years later that I met Solange and we married.

A number of years ago I received a letter from lawyers in Germany regarding the situation with you and the problems you were causing. It caused me to reflect on life and I felt great guilt for how I had treated Ilsa and you.

I discussed all this with Solange and Isaac Junior and suggested a plan to assist you. That plan was sent to Ilsa through the law firm and finally we all agreed. It was to get you away from the crime and troubles in post war

Germany and get you an education. I offered support to Ilsa but she declined. To her you were more important. I arranged the schooling at a Reform School in Ireland and then the plan to bring you to Aruba.

We were concerned about how you would accept life here and if you could stay out of trouble. Our concerns were valid. As you know there were some serious problems created by you, though as the years have gone by you have calmed and become part of our little society here in Aruba.

I have thought a lot about whether to tell you about the past. I have come to accept the consequences of my past actions and it is only correct you know the truth.

I am you father."

Chapter 8

Hans was bewildered. In his life he had never had any indication or thoughts other than that his father had died in the war. He sat quietly trying to compile the information that Jakob had just shared. Hans's feelings ran from anger to confusion, sadness and a strange happiness.

Jakob reached over the table and placed his hand on Hans's shoulder.

"We have time to spend together and you are one of our family. It will be different for you now."

Isaac Junior had remained quiet. He still worried that underneath Hans's demeanor there was still the potential for trouble. He would speak privately with Jakob and Solange later. Now was not the time.

"Hans I am pleased you now know the truth and that we are half brothers. I hope one day to be able to meet your mother. Jakob has not spoken much about her. Maybe now that will change."

Jakob looked at the watch on his tanned wrist. "Hans it is time to get you back to your business. You have customers for the afternoon. Tonight we will have a dinner at our home in Malmok. I would like to invite you, and if possible, your lady friend Irma."

"I will contact her. At what time should we arrive?"

"I normally spend the early evening in my garden and enjoy a cocktail with Solange before we have dinner. Isaac will you also join us for this occasion?"

Isaac smiled. "Yes I would be happy to bring the family and attend."

Jakob was happy. "We will have a nice evening. I love to spend those hours as the sun is setting over the Caribbean in my garden. It has taken Solange and me years to build the garden with all those exotic plants. It is truly one of my favorite places in the evening and to see the clouds reflecting an orange tint below their pink form is special. The colors blend with the orange, white and pink bougainvilleas."

The three of them stood and Isaac went to see Pedro and pay the bill. While he was doing this Jakob and Hans strolled out and waited in the heat on the dusty street.

"Jakob I am concerned that Isaac may be upset that I now know that you are my father and we will develop a bond. It is not my intention to allow for a rift to develop."

"Isaac is strong and has a good sense of things. He will be fine. I may speak with him privately."

When Isaac joined them they walked to Isaac's car.

They drove in silence to Palm Beach. Isaac pulled the car off the road and onto the reddish brown track that led down to the sandy beach where Hans's hut stood. Already the tourists were standing and waiting to be taken for their trip.

Hans jumped out from the rear seat. "I will see you both this evening around 6:00pm"

Isaac reversed the car and turned back onto the narrow poorly sealed road and proceeded north toward Malmok. In his mind his thoughts were running wild. He wondered whether Hans would continue to grow and stay out of trouble or had Jakob inadvertently created a situation that may become uncontrollable.

Within minutes they arrived at Jakob's home and pulled up onto the inclined driveway.

It was a scene of pandemonium. As they came to a halt, Isaac's children ran around the corner of the house armed with sticks in their hands shrieking and laughing. They were in pursuit of one of the stray goats that roamed the island. Isaac watched in horror as the goat ascended the steps at the front of the house and bounded inside the house. He and Jakob left the car in a hurry and started to run to the house. As they did so shouts came from the rear garden. Jakob stopped dead. He then turned and ran to the garden where he found Solange and Janelle, Isaac's wife, armed with a rolling pin and a broom chasing a herd of thirty to fifty goats who had decided to take a late lunch on Jakob's prized plants. There were young kids, old goats, white goats, brown goats and ones whose color could not be described. Jakob was mortified. The brightly colored bougainvilleas were partially torn from the ground, soil was scattered across the stone walkway he kept meticulously clean, branches of his rare palms dangled half chewed, and his garden of orchards was nowhere to be seen.

Jakob was furious. "Isaac, you find out who owns these fucking goats. They will pay for this damage and repair my garden."

Solange was worried that Jakob's recently diagnosed blood pressure problem could endanger him. She ran to his side and took his arm. "Jakob, Please be calm. We can fix this."

She and Isaac Junior escorted Jakob up the front steps and into the foyer of the house. Jakob let out a roar upon discovering a pile of the goat's finest on the hardwood floor. He shook off Solange and Isaac and raced into the kitchen where the young goat was munching on the carrots and food that Solange and Janelle had been preparing for the dinner. Isaac's children stood wide eyed not sure what to do. Jakob lunged forward and grabbed the goat in a headlock.

"Eat my plants and my dinner would you, you little fucker. I should take you to the abattoir and have you prepared for me to have goat stews for weeks."

Solange placed her hands behind his neck. "Jakob you must remain calm. Go into the living room and sit. Isaac, Janelle and I will look after this."

She gave Jakob a slight push toward the living room entrance then beckoned the others to join her in getting the goat out of the house and cleaning up the mess. She looked outside past Isaac's car and could not help laughing at the motley herd of goats wandering down the road looking for their next meal.

With the clean up done, Solange and Janelle took Isaac's car and drove to replace the foods that the goat had dined on.

Chapter 9

It was shortly before 6:00pm when Hans arrived with his lady partner, Irma. Hans escorted Irma to the back garden where he expected to find Jakob and the rest of the family. Instead he found the scene of destruction. Confused he walked toward the back door. As he approached he found them all sitting on the large covered deck.

"Jakob, what happened to the garden?"

Solange launched into the afternoons escapade and finally they all saw the humor and laughed off the incident.

Jakob stood and was introduced to Irma. She was a beautiful young Aruban woman with vivacious looks. She extended her hand and after Hans introduced her she went to each person to make her introduction, including Isaac's children.

Jakob was impressed. "Maybe this is what has stabilized Hans" he thought.

The evening progressed well. Irma charmed them all with her manners and outlook on life. Jakob wondered if the years she had been a nurse were reflected in her personality and attitude. Suddenly he found memories of Anke flooding into his mind. He remembered her kindness and how, as a nurse she found ways to soothe and charm people. The doubts he had recently experienced were back. Jakob started questioning himself mentally and admonishing himself for having done such foolish things in his younger days. He drifted from the conversation in the room and the presence of family into a daze of the past.

Solange watched from across the room.

"Jakob they are asking you for an opinion on the new developments. Are you listening? You seem to be far away."

Jakob snapped back into the situation.

 "Sorry I was thinking about a new business matter that is occupying my mind."

Solange studied him. She knew when he was lying and decided to leave it alone. Lately Solange had noticed an increase in Jakob's tendency to become lost in a thought he would not share.

Isaac and Hans were engaged in deep conversation when there was a knock at the front door. Isaac went to the door and opened it. Standing at the door was an attractive man in his late thirties. Isaac thought he looked familiar. His hair was a light brown flecked with grey and his complexion tanned. As they stood there, Carlita arrived at the door and beamed.

 "Isaac what do you think. This is Moreno. Today while you and Jakob were gone, I took the chance to shave Moreno and groom him. He is an attractive man. He still does not want to talk about why he is here or his past. I gathered he has had some hard times. When I was shaving him and cutting his hair I noticed scarring at the top of his back and neck. He is more relaxed and I hope that soon he will tell us more. I do not think he will harm us. Since he has been here his manners have changed and he has been very pleasant."

"I still advise you to be careful. We know nothing about him or the troubles he is involved in."

As they talked Moreno raised his hand and spoke quickly in Spanish. Both Carlita and Isaac understood him. He was giving a warning.

"Isaac he says he knows those men who were at your house this morning. He says to be careful."

Carlita spoke to him for a long time. Moreno just stood shaking his head.

"Isaac he does not want to say more. He still does not trust everyone. We will need to wait."

Isaac invited Moreno into the family dinner. Hans had watched the whole exchange at the door and soon found a way to introduce himself to Moreno. Hans had learned several languages during his schooling in Ireland and was proficient in Spanish. It wasn't long before Moreno and Hans were becoming best friends.

Chapter 10

Caracas, Venezuela.

Tomasso left "The Sicilian Club" offices and made his way to the luxury apartment he had rented upon his arrival in Venezuela. Upon arriving at the building, a uniformed doorman sprang to attention and opened the huge swinging glass doors with the gold handles.

"Good evening, Mr. Rossini. I must say you look very relaxed. Will you be staying in or will you need me to have your car ready for later?"

Tomasso chuckled and thought to himself. "If only you knew of my afternoon tryst with Yulia, you little twerp" but instead thanked the doorman and requested his car be ready for 7:30pm. He entered the apartment building and before taking the elevator to the penthouse suite, he stopped at the concierge desk.

"Good evening Carlos. I will be leaving early tomorrow morning and be away for a few days. Please hold any mail for me. Do not let anyone into my suite, including the cleaning staff. No one is permitted to enter when I am not here. Take this to assist in making that happen."

Tomasso pushed an American $50 bill into Carlos hand. Carlos flashed an exaggerated smile. "Yes of course, Mr.

Rossini. Will you require a limousine in the morning to take you to the airport? I can order one now for you."

"Yes. I am on the 8:00am flight to Aruba. I would like to leave at 6:00am."

Tomasso headed across to the elevator and rode up to his penthouse suite on the 30th floor. He unlocked the door and threw his case onto the low table in the living room. He proceeded to the bar and poured a scotch. He needed to prepare himself for the dinner meeting with the Palermo brothers. While they appeared to be charming to all those who were around them or met them, the Palermo Brothers were in fact the most ruthless members of the Club. They were Chicago's trusted lieutenants and oversaw the drug running operations in Colombia and the transshipment of the drugs through Venezuela. All the mob money from Chicago and Europe ran through the Palermo Brothers various businesses. Nobody questioned a Palermo brother. Tomasso recognized that he needed to be careful tonight. One slip up and he could end up one of the countless unknown bodies found each morning in the slums of the run down barrios. The Palermos had arranged a dinner meeting at a restaurant owned by a fellow Sicilian located on the western outskirts of Caracas in the district of San Pedro

Tonight they would be entertaining three key Venezuelan officials. The Chief of Police, the General in charge of Internal Security along with the Admiral responsible for the patrols along the northern coastline. All were on the

Palermo payroll. It was a small expense to ensure the Palermo Import and Export business ran smoothly and without any pesky official interference.

Chapter 11

At 7:30pm, Tomasso descended from his penthouse. He walked briskly through the lavish marble clad foyer and out to the sweeping circular entrance. He was pleased to see his huge black 1959 Lincoln Continental Mark IV parked and awaiting him. It was resplendent with its white wall ties, chrome tipped rear wings and tinted windows. The doorman sprinted across and held open the door for Tomasso who handed him a small tip and then slid onto the red leather seat. His signature red velvet gambling dice hung from the rear vision mirror. As a caution, Tomasso looked into the rear seat in case of any unexpected surprise. There was none there other than the bright pink and purple velour cushions that he and Yulia exercised frequently on their late night outings.

Tomasso started the car and slowly exited the driveway from the apartment building. The drive to San Pedro would be relaxing at this time of day.

Some 20 minutes later, Tomasso wheeled into the gaudy entrance of the **Santuario di Formaggio** restaurant. Statues of Venus and Adonis stood at the entrance of the portico, neatly trimmed Cyprus cedars lined the entranceway, a huge brightly lit replica of the famous Trevi fountain sent water spouting into the air. Tomasso shook his head at all these ostentatious and expensive decorations. The **Santuario di Formaggio** had been named by its owner, Alfredo Santaluca, after he had been defrocked and dismissed from the Catholic Church for sexual abuse of altar boys and the occasional nun. Alfredo loved the name he had given the restaurant..."The Shrine of Cheese."

Alfredo had hit hard times shortly after opening the restaurant and the Sicilian Club had graciously helped him out. In return the agreement was for it to be the secure and safest place for the mob to conduct their business.

Tomasso skidded to a halt on the loose white stone gravel at the entrance. A valet dressed in black trousers, a flame red jacket , white shirt and black bowtie walked quickly to the car and offered to park it in the spaces reserved for prestige customers. Tomasso handed the boy the keys and climbed the few stairs into the restaurant. He was soon ushered into a private room where the Palermo Brothers sat with glasses of red wine. They looked up at Tomasso with expressionless faces.

"Hey. Salvatore, Emilio.Hows youse guys doing?"

The Palermos simply stared ahead. Salvatore raised his hand a little off the table and pointed to a chair. Obviously Tomasso had been commanded to sit.

Salvatore fixed his stare on Tomasso.

"We not happy. The situation in Aruba is troubling. We have made some big investments there. So far we see no results. We contributed to certain politicians campaigns, invested into a bank and bought land. We have no progress. We were to get approval for building resorts and casinos. So far nothing. The boys back home are impatient. They are still furious about the Cuba situation and that fanatic Fidel Castro. We invested heavily in promoting Cuba as "Americas Playland". Advertisements on billboards and buses in New York with those huge color posters. Big investments into the casinos and hotels. We developed gambling venues for many events. We paid many of those crooked Cubans to help us and here we are....fucked! With the collapse of Cuba, you know we planned to make Aruba become the next Cuba. The political climate there is right and their economy needs us. That old oil refinery in San Nicolaas wont carry them forever. New refineries are being built on the other islands but they seem too stupid to realise this.

So tell me why we have not made any real progress. Tell us very slowly. Omit nothing and only tell us the truth."

Before Tomasso could answer, the drapes to the private cubicle were pulled back and a wine waiter enquired whether more drinks were required. Tomasso waited a minute before ordering a double scotch.

"I tell ya. I been wondering this too so tomorrow I go there and find out what that Tony Vitto has been up to. He is all talk. Remember you guys that he aint my choice but the fellas back in Chicago. Personally I would like to off him."

At that moment the maitre de entered, excused himself and announced their guest had arrived.

Salvatore looked across the table to Tomasso. "Before you leave tonight we will discuss this further."

Chapter 12

The maitre'de led the three Venezuelans to the private booth. The restaurant was quiet except the occasional outburst of laughter from one of the tables in the public dining area. The stillness of the private room was accentuated by the heavy drapes and carpet.

The Palermos stood as their "guests" entered and they shook each person's hand. Tomasso was introduced. He studied the three men carefully.

The Chief of Police looked to be around forty. He was stocky with a light olive skin and movie star looks. Tomasso thought to himself that this was a pretty boy on the take and not to be trusted. The General's features were sharp. His eyes were piercing and cold. This was not a man that Tomasso would have as a friend or trust. Finally, the Admiral extended his hand to Tomasso. The Admiral's mannerisms and approach were unlike the others. The Admiral had a sallowed complexion and silver hair that was impeccably combed into place. His teeth were bright and prominent when he smiled and he displayed the soft features of a diplomatic and privileged person. Tomasso thought "This is the person I can trust."

Salvatore ushered them to their places at the table. The waiter fussed with napkins and took the drink order. When he left they engaged in small talk and a discussion over the upcoming football tournament.

The maitre'd returned to present the restaurant's specials for the evening. Tomasso waited expectedly. He had always found that he was able to learn more about a person by observing the foods they ordered. "This will be interesting he thought."

"Tonight we have several items that are especially prepared for important patrons.

Firstly there is the Pork Tenderloin. This is prepared with freshly picked sage, sun-dried tomatoes, prosciutto, and heavy cream. It is rich in flavor. It is absolutely wonderful and one of our chef's specialties. It is served with medallion potatoes and asparagus.

Tonight we also have a delicious lamb shanks. The chef prepares the lamb shanks by slowly simmering them with fresh rosemary, garlic, tomatoes, and red wine. They are served with polenta, or roasted garlic mashed potatoes.

For steak lovers the chef has a special Steak Pizzaiola. This steak is a slowly braised beef cut of the finest tenderloin cut into medallions and seared. It is served coated with sweet, vine-ripened tomatoes. It is served on top of warm focaccia bread with an old sharp goat cheese.

Other specialties include wild boar, roasted pheasant, and a variety of freshly caught seafood.

Is there anything that interests you?"

The stocky Chief of Police and the General quickly ordered the steak. The Admiral pondered for a while and then requested the Pork Tenderloin.

Tomasso ordered fresh lasagna from the menu and the Palermos decided upon the Steak Pizzaiola.

The maitre'd thanked them and left with their orders. After he left the cubicle, Salvatore spoke.

"Gentlemen, we all know why we are here. I invited you here this evening to meet Tomasso. He is in charge of our project in Aruba. I am hoping that you will all find a way to cooperate with Tomasso. He needs to operate without the interference of your forces. He will need to transport exports from Colombia to our warehouses here in Venezuela. We expect that these shipments not to be disrupted by guerillas and other bandits. I am sure the General's troops can assure us that the shipments will proceed safely and without interruption."

Salvatore fixed his eyes firmly upon the Chief of Police.

"When the goods arrive here we do expect full protection from the Police forces you command. We are tired of the break-ins and vandalism at our facilities. This must stop as we increase the shipments. Do I make myself clear in this matter?"

The Chief of Police became visibly angry. His face flushed red and he shifted uncomfortably on his chair.

Salvatore pinned him with his stare. "My friend we have paid you well for services. We will continue to pay you. If you cannot perform this service I caution you that we will deal with both you and the problem. Is that a little clearer now?"

The Chief of Police nodded. "Yes but sometimes there are others in the force who I know participate in these things. I do not know who they are. I will make investigations and find these renegades."

"See to it" Salvatore barked back.

The Admiral had watched the exchange and spoke before the Palermos could dictate their demands.

"I have a plan already prepared. Simply, you will need to provide me with information in advance of the shipments from Venezuela to Aruba. I will need the locations of where the boats will depart from and the area they will dock in Aruba. Please remember it is only 14 miles from here to Aruba. We can provide support for part of the crossing but the Dutch and the Americans also patrol. We can distract them but cannot guarantee to stop them."

"We understand that and Tomasso is working to minimize the problem with the Dutch and Americans. We will arrange an introduction to a special contact for you. He is a Lieutenant in the United States Coast Guard and commands one of the patrol boats. His patrol area includes the waters off Colombia, Venezuela, Aruba and the Dominican Republic. He will provide you with excellent information and support. His actions will assist you in several ways. He will cause distractions, arrests and decoys that will convince others that your work is being performed well. You will listen to him and take instructions from him.

Now let me make the contributions I realize you are all waiting for."

Emilio snapped open a hard sided briefcase with a loud clack and removed three bulging manila packets. He handed one to each of the "guests" who in turn smiled and thanked the Palermos before pocketing the money.

Within minutes three waiters arrived with large silver trays containing their meals

Salvatore smiled. "Salud, gentlemen. Enjoy your meals."

Chapter 13

Malmok, Aruba.

Jakob had woken early. He dressed casually in a light shirt and shorts. Solange was still in a deep sleep. Jakob went to the kitchen and made a coffee. While he sipped the coffee he took some paper and left a note for Solange to inform her he had left for a long walk.

Jakob walked along the rough roadway past the curving shoreline of Arashi beach and the sand dunes. Instead of progressing down the wild coastline where the surf crashed in off the Atlantic Ocean, he turned right and proceeded to make a slow walk up the hill to the abandoned California lighthouse. The climb was long and hot. When he finally reached the top he was delighted to find he was alone with the exception of a few cunucu dogs that were sniffing around the ground searching for food scraps.

Jakob crossed the open area and found a large flat rock to sit on. He sat enjoying the cool trade winds that blew with some strength at the lighthouse location, while looking out over the Palm Beach area toward Oranjestad.

Jakob was finding events of recent difficult to comprehend. The progress of life in Aruba was confusing him and his patience for the changes was diminishing.

Jakob's joy was no longer derived from closing a successful business deal, but rather from spending time with his grandchildren who he took fishing or on adventure walks to the beach or in the cunucu.

Jakob reflected upon the past and changes that had occurred in his life. He was particularly encouraged that Hans had matured into an honest and hardworking man. He was pleased that he had disclosed the truth about being his father to Hans. Jakob was sure that this would assist Hans in continuing to move forward positively in his life.

Jakob allowed his thoughts to drift way back to the time in Europe. He wondered what had become of the friends and acquaintances he had made there. He resolved that he would return and visit with the intention of finding them and hopefully repairing any damage he had done.

It was noon before he started his walk back to the Villa. Along the way he encountered Solange sauntering toward him.

"Good afternoon, Solange. I have had a nice walk and rest at the base of the old lighthouse."

"I was a little worried. You have been gone for a long time. What did you do there all that time?"

"I have been thinking about my life and this morning I have made several decisions that I wish to share with you."

Chapter 14

San Nicolaas.

While Miguel and Alejandro awaited the arrival of Tony Vitto and Vincenzio, they drank the strong Dutch coffee they served at their bar. The time of 11:00am came and went.

Outside in the street, people were scurrying by, entering the stores and going about their daily life. Even though it was hot and the air filled with the bluish oily smoke from the refinery, this did not dissuade the shoppers.

"I suspect our friends are no longer planning on meeting us to discuss the business plans they seemed so eager to pursue."

Alejandro shrugged. "Miguel, I will wait until noon and then I must leave. There are matters I need to review with Isaac Junior."

At that moment the door swung open and Tony Vitto and Vincenzio walked in accompanied by a third person. They walked briskly to the table where Miguel and Alejandro sat.

Tony Vitto spoke.

"We are sorry to be a little late. We unexpectedly had our accomplice arrive this morning from Venezuela. Let me introduce him. This is Tomasso Rossini. He is a senior partner in our business. It is excellent that he is here as he will be able to explain our goals and answer any questions you may have."

"Would you gentlemen care for a cold drink or a coffee?" Miguel asked.

Tomasso responded. "A cold soda would be appreciated."

Miguel went to the bar and returned with glasses and bottles of soda.

"Tomasso, last evening Tony and Vincenzio spoke briefly of plans to invest in business here in Aruba. Can you please tell me some more?"

Alejandro was sitting quietly watching and listening intently. He was not convinced that these were legitimate businessmen.

"Before we talk, I wanna know more about youse guys. I aint gonna give away our plans until I know who you are."

Miguel described their lives on the Island from the time they were born through to the present. When he had finished the Italians sat in silence. Finally Tomasso spoke.

"So you are involved with the Klassens?"

"Yes. They are both friends and investors in business with us."

"That may be good then. Please leave us for a minute. I need to speak with these two before we go further."

Miguel and Alejandro returned to the bar. Several refinery workers walked into the restaurant looking to enjoy lunch there. Alejandro greeted them and advised them that the restaurant was closed for a private meeting. The refinery workers looked around and saw the Italians in deep but quiet conversation. Hands were gesticulating until Tomasso brought his beefy fist down on the table with a resounding crash which caused Miguel, Alejandro and the workers to stare across in their direction. Tony Vitto raised his hand in a small wave to signal that all was fine.

At that point Alejandro knew that these were no ordinary businessmen.

The refinery workers looked at Miguel and with lowered heads they left the restaurant.

Tomasso beckoned Miguel and Alejandro to rejoin them.

It was obvious that Tomasso was the boss and in no mood for anything but the business at hand.

"Miguel and Alejandro. My displeasure is not with either of you. Tony and Vincenzio have been here for weeks and during that time they have been unable to make the contacts that we need to establish our businesses. I am not happy with the delays. My partners are impatient. We are looking at more than just investing into a small restaurant like yours. I do not want to insult you but we need to purchase land and build resorts. Your restaurant is of course something we will want to buy from you. Our business is all about hospitality and making people happy.

Will you arrange a social meeting for me with the Klassens. I fear that these two may have created the wrong impression.

It is very simple. With the demise of the tourism business in Cuba due to that fanatic Castro, we need to establish another playground for the American tourist who wishes to escape the northern cold winters or enjoy the freedoms of gambling and an escape from the pressures of life in America."

Alejandro spoke.

"I will speak with Isaac Junior this evening. The Klassens are very strict in the way they do their business. I will ask them to set up a meeting."

Chapter 15

Palm Beach.

Hans was pleasantly surprised the next morning to receive a visit from Moreno who strolled toward him carrying a small paper bag. It was still early and there were very few tourists on the beach.

"Bon Dia, Moreno. What brings you here this morning?"

"I have come to share a breakfast treat with you and talk. There are some things you should know that may affect your family."

Moreno tore the bag open and handed Hans an arepa. Hans looked at it with curiosity. Moreno saw his confused look and laughed.

"The arepa is what we eat at breakfast in Colombia. It is a corn cake that is filled with a spicy seasoned meat. It is similar to the pastechi that you eat here in Aruba."

Hans bit into the arepa.

"I don't know why I have never tried one before. They are delicious."

Hans and Moreno leaned against the hull of Hans's boat and finished eating.

The fierce morning sun beat down upon them and gentle little ripples of waves licked at their feet.

Finally Moreno spoke.

"Hans there are no customers here. Can we go into the shade of your hut and talk?"

"Yes of course. If someone comes then I will need to leave and take them out on a trip. Maybe you should join us."

They walked back up the beach and into the dark interior of Hans hut.

"What is it you wish to talk about?"

Moreno was quiet for several minutes before he spoke.

"Hans I feel I can trust you. I understand from Isaac Junior that you have lived a life that has also had some difficulties. My life in Colombia was hard as well.

It is no mistake that I am here in Aruba. There are some others who have fled here. I know some of them and where they are.

Last night I went to San Nicolaas to a bar and met with them. It is important you learn about those Italian men and what they have planned here in Aruba.

They are very dangerous."

Hans was intrigued.

Chapter 16

Oranjestad.

Miguel had driven from the restaurant to Oranjestad on the chance of getting a meeting with Jakob, Isaac and Solange Klassen.

The drive was frustrating. The day was hot and his progress was slowed by herds of goats and donkeys wandering on the road. The road itself was in bad repair from the previous season's rains. Large potholes pitted the road and there were areas where the shoulder of the road had fallen away. Miguel cursed the conditions and wondered aloud how Aruba intended to attract wealthy tourists with such poor facilities. The trucks from the port at Oranjestad that carried freight to the refinery had also caused further deterioration.

After a drive of over an hour, which should have been around twenty minutes, Miguel pulled onto Main Street, Oranjestad. He parked and walked down several blocks until he reached the Klassen office building.

He entered the building and immediately encountered Isaac Junior who was escorting some visitors out.

"Miguel, it is good to see you. Why have you come here?"

"Isaac, I think we may have some problems arriving here on the island. It is important that I meet with you and the family. Is that possible? Is everyone here?"

"Yes. Jakob was about to leave and take the children out by Mangel Alto for a couple of hours fishing. Let me see if I can get them. Please, come and wait in our meeting room."

Miguel sat quietly reflecting upon the strange meeting at the restaurant. Something was not right. He valued Isaacs's sharp mind. He welcomed that the Klassens would listen and analyze the situation.

Minutes passed until Isaac returned with Solange and Jakob.

An office worker followed them and placed a large pitcher of iced cold water and glasses on the table.

It was Solange who spoke first.

"Miguel, Isaac tells us you have some concerns and that there may be some problems. What is happening?"

Miguel described the previous night at the bar and the meeting with the Italians at the "El Coco Loco."

When he finished they all sat in silence.

"This is what I see happening everywhere. Strangers are arriving here from Venezuela and Colombia. There is something developing here in Aruba and it is not good."

Chapter 17

After the meeting with Miguel was finished, Isaac made some decisions and announced that he would be away from the office for the balance of the day.

Isaac drove to the business of a local importer who was a friend of the family. Upon his arrival he asked to speak to Jose the eldest son. Isaac had gone through school with Jose and played sports with him. Jose had been best man at Isaac's wedding.

Jose rushed to meet Isaac.

"Isaac this is unexpected. Come to my office. Let's have a drink and talk."

Isaac walked with Jose through the cavernous warehouse to José's office. As they walked past the stacks of crates, Isaac could smell the aroma of spices and different fruits, including a pungent odor he could not recognize. He noticed some large white wooden containers with metal strapping. Stenciled on the side were the words:

DESTINATION: ROTTERDAM followed by a series of coded numbers.

While he was curious about them and why goods were being shipped from the warehouse he said nothing. As he looked around he noticed that there were more men at the business than normally. Something had changed in the business.

When they reached José's office, the air was cold. A large new industrial air conditioning unit had been installed. Isaac was aware of the costs associated with such a system. It confused him why such expense would have been made for a warehouse, then he recalled that while walking through the warehouse he had noticed how cool it had been. He assumed that maybe they had installed the system to help keep the imported produce fresh but this too seemed strange. The imported produce was delivered to the merchants almost immediately. There were definitely changes that had been made and defied logic.

Jose spoke. "Isaac you are such a busy man and I am wondering why you have come to visit on a business afternoon?"

"I am looking for some information and thought that you might be able to help. Our family invested into the new restaurant and club "El Coco Loco" in San Nicolaas. We have known the family who own it for years. Last night they had a visit from some Italian businessmen from Venezuela and again this morning. They wish to purchase the restaurant and also invest in other businesses here on the Island. We do not know these people. Have you heard of them or know anything?"

Jose's eyes darted to the door and around the room.

"Tell me more."

"I have told you all I know. I understand that they are Italian."

Jose shifted uncomfortably in his chair.

"Isaac, like your situation, my parents are getting older and less interested in running the business. My brothers and I see the expansion of the tourist business and with more people either visiting or coming to live on the island there will be a need for more imports. We decided to buy the business from them. We needed to borrow money to make the purchase. We went to the Aruba banks but none were willing to take the risk. Finally we approached the new Commercial Loan Bank of Aruba and made our proposal. We were not rejected and over a number of weeks there were visits from the Head Office of the bank from their executives in Venezuela. After a month went by we received an answer. The bank would be prepared to loan money to buy out our parents but subject to conditions. They countered the request for financing with the requirement for us to accommodate one of their fledgling businesses here. That business exports goods from Venezuela and Colombia. They provide their own staff and demanded we upgrade our facility here. The biggest changes were the air conditioning systems they say are needed to protect the products and also the security men that they demand be here all day and all night. We understand that the products are of extremely high value. As the warehouse is in the Free Trade Zone the authorities here are not interested in the operation. Nothing is unloaded or sold here in Aruba. We have divided the warehouse between import and export and those items that are brought in to the Free Trade Zone. The government is satisfied with the arrangement.

Isaac Junior was intrigued. He was aware of most developments amongst the businessmen. This was a major change and yet he had heard nothing.

"Jose what can you tell me about this new Commercial Loan Bank of Aruba. I have driven by the building but have not had any dealings."

"It is a bank owned by a Chicago company. They are shareholders and investors in many businesses in the US and Europe. I am aware that there are others here in Aruba who are now clients of that bank. Like us, the bank has invested in them as well as lending money. They have directors on our Board. So far in our relationship with them has been good. The company they wanted us to associate with operates by itself. We are happy."

"Jose, who else is doing business with this bank? Do you know if they have financed any others here?"

"Yes. There is a local radio station and also a newspaper into which they have invested heavily. I have been told that they are strongly represented to our government as well. This is a very powerful group. I am surprised you have not been introduced to them. The Klassen Group of companies would certainly be of interest to them. I can arrange an introduction for you."

"Not yet. I would like to learn more about this bank before then. I do not wish to seem ignorant when I meet them."

"I have to attend a meeting in a few minutes. Please send my regards to the Klassen family. I will speak to my brothers and maybe we can arrange a dinner party at our house."

"I would like that. Thank you"

Isaac Junior got up to leave. As he was escorted back through the warehouse he intently watched the operations. It seemed that all the new workers were either Latinos or Italian. Something was definitely strange.

Isaac Junior spent the balance of the afternoon visiting other business friends. He made the excuse that he was just in the local area and wanted to make a brief social visit.

At each visit he discreetly enquired about the Commercial Loan Bank of Aruba. He pretended that the Klassen Group was looking at some new ventures that may require additional financing. He was startled to find that many had already established relations with the bank. In each case he found the amounts were large and that the bank had imposed certain conditions on the borrowers similar to those on Jose's import business.

That night he went to Jakob's house. They sat in the garden and he shared his findings of the afternoon.

Chapter 18

It was 8:30pm when Isaac Junior left. Jakob stayed in his garden. While he sat there the crowing of the roosters running nearby the property was interrupted by the crack of a baseball bat hitting a ball at the local dirt packed baseball diamond. Cheers and cries of encouragement for the young players wafted through the warm evening air. Jakob was proud of the investment the Klassen Group had made in sponsoring junior baseball on the island.

Jakob reflected on the discussion with Isaac Junior. The changes he had seen in Aruba are real and not imaginary. Jakob is confused. Wearily he arises and returns to the house. Solange is at her desk writing.

"Jakob you look tired. What were you and Isaac talking about? You both spent hours together and it seemed to be a serious conversation"

"Solange, I have made an important decision. Isaac told me of some disturbing developments. I was unaware of things that I should have known. I fear I am losing my sense of business and stature amongst my colleagues."

Jakob proceeded to tell Solange about the Commercial Loan Bank of Aruba and its involvement in many of their friends' businesses. When he was finished Solange stood and went into the kitchen area to make them a hot chocolate drink.

"Jakob, I have been thinking and wanting to speak with you about us. I believe it is time for us to retire. You no longer have the energy you once did. Isaac is in control and capable of operating our companies. It is time for us to stop and enjoy what is left of our lives.

I have noticed you are having difficulty with some of the changes we need to make. Since the end of the war, things have changed a lot. There is no going back to the way things were.

Will you consider retiring?"

Jakob looked down at the floor for the longest time before he spoke.

"I came to Aruba under poor circumstances that I had created. I had friends amongst the whores and pimps in San Nicolaas. I knew most of the owners of the bars and stores. It is not like that now. The prostitutes are not friendly and are controlled by criminals. Owners of the bars and stores are threatened for money by these criminals. The police do nothing. In fact I believe many are involved with the situation. The refinery workers have also changed. Our Aruba is no longer the paradise it was for me when I arrived. This worries me.

Every day now I am thinking back to my younger days and how I made many mistakes. I wish I could undo some of them. I have betrayed many who helped me get through that difficult time."

"Jakob we do not need anything more. We have money, health and a strong family. Please consider my request."

Jakob left Solange in the living room. She thought back to the early years when she had first met Jakob. She had no regrets. He had been a good husband and father. She understood how big a change this would be for him. She worried a little and wondered how they would spend their time now. It seemed Jakob had always been occupied with some task.

She left for the bedroom and found Jakob snoring in a deep sleep. She smiled to herself. He had matured into a good man. She couldn't understand what had affected him so extensively in his younger years. She felt sorry for the torment he had experienced.

Chapter 19

Over the next few days Isaac made subtle inquiries about the Commercial Loan Bank of Aruba. The information he uncovered both surprised and concerned him.

Isaac looked at his watch. It was 10:30am. He picked up the phone and called his friend Jose. He was quickly put through to Jose.

"Isaac, it is good to hear from you again so soon."

"Jose I have been doing a lot of thinking since we met the other afternoon. Can I pass by and talk about some business and maybe then we can go to lunch at my friend Pedro's? It will be my treat."

"Certainly. Can you come now? I am not busy."

Isaac reached for his light jacket and called out to Solange that he was leaving for a meeting.

He drove the short distance from the centre of Oranjestad back to where the warehouses and commercial buildings were located.

Isaac parked at the rear of the building so he could observe the loading dock area. There was a truck unloading large dark blue oil barrels. Stacked on the dock there were pallets of materials wrapped in heavy brown paper sacks.

Isaac walked up to the dock and asked if he could enter through the back entrance in order to reach Jose's office. The men roughly refused him.

At the front entrance the receptionist was awaiting his arrival and immediately jumped up to escort him to Jose's office. She knocked on the door and entered. Jose was smiling and quickly walked from behind his desk his hand extended to shake Isaac's.

"Isaac, what is this business question of yours?"

"Jose we have been considering building on some of the land we had purchased years ago. With all the new developments here it seems the time is right. Unfortunately the timing is bad as we have made investments into other areas of our business. I am facing the question of whether to proceed and take a loan or to wait. You had mentioned your relationship with the Commercial Loan Bank of Aruba. I was wondering if you think it would be wise for me to introduce myself and our businesses?"

"Of course you should. They are looking for new customers. In fact, I am meeting with Jim Mastronardi, the bank President this afternoon. Let me call him and ask about bringing you along for an introduction."

Jose reached for the phone and without looking for the phone number dialed the Commercial Loan Bank of Aruba. Isaac thought to himself that Jose was obviously in frequent contact to have memorized the number.

Jose advised Mr. Mastronardi of the situation and requested the opportunity to introduce Isaac. He hung up and with a smile spoke.

"We will meet Jim at 2:30pm at his office."

Isaac considered the comment. Now it was Jim. He realized that the relationship was more than just that of bank manager and client.

"Jose, I parked near the rear shipping dock. It would be quicker if we could exit through the rear doors."

"No problem"

As they walked through the warehouse Isaac commented on the huge shipment of the dark blue barrels.

Jose looked across and replied.

"The company imports Ether from a supplier in Miami. It is stockpiled and exported from here to a hospital supply company in Colombia. By shipping this way, the Colombian duty is less."

"What are all those brown paper sacks?"

"It is a chemical compound for a plastic manufacturing firm in Cartagena. I am not sure what it is exactly."

Isaac noticed that some of the men loading the truck were staring at them. The looks were far from friendly. The majority of the workers appeared to be Colombian.

Isaac drove slowly through the backstreets of Oranjestad. Again the sidewalks were busy with people heading home or to restaurants for the long lunch break.

As they pulled up outside Pedro's restaurant, Pedro emerged wringing his hands together.

"Mr. Isaac, welcome back. Will you have lunch with us again?"

"Yes Pedro. Meet my old friend Jose. We went to school together and as young boys we got into a lot of trouble."

Pedro laughed and offered them a table in the window area that looked out onto the busy street.

"Today we have a very special lunch. Fresh caught Caribbean lobster. I recommend it. In fact I tried it earlier. It is sweet and tender. I can have it prepared with a bed of rice or some vegetable of your choice. For dessert my wife has made one of our Venezuelan delights, a quesillo."

Jose was confused. "What is a quesillo?"

"It is a sweet flan that is made from eggs and vanilla and caramel. It is a treat."

Over lunch Isaac asked many questions about the Commercial Loan Bank of Aruba.

"Isaac, the bank is part of a large conglomerate. It is privately owned by individuals in The Netherlands and The United States. They own a number of diverse companies in shipping, tourism, food and finance."

"Who are the owners?"

"The conglomerate is also owned by a number of different companies. There are no individual owners."

Isaac ate in silence thinking of the things he had seen in Jose's warehouse and the information Jose had provided. Conversation turned to small talk about family, sports and fishing.

They finished their lunch and left to take the short drive toward the area of San Miguel where the bank had its offices.

Jose and Isaac parked and walked across the empty parking area and into the bank. It was unlike any other bank Isaac had visited. There was a set of triple heavy glass doors. Each was security locked. A guard opened each one and escorted them to a side office.

Within minutes a diminutive man with slicked down jet black hair bounded into the office, loudly closing the door behind him.

"Good afternoon. Good afternoon. Welcome. It is good to see you, Jose."

He walked directly to Isaac and extended his hand.

"I am James Mastronardi. I am the President of the bank. I am very pleased to meet you. I am aware of the Klassen Group of companies. A very impressive operation you have."

"I am flattered but the praise should go to my parents who had the vision and fortitude to build the company"

"Jose has told me that you are looking into a new property development project. Where will it be and what type of buildings will you construct?"

"Years ago we purchased land that is a little inland on the way to the California lighthouse. Today it is covered in shrubs and Divi trees. There are several areas with large rock formations. We are thinking to build a Villa Park. The location receives a steady breeze from the trade winds. Some of the locations have excellent views of the ocean. I have spoken with Ministers of the government and they have encouraged us to build. It could be an exciting project for Aruba."

James Mastronardi nodded his agreement.

"It sounds like a project we would wish to participate in." At that moment there was a knock on the closed office door and it was cracked open. James stood and beckoned the person at the door to enter.

Isaac was shocked to see Tony Vitto and another larger and distinguished looking man enter. James was quick to make the introductions.

"Isaac and Jose. This is Mr. Rossini. He is a director of the bank and also a senior manager of our parent company. This is his assistant here in Aruba, Mr. Tony Vitto

This is indeed a fortunate meeting as Mr. Rossini is here from our Venezuela office."

Isaac looked directly at Tony Vitto before speaking.

"I have met Mr. Vitto before. We were to meet. Now it will not be necessary since I am dealing with Mr. Mastronardi."

Isaac detected a leer on Tony Vitto's face but ignored it.

"Well gentlemen, I must leave you now as I have appointments with some clients of the Klassen Group. It was a pleasure"

Isaac stepped forward to shake their hands. Jose was flustered. He did not understand what had happened.

As Isaac left the office he saw Vincenzio sitting in a chair near the lobby. He was wearing the same clothes and still perspiring heavily.

Isaac wheeled out of the parking area and drove in silence to Jose's office.

"My friend, I think you are associating with the wrong people."

Chapter 20

Business for Hans was bad on Palm Beach that afternoon. The strong winds whipped up clouds of stinging sand. The tourists had left the beach and retreated to their resorts. Hans was bored. He was unaware of the meeting that Isaac was having at the bank and was surprised when Isaac pulled up near the beach. The car door opened, Moreno exited and ran down to the hut. Isaac backed up, turned the car and left.

Moreno seemed eager. He burst into rapidly spoken Spanish. Hans raised his hand and commanded him to speak slowly.

"Hans I have important information. I need to ask you to come with me this evening. You will remember that I told you there were others here from Colombia."

Hans nodded.

"They have important information that will affect your family and some friends. I have arranged to meet them. They will only sell this information. It will be expensive. Can you come with me? Do you have the money?"

Hans studied Moreno. He was anxious but also possessed calmness.

"Where will this meeting take place?"

"There is a bar in Oranjestad. It is on a street behind the St Francis of Assisi church. The area is away from the main part of Oranjestad and the type of people there are rough. Bring only enough money to pay for the information. I suggest one hundred US dollars. Be prepared to hear things that will disturb you. After this meeting you will understand why I am in Aruba."

Hans was intrigued and wanted to press Moreno for more information. Moreno refused.

"Should I ask Jakob or Isaac to attend?"

"No. My friends will only speak to you. They have checked on you and trust you. They are unsure of the others. You will need to be careful after they tell you about the situation. They have enemies here who will think nothing of killing them if they are caught talking."

Hans decided he would arm himself with a knife to take with him.

"At what time are we to go there?"

"I arranged for 5:30pm"

Chapter 21

Palm Beach.

Hans and Moreno waited on the curb for one of the old buses that travelled down to Oranjestad. The winds were still strong and blew paper and debris through the street. After waiting for half an hour an old bus pulled up belching black diesel smoke. Its engine rattled and groaned as they pulled away from the curb. The twenty minute ride into the downtown was punctuated with brief stops along the way. Locals and tourists got on and off the bus. At one stage an 80 year old local carrying a rooster argued with the driver to get his way onto the bus.

The bus screeched to a noisy halt near the docks. Hans and Moreno jumped off and started their walk through the back streets toward the church.

They were soon in a rundown area. Hans was the first to find the bar. He started laughing uncontrollably. Moreno was confused.

"Hans. What is so funny? Please share the joke with me. This is a scary place to be."

Hans pointed to the broken and faded white sign with the blue lettering. The sign hung at an angle but on the fascia the name was clear and prominent.

It read "DE UITGEWOONDIE"

"Moreno, I speak Dutch and understand it well. That sign is excellent for this place. Look at this area. The houses are boarded up and run down and there are cholers walking around. There is hardly anyone decent walking around here. In Dutch the word has several meanings. It can mean derelict or you have had a rough time or sex many times that day and are exhausted."

"Hans the men we will meet will blend in perfectly here. Let us go in and wait. Be careful because they will have friends watching us."

They sat at an old stained table with uneven legs. A large very black woman glided over to them.

"OK...show me your money then I'll get you a drink. No bums or free drinks in here. Got it?"

Hans took a handful of coins from his pocket and laid them on the table which immediately tipped under their weight. Several rolled off onto the floor. Hans looked at the filthy condition of the floor.

"There's no way I am getting down there to look for them."

The woman returned with a large pitcher of pale beer and slammed it onto the table. More coins rolled off and onto the floor. She grunted and turned back to the bar.

Hans poured some of the beer into a murky glass and took a sip. He immediately knew the beer had water added to it. It was weak and tasted flat. Moreno watched him in amusement.

"Hans, in a place like this I suggest to stick to whiskey. It may be rough but at least it will have some taste and if you're lucky, you won't go blind."

They chuckled and Moreno called the woman in Spanish to bring whiskey.

After a few minutes four Latino men entered. They stood in the doorway while their eyes adjusted to the dimly lit bar's interior. Two of the men recognized Moreno and started toward the table. The others went to the bar.

"We will forget any introduction or names. Moreno knows us well. There is some information that we think will help the Klassen family but it will cost. Moreno did you explain this?"

"Yes. We have the money."

"How much did you bring? We want three hundred dollars."

"That is not what we agreed on. I arranged the amount of one hundred. This was the agreement. Don't get greedy. Remember I can also do you some harm."

The Latinos exchanged glances.

"OK. Pay now, then we talk."

Hans took a small yellowed envelope from his breast pocket. The Latinos counted the money.

When they were satisfied the older one spoke.

"We fled from our home country of Colombia some time ago. We came to Aruba as we thought it would be safe for us. We had been in Venezuela first. We had been working with others doing construction. We were hiding from a gang who operated a large drug operation in Colombia. We did not know when we started working the construction that it was connected with the drug gangs in Colombia. They were bringing the drugs across the border into Venezuela and shipping to America. We were threatened with our lives unless we stayed quiet and worked with the smugglers. The gangs were Colombian but the brains and money were the Italian Mafia. There were hundreds of Italians in Caracas.

We were scared and fled to Aruba. When we came there were no real gangs from Colombia, just a few loners selling drugs. We thought we were safe here."

Hans was getting impatient.

"So why is this so important to me?"

"We know the Klassen family. We have seen pictures. My brother is here in Aruba. He is a gardener. The other day he saw two of the Italian Mafia from Venezuela at the home of Isaac Klassen. One of the men is an enforcer.....a killer. We think that your family has been selected by them to operate some of their criminal activity.

I work at the Import company and Isaac has been there twice. There are strange things happening there. They are shipping chemicals to Colombia for the production of drugs."

"How do you know all this?"

"Before we ran away from Colombia we were forced to work with the peasant farmers. They are growing coca leaves. America has a new drug need. They want cocaine, and lots of it. The peasant farmers are paid well but those in the drug factories are prisoners. They are slaves. The factories are guarded by armed men. Some are soldiers who have deserted the army and taken their weapons.

We spent a year trying to escape. We learned about Aruba from an older man who is enslaved at the factory. He was from Aruba. He told us of the country and the life here. His name was Juan. He was kidnapped at sea when he saw a drug transfer taking place. He said he was a simple fisherman. The smugglers knew him and were cousins. Instead of killing him they took him captive and put him in the factory. He was a good man and a hard worker."

Hans could not believe what he was hearing.

"Please let me speak with Moreno privately. We will talk further. Wait over there at the bar."

Hans spun to Moreno.

"Do you realize what we have just been told? If this is true about Juan, and it is the same person, then he was one of my father's best friends. The family still looks after his wife. You know her. It is Carlita."

Moreno gasped. "That cannot be true."

Hans went quiet as he thought of all that he had just heard.

"Moreno, do you trust these men?"

"Yes. They have been through terrible times. It was I who asked them to share this information with you."

"Please call them back and inform them I will pay them well to provide more details. I need to know where Juan is held and what it will take to rescue him."

Moreno turned to the bar and motioned the men to rejoin them.

When they were seated Moreno spoke in a low voice and relayed Hans' request. The two Colombians left the table and joined the others at the bar. With their heads bowed together they entered into a deep discussion.

Moreno watched them closely. One of the men who had sat and watched approached.

"I believe I have the details you will need. Return tomorrow at the same time with five hundred dollars."

Chapter 22

The four Colombians left the little bar. Hans was impatient.

"We need to go. It is important that I share this news with Jakob and Isaac. Let us take a taxi."

Hans reached into his pocket and placed some paper money down on the table. He called to the lady and pointed to the money. She grunted some words and waddled across to fetch it.

They found an empty taxi at the entrance to the docks. Hans piled into the front seat and Moreno crawled into the rear.

Hans made a startling decision.

"Moreno this is all really important. I am going to get Carlita in Savaneta. She needs to hear this. We will pick her up and take her with us to Jakob's home in Malmok.

Hans gave instructions to the driver and they sped off in the direction of Savaneta. It took twenty minutes before they pulled into the drive of Carlita's Villa. She was outside hanging some clothing on a makeshift line.

"Carlita, you must come and join us. We are going to Jakob's house. It is very important you come with us."

"Is there a problem? Is someone hurt? Why this rush? I am washing right now."

"Carlita, all of that can wait. What I have learned is important and you must be with us. Bring some extra clothing. I suspect you may stay the night."

Carlita was perplexed. She ran into the house and emerged with her battered little case.

Hans opened the rear door of the taxi and she climbed in beside Moreno.

"What is going on?" she asked.

"It is best we are all together to discuss things. We will soon be there."

Thirty minutes later the taxi emptied them at Jakob's. The driver, sensing urgency, had driven fast.

Hans rushed ahead and into the house.

"Quick, please call Isaac. I have some very important things to discuss. He must come now. Tell him to bring Janelle."

Everyone was curious and getting annoyed at Hans for not speaking immediately.

Time seemed to drag before Isaac arrived with his wife.

"What is so important to interfere with people's dinners and evenings?" It was plain to see that Isaac was not in a good mood. The meeting at the bank had soured his afternoon.

"Let's all sit in the living room. I will start with the best news. Earlier this evening, Moreno and I met with some of his fellow countrymen. They had escaped from a drug operation in Colombia and sought refuge here in Aruba.

During our conversation they mentioned that they had learned of Aruba and life here during the time they spent working at a drug factory in the jungles of Colombia. When we questioned them they told us of a man who was imprisoned there. His name is Juan. They say he used to be a fisherman."

Carlita tried to stand but slumped and fainted on the floor. Jakob's jaw hung open. Solange appeared to be in shock.

Finally Jakob spoke. "How do we know this is the truth?"

Hans went on and told them of the other details. It seemed too coincidental for it not to be Juan.

"There is more. There is a lot more. These men worked in Venezuela and unwittingly became employees in construction projects run by the Mafia. The brother of one of them observed the visit Isaac received at his house from the Italians. The Colombian men know them. They are Italians from the Venezuela Mafia. One of them is an enforcer....a killer.

Isaac you must be careful."

Jakob shook his head. "Trouble has arrived in our paradise I am afraid. What do we do with this news?"

"I am meeting with them again tomorrow evening. I have agreed to pay them for information on where the drug factory is located. I have asked for details about the factory, the guards and other information."

Isaac spoke "I will come with you."

"No Isaac. I think only Moreno and I should go. These men are nervous. I am sure we will get what we need from them. Please do not do anything foolish. Carlita, please do not tell Miguel or Alejandro about this yet. Let us get more detail then we can plan."

Jakob looked across at Solange. She nodded.

"Isaac and Hans. We were going to wait until the weekend but I think this is the right time to tell everyone. Solange and I have decided to retire from Klassen Group businesses. We will stay for a while as you make the changes necessary for the company to continue and grow. We are tired and it is time. With what you have told us tonight I am afraid I do not have the stamina or the drive to deal with these new forces. We will be there for you both. Isaac we are leaving the business to both you and Hans jointly."

Chapter 23

When Hans had left with Moreno, Solange settled Carlita into bed and then returned to join Isaac and Jakob.

"I do not understand your decision to leave the company to both Hans and I. Hans has never really worked in the areas of property development or finance. This troubles me. Why did you do this?"

Solange placed her hand on Isaacs's knee.

"Why do you want to involve Hans? He has never shown any interest in the companies other than the water sports one?"

"Hans has changed. He has built his business well. He is serious with Irma and she confided in me he wishes to marry her."

"Be calm. We have reasons. Isaac you have always excelled academically. It often seemed that there was no puzzle that could defeat you. I admire how brilliant your mind is. Hans is not so brilliant, but what he lacks intellectually he makes up for in other ways. Hans grew up the hard way in post war Germany. He was associated with street gangs, in trouble with the law and involved in fights and bad deals. Those days are a long way behind him now.

Our thinking is that with your brilliant academic mind and Hans' "experiences" you will make a good pair to operate Klassen Group. This is especially true now that we know that there are forces at play in business here that are not so ethical. I believe you will both look after each other's interests. I am tired and will now go to bed."

Part 2

"Things have a way of Happening"

Chapter 24

Because of the upcoming changes, Isaac and Moreno changed the meeting with the Colombians. Over the next week, the Klassens planned the announcement of their retirement from business in Aruba.

Invitations were sent out to various business leaders, politicians and local press to attend a social event planned for the following Tuesday afternoon.

Isaac Junior confided with Hans and discussed his meeting with James Mastronardi of Commercial Loan Bank of Aruba. Together they agreed that a further meeting was required and that they would advise the bank that the plans to proceed with further development were not going to proceed until all the changes in the companies were completed. They decided to meet with James Mastronardi before the official announcement was to be made.

For days Isaac Junior spent hours with Hans explaining to him the intricacies of the operations and advising him about particular key staff members. Hans was a keen learner and grasped the information quickly.

"I have arranged for a meeting with James Mastronardi this coming Friday afternoon. He is eager to meet. I did not tell him why we need the meeting. He will be surprised."

Hans nodded as he absorbed this information. Finally he spoke.

"I am planning to hand over the operations of my water sports business to Miguel's nephew so I can be active in the business here. He has been working the boat for months now. The tourists love him and he receives many tips. They love his yarns and tales of the history of the island. Many often invite him for a drink or dinner that evening. He is a natural guide and has a strong sense of authority. The other young men on the boat respect him. He has shown me that he is both smart and fair."

"I think you have made a good choice in selecting him."

Isaac Junior reached across his desk and pulled the black phone toward him. He then flipped through some business cards until he located the card for James Mastronardi and dialed the number.

The phone at the bank was answered by a man. Isaac requested to speak with Mastronardi. He was asked to identify himself which he did. Moments later a charming James Mastronardi came onto the line. His words were smooth and jovial.

"Certainly and at what time shall we schedule to meet? Would you like a lunch meeting? It is a Friday afternoon and, as you know, not much happens in Aruba on such afternoons. As it happens, Tomasso Rossini will be here and I will ask him to join us."

"No we are very busy at present and will not be able to have a lunch meeting. I have some serious business to attend to that afternoon. I will be attending the meeting with Hans, a family member."

James Mastronardi was confused. He had heard of Hans but did not understand his relationship with the family. He wondered why Hans would be attending and what possible business he may have within the Klassen organization.

"I look forward to our Friday meeting."

He hung up the phone and called to his assistant to find Tomasso Rossini and Tony Vitto. This was an important development and he wanted all the assistance he could gather to land the "big fish" that was the Klassen business.

The assistant diligently phoned around the businesses in which the bank had invested until he located Tomasso who was with Tony Vitto at the import/export company. They were angry at being interrupted in the middle of their business with Jose. A lesson was being taught and Jose was neither happy nor receptive.

Tony Vitto was making threats when the phone jangled alive with James Mastronardi. He snatched the phone from Jose's hand and listened intently. He threw to phone back to Jose.

"You little worm. Youse lucky this time but we be back to finish this business. Ya got it? I think you need to learn quick that we are the bosses now. You do what we tell you."

Tomasso and Tony Vitto turned and kicked open the office door. Vincenzio had sat outside to make sure that no one entered during the "lesson."

As the trio walked through the cavernous warehouse, Tomasso grunted "That little paisano needs to learn very quickly that our orders need to be followed before his shitty business of shipping bananas and coconuts. We are the bosses now regardless as to what he thinks."

When the three men had left, Jose called Isaac Klassen.

"Isaac, we must speak urgently. Can we meet?"

"Jose what is so urgent? You and your family are our friends and yes we can meet. What is so important?"

"It is best for me to tell you of some developments, but I must do this directly with you. You need to be careful. Some bad changes are happening here."

Jose sounded panicked and frightened. Isaac was concerned.

"Jose, do you wish to come here?"

"No. There is an old bar near Savaneta. It is owned by a Chinese family. It will be safer to meet there. We will be away from Oranjestad and the eyes of some who may now be watching us. If I leave now we should be able to meet in an hour."

Isaac looked out of the large second floor office window. It was late November. Dark black clouds hung in the sky and fierce lightning flashed accompanied by the roar and claps of thunder. The rainy season had arrived. The road to Savaneta would probably have some surface flooding along with the construction to fix the huge holes created by the constant flow of heavy trucks to the refinery in San Nicolaas.

"I will meet you there. Hans will be with me."

After explaining the call to Hans, they left the office in Oranjestad and started the slow drive to Savaneta.

The drive was slow and tedious. They crawled past the road construction that was in progress for the access to the airport. Before the incline to Balashi the road was awash. Water flooded across the loose seal. Several cars sat abandoned with water above the bottom of the doors.

Isaac carefully navigated the obstacles until he reached the crest of the small hill at Balashi and took a right turn down toward Spaans Lagoon and over the bridge that lead to Savaneta.

It was almost exactly an hour when Isaac and Hans pulled into the dirt area behind the brightly painted house that also served as a restaurant and bar.

Upon entering the restaurant they were immediately greeted by a young Chinese man dressed in a crisp white shirt and tight black trousers. On his feet were open sandals.

He ushered them to a well worn old table and placed two handwritten menus in front of them. Isaac raised his hand.

In halting Papiamento he explained that they were there for drinks only.

Hans scanned the darkened interior. At several of the tables, local fishermen sat with bottles of open beer playing dominoes. Every so often a shout would erupt from one of the tables followed by a sharp crack as the dominoes were slapped down by the winner.

Isaac and Hans ordered beers and sat waiting. Soon two hours had passed. Isaac wondered if the storm had made the road impassable.

After three hours had gone by, Isaac asked to use the restaurant phone. He called Jose's office and was informed that Jose had left three hours earlier.

Isaac was concerned. Could there have been an accident he wondered.

He called out to Hans and after paying for the drinks they ran to their car for the return trip to Malmok.

Chapter 25

That evening Isaac went to visit Jakob. He discussed the day and the strange situation with Jose. Jakob said nothing.

Solange joined them and they sat quietly enjoying a heavy Dutch coffee and cake. Finally Jakob spoke.

"Isaac I am aware that there have been some strange events recently. I know Jose's father and family well. I will go in the morning to make sure all is well. I am sure that the reason that Jose did not meet with you is because of the storms. They have been bad this afternoon."

As Isaac stood to leave the telephone rang. Solange walked quickly to the small table upon which it was located. She answered it and stood motionless, listening to the caller. She emitted a gasp and beckoned Isaac to take the phone.

"This is Isaac. Who am I speaking with?"

"Isaac, it is Carlos. There has been a terrible accident. My brother Jose is badly injured. Can Jakob and Solange come to our house? My parents are upset. I need someone to be with them while I attend at the hospital."

Isaac explained the situation to Jakob and Solange who stood immediately, while nodding their agreement.

"Carlos I will drive them to your parent's house. Hans and I will meet you there."

Isaac called Hans and told him of this development. He arranged to pick him up.

The rains had ceased when they arrived at the house. Carlos was standing in the doorway. He was agitated and in a hurry to leave for the hospital.

On the drive to the hospital, Isaac asked about the accident.

"It was at the location of the bridge at the end of Oranjestad. A car pulled across the road and hit Jose's car from behind forcing it off the road and into the small river. The car that hit Jose was travelling fast and sped away after the accident. It seemed that this was deliberate. Why would anyone want to hurt Jose? We are honest people and treat everyone well."

Isaac thought back to the panicked phone conversation of earlier that afternoon. Jose knew something that someone did not want others to know. He was concerned.

They drove on in silence. Isaac's mind was racing.

Chapter 26

Darkness was setting in when they arrived at San Pedro di Verona Hospital in Oranjestad. Isaac parked the car and the three of them ran across to the main door. They asked for details and were directed to a room on the second floor.

The wait seemed endless. Finally a white coated Doctor and a nurse entered the room. Introductions were made.

The Doctor placed a folder and papers on the table in front of him.

"I am so sorry. By the time we received the patient there was very little we could do. His neck was broken, his lungs were punctured and a number of bones were broken. He passed within minutes of his arrival here."

Carlos let out a piercing scream. Tears rolled down his cheek. "No, that is not possible. He is my brother and my best friend. I want to see him. I want to see him now."

The Doctor spoke. "I think it is best you wait. The accident has made his appearance difficult. Please let us prepare him for you. It will not take us long."

Carlos was now shaking in anger. "Who did this? Why? Are there any others who were injured?"

Yes. There was a worker from one of the fruit stands who was starting his bike ride home. He was hit by the car. His leg is broken. He is angry. I will ask if he will speak with you. The authorities have been asking him many questions. Let me check."

Carlos slumped down into a chair and started to mutter incoherently. The Doctor signaled the nurse who produced a syringe and after filling it from a small glass vial proceeded to inject Carlos.

The Doctor spoke. "He has gone into a mild shock. This often happens with immediate family members. I will go now and speak with the authorities. They will want to speak with all of you. We will need to discuss the arrangements for the body. Who will do that?"

Isaac spoke immediately. "I will take that responsibility. We are close to the family and Jose was one of my best friends. I fear that the family will have a very difficult time with this death."

After the Doctor and nurse left the room, the three waited. No one spoke. The shock and impact of the accident was evident.

Isaac looked around the room. It was a depressing sight. The walls were painted a sickly pale sea green. The floor was covered in nondescript linoleum of a light grey with flecks similar to used chewing gum streaks as a pattern. Isaac wondered to himself who chose such colors for hospitals. Every hospital he had visited seemed dull and dreary. From overhead bright and glaring fluorescent lighting beamed down giving everyone in the room a sickly white appearance.

There was a rap on the door which swung open and two large officious Dutchmen entered. They introduced themselves as the officials investigating the accident. Their manner and demeanor was abrupt. Isaac recognized the taller man from some charity events he had attended.

"I am Richard van de leek and this is my partner Evert Joost. We are sorry for your brother's loss, Carlos. We are trying to gather information and understand what happened. From the reports of the man who witnessed the accident it seems that it was deliberate. This concerns us greatly."

Isaac spoke loudly. "Please tell us what you know."

"From what we have been told by the witness and some others in the market area the car that hit Carlos was driven behind him and when they reached the bridge it tried to pass but turned against his car forcing it into the railing and off the bridge. The car then backed off and sped away into the back of Oranjestad. We have made inquiries but have not received any information."

Isaac, Hans and Carlos hung on every word.

"Carlos, was your brother involved in any bad situation that you are aware of?"

"No. Recently we had added to the business. Things were good. Our family business was growing and we were planning to expand to handle the new opportunities that the increased tourism was creating. We had arranged new banking and everything was progressing well."

Everet Joost was recording every word that Carlos spoke. Occasionally he would exchange looks with his partner.

An hour passed. The nurse who had injected Carlos returned. She spoke to Carlos and checked his blood pressure. Satisfied that he was calmer she recommended some medicines to help him remain calm for the next little while.

The two Dutch officials left the room.

Hans stood and addressed Carlos.

"Come Carlos. Let us take you to your parent's home. There is much to be done now. We are your friends and are here to help."

Carlos thanked the nurse and told her that members of the family would return in the morning to make arrangements.

When they left the hospital, the rains had stopped. The air was warm and humid. The trade winds had returned and a full pale moon lit the ground.

The trio climbed into Isaac's car for the trip to Carlos' home. It would be a sad and difficult night. Isaac did not look forward to the conversations that needed to be held with the family. Out of a sense of loyalty he would stay and assist.

Chapter 27

Vincenzio cursed. A loud scraping sound was coming from
the front wheel area of the old nondescript Black 1942
Ford. Vincenzio looked in the rear vision mirror and saw
Tony Vitto following at a discreet distance. Vincenzio
hoped the old car would make it to the location they had
chosen to abandon the car. It was likely that the police
were already alerted that the car had been stolen from the
cunucu house in Noord and were assuming it was the
same car that had rammed Jose.

Vincenzio drove slowly and carefully. They did not need
the car to breakdown before reaching the area. The old
Ford had been chosen as it did not draw attention.

As they reached the road to San Nicolaas the rains started
again. The rain was heavy and lashed down on the cars
making it difficult to see oncoming cars or obstructions on
the road. Vincenzio was worried and sweating profusely.
He wanted to stop for the fear of hitting something or the
car stalling. He slowed to a stop and pulled over to the side
of the road, jumped from the driver's seat and ran back to
Tony's car.

"This weather is making it too hard to see. That old car has
bad wipers. I cannot see."

"Let us proceed a little way. Earlier I had noticed a track ahead on the right. We will pull off there and wait."

Lightning flashed and the rains continued to cascade down as they waited in the little clearing. The occasional truck rattled by on its way to the refinery.

The weather matched Vincenzio's mood. Foul and intense.

After approximately fifteen minutes the rain stopped as quickly as it had started. Vincenzio fired up the old Ford and pulled out onto the now flooded road. The old car's design allowed it to clear the waters which were flowing across the road.

Slowly they inched up the incline and continued their journey to The Colony area.

As they reached San Nicolaas the lights from the brightly lit refinery and bars illuminated the town. Vincenzio wished he could stop and expel the demons that possessed him after an assignment. Knowing better he continued through the streets and finally swung right to climb the hill toward The Colony. He glanced in the rear vision mirror and noted a car between him and Tony Vitto. He cursed as they wanted no witnesses or to draw attention to themselves.

He slowed and pulled over. The car raced by them. He assumed the occupants were in a hurry to get to the Lago Esso Club for the entertainment and social activities.

When the road was deserted they pulled out and continued through the Seroe Colorado district. Vincenzio looked at the neat settlement that had been built to house the oil company workers. He wondered what a job like that would be like with a wife and family.

As they drove on the road turned hard right toward Baby Beach and the Esso Club. They continued until an entrance emerged at the back of the refinery.

Vincenzio slowed and scanned for the road that headed off to the left and up a hill. A herd of goats were grazing on the side of the road and blocking the entrance. Vincenzio was in no mood to wait. He dropped the car into first gear and proceeded to run through the goats. Sensing danger the goats scattered. Vincenzio laughed and continued to drive. The road became narrow and steep. The recent rains had caused large washouts. After carefully navigating the treacherous conditions, they arrived at the top next to the rusting large gun placements that had been built by the US Army Engineers to defend Aruba's south coast and the refinery from invasion or attack. Vincenzio stopped the car and walked back to speak with Tony Vitto.

"OK boss. What we gonna do now?"

"Drive over to the edge of that cliff. Be careful. The ground is soft and the soil loose. Stop about 10 feet back from the edge."

Vincenzio edged the old Ford to the edge of the cliff. He got out of the car and walked to the edge and looked down. The wild surf was crashing in on the rocks below. Huge white caps surged as the ocean unleashed its fury against the coast.

He turned to see Tony walking toward him carrying a large red round gasoline can. Tony stopped at the old Ford and poured gas in the back doors and over the front of the car.

When he had completed this task he returned to his car with the can and threw it into the trunk.

Tony walked to the old Ford and beckoned Vincenzio to help him. They pushed the car to the cliff's edge. Tony motioned to stop. He reached into his coat pocket and lit a Molotov cocktail he had been carrying. He threw it into the Ford. Quickly he and Vincenzio pushed the now flaming car over the edge. They stood back and watched as it cart wheeled done the bank. Pieces flew from the body of the car before it crashed onto the rocks and exploded.

Tony loved it and laughed.

"Let's get the hell outa here. Let's go to that bar that those Aruban guys, Miguel and Alejandro, own.

Vincenzio grunted his agreement and while soaking wet piled his body onto the front seat of Tony's car.

Chapter 28

San Nicolaas, Aruba.

At the "El Coco Loco" club, Miguel and Alejandro greeted their friends and patrons. Since they had met with the Italians there had been a change in the type of customers. More businessmen were frequenting the club. In addition Miguel was disturbed at the increase in prostitutes who were constantly in the bar area. His attempts to send them away were often met with resistance by their male companions.

As the evening wore on the level of conversation swelled and a mixture of cigarette and cigar smoke filled the club. Alejandro was unhappy.

"Miguel we can no longer control the club. There is drunkenness, drug dealing and prostitution happening here. This is not the club I want anymore. It is against our beliefs and morals. I think we should look at the offer that those Italians wanted to make us. There are many better ways for us to live."

Miguel looked around at the patrons. He turned to Alejandro and nodded his head.

"We have started several very successful clubs over the years. I think it is time for us to retire from this business. It is no longer the same. We always had fun with the refinery workers. When the occasional one got drunk there was always a friend or coworker to take him home. Now these customers get nasty and fight. I agree and we will contact the Italians. Let us sell. I will contact Isaac Junior to advise and assist us."

"Miguel I will not be sad to leave this business. I am tired and ready to try new things."

While they were talking Vincenzio and Tony Vitto walked in. Both men were disheveled and wet. They did not look happy. Vincenzio stormed up to the bar.

"Gimme the best bottle of Scotch you have and some glasses."

Miguel reached into the cupboards beneath the bar and withdrew a bottle. He sat it on the bar surface along with two small tumblers.

Vincenzio scowled and snatched up the bottle. As Miguel and Alejandro watched he pushed his way through the crowded room and joined Tony Vitto. He then turned to a table where some men sat drinking beer. Miguel and Alejandro had not seen these men before. Vincenzio seemed to shout something and the men quickly left the table. Vincenzio slid his huge frame behind the table from where he could monitor the activities in the club. Tony Vitto sat at the end of the table.

It was obvious that the two had been involved in some situation. Tony's cool manner had been replaced by nervousness. He continually looked around at the other customers. Every so often he would lean forward and engage Vincenzio in quiet conversation.

Miguel decided to visit with them. He crossed over to the table.

"Bon Noche mi Amigoes. Alejandro and I have spoken and we are ready to sell the club. When will we meet to discuss this?"

"We are busy with another matter here. It will have to wait until next week....maybe two weeks."

Miguel shrugged and returned to the bar.

"Alejandro this is not the correct time to discuss the sale. They are not in the right mood. I suggest we leave them alone tonight."

Vincenzio's mood darkened further as the Scotch infiltrated his system. When he had consumed six glasses he turned to Tony Vitto.

"Tony, go and leave me. I am going to have some female companionship tonight. I will meet you in the morning at our hotel."

Tony was not happy.

"Vincenzio, I want you to be careful. There is a lot we are responsible for. Remember that the Palermo Brothers are unforgiving. We have many tasks to complete here. Don't mess up."

Tony slid off his chair and threw some money onto the table. Vincenzio sat alone surveying the possible targets of his desire. He spotted a young attractive Colombian girl who was laughing with a group of young men. He watched as she started to work the room. Her gaze finally settled upon Vincenzio. He smiled and raised his finger. She sidled over to him.

"You buy me a drink? Maybe something more?"

Vincenzio leered at her. She was beautiful. He wondered why such a pretty girl was a whore. Then he remembered the time he had spent in Colombia and the destitute barrios.

"You speak English? Espanol? You looking to make some money? How much?"

"Please be slow. What is your name? Mine is Doris Daze."

Vincenzio shook his head. He could never believe the incredibly bizarre working names these girls gave themselves.

"OK Doris. What do you want to drink?"

"I like the champagne. It is good for a special girl like me."

Miguel had been watching from the bar and hurried across when Vincenzio waved to him.

"Please Miguel. Champagne for the girl. Not too expensive."

Miguel returned with a small half bottle and a champagne flute. Doris was all smiles. She moved to sit next to Vincenzio and pushed against him.

"For $20 I can be your Chiquita for the whole night. I will make you very happy. You will need to sleep all tomorrow I am sure."

They finished their drinks and Doris ordered yet another. Vincenzio was getting frustrated. The events of the day were in his mind and he wished for a distraction to clear them.

"Doris I wish to leave. I will pay you the $20. Maybe a bit more."

Doris swung her long legs out from under the table and eased onto to feet. Vincenzio marveled at her beauty and his luck.

He waved to Miguel and strode to the bar and dropped some US Dollars on the wooden surface. Miguel scooped them up and smiled.

Outside the bar the street was alive with street music, old women selling foods, furtive men openly selling drugs and pimps standing on corners.

Doris slid her arm through Vincenzio's and led him down a small laneway to an old white and blue adobe. The laneway was dark and foreboding. Vincenzio noticed a group of Latinos near the end of the lane. They glanced at Doris as she passed by.

The adobe was small and poorly lit. The front door was open to the street and some girls were in the rooms on the ground floor. Doris took Vincenzio's hand and pulled him over to the staircase that led to the second floor.

Doris opened the door to a tiny bedroom. In the centre was an old iron bed covered with yellowing sheets. An old wooden dresser stood against the wall. The room reeked of marijuana fumes and stale cheap perfume.

Doris sat on the edge of her bed and extended her palm.

"I need you to pay now. I must give money to the house before we start."

Vincenzio reached into his jacket and handed her a $20 note."

Doris left and soon returned. She sat back on the bed and unbuttoned her blouse. Vincenzio was excited. Doris crossed over to him and assisted him in removing his shirt. The smell of two day old stale perspiration oozed from him. Doris ran and jumped under the sheets while emitting a squeal. Vincenzio became more excited. He dropped his trousers and stood looking at her. Naked his 300pound body seemed huge.

Doris started giggling uncontrollably. She could not stop. Vincenzio was confused.

"What is so funny?" he asked.

"You." Doris pointed at his penis.

"I have never seen one so small. I do not have condoms for babies. It is the size of a three year old boy. I think a toy balloon might work." With this she roared laughing.

Vincenzio was incensed. After the day he had he was in no mood for this. He lunged at her and slapped her across the head. She screamed a piercing scream and fell to the floor. Vincenzio rushed at her and kicked her hard in the ribs.

There was the sound of heavy footsteps pounding up the stairs. The door flew open and four young Colombian men burst in. Vincenzio ran at them but the younger men were too fast. With knives drawn they descended upon him waving them through the air as they did so. One of the knives made contact and cut a large slash just above his flaccid penis which had shrunk further during the melee

Blood spurted from his stomach. One of the larger young men grabbed Vincenzio in a headlock and dragged him from the room to the stairs and pushed him down.

Vincenzio lay naked at the foot of the stairs bleeding profusely. As he tried to stand his clothes were thrown down on him.

Vincenzio attempted to run from the adobe into the lane. Once outside he found a path that lead to a garage. He limped down the path and lay on the ground. After regaining his breath he awkwardly pulled on his clothing.

After attempting to clean himself he stumbled to Main Street where he found a taxi. He fell into the back seat and gave the driver the name of his hotel. The driver questioned Vincenzio's condition but quickly drove when shown a wad of money.

At the hotel Vincenzio crashed into his room and collapsed on the bed. Tomorrow would be different he decided.

The morning rolled around and Tony Vitto loudly knocked on the thin front door. Vincenzio dragged his beaten body to the door.

Tony stood gaping at the sight in front of him.

"What the hell happened to you?"

Vincenzio told Tony of the escapade.

"We cannot let you be seen like this. It is time to call in the services of one of those Doctors we have financed to help build a fancy clinic. They will be told to keep this quiet."

Tony left to return to his room and determined which Doctor and phone him. After, he returned to Vincenzio's room

"This is not a bad thing. People will have seen us at "El Coco Loco" and with the fight in the brothel they will be able to check us out in case we are suspected of any involvement in Jose's accident and the ditching of that piece of junk Ford."

Vincenzio attempted a smile. That is when Tony noticed the two broken front teeth.

"Shit, another complication that this gorilla has created," he thought.

Tony left the room and walked to reception to use the phone and call a particular Italian Doctor whom he knew could be trusted with mob matters. The phone rang and rang before it was answered by a somewhat impatient receptionist. He gave her his name and need for a house visit. In the background the Doctor's voice was asking who was calling at such an early hour. Tony heard her call his name. Within seconds the phone was snatched up by the Doctor. Tony gave instructions and a description of the injuries and the need for discretion. The Doctor acknowledged his comments.

Chapter 29

It was early Friday afternoon when Isaac and Hans left the office for the meeting with James Mastronardi at the Commercial Loan Bank of Aruba.

It was a beautiful sunny Aruba afternoon. Gentle trade winds carried a cooling breeze from the East. The palm trees swayed in a lazy dance. If it wasn't for the meeting Isaac would have taken his children to the beach and maybe some fishing from the family's restaurant pier. He loved days like today and cursed at the task he and Hans had ahead of them.

During the drive to the bank, Hans told Isaac of the late night visit he had received from Miguel and Alejandro. They had told him of their desire to sell "El Coco Loco" and the reasons in wanting to do so.

Isaac was quiet. "I think Jakob is correct. Troubles have arrived in our paradise. Do we let these people continue to infiltrate our society and lives or do we find a way to stop or at least slow them down?"

They drove on in silence, reflecting on that question.

Hans thought back to his rough days in Germany immediately after the end of the war. He had lived on the streets and fought and run a sizeable black-market operation. Hans was feared amongst the other gangs. He never allowed anyone who crossed him personally or in a shady deal to go free. Given the nature of his business activities it was impossible to report him to the ruling authorities at that time. Hans had established a clique of loyal lieutenants who protected him and his gang interests. Rumors circulated about Hans and the fate of those who ran up against him. Here in Aruba after settling into an honest and hard working life, Hans was disturbed that troubles were again surfacing. He did not want to return to the former life he had once had or live with the possibility of troubles once again.

They drove slowly past where the old Eagle Refinery stood and turned inland to where a few new industrial buildings had been built. The area was uninspiring and desolate. For all its beauty, this part of Aruba seemed incongruous.

Finally the grandiose entrance to the bank came into their view. Large boulders had been placed either side of the entrance to create a "natural" feel. The curved driveway lead into a covered entrance and to a paved parking area just further beyond.

Isaac drove carefully through the entrance area while intently observing the people standing around.

There were few that he recognized. He pulled across to the empty parking space reserved for visitors.

Once parked he and Hans walked back to the huge glass doors that were opened by a burly security guard. Isaac announced his scheduled meeting with James Mastronardi. He and Hans were directed to sit while the guard telephoned someone. Within minutes a short stocky Aruban woman marched into the reception area. "Bon Tardi. Follow me please. Mr. Mastronardi and Mr. Rossini await you in the conference room.

Isaac shot a look at Hans. There had never been any mention of Rossini attending the meeting. Isaac motioned Hans with his hand to remain calm.

The woman stopped at a large teak door and swung it open.

"Mr. Mastronardi will see you now."

Upon their walking into the conference room, James Mastronardi bounded forth with his hand outstretched.

"Welcome, welcome. You have met Mr. Rossini before. Given that this will be such an important meeting and the fact that the Klassens are so important here in Aruba, I thought it appropriate to invite Mr. Rossini as he is a director of the bank and also of our parent company.

Isaac attempted to hide his distaste of the man. He had severe reservations about Rossini and the role he was playing in the events unfolding in Aruba.

James Mastronardi stood and offered them coffee or if they wished, stronger drinks.

"I would like to get to our business immediately as Hans and I do have another couple of business matters we will need to attend to after this meeting. Thank you but we are fine. I suspect that we will not be here for a long time."

James Mastronardi frowned. Something was not right. In all previous meetings with borrowers and partners, the customers were always polite and feigned an air of subservience to the bank with its power and money. Isaac and Hans seemed different.

"All right then. Shall we commence? Did you bring a portfolio of your financial affairs and the interests into which the Klassen Group is invested?"

"Mr. Mastronardi, we have made several significant changes since we last met. Jakob and Solange, my parents, will be announcing their retirement from the business this Tuesday at a function to be held here in Oranjestad. I am sure you have received an invitation to attend and I hope you can. There are going to be many changes in our company. Hans and I will be taking over complete control. The legal papers have already been executed. Given these recent events, we have decided not to proceed with any banking changes nor will we embark upon the new development projects. We will wait some months and then re-evaluate. At present our plan is to leave everything operating the way it is. In fact we will probably sell some of the smaller businesses that take so much time to manage. We will of course keep the water sports company and restaurants on Palm Beach. In fact Han's company will become part of our larger water sports operation. It has done very well."

Hans smiled a gracious smile at Mr. Rossini who was sitting red faced and obviously angry.

Isaac stood. "Gentlemen, I believe we are finished here. As we progress with the company we will keep you advised of any assistance you could offer."

They stood and after shaking hands walked to the large teak door and waited to be escorted from the bank.

In the car Hans could barely control himself. He howled with laughter.

"Rossini. You should have seen his face as you announced our plan. I know you were watching Mastronardi but I wish you could have seen the change. It was like a storm coming over the horizon."

"Hans we must be careful. These are dangerous men. We must not provoke them. They have an agenda and we have upset it."

Chapter 30

San Nicolaas.

The weather had changed over the past weeks. Hans enjoyed the drive down to San Nicolaas from Malmok. There was construction of new roads in anticipation of the increase in tourism and the need for better transportation. The new fledgling bus line was operating and while naïve and deficient the taxi service was slowly expanding. Hans observed the new vehicles as he drove. He wondered if the Klassens should start a business to transport tourists and locals. He would talk with Isaac and Jakob about this later. Today he had important business to discuss with Miguel and Alejandro.

As he drove through Savaneta barefoot children ran beside the road chasing hoops and some in a group chased a football. There was an innocence that Hans realized had been missing in those years in Germany. A dark brown rooster with a red neck and a high protruding tail ran into the street in front of his car. Hans braked to a halt. A shy boy approached the driver window and put out his hand for money. Hans shook his head and gently eased the car forward. He had never seen anyone beg for money before in Savaneta. This was new. He wondered if it was an isolated event or if things had changed. He dismissed the thought from his mind and continued on to San Nicolaas.

He swung up the narrow entrance of Main Street and drove to the "El Coco Loco". The doors were locked and no lights were lit. Since the sale of the club, some modifications were being made. Miguel and Alejandro had agreed to stay and assist until the work was completed.

Hans parked near the wall that separated the refinery from the rest of the town and walked back to the club. He rang the electric buzzer above the door and waited. Alejandro arrived and looked through the window. Satisfied, he opened the door and admitted Hans.

"Bon Dia Hans. Come in. As you can see the old club is getting many new changes. I will get Miguel and we will go to the "Pink Panty" for lunch. It is always entertaining there. Sometimes the food is good. We can only hope it will be good today."

Hans laughed. The "Pink Panty" had an interesting reputation. Its exterior was painted in a bright pink with heavy iron bars welded over each window. The front door was painted a crimson red with antique coach lights mounted either side. The interior had a fake marble floor with heavy mahogany tables upon which brass candle holders sat. A greeter dressed in traditional East Indian dress met all patrons at the door and escorted them a table. It was an eccentric and bizarre place, neither Indian, Aruban or for that matter any other ethnicity.

The three sauntered up Main Street in the sultry heat of the mid day until they reached the restaurant. They were greeted by the man with the false Indian accent and shown a table.

Conversation quickly turned to business and recent developments in the town. Miguel described how many bar owners who had rejected involvement with Tony Vitto and Vincenzio had experienced problems with deliveries, delays in maintenance and troubles with the authorities. Miguel was certain that these were not isolated events. He told Hans of friends who were forced to hire men from Colombia and Venezuela by Vincenzio. These men had no experience in bars or restaurants and very seldom arrived to work but were able to obtain government papers.

Hans listened intently.

"My friends, Miguel and Alejandro. It is best that you have sold the club. Isaac and I agree that there are some bad influences at work here in Aruba. We hope that they will not succeed and soon will realize that Aruba is not another Cuba where they can influence and buy everything and everyone. I have come here today to discuss an offer from the Klassen family. We have a proposal for you. There are many things happening and we want you to join with us. Now that Jakob and Solange are retiring both Isaac and I will be taking over all the operations. We have decided that we will concentrate on the resort and land development business and sell some of the other businesses. Isaac and I wish to offer you a partnership where you can purchase the pier restaurant and water sports company. I will be combining my little company with the Klassen Company."

Miguel and Alejandro sat shocked at the announcement.

"Yes of course we are interested but how can we pay for this?"

"Isaac and I have a plan. If you wish to proceed we will discuss this later."

Silence descended over the table. Each person was deep in thought as the foods arrived. They had all decided upon the Indian lunch menu to share. Plates of Nam, papadum, curried goat and rice, lentil soup, creamy cold peas and a mulligatawny soup were served.

They ate in silence until Alejandro spoke.

"When can we make arrangements?"

"I will speak with Isaac and Jakob tonight. Solange will not be able to participate as her old ailment is bothering her and she is not well."

Hans watched the brothers as they ate. He wanted to tell them of the news that Juan may still be alive at a remote jungle location in Colombia but feared how they would react. In time they would be told.

Chapter 31

After the announcement of Jakob and Solange retiring from the daily business, Isaac and Hans prepared the agreement for the purchase of the restaurant and water sports operations by Miguel and Alejandro. A date for the transfer was agreed upon that would allow Miguel and Alejandro to prepare and hire certain people with whom they had employed in earlier ventures.

Weeks passed and Isaac was becoming concerned. He was receiving frequent visits from various contractors that they used for work in their construction activities. A disturbing pattern was emerging. In general discussions he held with the owners, Isaac was learning that all of them had rejected loans or business involvement with the Commercial Loan Bank of Aruba. Isaac said nothing of his suspicions to anyone.

As he and Hans sat together reviewing plans for the building of a new resort, Moreno burst into the office. He was speaking rapidly and in Spanish. Isaac held up his hand.

"Moreno, please relax. Tell us in English what the problem is."

"Isaac, Hans there has been a big accident. You must come right away. "

"You must come and see. It is destroyed. All of it."

Isaac and Hans were confused. They grabbed a set of car keys and with Moreno walked briskly to the car. They drove rapidly to Palm Beach where Hans had established his water sport operations. They drove down the narrow dusty track to the sand. The air smelled strongly of a smoke tinged with an earthy smell. Isaac pulled the car up and all three jumped from it and ran to the sandy edge of the beach. The shack and kiosk that Hans had built as an office and storage area was gone. Black smoldering embers lay in the sand. Scorched papers blew around. Small wisps of bluish smoke twirled up from a few boards that were still burning.

Half burnt life vests, snorkeling equipment and diving gear lay in the remains.

Hans was furious.

"How could this happen. Was it one of the boys smoking? I have insisted that smoking was not allowed in our office or on the boats."

At this Hans spun to look out at the moorings where his boats were secured each night. The boats were gone. Hans felt some relief. The kiosk and shack could be rebuilt easily.

As he continued to look out over the turquoise waters of Palm Beach he noticed very small waves breaking at the surface where his boats normally moored. He continued staring out and made out the shape of the deck of one of the boats breaking the surface of the water. Hans ran to a neighboring competitor and asked to use a boat.

Hans, Isaac and Moreno piled into the boat and motored to the moorings.

Hans stood in the boat and watched as the deck of the submerged boat floated just below the surface. His second boat was nowhere to be seen.

Hans's fury erupted.

"Who the hell did this? Why? What is this all about?"

Isaac remained quiet.

"Hans I will tell you of things I have learned over the past few weeks. I believe we will be able to determine who did this."

Hans spun and shouted at Isaac. His temper had flared. Moreno grabbed at Hans's shoulder.

"Hans, Isaac lets tow the boat back to shore. I will get one of the boys and we will start a search for the other boat. I will dive in the area around here as I believe they probably sunk it. I am sure we can rebuild the shack in 2-3 days. The boats are the most important."

Hans calmed somewhat but was in no mood for any conversation.

They motored back to the shore.

Chapter 32

Once back on shore, Isaac took Hans aside and away from Moreno and the boat boys.

"Hans, our company has worked with many contractors over the years. We had some special people to help when we built the pier and restaurant. I will contact some of them to salvage the boats. I am sure we can save them. I have an idea who did this and why. I will tell you all when we are back at the office."

Hans's face was thunderous.

"I will stay here with Moreno and the boys. I need to plan the rebuilding. I will come back to the office later this afternoon."

Isaac turned and returned to the car. As he drove to the office he thought of the events that the others had experienced. "Things are getting out of control" he thought. "We must stop this now."

Upon entering the office, the receptionist ran across the entranceway with a manila envelope in her hands.

"Isaac this was delivered by a strange man about thirty minutes ago. He said it was important and personal."

Isaac looked at the envelope. There was no stamp or other identifying mark. He thanked the receptionist and proceeded to his office. Curious he sat and opened the envelope. Inside was a single sheet of thick white paper. Isaac withdrew the paper and turned it over. Typed in large letters was the following:

"Things have a way of happening"

Isaac thought back to when he had heard this before. He remembered. This now confirmed his suspicions.

He sat quietly contemplating their next actions. It was time to tell Miguel and Alejandro of the possibility of Juan still being alive in Colombia. He would also speak with his business associates and spread the word about what he had learned.

He picked up the white piece of paper and stared at it.

"Ok then. It is time to fight back. Things have a way of happening that can be positive as well," he thought.

He called for his secretary to join him. After she entered his office he handed her the paper. She read it and frowned. She was confused.

"Please have this framed. I want to hang it here in my office as a reminder of what has happened and what needs to be done."

The secretary nodded and left his office with the paper very confused.

Chapter 33

It was late afternoon when Hans arrived back at the office. Isaac joined him in his office.

"Hans I wish to meet with Jakob. It is time we discuss the many strange things that have happened over the past few months. I would like you to join us. I have sent a message to Alejandro and Miguel that we wish to meet with them this evening at Jakob's home. It is time to tell them of the meeting we had with those Colombians and their comments about the whereabouts of the drug lab and the man who might be Juan."

"After the destruction of my little business I would wish to be there when you speak with Jakob."

After the staff had left the office, Isaac called Hans to lock up the doors and meet him at his car.

The drive to Jakob's home was slow. Neither spoke on the way. They were preoccupied with thoughts of the problems that had surfaced over the past few months.

Isaac pulled the car into the entrance of Jakob's home. He left the engine running and jumped from the car to get Jakob. He rang on the bell and opened the door calling Jakob who arrived almost immediately.

"Isaac, will you come in?"

"No. Will you join Hans and me? We are going for a beach walk and discuss the issues that have arisen recently. We need your advice."

"Certainly. Wait while I let Solange know and fetch a jacket."

Isaac waited and when Jakob was ready they walked to the car. Jakob was pleased to see Hans.

"It must be important to have you both wanting me."

Isaac drove a little north to Arashi Beach. He pulled the car off the dirt road and onto an opening covered in a growth of sunburned high grass. They all exited the car. Hans and Isaac bent and removed their shoes. The white sand was still warm from the heat of the day's sun. They started their walk toward the north. On their left, a gentle low surf crashed onto the beach creating a relaxing calm.

"Jakob since you left the company we are having many problems. It seems that these problems have only started in the last six months. The contractors and suppliers we have used in the past are reluctant to commit to dates or prices. When I confront them I know they are being less than honest with me. There is a common factor. All of the companies we are experiencing these problems with are the ones that have established relationships with the Commercial Loan Bank of Aruba. I believe they have been forced to trade with the others who are also the bank's clients. It is my belief that the individuals at the bank are determined to punish us for refusing to transfer our business to them and told these companies not to cooperate or work with us.

Today Hans found his shack on the beach burned and his boats sabotaged. As well, I received a cryptic message at the office. It was a sign and contained the words that Tony Vitto had used when I refused them to do business at my home. I firmly believe they want to cause us damage. I am worried for our safety. I also believe that they were involved in that accident that killed Jose. His import and export company has been renamed as ExImFreight Aruba. It is handling strange shipments of chemicals and Trans shipping large shipments from Colombia through the Free Trade Warehouses. This is not the company Jose and his family developed. Their company simply handled food and produce. Now it is chemicals and equipment. There are a number of foreign workers at the warehouse.

I have investigated this situation. We know the owners of these companies well. Many had been to our homes and we had visited them. Now they don't want to speak with us.

It is time to stop this.

Things are out of hand. Moreno had warned us about these men. They are bad and are associated with that bank. We need to find some way to stand up to them and help the others get away from their grip."

Jakob said nothing. A silence enveloped the three as they continued walking. The sun was setting over the

Caribbean. The ripples on the water caused the late sun's rays to break up and sparkle on the surface.

Jakob walked down to the water's edge and picked up a flat smooth sided stone. He reached back and threw the stone. It skipped across the surface. Jakob stood looking out at the trail it had produced on the water.

He stood for minutes in total silence before turning back to Isaac and Hans.

"I do not have a solution in mind but I have some ideas that I wish to explore. I will do this and then we can talk further. This situation must be handled very carefully. You are correct. These are dangerous men and criminals."

"Jakob there is more to tell you. I have invited Alejandro and Miguel to your home this evening. It is time they are informed of the information that the Colombians provided Hans and Moreno. I think that Vincenzio and Tony Vitto are somehow involved. Before we take any action we must tell Miguel and Alejandro. If Vitto and Vincenzio become aware that we are working against them they may create more problems. These could be aimed at Miguel and Alejandro's new business or even against Juan, if it is him at that drug lab in Colombia.

"I have heard enough. I will think about this and speak to certain people. I will contact you both after that."

They started to return to the area where the car was parked. Jakob raised his hand.

"Let us stop and sit here for a while. I wish to watch that beautiful sunset."

The three sat on an old tree trunk that had washed up onto the beach and watched as the giant ball of the golden sun slipped low into the ocean and painted to overhead clouds. Where the rays did not reflect on some clouds, they contrasted in a soft grey.

"You cannot paint a beauty like that. There are some nice paintings but none capture the softness or warmth of the air during this spectacle."

Hans spoke. "Jakob you have become a real poet since your retirement."

They all laughed.

"Yes I may be enjoying my garden, the cactus studded island, the large outcrops of huge rocks, the seas and beaches, but don't be fooled. You will appreciate that when you see the plan I have devised to deal with that bank and assist our friends. Now let's go back to my home for a cold drink or two before Miguel and Alejandro arrive."

Solange was lying in a lounger near the entranceway to the house enjoying the warmth of the early evening. Isaac looked at her in the receding soft light. She looked drawn and tired. He had noticed that she had not seemed lively or well for the last few weeks. He went to her.

"Solange are you feeling well? You look tired. Is there anything I can get for you? Would you like a drink or possibly something to eat?"

"No I have no appetite. A fresh juice would help. Can you get me a blanket? Even though there is sun I feel cold."

Isaac was concerned. He remembered the story that Jakob had told him of when he and Solange had first met and of the cane she had used as a result of an earlier ailment. Was it returning? He looked back at her as he was leaving to get a juice from the kitchen. She seemed pale and lifeless.

Hans and Jakob had left to talk in the back garden.

Isaac returned with the juice. Solange took it with a shaking hand and attempted to guide it to her lips. The juice slopped over the edge. Isaac quickly reached for the glass and assisted her steady it to her lips. He covered her legs and chest with a light blanket.

"Oh, Isaac. Don't get old. I am becoming a decrepit old lady I am afraid."

"Don't talk such nonsense. You are young in your mind. You are just having a bit of a bad spell. It will pass."

Solange looked up in to Isaac's eyes.

"My dear boy I don't think so."

She went quiet. Isaac reached down and held her hand. She started to sob softly. Her eyes filled with tears. Isaac felt numb. He was unsure what to do or say.

"Isaac it is not me that I feel sorry for. It is Jakob. I worry what will happen to him if I was to die. During all our time together he has been active and energetic. He is smart and I have enjoyed our life so much. He taught me many things about life and people. If something happens to me I want you to promise me you will look after him and make sure he stays active."

"Solange it worries me that you talk like this. Is there something you know that you are not telling us?"

Solange lay in silence. Minutes passed. The skies darkened as the night encroached. Isaac had pulled up a garden chair and sat with her. It was obvious that Solange knew more than she was telling him.

"Please take me in. I will go to the living room. I want to be there when Miguel and Alejandro arrive. I will stay and listen. Maybe I will have an idea."

As Isaac bent to help lift her from the lounger, Moreno arrived. From the look on his face, Isaac could tell he was shocked when he saw Solange.

Isaac looked firmly at Moreno and shook his head. Moreno smiled at Solange and walked forward to kiss her cheek. This was the first sign of softness that Isaac had witnessed from Moreno. Together they assisted Solange to a large chair in the living room and gently lowered her into it.

Chapter 34

Miguel and Alejandro were late arriving.

"Isaac we are sorry. Today we had more problems at the restaurant. The barman left us and the deliveries for this evening's kitchen were late. We had a visit from Vincenzio and Tony Vitto. They seemed to be delaying us and were asking many questions. They say our old club in San Nicolaas is doing well and they have set up gambling and girls in the rooms off the club. This is not what we wanted. We can do nothing now."

Isaac took Miguel by the elbow and assisted him to a large couch.

"Here. You and Alejandro sit here. Can I get you a drink? We must start soon as Solange wishes to be present and she is tired and not feeling well."

As Isaac left to get the drinks, Jakob, Hans and Moreno entered. Greetings were extended. Isaac returned with the drinks. Upon seeing the others he again offered to get some refreshments for them.

When they were all seated, Hans spoke.

"Miguel and Alejandro. We have received some information that is important for you to know. Moreno and I received this couple of weeks ago. We did not tell you then because we needed to check it and the people who provided it to us. We have made these checks and it seems the information is correct.

Moreno is from Colombia and has contact with other Colombians who are here in Aruba. It was through these contacts that he found out about this.

Isaac and I ask you to forgive our delay in telling you this, but we wanted to be sure that what we were told is correct.

Moreno and I met with a small group of four men who have come to the island without papers. They are concerned that they are not sent back to Colombia. The men all know of the activities of that Tony Vitto and his accomplice Vincenzio. They warned us about them. They are with a large crime group from Venezuela that is run by the Palermo Brothers on behalf of the mafia in Chicago. Their main interests are in gambling, prostitution, drug trafficking and production and smuggling. They have powerful backers. We have also determined the Commercial Loan Bank of Aruba is a front for them to move money. In fact they are loaning money to businesses here in Aruba to take control of them.

What we are about to tell you is sensitive and you must not let anyone know of it. I should tell you that outside of our family and Moreno and Carlita, no one else knows."

Miguel jerked his head toward Hans at the mention of Carlita's name.

"Please tell us. What can be so important?"

"The men we met had escaped from Colombia through Venezuela. While in Colombia they were forced to work with the peasant farmers who grow the coca plants. The coca plants are processed into the drug cocaine at a drug lab in the jungle. For a year they tried to escape from the compound which is heavily guarded by armed men. While working at the lab they became friends with an older man. He claimed to be from Aruba and had been a fisherman there. They told us his name is Juan. "

Miguel and Alejandro stared at Hans in shock.

Miguel was shaking. "Is this true? Can we meet these Colombians? Where is this lab in Colombia? How do we get there?"

Jakob stood and held his hands outstretched in front of him.

"Miguel, Alejandro please calm down. I know that this is exciting news for you. I understand that you want to know more, but we must proceed very carefully. If what we have been told is true and correct, then those men from Venezuela must never get to hear of this. They are dangerous and will do whatever and kill anyone who gets in their way. We believe that they were responsible for the car accident that killed Jose from our friends' export and Import Company.

We are telling you this now as we have had the time and opportunity to check out the possibility that it is our Juan. Remember that Juan is a name used by many. It seems that it is Juan. Now we must decide on a plan to get Juan home."

All heads turned toward Solange as she quietly interrupted.

"My family still has a business in Colombia. It represents exporters and growers of coffee beans. The company is old and operates without interference from the government or others. It is run by a couple of my cousins. It may be possible to use my contacts there. I will contact Florida and ask for their personal contact information."

Jakob was disturbed.

"Solange you have been ill. This is not something you should get involved with."

"Jakob I must. Carlita is one of my best friends and if this is true then I owe it to her to try and bring her husband back home. I have my own money and will use that to finance his rescue."

Jakob and Isaac were surprised at the determination and decisiveness in her comments.

"Solange I am sure you want to help. I understand that, but you need to get well and look after yourself. I am sure that any plan to rescue Juan will be difficult and challenging. I worry that it will be too much for you. It will be very emotional for you and Carlita."

"Jakob don't make me angry. I am going to do this. Nothing short of death will stop me."

After the years of marriage and working with Solange, he knew when to stop. It was a situation where Solange would not be swayed.

Chapter 35

As the evening progressed, different ideas were discussed. It was late when a decision was made to arrange for another visit with the four Colombians who had the information on Juan and his whereabouts.

Jakob spoke forcibly. "Moreno these are your countrymen. I want you to set up this meeting immediately. Miguel and Alejandro you are to do nothing. Isaac and Hans you will pay close attention to the business as I am concerned that more problems may arise as a result of those Italians. I am taking control of this. I will go with Moreno to the meeting and after that we will review and plan."

Isaac tried to object. Jakob swiftly quieted him. Hans had been silently listening and watching the discussions. In particular he was sure that he detected that Alejandro was uneasy. Hans was unsure why, given the news that Juan may still be alive.

Solange looked at Moreno. "When can you contact those men?"

"It is still early and there is a Colombian restaurant in Ponton, the area behind Oranjestad. I am sure they will be there. If they are not there I will get a message to them. One of them works at the import export company. We could get him there but I worry that might make others suspicious. If Hans can drive me I will go now."

Hans was pleased for the opportunity to leave the house. He had continued to observe Alejandro and in his mind he was sure that something was wrong.

As they drove in toward Oranjestad, Hans turned to Moreno.

"I was watching Alejandro this evening. He did not seem to be relaxed or happy to hear that it might be Juan. His behavior seemed strange for someone receiving good news."

Moreno said nothing. They drove on to Ponton and Moreno directed them to drive off the road and onto a worn dirt track that led to a small brightly painted orange adobe. There were bikes and some cars in the dirt parking area.

"This is it. We will go in. I suggest you do not speak. Let me do the talking. Many here will have fled from Colombia and will be nervous to see someone entering that they do not know. I will assure them that you are to be trusted."

They pushed open the wooden turquoise door and walked into the dimly lit room. Smoke filled the air. At the tables groups of men sat playing cards and Dominoes. As they entered the loud conversations fell silent.

Moreno held up his hands.

"Friends I am looking for someone I met a while ago. I think he could be here tonight. My friend here has work to be done and wants to hire him."

Moreno looked around and spied one of the men sitting at the bar. Moreno waved to him and crossed over the room to the bar. The man faced Moreno and Hans with an expressionless look. He recognized Hans from the earlier meetings.

Moreno ordered them a round of Aguardiente, the potent and fiery drink of Colombia. He placed a $20US note on the bar and instructed the server to keep their glasses full.

"We wish to arrange another meeting. The relatives of the man you call Juan want to find out more. Can you make this meeting happen?"

The Colombian sat in silence. His eyes scanned the crowded room until he found one of the others. He beckoned him to join them at the bar.

In rapidly spoken Spanish he relayed the request from Moreno. The man looked at both Hans and Moreno.

"Yes we can do this. When?"

Moreno replied, "As soon as we can. It is important."

"Let us go to the place where we first met. "De Uitgewoondie in Oranjestad. We will bring the others with us. Again, this will cost money."

Hans scowled at him. "There will be a lot of money if we hear what we need and even more if we get help from you and your friends."

At the mention of this the Colombian smiled and nodded.

"We will be there in an hour."

Hans and Moreno finished their drinks and after telling the barman to keep all the change, they left the club.

The drive to Oranjestad was short. Hans was concerned. The area where the bar De Uitgewoondie was located was rough and quickly deteriorating into a place for drug addicts and drunks. It was a bad area to visit during the day, but many times worse at night. Even the policing authorities avoided the area. He pulled the car up onto the sidewalk. Hans ensured that it was locked and there were no items on the seats that could attract attention. He looked across to the San Francis church and noticed a man huddled in an old blanket. He walked over to him.

The man looked up at Hans who was startled to see it was a relatively young man. Hans addressed him in Dutch. The man grinned and held out his hand.

"That is my car over there," Hans said pointing to the car. "If you watch it for me I will pay you when I return. I do not want it damaged or the windows broken. Will you do this?"

The man held his hand out again. Hans took another $20US bill from inside his shirt pocket and held it in front of the man.

"You will get this and maybe some more when I return if the car is without damage."

The man replied in an educated manner. They agreed and Hans wandered off with Moreno in the direction of the club.

Chapter 36

They entered the club. A bare light bulb hung from the ceiling and was the only source of light. The temperature was unbearable and an old five bladed fan beat against the air in a vain effort to cool the place. Hans looked around carefully. There were only three men in the club. One was passed out at one of the rickety old tables. The other two were at the bar and arguing about something trite. In their drunken state they probably couldn't remember what the topic was. Hans and Moreno took a table near the front in case they needed to leave quickly.

A waitress with the personality of a rattlesnake demanded they order drinks. She listened to their request and then demanded money.

"Aint no fuckin drinks without it honeys. This aint the fuckin Ritz."

Hans placed some coins on the table. She eyeballed them and made a quick count.

"You guys can do better that that. Gimme me some dollar notes then I look after you with classy service all night."

Hans chuckled and threw a $5US bill onto the greasy table top. The waitress smiled exposing her missing front teeth.

"Danki my honeys"

She lumbered her huge girth back to the bar and returned to the table with a cheap bottle of rum.

"This shit should kill ya troubles. Now I tell ya. No trouble or I will havta beat the shit out of yas and throw you out. We have class here."

Hans looked at Moreno and the two of them burst out laughing. Hans could not recall a more ludicrous setting he had been in. Even in post war Germany the clubs in the rundown areas were better than this shithole.

It was almost an hour later when the four Colombians arrived. Chairs were dragged to the table and Moreno spoke.

"We have rum. I will order more for you." He turned and called to the waitress. She was not amused. She floated like a schooner under full sail and slammed the bottle onto the table. She stood with her hand extended in front of Hans. He dropped a couple of dollar coins in her hand. She scowled and muttered something in a language that neither Moreno nor Hans understood.

The Colombians were bewildered at the exchange.

Moreno waited until the drinks were poured.

"I am here to ask for more information and assistance. We need to know more about this man Juan from Aruba who you claim is imprisoned in a drug lab in Colombia. We need to know where this camp is located and how it is guarded."

The older of the Colombians spoke first. "You are asking a lot. The location of these operations is kept secret. If we say too much we will make it dangerous for us and others."

"We understand this. What you tell us will be between us. You will be safe."

"How can you make this promise? There are people here in Aruba who are aware of our situation and that we escaped this place. For a small amount of money they will betray us to those Italians and those who deal the drugs. This sounds too dangerous for us. We told you about Juan in order to get some money. We were broke and struggling. We cannot tell you more. There are people here and in Venezuela who will find us and kill us. If we could do this safely we would. It is just too dangerous."

"We understand the danger. Tell us about this man Juan. Surely you can do that without being worried."

"No. There was something he told us. There are some here In Aruba who know he was taken captive. He was angry at times and spoke of them."

Hans looked at Moreno with an expression of confusion.

"Do you know who these people are?"

No one spoke. The Colombians glanced at each other.

"I think it is time for us to leave. You are asking too many questions that will get us and you killed."

As the Colombians stood to leave Hans spoke out loudly.

"There is a lot of money to be made by helping us. Go and think about it. Moreno and I will be back here tomorrow at six. If you want to earn that money then we will talk. If you do not come we will start to ask some others here and in Colombia. We do have contacts as well."

As the Colombians were leaving, the one who Hans assumed to be the leader stopped. He addressed Hans.

"If you can show us that we will be safe then we will have something to discuss."

The group continued through the door out onto the dusty street and faded into the night.

The waitress arrived at their table.

"Now you git. I tired. Goin home. I ready to throw those bums out." She pointed to the unconscious man and the two drunks at the bar.

Rather than get into an argument with her highness, Hans and Moreno left the club.

As they walked to the car, Hans looked around for the street bum who he had bribed to watch his car. He was nowhere to be seen. Hans swore beneath his breath.

He unlocked the driver door and was about to slide onto the seat. There, with a grin on his face was the bum.

Hans was perplexed.

"How did you get into my car? Did you damage it? What are you doing in my car?"

The bum laughed out loud.

"You mistook me for a street bum. I am not. I arrived in Aruba a few days ago and have yet to find somewhere to live where I will be happy."

"Who are you?"

"I am a former Marine. I trained in jungle warfare. I have been in the jungles of Indonesia, Venezuela, Colombia and Suriname. My time with the Marines was up. I had been to Aruba before. During my time here I was content and decided to return and try to start a business. I received special training while in the Marines. I am considering an adventure company for the tourists who visit here."

Moreno stepped forward. "I know a woman who will rent you a place to stay until you find your own. We can take you there now if you wish."

"Yes but don't try any funny moves. I received Commando training and the lethal moves. It would be a huge mistake to try anything."

Hans opened the trunk and the former Marine threw his paltry belongings in.

Moreno directed Hans to drive behind Oranjestad and to a low Villa behind a tall stucco wall.

"Wait while I go in. I will explain and ask if she has a room to rent."

While Moreno visited with the owner, Hans spoke with the Marine. They talked about the military and Hans told him of the days he spent in Germany and the education he received in Ireland before coming to Aruba. The two were quickly developing a rapport.

Moreno returned with an older woman. He introduced them. She looked at the Marine closely before speaking.

"You need somewhere to stay? I have a room I will rent. No cooking. Only got one bathroom. How long will you stay?

The Marine shrugged. "A week or possibly two."

"Ok. You need to pay me first. You seem OK. Come with me and I will show you."

The Marine fetched his possessions from the trunk. As he was leaving Hans called to him.

"What is your name? If you want to work I own a water sports company on Palm Beach. I need someone to assist with the boats. If you want a job come and see me I will be there in the early morning getting the operation prepared for the day. You will see my shack. It is called "Water Pleasures."

The Marine called back. My name is Adrien. I will be there in the morning. Good night."

Chapter 37

Governor's Bay, Aruba.

The phone jangled continually. Tomasso Rossini cursed and pulled himself from the lumpy bed with its kapok mattress. God, how he hated Aruba and those dammed Dutch who had settled it and imposed their stupid customs and ideas of comfortable furniture. They could certainly learn from us Italians.

He snatched the receiver off the old black phone. He reached for his watch on the side table. It was 5:00am. Who was ringing him at this hour?

"Pronto."

"Rossinni. This is Salvatore Enjoying your vacation? We hear things. We need you; Vitto and Vincenzio back here in Venezuela now. We hear from some of our friends that there is suspicion about things there. They say there is talk about that car accident and the problems at the Bank. It seems that Vincenzio has done some things to anger the Klassens. He was settling some personal issue he had with them. He acted stupid. He was not to do damage to their businesses. He was responsible for the destruction of the water sport operation on the beach. We had forbidden him from acting alone or settling personal vendettas. It was our plan to slowly get the Klassens as partners. Now it is in jeopardy. We need you to get out today and return. Vincenzio is in trouble with the bosses. Get home today or you too will be asked for reasons why you shouldn't pay for the Aruba mess. No one is happy with all that has happened there. Remember we have a meeting that will be with our US Coast Guard friend soon. You must be here for that."

Before Tomasso could respond the line went dead.

Silently he was thrilled to be leaving Aruba. He thought of his luxury apartment and of his life in Caracas. He wondered how people in Aruba could be happy when there was no real life. There were no real clubs or entertainment like that of the city.

He rang the room where Tony Vitto and Vincenzio were. Impatiently he waited while the phone rang and rang. Frustrated he pulled on his clothes and marched down to their room. He hammered on the door until a bleary eyed and hung over Tony Vitto pulled it open. Without speaking Tomasso pushed his way in.

He poked his head into the bedroom where Vincenzio lay snoring. He returned to the kitchen and filled a glass with water. He walked back to the bedroom and threw the contents over the sleeping Vincenzio's face.

Vincenzio sprang from the bed with clenched fists prepared to take on whatever situation had presented itself. Seeing Tomasso he quickly dropped his raised fists.

"What the hell? It is early. Why are you here? I need my sleep. Fuck off."

"My friend, you have no choice. Get dressed now. The Palermo Brothers want us and especially you back in Venezuela immediately. Get dressed and after we find some breakfast we will go to the airport. I will go and pay the hotel for the use of these rooms. I will meet you in the lobby area in ten minutes."

Tony Vitto stood with his mouth drooping open.

Tomasso spun on his heel and proceeded to the reception desk. He felt exhilarated to have confronted Vincenzio. He had never liked him.

At the desk Tomasso hit the ringer on the silver bell. A blurry eyed clerk emerged from the office behind the reception area.

"Good morning. How may I assist you?

"We have business that requires us to travel this morning. I need to check out and pay for the rooms. I will pay for both mine and my business partners."

Tomasso gave the information to the clerk who took considerable time to prepare the bill. Tony Vitto and Vincenzio arrived as Tomasso completed the transaction.

"We will find somewhere to get coffee and breakfast in Oranjestad and then go to the airport. Salvatore was in a foul mood. I suggest we return Caracas as fast as possible."

Chapter 38

Jakob's House, Malmok

Isaac and Hans did not return to Jakob's house that evening after meeting the Colombians. It was morning when Isaac and Moreno decided to visit and discuss the developments of the previous evening.

Isaac was surprised to find Solange enjoying a coffee at the garden table on the front balcony's patio. He hurried up to her. The tiredness he had seen the night before was gone though she still seemed weak.

"Please come and join me. I have been given a gift of some nice Dutch coffee. It is so rich. I really like it."

"Where is Jakob? I want to tell you both of the meeting last evening."

Solange was about to stand and get Isaac a coffee.

"No Solange. I will get myself a coffee. But where is Jakob?"

"Go get your coffee then we will speak."

Isaac found the coffee percolator on the kitchen stove and poured himself a large mug before returning to sit with Solange.

He looked out at the view of the Caribbean Sea from the balcony. In the early morning sun the waters reflected the soft hues of blue dotted with small boats which Isaac assumed were local fishermen.

"Jakob went down to swim in the ocean this morning. It seems he is invigorated by all this news of Juan and a plan to rescue him. I worry about him. He is not the young impetuous man he once was. After last night he is acting like a teenager. I beg you not to get him too excited. Remember he has some issues with blood pressure."

"No I will not excite him. In fact when he hears of the situation with the Colombians he will be disappointed I believe."

She wanted to ask more but decided to wait until Jakob returned and joined them.

"I am both worried and pleased. Jakob has been reflecting on his past and all the problems he created as a younger man. He is sorry for his treatment of certain people. It has been preoccupying his mind. For days he will go quiet and lose interest in our life. I cannot break him out of these moods. I explain that times were different then. There had been a war followed by a depression in the economy followed by yet another war. Times were uncertain and survival was hard. He will not hear that and blames himself for leaving behind a peaceful life in Canada and the death of his wife. Some days his mood is so dark that I cannot even speak with him. I worry he will do something stupid. He is a smart man but loses vision when he revisits the past. I don't know how to deal with all the demons he faces during those moods."

A voice called from the street and they saw Jakob walking briskly toward the driveway. For moments he was obscured by the towering cactus plants. He emerged with a white towel wrapped around his neck, wearing a swimming costume and sandals. For those who did not know Jakob he could be early forty. He soon reached the house and disappeared into a lower door.

Even though it was early morning, Jakob arrived with a beer in hand. He was in a great mood.

"There is nothing more refreshing than an early morning swim in that little beach of Boca Catalina and the walk back here to our beautiful house. This morning there were turtles swimming over the reef. They are so graceful and beautiful. Just like you, my Solange."

 "Oh, Jakob. Behave yourself. Isaac and Moreno are here to tell us about the meeting last night with the Colombian men."

Jakob lowered himself into one of the wicker chairs and sipped his beer while fixing Isaac with a steely eye.

"All right my son, tell us what happened."

"We did not get any more information. Moreno tells me that the Colombians are scared for their lives and refused to help us. They claim that those Italians have others on the island who report to them. They fear that if they tell us what they know it will be traced back to them and cost them their lives. Unless we can protect them we will probably not get the information we need."

Moreno turned to Jakob. "If you lived in Colombia you would understand. The gangs who control the drugs are lethal and have tentacles that reach high into the police, army and government. If you are suspected to have caused them trouble it is unlikely you will live long. The gangs fear nothing."

Jakob stroked his chin and did not respond. His thoughts were focused on finding a way to get them to talk.

"Thank you Moreno and Isaac. I am going to think about this. Go and do your work. Before you leave to meet with them again we will talk. I have some ideas."

Chapter 39

After Isaac and Moreno departed Jakob and Solange remained on the patio. The sun was becoming hot.

"Jakob I think I will go inside now. Will you join me?"

"Yes and I think we need to decide whether we will continue to investigate if it is Juan and how we could help him."

As the morning turned to noon, Solange and Jakob despaired that there was no easy solution to get the Colombians to share what they knew of Juan and where he was imprisoned in Colombia.

Jakob decided to walk up to the old lighthouse. It seemed to help him think through problems. He put on some light shoes and announced to Solange he was leaving.

Solange was not happy. "Jakob you are not so young and fit. Please reconsider as I worry so much about you going up that steep hill."

As Jakob was about to leave, the skies darkened and thunder clapped. Within minutes torrential rain fell. Jakob stood with the front door open watching the rain puddle and flood on the path. From the time since he had jumped ship and lived in Aruba the tropical rainstorms fascinated him. More thunder roared and lightning flashed and sparked through the dark clouds. Solange moved behind him and reached up to massage his neck.

"Jakob I have an idea that may help us with the Juan problem."

She pulled Jakob back and into the living room before telling him of her ideas.

"I know how much Juan meant to you. You were both close friends. I know you want to help. This is what I am thinking."

Solange talked for the longest time explaining her ideas. Jakob sat and listened without commenting.

When she was finished Solange left and phoned Isaac.

"Isaac please come and drive me to the bank. I have important business I need to look after."

It was almost an hour later when Isaac arrived to take Solange into Oranjestad to her bank. They drove slowly along the flooded muddy roads. Rain water splashed from the wheels of the cars and drenched a herd of goats munching on the tall grass that grew on the side of the road.

"What is this important business?"

"It is family business. I need to deal with a matter back in Florida. I may need to travel there, but first I will deal with a financial situation."

Isaac knew when Solange did not wish to disclose anything and this was one such occasion.

He stopped at the front of the National Bank of Aruba and jumped out of the car to open the passenger door and escort Solange up the stairs and into the bank.

"Thank you Isaac. Now please go back to your office. This is personal business. I shall phone you when I am ready to be taken home."

There was no point in arguing. Isaac ran back to the car and started the drive back to his office. During the short drive he wondered about the meeting with the Colombians. He did not know how to find out more about Juan without creating a problem.

It was early afternoon when the phone rang and Solange advised him she was ready to return. As they were driving she asked Isaac to stop and see if Hans and Moreno could join them. Isaac changed direction and followed the recently paved road to Palm Beach. When they reached the beach he drove down to the newly built shack. Because of the rains there were no tourists. Isaac told Hans that Solange wanted them back at the house. Hans agreed.

"I will close up and come, but first I need to pay the staff. Moreno and I will be there in thirty minutes. The former Dutch Marine, Jan started work for me this morning. He is smart and strong. He impresses me and reminds me of friends back in Germany."

He returned to the car and told Solange. She smiled but again the tired look had returned to her face. The day was proving to be too much for her to handle.

At the house Isaac assisted her to the front door and into the living room. He called to Jakob who arrived in seconds.

"Solange has asked Hans and Moreno to come here. She wants us all together for a discussion."

Promptly Hans and Moreno arrived. Barely thirty minutes had passed. They joined the others and waited for Solange to start speaking.

"I have told Jakob of my ideas to assist in finding and helping Juan escape. I have withdrawn funds from the bank today for Hans and Moreno to pay the Colombians tonight. "

Hans objected. "That will be wasting money. They told us they would not help as they are scared of the consequences."

Solange interrupted. "Hans be quiet until I finish. As you all know I have business interests in addition to the company here in Aruba. I intend to use my position and influence in those other companies to make it safe for the Colombians. While I was at the bank I had them assist in making arrangements for Jakob and me to travel to Miami. We will leave tomorrow morning. The flight will leave at 9:00am. Isaac will drive us to the airport and wait until the flight has left. Should anyone ask I am travelling for a medical visit with a Specialist. We will return in a day or two.

Tonight Hans and Moreno you will meet the Colombians and try to find out more. I have taken money and I want you to use it to convince them to help us. Tell them that we have a plan that will make it safe for them. Arrange another meeting three days from now. I am sure they will be pleased with the arrangement."

Other than Jakob the others were confused and curious.

"I will not say anymore on this subject until I return. Then we will be able to plan."

Jakob looked at their faces and grinned. He was enjoying the atmosphere of suspense and the unknown.

Chapter 40

Shortly before six Hans and Moreno strolled up from the dock area to the club for their meeting. Even in daylight the area was decrepit and ominous. They reached the club and entered to find the Colombians had already arrived. There were two others with them.

Hans and Moreno joined them at their table.

"We have brought friends with us who also escaped from the drug gang. They know some things that are important. I told you we will need payment before we can tell you anymore. Even if we tell you what we know there is still the problem of the Italians finding out and killing us. We will give you some help but you must then leave us alone."

"You need not worry. If you are asked questions tell people that we met you because we are looking for men to work on a new construction job. I have a payment here for you, but first we need to hear what you have to tell us."

The group exchanged looks and finally one of them spoke.

"The area is far inland. It is called Caqueta. The drug operation is built on the Yara River. It is a hard place to reach. The drug gangs bring supplies of chemicals to the lab by boats. It is too hard to bring them through the dense jungle. The place is heavily guarded. There are militiamen in the area but most are working for the gangs. They are not to be trusted. The man you ask about, Juan, is in this compound. He is living in barracks they have built. There are other prisoners there. During the day they work to produce the cocaine or bundle the marijuana for shipping. We can help you locate this place on maps but we must be paid first.

Hans opened an envelope and took out $100US and placed it on the greasy table surface.

The Colombians looked at it and laughed.

"Do you think all of our lives are worth only one hundred dollars? No. We will leave. It is not worth risking ourselves.

As they arose to leave Hans raised his voice and commanded them to sit. Others in the club turned to watch hoping for a bar room fight. The group froze.

"That's better now sit back down. We will negotiate a price that everyone will be happy with."

Hans signaled the waitress to bring a bottle of rum. The negotiating began. Moreno cautioned his Colombian countrymen not to get greedy and offered that there could be future money and jobs. He had their attention.

Hans spoke. "I need a commitment from you all that in three days we will meet again. I do not want to meet here. We will meet in San Nicolaas. There is a bar there where I know the owners. We will need privacy as we will be discussing serious things."

The Colombians started to complain about the distance and time to get to San Nicolaas.

"If you are interested in making lots of money I suggest you be at The New York Bar at 7:30pm. We will be waiting for you."

Chapter 41

Caracas, Venezuela.

The flight from Aruba arrived in Caracas at noon. Tomasso Rossini was eager to meet the Palermo Brothers. He was worried. The work in Aruba had not progressed well. He was anxious. As he reflected on the failures he realized that Vincenzio had created situations that exposed them. He wondered whether it had been necessary to kill Jose and steal that car. Vincenzio had acted alone with local thugs to sabotage the Beach business of Hans Klassen.

Tomasso had learned enough about Hans Klassen to know that he would seek revenge. The Klassens had the resources and contacts to find those responsible. It was important that he convince the Palermos that Vincenzio had acted alone and without telling either of them his plan to destroy the business. Neither he nor Tony Vitto would have approved as the risk of exposure was too great.

Tomasso wondered what the Palermos would do. Their brand of justice was quick and final.

After retrieving his baggage, Tomasso hailed a taxi and went immediately to his office. He left Tony Vitto and Vincenzio at the airport. He did not want them with him when he met the Palermo Brothers.

He arrived at the office building and took the elevator up to his second floor office. He opened the door and found

Yulia at her desk manicuring her long cat like nails. She looked up as he entered.

"Well the big boy is back. You have a nice tan. It makes you look more handsome. Let me get you the messages. There were many people who wanted to meet you. I think this is the most important. Salvatore Palermo phoned an hour ago he wants you to call him immediately. He was rude and insisted that I make you call him. Here are the other messages.

She leaned forward over her desk to hand Tomasso the sheath of handwritten messages. As she did so she bent in a manner that caused her large appendages to partially bobble out of her loose blouse. She had missed the daily trysts with Tomasso and was trying to get his interest. Tomasso was too preoccupied with the issue of the Palermos.

"Yulia I must call Salvatore and possibly go and meet with him. I will be back later and take you for a dinner. You can tell me all that has happened and what I need to know over dinner. Afterwards we will go for drinks at my apartment."

Yulia literally purred. She knew what this meant and battered her artificial eyelashes at Tomasso.

"Sure Boss. I will be ready."

Tomasso opened the door into his office and grabbed the phone to call Salvatore Palermo. Tomasso was ordered to go immediately to the Palermo's office. Without hesitation he left the office and instead of driving he waved down a cab. After Aruba the traffic in Caracas was hectic. Horns blared and drivers shouted obscenities at each other out the open car windows. Tomasso liked the busy and loud pace of life in Venezuela.

He arrived at the Palermo's office and was taken by a secretary to a closed off area at the side of the main office area. She knocked and waited. A voice called for them to enter.

The secretary opened the door and stood to the side. Tomasso walked in. Salvatore and his brother Emilio sat at a table. There was a platter of veal sandwiches and other pasta dishes on the table.

"Tomasso you have had a long day so sit and join us as we eat. You can explain the situation that happened in Aruba. We are not happy. The bosses in Chicago are furious and calling for someone's head. I hope it won't be yours."

Tomasso sat and presented the actions that Tony Vitto had taken with the Commercial Loan Bank of Aruba and the investments that had been made into local businesses that they considered strategic to the drug trafficking and smuggling activities.

The Palermos listened without speaking. When Tomasso had finished, Emilio, the quieter of the brothers spoke.

"Tomasso what about those other things that happened?"

"I don't know what you mean."

"I mean the killing of the son of the owners of the export company, beating up that prostitute who worked for one of our friends and the destruction of the Klassen's water sports company?"

Tomasso was shocked. He was amazed that the Palermos knew of these events.

"It was Vincenzio who destroyed the water sport company's beach shack and sunk the boats. He paid some locals on the island. They were probably from Venezuela. I made the decision to remove Jose. He was about to crack and tell all to Isaac Klassen. It was necessary."

The Palermos stared ahead at Tomasso. Finally Salvatore spoke. "We heard of the meeting you attended at the bank with Isaac and Hans Klassen. I think that you and Vincenzio made it personal."

"No. I did not. I was aware that Mastronardi was working on another plan to get their business. I would never interfere."

Salvatore fixed his gaze on Tomasso. "Before you left for Aruba you made an interesting comment to me. You might recall that comment. You told me you wanted to off them. It is now time for you to do just that. Only Vincenzio though. He has become a liability. No one operates their own agenda without our approval. He has broken the rules. See to it that my order is carried out and it serves as a reminder to others in our organization that we will not tolerate actions like that."

When he finished Salvatore reached across the table to a plate of meats and sausage. He took a cold cabanossi and placed it in his mouth like a cigar as he chewed the ends.

"Come now. You have your direction from us. That is enough talking business. Join in and eat with us."

Tomasso was scared and sweating profusely. He reached and took a plate of freshly prepared pasta and a glass of the red table wine.

He was annoyed. If it wasn't for that dammed island of Aruba and the mob's desire to run resorts and casinos and bribe the politicians there, none of this would be happening. He hated Aruba even more. In his mind it would never be a replacement for Cuba. He closed his eyes and momentarily thought back to the many nights he had partied at the clubs in Havana.

"We are not pleased with your performance or that of Tony Vitto, but understand the difficulties that exist in Aruba. You will take Vitto with you and attend to dealing with Vincenzio. The matter is to be done now, before we receive our friends from the US Coast Guard. Do I make myself perfectly clear?"

Tomasso clearly understood the message.

"Now tell us all that happened while you were there.

Tomasso refilled his glass of wine and spent the next hour recalling the past weeks in Aruba.

When he had finished Emilio spoke.

"Tomasso the visit from our US Coast friends is very important. You will bring Tony Vitto to the meeting. You and Tony have met them before and will be able to provide introductions and assist us. We will have the Venezuelans you met at dinner attend as well. The bosses are counting on us to make this a success."

Tomasso realized that this was to be an important meeting. To expose the identities of the Venezuelans and their friends from the US Coast Guard meant that a large deal was planned. There was high risk.

"I will speak to Tony. We will go to the ship when it has docked and port formalities are complete. I will take them to the **Santuario di Formaggio** restaurant. You will need to tell me the time for this meeting."

"You will be advised. Now get Vitto and have the matter we discussed dealt with."

Tomasso was dismissed.

Part 3

"All at Sea"

Chapter 42

Key West, Florida, 1961.

For days heavy rains had fallen in Florida. Finally the weather had cleared and as the early morning dawn of May 5th, 1961 was starting to break the 82 foot long US Coast Guard Cutter, *USCG Pearl* was preparing to push back from its mooring and start what was to be a long journey to the islands of the Caribbean and the shores of Venezuela and Colombia.

On the bridge Lieutenant Jeremiah Slate stood drinking the acrid dark and bitter coffee for which the ships mess was well known. He and his buddies watched as some of the men on the dock and the ship's deck skittered around and prepared the ship for its voyage.

Other crew members stood at the ship's railings experiencing the anxiety of not knowing when they would next see their loved ones.

Slate's uniform reeked of stale smoke from the French Gitanne cigarettes he had traded with the sailors from a visiting French Navy Frigate. He shook one from the dark blue packet and slid it to his lips. Clouds of putrid smelling smoke filled the enclosed bridge area. Although smoking on the bridge was prohibited, Jeremiah did not care. This vessel was under his control.

On the dock wives, girlfriends and children waited to bid farewell to their husbands or partners. There was no one there for Slate. He was in many ways a loner.

Slate resented leaving on a patrol at this time of year. Spring was arriving in his beloved home state of Connecticut. He missed his home and his many lady friends, most of whom he had mistreated.

Slate swore out loud to his mates. He hated the possibility of the shitty weather they would probably encounter during their patrol. Hurricane season in the Caribbean was arriving and this particular year was predicted to be an extremely active season. Already the first tropical storms had developed and done their damage, leveling shelters in Haiti and The Dominican Republic. Slate envisaged fishing the remains of drug smugglers' bodies from the oceans. At least whatever remained that the sharks had not eaten. The drug traffickers would have attempted to have made the crossings to Florida in their poorly made boats on those ill fated trips.

He took a long last look to shore and recalled the previous nights partying at the infamous Red Parrot Club.

At 5:30am the radio crackled and commands were barked back and forth to get the ship underway.

This particular morning the waters were busy with all types of craft. The United States was launching Alan Sheppard on Freedom 7 to be the first American in space. Small craft were heading out to try for a better view of the launch which was scheduled for 9:30am from Cape Canaveral. Lt Slate was not impressed. Smaller Coast Guard patrols were escorting the pleasure boats away from the shipping lanes.

Lt. Slate had been with the USCG for 7 years and time had jaundiced him. He no longer had the enthusiasm or belief in the role he played. His paltry salary hardly afforded him the luxuries he believed he needed to portray his image as a successful Officer.

Slate thought back to his earlier life. It had been one of both privilege and trouble. Born into a family of wealth in Hartford, Connecticut, he had been schooled to assume a managing role in the expansive insurance empire the family controlled. Slate's early years of education had been without incident. At age seventeen he joined in with a gang of criminally intent boys. It was only a matter of time before drugs and burglaries became commonplace to him. Then an event occurred that would forever change his life.

It was Halloween. The weather had remained relatively warm. Slate went to a costume party with his undesirable friends who were intent on creating trouble. Slate decided to stay away from them that night and spent the majority of the night with Lise Franchette, a popular and beautiful French girl. Her father was a partner in one of France's largest insurers and the family was in Connecticut while he negotiated a merger.

Slate danced and joked with Lise until the function ended. As he was leaving to escort Lise to her home, his friends called to them to join them at a favorite bar on the waterfront. Slate was reluctant. There were too many problems that happened at that bar. He told Lise not to go but she insisted since she was having so much fun. Slate took her by the arm and helped her into the rear seat of the friends' Cadillac convertible. Shrieking with laughter they set off in the direction of the bar.

Slate became concerned when the Cadillac turned and headed in the direction of Westport. He shouted at his friends to turn back and was met with a heavy blow to the face. Slate crumpled under the blow and momentarily lost consciousness.

Slate awoke to find himself on the ground in a park. Lise was tied to a tree. Her clothes had been partially stripped from her.

Two of the gang had finished with her and were standing back smoking and watching as the third member thrust himself into her. She screamed but to no avail.

Finally expended, the three gang members sped off in the Cadillac but not before they untied and threw Lise on top of Slate. He tried to calm her but she became more hysterical, screaming and shouting. Scared and worried about being found in this situation, Slate hit her hard over the head in an attempt to calm her. Blood spurted from a cut he inflicted on her head. She slumped forward in an unconscious state.

As he tried to drag her to a secluded area, a police patrol car with white and red flashing lights and siren screaming screeched to a halt. Two officers ran across the short cut grass to the couple. Slate was grabbed. His arms were pulled behind him and he was handcuffed and taken to the local precinct.

Hours of investigation ensued and Slate was finally arrested and charged with rape, assault and forcible confinement.

Over the next week the family used every political and financial connection at their disposal to cover up the incident. Slate was kicked out of school and spent hours at the family home. For him it seemed hopeless. He was angry. He had done nothing yet he could not prove it.

A trial was scheduled. Before the trial could commence, Lise Franchette provided a statement that exonerated Slate, but the damage was done.

In desperation, Slate's father called on politicians and members of the Navy who he had supported. After some cajoling and compensation, Slate was accepted into Naval training school. He studied and became a prized student with above well above average standings. He was accepted for an officer training program. It was too late. The damage was irreparable.

Lt Slate thoughts returned to the ship as shouts arose from the dock below. The ship pulsed with vibrations as the huge diesel engines engaged the propellers and the ship slowly slid back toward the channel.

The ship moved cautiously down the channel. Jeremiah looked across at the shore and the lights of the buildings as they faded into the dawn's growing light.

Chapter 43

For the next two hours the ship sailed slowly south from the shore. Lt. Slate monitored their progress with the ship's navigator. At 09:00 an announcement was made throughout the ship. A meeting of all hands was to be held at 09:30 on the mess deck to provide details of their mission. No details had been provided to the crew and Slate had only been provided a brief report and an envelope containing further detailed information that was to be opened once the ship was underway.

Slate took the envelope from the small safe beneath the chart counter. He examined it and noted the US Coast Guard Insignia was accompanied by a State Department Stamp, an unusual combination.

He carefully tore open the envelope and removed its contents. There was a five page briefing report on the purpose of the mission and the locations in which it was to be conducted.

Slate read the report with mild interest until he reached a part of the report that had been prepared by Military Intelligence. He sat and read each detail of this section of the report. Intelligence sources had learned of a sophisticated smuggling operation and the proceeds were being funneled to arms procurement by certain criminal organizations and political foes. Slate read on and was shocked at the level of detail and the individuals involved.

According to the report the type of drugs being smuggled to the US were changing. During the 1960 period there had been a huge increase in the drug cocaine. Previously marijuana had been the most commonly smuggled. The tastes of drug users were changing. The report provided a brief summary of the impact of this drug and its danger. Slate read on. He was not sympathetic to those who relied on drugs. The ability to make money from the trafficking was another matter and one that Slate benefitted from.

At 09:30 Lt. Slate addressed the assembled hands on the mess deck. He looked at his crew for this patrol. There were forty seamen and six officers. They were young with ages between eighteen and twenty-four. For some this was their first trip to sea. In his mind Slate could visualize problems. No Captain or Commander enjoyed sailing with rookies on their first trip. There were always problems. Slate took the bullhorn and addressed the crew.

"Gentlemen. Welcome aboard for this mission. I can now disclose the nature of our trip. We have been assigned a patrol duty in the Southern Caribbean. Intelligence and surveillance ops have determined a significant increase in the smuggling of drugs from South America to the US and similarly the smuggling of goods and weaponry from the States to criminal organizations. Our mission is to locate and intercept these smugglers. Our operation will be supported by the US Coast Guard base in Puerto Rico should we require assistance. The duration of our mission will be three weeks. In addition to our patrol duties, I have a communiqué from the State Department which advises that we will make a goodwill visit to Venezuela. The Venezuelan authorities have been contacted and advised of our visit. We will be docked for a three night stay. During that time there will be shore leave. Those wishing to go ashore will receive a full briefing from the US Military attaché who is stationed at the US Embassy in Caracas. We will dock at the port of La Guaira. Remember we are their guests while in port and all who go ashore will conduct themselves appropriately.

For those sailors who are making their first voyage be warned that this is a working patrol and not a luxury cruise. You are required to be in a state of readiness at all times.

I remind all crew that while playing poker or other games for relaxation in the evenings, gambling of any sort for money is strictly forbidden.

Crew, dismiss."

The sailors broke rank and made their way back to their cabins or assigned duties.

"Lt. Slate that was excellent and provided the men with the knowledge they need. It can get awfully lonely out here and then questions arise in their minds regarding the value of the patrol."

Slate looked at the Officer who had spoken. His name was Johnson. He recently transferred from Virginia and had not sailed with Slate or the other officers previously. Slate was wary of him. Over the years Slate had developed friendships with the group of officers and had sailed with them on each voyage. All were aware of the dealings Slate participated in and each got a cut. Slate had a loyal bunch. This new officer presented a concern as he seemed straight and had a "by the book" attitude.

Slate thanked him for his comments and excused himself as he had business of his own to conduct in his cabin.

Chapter 44

Slate loosened off his uniform and even though it was early morning he grabbed a bottle of rum and poured himself a large shot. He dreaded the three weeks of boredom he was facing.

As the commanding officer, Slate's cabin was divided into private quarters and a separate office area. He slumped into the thickly padded leather chair behind his desk and was looking through a pile of radio messages when there was a knocking at the door.

The door opened and Hector Ramirez poked his head in.

"Can I join you Jeremiah?"

Slate had known Ramirez from his days in naval school. He was as close as a best friend that Slate would ever have.

"Yes come and join me. Want a shot of this fine Jamaican rum?"

Ramirez nodded and laughed. He pulled up a chair and took the glass of amber liquid that Slate held out to him.

The cabin was stuffy and smelled strongly of oil and diesel. Slate got up and went to the air circulating controls and selected the highest setting. Within minutes the strength of the fumes decreased.

"Jeremiah you knew about the goodwill visit to Caracas before we left. Are you expecting to see our business friends while we are in port?"

"I had sent a private telegram to Tomasso Rossini advising him of the possible dates. His dimwitted secretary responded. He is in Aruba with two others from the firm, one who I know well. It seems like there is something planned for Aruba. I am surprised that they would send three men to conduct simple business. Tomasso's secretary advised that he has been in Aruba longer than he had planned. I am friends with one of the other men, Tony Vitto. Tony and I grew up together in Connecticut. Tony was one of those at the Halloween party the night that Lise Franchette was raped. He had tried to stop the others and refused to get into the car that night. Tony and I did get into some bad situations. I lost contact with him for a while after he moved to Chicago. It was in Chicago that he became involved with the mob. It was Tony who introduced me to Tomasso and suggested we work with them. He has been our contact for the little business operation we have. I will try to meet with him in Caracas. I had received a call from Tony a few weeks ago. It seems they have things to discuss with us. I will be sending a message from the next port we dock at. It is too dangerous to use the ship's communication system. Those communications get seen by too many."

Ramirez chuckled and sipped at his rum. He reached into his breast pocket and removed a small pack of cigars. He reached over the desk and offered one to Slate.

"Finest Cubans from Florida," he laughed.

Slate took the cigar and soon the cabin was filled with smoke as the two sat drinking and smoking.

It was shortly before the noon and the first lunch sitting in the mess. Slate and Ramirez decided to join a couple of the other officers for the lunch. It was a bland meal. Lunch consisted of a watery mushroom soup and a piece of fried chicken with boiled white rice.

Slate thundered. "What in God's name is this crap? Get me whoever is in charge of the kitchen. I want to speak to him now."

Moments later a young chef dressed in his kitchen uniform was escorted to Slate.

"We are to be at sea for three weeks. The men cannot eat this. The ship was fully stocked with steaks, vegetables, pastas, cold cuts and other foods. Why have you made this miserable mess? I demand you immediately return and prepare a more substantial meal. Do I make myself clear?"

The young chef blushed and nodded. He attempted to speak but was quickly cut off by one of the other junior officers. He scurried away back to the kitchen.

Slate and the other officers laughed at the lecture the young chef had just received.

While waiting for replacement meals the men drank coffees and smoked. New plates were served to them twenty minutes later.

Slate inspected the new meal. It consisted of a thick rich tomato soup and with a thick slice of Virginia ham floating in a raisin sauce with beans and mashed potatoes. Slate smiled.

"That is more like it. Tell that chef's superior officer that I expect no less than meals like this to be prepared for my crew. If he cannot perform this duty I will radio Puerto Rico and arrange a replacement chef. His future will be pretty bleak if I need to do that."

Chapter 45

Throughout the afternoon the ship sailed south without incident. The seas became more turbulent and the ship started into a lazy roll as it mounted each wave. A number of the younger crew gathered on deck to view the sunset and take photographs to show their family and girlfriends. There was a mood of calmness developing amongst the men on the ship.

At 18:00 hours the first dinner sitting was called. Those assigned for this sitting soon filled the mess. The mess was nondescript. The walls were painted in a light dull grey. Blinding overhead fluorescent lights lit the interior. A large counter ran the length of one wall where the men would take their trays and select their meal from several available selections. In the mess the level of conversation was loud but every once in a while it ebbed.

When 19:00 hours arrived, the second roster of hungry men arrived. They bantered with the stragglers who had remained at tables from the previous sitting.

Slate was late arriving at the head table which was reserved for the senior officers. He looked around the mess at the men and sensed the atmosphere. It seemed that this patrol was starting well. He hoped it would be routine and without too many events.

When the meals were complete, kitchen staff cleared and cleaned the mess hall in preparation for the evening when the men would play cards, read or sit talking with each other.

Slate could not be bothered with this mundane and boring activity.

"Ramirez, would you find a few of our special friends? I will entertain in my cabin tonight. We need to plan for the business ahead."

Hector Ramirez grinned and left to fetch those officers loyal to Slate and a part of the dirty schemes he operated.

The night grew late. Copious amounts of liquor were consumed and the cabin filled with cigar and cigarette smoke. It was definitely an exclusive club. The officers began to leave Slate's cabin and find their way to their own quarters shortly before midnight.

Slate decided to make one final visit to the bridge before retiring for the night. Even though he had drunk many glasses of rum he was steady and coherent. He smiled to himself and thought "Practice makes perfect."

On the bridge there were two officers and another seaman who was controlling the ship. Slate looked behind the chart storage shelving and into the radio room where two men sat monitoring communications. Occasionally one of the men tore of a message from the secure teletype machine and scanned it to determine its relevance to the mission and who should receive the communication. Slate had the highest regards for the radio ops. On a large and empty ocean they could be the only lifeline. He made sure his radio people were well taken care of.

Satisfied with what he saw, Slate retired for the night.

It was early morning when his intercom buzzed him awake. He rose from his bed and pressed down the button to respond.

"Lt. Slate. What has happened that needs my attention?"

"Lieutenant, Sir. There is an important operational command for you. Should we bring it to you or will you come to the bridge? It is rated high importance."

"Give me some time to dress and I will be there."

Slate cursed. "Here we go. One day out and the bullshit starts. What can be so important? We are not even in the Caribbean waters yet. Probably it's just some stupid pleasure boaters who have got into trouble."

After a quick shower and dressing Slate proceeded to the bridge. Upon his arrival he was handed a mug of the infamous coffee and a folder containing a transcript of the radio message. He sat the coffee down on the chart table and opened the folder.

The message had all the normal bureaucratic wording at the beginning including an 'Eyes only" heading and various confidentiality and other warnings. Slate scanned down to the main body of the message and read the following:

USCGC Pearl / Caribbean Patrol / May 7, 1961.

Unidentified vessel under reconnaissance has been identified as possible transport for illegal activities. Vessel is not flying the flag of any country and is of unknown registry.

The ship is at coordinates Latitude23°52' and Longitude 73°47' For the past three days ship has moved slowly in a circular pattern. No radio contact. Unknown if vessel is in any distress or its purpose.

You are commanded to intercept and engage with this ship. It is in International waters and you will adhere to protocol.

Acknowledge.

Slate was pissed. Shit. So early in the mission.

"Hey, Radio ops. I need more information. Contact base and get me a complete description of the ship, the time it was last seen, who has reported this and any other pertinent information."

The young operator eagerly started the communication back to base.

"Fuck. I haven't even had my powdered egg breakfast yet. This is going to be a long day'" he muttered to no one in particular as he stormed away from the bridge. He needed to enact the operational plan and required information from his office.

As he was retrieving the documents the radio room buzzed him again on the intercom.

"Lieutenant, I think you should come and read this latest transmission."

Slate called his two subordinate officers to meet him immediately in the radio room.

He ran along the outer deck to the narrow stairs that led up to the bridge. Within minutes he was joined by his junior officers.

The radio operator handed him the transcript of the last transmission which he read quickly.

"We have been ordered to intercept a suspicious vessel. I have just received this information. This vessel is no more than 12 nautical miles ahead of us. Order all your men into full operational status. Make sure they know that this is not a drill. It is the real thing. We have no idea of what we will encounter ahead."

Slate called for the ship's navigator and after a quick discussion showed him the coordinates. The navigator took the ship's position and ordered a course correction that would take them to the unknown vessel's location.

Chapter 46

Lt. Slate checked the time and made an entry into the ship's log. It was 08:00. The early morning sun shone brightly on the deep green waters. A stiff easterly wind was blowing, creating little whitecaps on the water. The ship rose and fell against the swell and the low waves.

On the bridge, a junior officer called to Slate.

"Sir, we have the ship on our radar. We estimate a rendezvous in about thirty minutes."

Slate called to Hector Ramirez. "Please prepare the boarding party. We must be careful. All of our attempts at radio contact have been ignored. I am treating this as a hostile encounter. Arm the men and get the inflatable ready to be lowered."

Hector strode off to the rear deck and spoke to the group of assembled sailors.

Within fifteen minutes, the target of interest became clearly visible. Flocks of screeching seagulls circled above the boat which was barely moving. Slate stood scanning the decks of the rusting hulk of a ship looking for activity. There was none which he found confusing. Normally they would be greeted by some crew on deck of the vessel as they approached. Something was wrong here.

Slate called out "Ramirez. I am going to heave to and wait back here. On your approach I want you to pass by the stern of the ship. I see no flag flying. This could be a stateless vessel. Check for any identifying information and radio back to us."

Ramirez nodded and turned to rejoin his men in the boarding party.

The *USCG Pearl* slowed and finally stopped back from the boat and to the starboard. Ramirez shouted to launch the inflatable.

Ramirez and his party sped away from the *Pearl* toward the stern of the ship. Within minutes the radio on the bridge crackled.

"Lieutenant I can make out the ship's markings. They are barely readable. The ship is *"Antilles Adventurer"*. It shows the country of registration as Liberia. I do not see any signs of life. I will hail them on the bullhorn."

Ramirez proceeded to hail the ship as the inflatable circled. After several minutes two men appeared on the deck.

"Lower your gangway and prepare to be boarded for a law enforcement inspection. We are the United States Coast Guard."

He repeated the message several times until the gangway was lowered. He commanded the boat be taken alongside and tethered to the gangway.

"I want one man to stay here at the helm with the motor running in case we need to retreat quickly."

Ramirez hauled himself out of the inflatable and onto the narrow rusting iron stairs of the gangway. His men followed close behind as they ran up the gangway to the deck.

At deck level they were met by an older burly man with grey crew cut hair. He was dressed in old fatigues and was carrying a rifle.

"United States Coast Guard, drop the rifle. We are armed. We are here to inspect your papers and cargo."

The man bent and placed the rifle on the ground behind him.

"Do you speak English?"

"Yes. I am the First mate. We are in trouble. We left the Port of Belin in Brazil with a cargo of Soybeans and Sugar. We are destined for Galveston, Texas to offload. Three days ago we experienced an electrical fire onboard. We have lost all communications. Our radio and radar are out of service. I made the decision to slow the ship and sail in large circles hoping that we could attract attention to our situation. I am pleased you are here."

Ramirez was not convinced. "Where is the Captain?"

"We have another problem that is serious. Shortly after sailing for Brazil one of the Filipino crew members became ill. Within days the illness spread throughout all the crew, including the Captain. He is below in his cabin. I can take you there. "

"No. Wait and I will radio my ship."

Ramirez grabbed the radio from his vest and called the *Pearl.* He informed Slate of the situation.

Slate pondered the news. He finally called to the ship's Doctor. "I need you to get you the medics together and cross over to that ship. They are reporting an illness that has affected all their crew. You will need to take precautions."

While the Doctor assembled his equipment and men, another inflatable was quickly lowered into the rising and falling sea.

Very little time passed before the medical crew arrived at the *Antilles Adventurer's* gangway and slowly unloaded small white cases of medical supplies to the men from the boarding party who were waiting on the gangway.

Once he reached the deck, the Doctor addressed Ramirez and his men.

"Do not accept any coffee or food. We do not know what we are dealing with. I will visit with the Captain and attempt to diagnose what the illness is. The medics have brought surgical face masks that I ask all of you to put on immediately. We do not want to spread whatever this to the crew on the *Pearl*. He then turned to the First mate.

"Please take me to the Captain's cabin."

Ramirez stopped him.

"We have not been below. This could be a trap. I will accompany you with two of my men."

The Doctor shrugged. "As you wish."

Chapter 47

Slate paced back and forth on the bridge. He was annoyed. This would probably delay the visit to Venezuela and his "business meeting" with Tomasso Rossini and Tony Vitto. Before leaving port he had earlier communication with Tomasso and it seemed that timing of the meeting was critical. Slate became further annoyed. It was likely that he would need assistance from other Coast Guard ships in the area. He radioed the base with a report of the intercept and the findings. He was advised to wait further instruction.

He looked out at the floating derelict of a ship and wondered when there had been any maintenance performed. It was a typical tramp steamer....poorly maintained and probably lacking survival equipment. He could only imagine what the crews quarters looked like. Slate had been on similar ships and seen the squalid conditions.

"Why is it up to us to save these wrecks and their scabby crews?"" he wondered.

On the *Antilles Adventurer* Ramirez requested the ship's log and cargo documentation. He scanned it and then called for two of the boarding party to accompany him to inspect the cargo holds.

As Ramirez was about the leave the Doctor appeared. He had a serious look on his face.

"I have examined some of the men. It is a serious situation. All of the men I examined are covered in the rash that comes with typhus infection. Some are complaining of extreme headaches and high fevers, while others are too weak to move. They are infected with Epidemic Typhus. This is a bacterial disease that is highly infectious. It is caused by body lice. I suspect all the crew sleeping areas and clothing contain these lice. There is no vaccine for this. Most of the men are in an advanced state and I fear they will die through lack of treatment. I will not be able to treat these men. We must find help. The ship needs to be quarantined. I suspect that there are other serious health problems. While leaving the crew area I disturbed some rats chewing on some type of food. This ship is unhealthy and a risk to all onboard."

Ramirez called his men to return immediately to the inflatable.

He radioed Slate to update him on the situation.

Slate listened and commanded Ramirez to return to the *Pearl*.

Upon his return Ramirez hurried up to the bridge. The other officers were crowded around awaiting his full report on the ship and the condition of the crew. As he started to speak the radio Officer entered with a paper in his hand.

"Lieutenant, this is important. It is from USCG Base in Puerto Rico."

Slate snatched the paper. "God," he thought, "what a day this is turning out to be."

"Thank you"

He read the communiqué over and then handed it to the group who were standing around expectedly awaiting orders. After reading it some of the group let out a shout of happiness.

Slate turned to those who had not read the document.

"There is a US Navy destroyer nearby. We are ordered to stand by the disabled ship until it arrives. They will assume control of the situation. I will need to advise them of the health situation onboard that ship."

Slate quickly dictated a message to USCG Base in Puerto Rico. It took minutes before a reply was received ordering them to stay off the ship.

An hour passed by before the shape of the dark grey destroyer appeared on the southern horizon. It sailed toward them and a small launch was dropped to the water. Men in water protective suits climbed down a small ladder and jumped into the boat which then sped toward the *Pearl*.

Slate ordered a boarding ladder be dropped. The launch moored below the ladder and soon Slate was surrounded by Navy officers from the destroyer. After a quick briefing they asked to speak with the ship's Doctor.

Slate requested the men to follow him to his office where they could speak privately. The Doctor described the conditions onboard the ship and the state of the crew members he had examined.

The senior officer from the destroyer spoke quickly into the portable radio strapped to his chest.

There was a considerable pause until the radio squawked into life.

"This is Captain Rogers of USS Fitzroy. We have reported the findings to Headquarters. They are establishing communication with other countries to determine what assistance can be rendered. You are commanded to stay at the scene while this matter is reviewed."

Slate was both relieved and annoyed at this situation. He had other more important things on his mind.

The decision came quickly. The radio crackled to life.

"This is Rogers again. We are informed that The Bahamas do not want this ship or these men in their waters or port. We have received similar refusals from other nearby islands. No one wants this ship in their port. Our instructions are to take the crew aboard and quarantine them. After they are evacuated our instructions are to scuttle this ship."

Slate was thrilled. He had silently been hoping for some action. He announced the plans to the crew. A number of the crew appeared on deck to watch or photograph the sinking.

The ship rolled lazily in the calm seas. The late morning sun added a theatrical feel.

Black inflatable Zodiacs ferried their way back and forth between the freighter and the destroyer carrying the sick men. When it was confirmed that all of the crew had been removed, a team of Navy divers clad in black diving suits climbed down into a larger inflatable. Large crates were loaded down to them from the deck. After the cargo was secured, they accelerated away from the dark grey hull of the destroyer to the dirty rusting freighter.

Six of the divers entered the waters and clung to the side of the boat while yellow rectangular packets were passed to them. In teams of two, the divers swam toward the freighter and dived below the surface when they were about fifteen feet from the hull to attach the explosive charges to the ship.

The crew of the *Pearl* was enjoying the show in the near perfect weather.

After almost thirty minutes the divers surfaced and swam back to the inflatable. They were pulled aboard and returned to the destroyer.

Slate was watching from the bridge when the ships radio beeped. One of the officers acknowledged the incoming call.

"This is Captain Rogers; I request that you sail back and away from the *Antilles Adventurer*. The charges have been set and we are ready to detonate."

Eager to witness the explosion, Slate ordered the ship to a location next to the destroyer.

The *Pearl* shook and pitched to the side from the force of the explosions. A huge plume of water rocketed into the air from the centre of the hull. The ship broke into two pieces and started to fall back on itself as it slid into the waters.

A huge cheer arose from the men on the deck. Waves were exchanged between the sailors on the deck of the destroyer and Slate's crew.

Slate and the Captain of the destroyer engaged in some small talk by radio before orders were issued for the Pearl to continue on its mission.

Chapter 48

As they continued their voyage south, the weather changed. The bright blue of the sky assumed light grey color as it became overcast. Slate had seen these conditions before. He immediately called for updated weather conditions. A tropical storm was forming in the Atlantic and was predicted to pass through the northern Caribbean. He ordered the ship's navigator to the bridge. Together they checked the storm's reported location and their planned course. A new course was plotted that would take them away from the coastline and further out into the Atlantic, as the storm was tracking toward land.

Slate called for the Chief Petty Officer.

The tall gangly young officer arrived on the bridge within minutes.

"Due to a storm we are changing course. We will be sailing into heavier seas within the next couple of hours. Brief the men on this change. Have them prepare for rougher waters."

The Chief Petty Officer confirmed the order and left to call the men together.

Slate was concerned. He had provided the Venezuelan connections with the arrival dates and it now seemed that it was unlikely those dates could be met.

As Slate stood drinking the putrid liquid that passed as coffee, he experienced the increased roll of the ship. Soon the bow was pitching high into the air as the high waves smacked the ship. Without warning torrential rains smashed against the bridge windows reducing their visibility.

The door crashed open and Ramirez, dressed in protective rain gear was blown in. The wind howled through the open door scattering papers and carrying sheets of rain. Slate cursed Ramirez. His coffee drenched his white shirt and splashed down his chest. The remainder of the coffee flew from his mug and landed in his lap, scalding his penis. At this point Slate became livid and jumped toward Ramirez grabbing him by the shoulders.

"Look what you have done, you imbecile."

Ramirez staggered back. The others on the bridge moved away sensing a fight was imminent. Slate composed himself quickly. He shouted to Ramirez. "Take over while I change uniform. You can really be an idiot at times."

Slate attempted to walk back to his cabin. The roll and pitching of the ship threw him from side to side of the narrow corridor.

As he was reaching his cabin door, one of the new seamen tried to pass him. The situation worsened. The seaman was seasick and could no longer hold back. He projectile vomited. Slate was drenched in yellow slimy vomit from below his chin and over his coffee stained shirt.

Slate reached out and firmly pushed the young sailor sending him crashing to the floor. Furious Slate opened his cabin door while pulling off the soggy and smelling clothing. He quickly tried to shower. The motion of the ship made it impossible. Holding onto anything that could steady him Slate found a new uniform. He tried dressing. As he attempted to put the trousers on a huge wave caused the ship to pitch high and crash down. Slate was thrown off balance and fell. He slid across the floor and his face crashed against the legs of his luxurious leather chair. Blood spurted from his nose. The top of his head collided with his desk which resulted in a huge gash. He lay on the floor unconscious.

An hour passed. On the bridge the officers were concerned with Slate's absence. Attempts to raise him on his cabin intercom failed. Ramirez asked one of the officers to go to Slate's cabin and check on him.

The officer knocked loudly at the cabin door. There was no response. Apprehensively and fearing a tirade from Slate, he cracked the door open. He gasped when he saw Slate lying face down on the floor in a huge pool of blood. He ran across the cabin and pressed the button to summon the bridge.

Within minutes the ship's doctor and medics were in the cabin. They examined the injuries.

The Doctor spoke. "He is going to need stitches for that head wound. Help me carry him back to the sick bay. We will clean him up and treat him there."

The medics grasped Slate beneath his armpits and awkwardly shuffled him back to the medical quarters.

The Doctor anesthetized Slate. The wound was deep and bone was showing. After the stitches were completed and Slate cleaned they laid him in a cot. He muttered occasional incoherent words and sentences.

The Doctor was worried.

"I suspect he has a concussion. We will need to keep him sedated and observe his behavior."

The Doctor was about to contact the bridge when Ramirez arrived.

"How is Lt. Slate? I am second in command and if he is incapacitated I will need to assume control and make an immediate report to base. Will we need to have him airlifted? I will need to advise them."

"No he will be fine. He has a mild concussion and a couple of minor cuts. Give him a day and he will probably be back in action. He is a tough cookie."

"I will need your report to include in the ship's log. Please prepare it for me today."

Ramirez looked across at the inert Slate who lay with a half grin on his bruised face.

He wanted out of the sick bay. The smell of disinfectants and medications in the warm room was causing him to become nauseous.

"Ramirez, I suggest you radio in an event report in case this develops into a more serious situation."

Chapter 49

Hours had elapsed since the *Pearl* had encountered the edge of the tropical storm. Now the skies were blue and a mild breeze blew.

On the bridge Ramirez was approached by the navigator.

"I suggest we take a look at our current position and course. We made a drastic course change to avoid that storm. We cannot continue on that course. We are heading too far out to the east. We need to make a corrective change now. Here, look at these charts."

The navigator laid out a large marine chart on the table. He pointed to the ships present position and using a protractor and ruler placed them to calculate the new bearings required to take them south and deeper into the Caribbean to their destination port of La Guaira, Venezuela, 9 miles from Downtown Caracas where they were scheduled to meet with Tomasso, Tony Vitto and others involved in the drug trafficking ring.

Ramirez queried the navigator.

"We are meant to dock at La Guaira in 2 days. After the delays due to the storm and the intercept of that freighter will we be able to arrive on time?"

The navigator pulled up a stool and sat calculating.

"Yes at this speed and assuming no further stops we will get there early morning. We have made good time regardless of the situations we faced. The ship is not running anywhere near full speed and we could arrive earlier."

Ramirez nodded his approval. The navigator handed the new course coordinates to the helmsmen. A course correction was made.

They cruised on into the night, unaware of the events about to unfold.

That night in the mess, the men gathered to talk, smoke, drink and play poker, cribbage and other board games. While gambling for money was prohibited, many ignored the rule. Most played for token amounts of a dollar or two. No one got upset at losing, unless they had joined in a game with Joe Stubbs. It was common knowledge that Stubbs took his gambling seriously and only played for high stakes.

Joe Stubbs had sailed with Slate and his crew for several years. Though he had a volatile temper the crew essentially accepted him and avoided situations involving gambling or money.

Stubbs was sitting alone when one of the new junior seamen wandered into the mess. He was full of bravado. The older crew members had watched his antics since the beginning of the cruise. He joined a group at one of the poker tables. No one made any attempt to welcome him.

Amongst the crew he was thought to be a hothead and full of himself.

He reached into his back pocket and took out his wallet from which he removed several large bills. The men at the table looked and folded. Most got up and left. The young seaman looked around for another player. Stubbs was the only other player left in the mess.

He had heard of Stubbs's reputation but dismissed it. In his mind there was no better player who could beat him.

"Hey Stubbs. Want to wager one with me?"

Stubbs looked at the kid. He was muscular and swarthy. If it wasn't for the uniform this could be a gang member on the streets of New York.

"Sure kid. How much are you in for?"

"Let's make it worth my time Stubbs. I'll bet $200."

Stubbs took an instant dislike to his arrogance.

"Sure kid. I'm on. You got the money though? I don't lose and expect you to settle immediately/"

"And if I don't, then what?"

"I guess you'll soon find that out if you try anything."

The game started. Some of the sailors came and stood close to the table. It wasn't long before Stubbs was winning. The young sailor tried to remain calm but became flustered as the losses mounted.

It was late when Stubbs finally called an end to the game. He stood and held out his hand for payment. The young sailor sat motionless.

"Come on boy. It's time to settle up."

"I'm a little short. I'll settle after next pay."

Stubbs was furious. Throughout the game the young sailor had antagonized him.

"No, that wasn't the deal. You pay now."

"Says who? I told you I'll pay you in a couple of weeks when I get paid."

Stubbs was incensed. He sprang toward the sailor and grabbed him by the shoulder. Within minutes a full brawl was in process. Stubbs held nothing back. Fists flew and the thump of them landing on the young sailors face and chest could be distinctly heard,

"Stop it Stubbs. Enough. I think he has learned his lesson. Stop now before it is too late."

Several of the crew ran forward to restrain Stubbs. The young sailor lay writhing on the floor. Several of his teeth were on the floor in front of him.

It was minutes before Ramirez arrived in the mess. He looked at Stubbs and the sailor on the floor.

"What the fuck happened here?"

No one wanted to speak. There was total silence except for the distant pounding of the diesels laboring to power the ship through the ocean.

"Someone speak now and make it fast. You are all witnesses and unless I get an account of this you will all be written up and held."

Amongst the crew there was a shuffling and a voice sounded and the recently arrived officer, Johnson walked forward.

"There was a fight over a gambling debt."

That was enough for Ramirez. It was bad enough that Slate was incapacitated but this needed to be dealt with. As he assessed the situation, he thought "The men must recognize who is in control here."

"Stubbs and you! What is your name? You are under arrest and will remain here while I call the policing officers to accompany to the brig. Stubbs you know the rules regarding gambling and fighting on board."

Ramirez ordered Johnson to summon the officers to take them to the cells.

As he was about to leave the mess the ships klaxon sounded.

"Now what?" he shouted and stated off at a quick pace to the bridge.

On arrival on the bridge he joined the group who were standing looking to port with their binoculars.

"Sir we have spotted flames off in the distance. It appears to be a burning boat. We estimate it is at a distance of 2 miles. What are you instructions?"

Ramirez took a pair of the binoculars and studied the burning craft.

"It is clear in our mandate that we are to assist vessels in trouble and also offer assistance for medical and other emergencies. This is definitely a situation we will need to assist.

Have radio ops contact base. Have the base issue a broadcast to all other ships in the area. Find out if there have been any distress signals."

He continued to study the burning boat. It sat low in the water. As he scanned the water around the scene, he noticed some large items bobbing in the water. Curious he commanded the ship to approach at a low speed.

As they drew closer Ramirez identified the floating objects as bales wrapped in sacking. "Probably marijuana," he thought.

"Prepare a salvage party to secure those bales and bring them aboard."

The cutter shone high powered searchlights onto the situation. The salvage crew carefully searched for the crew or any survivors. There were no signs of life. They attached ropes around the bales and signaled the men onboard *Pearl* to winch them aboard.

Ramirez went down to the aft deck. He surveyed the recovered bales. It was a huge shipment. One of the men slashed open a bale. Inside were hundreds of plastic wrapped packages of marijuana. A larger pack wrapped in blue plastic and stamped with a strange logo fell from the bale onto the deck floor. Ramirez strode forward, bent and picked it up. It felt heavy and sponge like. He took the crew members knife and cut a small slit in the top. The package was full of white flour like powder. They had just salvaged a shipment of cocaine. Ramirez looked at the men gathered around watching.

"I am taking this to Lt. Slate's office. It is evidence we will need."

He ordered the burning remains sunk and retreated with the package of cocaine.

Chapter 50

Slate awoke with a pounding headache. He swung his legs from the bed and shakily stood. He attempted to walk to the latrine but was stopped by a medic

"Sir I will assist you. There was a lot of blood lost. You will need to rest today."

"I am fine. Get someone to fetch me a new uniform from the wardrobe in my cabin."

He sat back on the bed and waited for his uniform to be delivered.

After dressing he cautiously made his way up to the bridge and upon entering he read the ship's log. Interested to learn more about the incident with the burning boat and the drugs he requested Ramirez to join him.

Ramirez swore. It was only a few hours since he had gone to get some sleep after an active night of commanding the cutter. He was tired but knew better than to delay and keep Slate waiting. He quickly dressed and proceeded to the bridge, stopping at the mess for two mugs of the foul coffee.

On the bridge Slate was standing alone deep in thought.

Ramirez looked at him. He wore a massive black eye. His hair had been cut back above his right eye by the medics in order to disinfect and sew up the gash. He had bruising on his neck and his lips were swollen.

Ramirez handed him a coffee.

"It seems you have had an active night. Tell me. Has the drug matter been reported to shore yet?"

"Yes we radioed that we had fished some bails of marijuana from the sea. We advised that an estimate of the weight and number of bales will be sent today."

"Let's go to my cabin and talk further."

Slate looked over the group of men. Officer Johnson I am temporarily handing over control of the ship to you. I will be in my cabin conferring with Ramirez if you require me."

"Yes sir"

In the cabin Slate went to his desk and removed the bottle of rum.

"This is better than that god dam medicine they pumped into me. I want to know more about last night and that burning boat. It doesn't make sense that the boat was left burning with no crew and all those drugs floating in the sea. There is something wrong with that."

Ramirez described the scene and their actions. Slate's interest piqued when the packet of cocaine was mentioned. Ramirez left to bring the package back for Slate to inspect.

"Who else knows about this cocaine?"

"Not many. I believe that only the men who were inspecting the bales know."

"I have an idea. Have all the bales opened for inspection. Get the cocaine removed from them and securely stored in the aft hold. Have one of our guys guard it.

Now please tell me what the hell happened in the mess with Stubbs and that new seaman."

"Stubbs won a poker game. The young guy couldn't pay the debt. He became abusive to Stubbs and a fight broke out."

Slate was quiet and waited some time before responding.

"We have no option but to deal with this. Too many saw what happened and I need to maintain order, especially on this trip. I want to delegate that new officer, Johnson to handle this matter."

Slate went to the intercom and ordered Johnson to his cabin.

"Johnson, are you familiar with the Uniform Code of Military Justice? I believe you would have studied and made aware of the code. I want you to conduct a hearing and implement the penalties as prescribed. I want both men written up and a 'Conduct not becoming' entry made against them. I want them both off this ship. You will make arrangements with the Embassy in Venezuela before we dock to have these men removed."

Johnson smiled. Unknown to either Slate or Ramirez he was an authoritarian. This was exactly the type of assignment he loved. He felt his sadistic character bubble inside him.

He saluted Slate and spun on his heel to undertake his duty.

As they continued the southward trip, changes in the water and weather were evident. The winds were warm and soft. The ocean had taken on a lighter blue hue.

Slate returned to the bridge and looked for the navigator.

"When can we anticipate arrival in La Guaira? We need to notify the port. This is one port where they insist on a pilot being aboard at time of arrival and docking. We will also need to notify the customs and immigration authorities and update the Embassy with our arrival info."

"I am anticipating an arrival time of 15:00hrs. In spite of the delays we have made excellent time."

Slate ordered the radio ops to relay the arrival information to the port authorities.

Ramirez. Come with me. I need to discuss matters with you privately."

They left to bridge and instead of heading to Slate's cabin headed to the mess. It was empty except for some staff cleaning.

Slate took the furthest table in a darker corner and indicated to Ramirez to get coffees and join him.

"What is it you want to discuss?"

"Tomorrow you and I will meet with Tomasso and Tony Vitto. There is to be a dinner with others they work with. I understand we will not be the only guests. I am thinking that we arrange for that cocaine to find its way to their operation. Of course we will expect payment. I am going to have a personal message sent to Tomasso. He has a different civilian name. I will make it look like we are accepting a dinner invitation with him. This will not arouse any suspicions amongst the hierarchy. It will seem like the two of us are meeting up with an old friend."

"That is fine but how will we get that cocaine off the ship?"

"This visit was arranged a long time ago. Ostensibly it is a goodwill visit. The men will be going ashore. As you know we have several crew members who are with us in our ventures. I will arrange for them to take some. We will spread out the removal and delivery."

Ramirez nodded his approval.

Chapter 51

Caracas.

Tomasso longed for lunch. He wanted to gorge on the delicacies a large serving of *pabellón crioll*. It was a simple dish of shredded beef and black beans served on a bed of white rice. Tomasso had it with a fried egg and fried plantain.

Saliva dribbled from the corner of his mouth as he imagined the taste and the aroma. It was so over powering that he almost forgot Yulia kneeling between his knees.

He wondered what was better. Was it a good meal or crazy sex? He had plenty of time to find out.

Tomasso was groaning and moaning as the desk phone rang. He let it ring until it stopped. Yulia looked up at him and grinned. Her job was done.

She was composing herself when the phone rang again. She slowly picked up the receiver and announced Tomasso's office.

Her face became serious. It is Salvatore Palermo. Tomasso hobbled to the desk, his progress impeded by the trousers draped around his ankles.

"Salvatore. Greetings. What can I do for you?"

"Has that business with Vincenzio been handled?"

Tomasso thought back to the evening earlier in the week when he and Tony Vitto had driven to the poorest of the slum barrios. Vicenzio was told his services were needed to collect on a drug debt. They had driven slowly into the back streets and through the dirty narrow cobblestoned street lined with multi colored house in disrepair. Barefooted kids dressed in rags had run beside the car hitting the windows and begging for money. It was unusual for a car such as the Lincoln to venture into the barrio. When they had reached a darkened cul-de-sac and Tony pointed to the door of a dilapidated house. Vincenzio had eased his huge frame from the car and started across to the house. He was no more than ten feet from the car when Tony called out to him through the car's open window. Vincenzio turned and Tony fired shot after shot from his Glock pistol. Vincenzio slumped to the ground. Some teenage boys arrived. Tomasso called them over and arranged for them to get rid of Vincenzio's body. He handed them some American dollars with the threat that he would return if they failed.

His mind returned to the call. Salvatore was talking quickly.

He listened in silence. He beckoned to Yulia to bring him a pen and some paper. He scribbled down the address, information and names that Salvatore gave him.

There would be no time for that leisurely lunch with Yulia and her girlfriend.

Tomasso looked at the notes he had hurriedly written. The US Coast Guard *Pearl* was arriving that afternoon and the dinner was arranged for late that night. He called Tony Vitto and instructed him to meet him at his apartment at six. Tony agreed. Next Tomasso called his man on the docks. He needed access to park his car and meet with Slate and Ramirez.

He had no sooner finished when Yulia handed him a note. "This was sent you from an American ship. It seems you have a friend visiting later. The note says he is bringing you a gift and that he needs you to meet him. Should I respond?"

Tomasso frowned. The reference to a gift was a coded way of telling him something but he was unsure what that message was.

"Yes please respond. Ask him if I need anything special to carry the gift."

Yulia scurried away to perform her most important task of the day.

An hour passed before she received a reply.

"Tomasso your friend says that a large case would help."

Tomasso shrugged. "I have no idea what that could be. I will be surprised."

He did not want Yulia to know too much. She was stupid enough to tell everyone. "One day soon I will get another to replace her," he thought.

Yulia saw him looking at her intently and walked over to him. She slipped her hand suggestively around his waist.

"Maybe not so soon," Tomasso thought.

Chapter 52

Slate had dressed in a fresh uniform for their arrival. He wore his hat with the peak drawn down over his forehead and dark glasses to cover up the wounds.

The afternoon was early when the launch carrying the harbor pilot approached. The gangway was lowered and two men jumped from the launch onto it. They ascended to the deck where they were welcomed aboard by the Chief Petty Officer and escorted to the bridge.

Slate advised the pilot that his presence was a formality on the US ship. He was cordial and explained that the helmsmen would take the ship in under the pilot's direction. The pilot was not happy and reluctantly agreed.

The man accompanying the pilot was with the port authority. He requested papers on any cargo they were carrying.

Ramirez shot a look at Slater who barely flinched.

"No but we did an intercept of an abandoned boat. There was a large amount of marijuana which we confiscated. It is secured on deck. I believe that this was declared by the Department of State when updating your people on our arrival. I understand full clearance has been given."

"I will need to speak with our Customs Officers. It is likely that the cargo will be impounded here."

"We made the intercept in International waters and under appropriate law. The confiscation met all the legal requirements and is property of the United States Treasury. We will object through diplomatic means."

Slate did not object too strongly. He knew that the Venezuelan Customs officials were corrupt. Within twenty four hour the marijuana would probably be back on a boat destined for Aruba or Curacao for shipment onto the US and Holland. He had seen it all before.

Slate stood thinking. Why did the governments try to stop this trafficking? It was clear from the demand in the States, Canada and Europe that a huge number of people were users. He thought of the millions of dollars that were spent each year in a losing battle. He was personally aware of elected officials in his home state who were users. In addition there were other Coast Guard members who were active in dealing. To Slate it was all a high priced farce. He no longer cared about the ethics and to him it was a profitable business and one he willingly participated in.

The pilot demanded the ship slow to allow a tug to take the hawsers and tow them to the dock. The ship involuntarily lurched as the tug made heavy contact.

"Shit," shouted Slate. "Ramirez, go check if there is any damage. These bandits need some serious maritime lessons."

The pilot glowered at Slate. The feeling was mutual.

The ship was alongside and being pushed a mooring position when Slate observed a light grey US Embassy car travelling down the dock to where they would drop their gangway. They had no sooner berthed when a couple of MPs accompanied by a khaki uniformed officer exited the car. They stood at attention at the base of the gangway. The officer made his way up to the deck. Slate descended the stairs from the bridge and went to meet the man. As he did so, he noticed a preening Johnson standing in wait.

The officer from the car introduced himself.

"I am here from the Embassy to arrest and transfer the two men you have in custody. We will be handling the issue. I will need all the paperwork including the incident report."

Johnson was brimming with pride.

"Yes, sir. I have it all here. I have arranged for their personal effects to be packed. They are ready for transfer to you."

Slate was amazed at Johnson's perverted efficiency.

He arranged for the transfer paperwork to be signed and sent for the imprisoned sailors.

It took only a couple of minutes before the shackled men were brought on deck and guided down to the waiting MPs. As he stated his descent, Stubbs turned and glared at Slate who wondered just how much he knew of the drug operation he and Ramirez were running. He was a little concerned. It was never his intent to have Stubbs incarcerated and discharged from the service. In his mind Johnson had gone too far.

The Embassy officer strode over to Slate.

"Later this afternoon there will be a visit from the Military Attaché. The men are to receive a full briefing from him before going ashore. This is a dangerous place and the port of La Guaira is particularly unfriendly. Please wait until then before allowing the men to leave the ship."

He saluted and returned to the car. The MPs had roughly marched Stubbs and the other sailor to the car.

Slate and Ramirez observed the arrival of a couple of women on the dock. The word had circulated that an American ship was in town. The prostitutes grew in number as they watched from the deck. The women were chattering and whistling and calling out to ship offering their services.

The Chief Petty Officer approached.

"We have commenced refueling and removing garbage from the ship. The engineer is concerned. He wishes to have an inspection made of where the tug boat slammed into us. He fears that there may be buckling of a plate. If this is the case we will need to return to a port for repairs."

"Go ahead and perform the inspection. I will be leaving the ship for a personal visit with friends later this afternoon. When will the inspection be completed?"

"I can start it immediately. I have a crew ready. We were awaiting your permission."

"Undertake the work and report to me as soon as the inspection is complete."

Slate remained on deck looking at the harbor and its surrounds. It was a typical dirty working port with all the normal blemishes. Bored, he retired to his cabin for a sleep in advance of the important meeting.

He woke, showered and dressed a little before six and made his way to the bridge. He took the ship's log and read the recent entries. Johnson had entered a damming report on the fight and the removal of the offenders. Other than some mundane and routine entries there was nothing of consequence. He looked for the Chief Petty Officer's report on the inspection of the hull. Unable to locate it he called for him.

The flustered Chief Petty Officer arrived with a clipboard. Some papers were clutched in his hand.

"The inspection is complete. I am sorry for the delay in reporting. There is some difference of opinion about the extent of the damage. The impact has dented a plate. The inspection of the plate and the welds and rivets showed that there was no water seepage. The engineer is content to leave it and continue the mission. His assistants are worried that the plate could buckle further in heavy seas. The decision will be yours Lieutenant."

Slate took the report and read it in detail.

"I will report a 'damage to vessel' incident. I am accepting the senior engineer's decision. We will continue the mission."

On the dock the mood had become festive. There were women with armfuls of hats, shirts and other cheap souvenirs they hoped to sell to the sailors. An enterprising couple had set up a grill. Smoke billowed from the 44 gallon drum that had been cut in half. The drum contained the burning wood and embers. Unknown objects were cooking on the chicken wire secured over the top of the drum.

An Army jeep drove down past the activities on the dock and came to a halt at the base of the gangway. A young dark haired man in a crisp uniform emerged from the jeep and made his way up to the deck. Slate went to greet him.

"Permission to board. I am Adjutant Cruz from the Embassy. I am here to brief the men before they go ashore."

"I have advised the men that you would be coming. I will have them report to the mess. Would you like some of our renowned coffee while you wait?"

"That would be appreciated. It's been sometime since I tasted good American made coffee. The coffee here is mainly from Colombia. It is good but not like the coffee from home."

In the mess, Slate poured Cruz a large mug of the ship's coffee. Cruz thanked him and took a long sip. His face distorted and he pursed his lips. Slate watched with quiet amusement.

The men dribbled into the mess. Some pulled up chairs or sat on the benches while others leant against the walls.

"Good afternoon gentlemen. Welcome to Guaira and Venezuela. My name is Cruz. I am the Military Attaché here at the US Embassy in Caracas. It is my duty to provide you with an orientation before you venture ashore for leave. Please ask questions during this briefing.

You have docked in the old port of Guairá. You are approximately 9 miles from downtown Caracas. The area of Guairá is not a friendly or safe place to be. There are frequent armed robberies at both knife and gunpoint. I advise you not to travel alone. It is the conclusion of the festival 'Diablo's Danzantes', a supposedly religious festival involving the famous scissor dancers. It is a very old festival and has been celebrated for years. Unfortunately there are many drunken or drugged party goers on the

254

streets. You will be approached to buy drugs or the services of a prostitute. Be careful. These people do not like it when they cannot make a sale. You will be followed and harassed as you will be in uniform. As with elsewhere in the Caribbean and South America there is real poverty and a common belief that all Americans are wealthy. Be on your guard. You need to travel in groups of three or larger. This is important. Be on the lookout for the street urchins who are expert pickpockets.

This is a sample of what to expect here in the port.

I recommend you take a taxi into Caracas. Do not let the taxi driver talk you into going to Silencio. It is no better than Guairá and in fact is worse in certain areas. In Caracas you will find entertainment, shops and restaurants. It is a sophisticated city. Again expect to be approached many times. Be polite but firm. Do not waiver or show interest or they will not leave you alone. In Caracas there are many brothels. Prostitution is legal here. If you go with a girl make sure she is legal. Ask to see the card that is issued by the government. Check it is current. These girls are examined for sexually transmitted diseases weekly and their card updated.

Should you find yourself in any form of trouble do not rely on the cops here. Many are corrupt. I suggest you take some money and keep it separate from the funds you want to spend in case you need to bribe a cop. If you get into a situation call the emergency number for the

Embassy. I have a card here that I will distribute at the end of the briefing.

Cruz droned on and answered questions from the men. At the end of an hour the briefing was over.

"Lieutenant Slate. Thank you. I hope the men will stay out of trouble here. I hope that one day soon you will come and visit me at the Embassy. It will be my pleasure to reciprocate and serve you one of our famous coffees."

The two shook hands and Cruz strolled along the deck toward the gangway stairs.

Slate was watching him when he noticed the 1959 Lincoln Continental Mark IV parked a discreet distance away from the festival on the dock which had grown in size. It was a carnival of sorts. There were men in strange dress playing guitars and others singing. It seemed impossible for such a friendly setting to disguise the ugly truth that was Guairá.

Slate went to Ramirez cabin.

" Tomasso is on the dock waiting for us."

"Did our men prepare the packages for us?"

 "I checked earlier during that briefing. They are waiting to leave with us."

There were four men waiting in the mess for Ramirez and Slate.

"Follow us down to the dock. Stay close. Our friends are waiting on the dock. Their car is parked near the cargo shed. It is a black Lincoln Continental. You will recognize it. Saunter up and make out you are asking directions."

Slate and Ramirez were greeted by Tomasso and Tony Vitto with hugs and vigorous handshakes. Tomasso looked at Slate's injuries.

"What the hell happened to you?"

"There was a little onboard accident. I got thrown during a storm. Hit some furniture."

The four sailors approached the car.

"Tomasso is there a quiet bar nearby where we can stop for a drink with our friends here?"

"Yes. Squeeze in and I will drive us there/"

All eight squeezed into the spacious car. There was a lot of laughter and Tomasso's pink cushions were used as boxing gloves. Within minutes Tomasso pulled up at a rundown bar appropriately named 'Un desolado paraiso'.

Ramirez laughed. "What a name."

The others asked him for the meaning.

"It is 'A desolate Heaven'.

Tomasso led them into the empty bar. Upon entering he was recognized. The barman sprang into action and brought beer and rum to the table they selected.

"Tomasso we have a "gift" of sorts. It is business related. Please take out the packages."

The men removed the packets from different parts of their bodies.

Tomasso's eyes bulged. He saw the logo on the plastic wrapping.

"This is from Colombia. It is meant to be the best. Where did you get this?"

"Let us just say it came into our possession. Do you wish to buy?"

Before Tomasso could answer Tony Vitto interrupted.

"How much do you want? Is this all of it?"

"Yes. We will leave our friends here and go to our dinner appointment. We will discuss price on the way."

Slate did not want the other men to hear the value of the drug.

They left the four sailors in the bar and returned to the car for the drive to the restaurant and the important meeting.

Slate slumped back in his seat and watched as they drove through different barrios on the way to the **Santuario di Formaggio** restaurant. He wondered what the night held.

"Tomasso that little gift is easily worth $15.000 dollars. Will you pay that? I know the dealers will sell for double that amount."

Tomasso thought about the price for several minutes.

"Yes. I will pay that. This deal is between Tony and I and no one else or it is off."

"We have a deal my friend."

Chapter 53

Throughout the drive, Tomasso chatted amiably with his passengers. He chose to drive through a scenic route to the restaurant avoiding the early evening traffic.

"My friends we will say nothing of our little transaction. That is strictly business between Tony, me and you. Tonight you will meet with some other important guests."

It was shortly before seven when they pulled up in front of **Santuario di Formaggio** restaurant with its gaudy entrance statutes. Alfredo Santaluca, the owner, bounded down the front entrance steps to welcome them.

"Bon Noche. Bon Noche. Welcome back Tomasso. The Palermos are waiting in the private lounge for their guests to arrive. Tonight will be special. Our chefs have produced a magnificent Italian dinner for this gathering. Come in and enjoy."

Slate and Ramirez exchanged looks. The profuse welcome exceeded their expectations.

Together with Tomasso and Tony Vitto they climbed the faux marble stairs and crossed the foyer into the luxuriously appointed restaurant.

Alfredo walked briskly ahead of them and gently pulled back the heavy drape to announce their arrival. The

Palermo brothers stood and stepped forward to be introduced to Slate and Ramirez. When they were seated, Salvatore turned to Slate.

"Lieutenant, was it an uneventful trip?"

Slate replied and described their two encounters on the voyage.

"Lieutenant, how long will you be on patrol in the Caribbean?"

"Salvatore that will depend on a number of factors. We are under the command of the base in Purto Rico for this mission. They will ultimately decide the duration. Since we are able to refuel at extremely low prices here in Venezuela and replenish food and supplies it is possible our trip will be extended."

Salvatore took in every word. His dark eyes scanned Ramirez. He stood and addressed Slate.

"I need to speak privately with you. Follow me please."

He led Slate out of the private room and turned left down a narrow corridor. At the end of the corridor on the right was a pale grey blue door. He reached into his pocket and removed a key to open the door. Inside there was a basic office. Three phones sat on the desk. Piles of invoices and documents lay in an in basket. The room was non descript and its decor defied its place in the restaurant.

Slate was concerned.

"We have had a good relationship over the past couple of years. We have paid you well and protected you from scrutiny of some very nosy officials in the States. I need for you to vouch for Ramirez. He has been with you now for about a year. Do you fully trust him? What we will discuss tonight is very sensitive to our whole operation here. If there was a leak it would compromise our people in Colombia, Venezuela, Aruba, Florida and Holland.

Tonight you will be introduced to Admiral Maduro. He is the senior authority for all Naval operations for the North coast of Venezuela. He is one of our men. He has influence that reaches the top circles of both the military and our politicians. I suggest you listen very carefully to him.

Now tell me why you trust this Ramirez so completely."

Slate bent forward in his chair and reached for the pack of locally produced Belmont cigarettes.

Salvatore watched his every move.

After resting back into the chair and with clouds of acrid smoke drifting from the cigarette, Slate responded.

"We have had a number of encounters with drug traffickers, weapons smugglers, contraband exporters and others. Some of the seizures were incorrectly reported by Ramirez and his accomplices. The proceeds from the disposal of goods to our friends have always been accurately disclosed and paid out. I personally have had his records checked. He is clean. A couple of arrests when he was younger for selling alcohol to minors and some traffic violations. I have also put him to the test to deal with some very difficult tasks involving a street gang that we suspected had a plant in our little groups. The problem was solved and we havent had any since. He is motivated by money. His career with the Coast Guard has presented some unique opportunities. I suspect he will leave the service and continue in this line of work."

"I will hold you personally responsible for any problems with him or the carefully planned job that we are about to launch. Now let us return to the others."

They returned to the private cubicle and found the others smoking and drinking wine while chatting amicably.

Chapter 54

There were voices outside the private cubicle. The conversations ceased. The drapes were pulled back and the distinguished looking Admiral entered. He went to Salvatore and Emilio and profusely shook their hands. He continued on to Tomasso and Tony Vitto next. He then stood to attention and faced Slate and Ramirez. His eyes did a cursory inspection of their dress uniforms. He addressed them in perfect English with a slight British accent.

"Welcome to Venezuela. It is a pleasure to greet fellow officers. I hope your voyage here was uneventful and that you can enjoy your brief stay here. If there is anything our naval offices can assist with you are welcome to contact me and I will arrange this."

"Thank you. We will only be in port for two days and then back on the high seas."

Salvatore watched as the conversation wound its way to issues of life in the Coast Guard. Maduro was fascinated and hung on every detail. After fifteen minutes, Salvatore called them to sit around the dining table.

"Gentlemen. You are here tonight as our guests. There are matters that we need to discuss that relate to our business and the roles you will play.

In the last couple of years our organization in the US has observed a change in the product demand. We will continue to ship marijuana but increasingly the demand is now for cocaine. Our associates in Colombia have been able to meet this demand and in fact have increased their production of it. I understand that the process of producing it is not difficult and in fact the farmers are eager to grow the coco plant as it is easy to grow and more profitable than their other crops. Supply is not a problem. Contacts in the Colombian government and police make it possible to conduct our business without interference. Our problems lie with the transporting of the drug from Colombia to Venezuela and on to the US and Europe. We have established relationships with certain individuals here and in other countries to assist and protect our business. Most recently Tomasso has been busy In Aruba. We have invested in companies who will benefit our interests. We have taken a major investment in a company ExImFreight that handles the import and export of goods through the Free Trade Zone."

Salvatore reached behind him and remove a large envelope from a bench. He opened the envelope and removed copies of two enlarged photos which he handed to Maduro, Slate and Ramirez.

"These are pictures of two boats we recently purchased for ExImFreight. Study these pictures. As you can see, one is a freighter and the other a fishing trawler. The trawler is here in La Guaira and the freighter is in Barcadera, Aruba.

The trawler is supposedly owned by a couple of fishermen here. It is used to transport fish and other items to Aruba. The freighter is used to ship goods to Colombia and return with our product.

Please study these pictures. We do not want either the Venezuelan forces or the US Coast Guard stopping these boats.

Admiral Maduro. You will find a way to instruct your men that these are secret vessels employed by Aruba and Venezuela to gather intelligence on smuggling activities.

Lieutenant Slate. You will declare to your crew that these boats are known and exempt by your government from search.

Do either of you see any problems?"

Both Maduro and Slate shook their heads.

Salvatore reached into the envelope a second time and withdrew a couple of typewritten sheets.

"Here is the schedule of the sailing dates. In addition you will see reference to the operation of our smaller craft. These will take shipments to Aruba for trans shipment to Holland. All of our boats will be identifiable as they will fly decorative flags with a large blue fish on them. Do not stop these small boats. We will send some decoys out as well. You will stop these and arrest the crew and seize the drugs onboard. The use of these decoys will enforce to your superior command and base that your mission is succeeding and maintain your credibility.

We will be making some shipments within the next week. Be prepared. Be sure that our boats are not intercepted or delayed. After the special goods are delivered to Colombia and our products received in Aruba you will receive your payments. Now let us have an enjoyable evening."

Silence fell as the group sat reflecting on Salvatore's words.

Salvatore summoned Alfredo Santaluca and enquired about the evening's special meals. He badly wanted to show his influence and control.

The Admiral was perplexed.

"Salvatore there is a matter that troubles me. How do we communicate? I am sure that Lieutenant Slate's shipboard communications are monitored. For me it is easier as we are in the same country."

"We have a plan for this. There is a transmitter/receiver that has been modified for our use. We will be providing these units for you and Lieutenant Slate. They are compact and easy to operate. The frequencies they use are off the marine bands. For obvious reasons I suggest you use the codes we will provide you. There will be no use of anyone's names or identification of the activities. This plan has been in preparation for some time now. Familiarize yourselves with the units. They are easy to operate."

Accompanied by his head chef, Alfredo Santaluca drew back the heavy drape and joined the group.

"Gentlemen for tonight we have prepared a very special dinner in honor of the guests of the Palermos. I have my chef Enzo here who will describe the meal for you."

"Buona Sera gentiluomini. I have prepared for you foods for the Gods. You can choose your meal from the following dishes.

We have osso bucco, our special veal shanks, or you may wish to try our Braciola, which is Italian Beef rolls in a rich tomato sauce. If you do not want meats and prefer fish, then I have made Cacciucco. This is a recipe from Tuscany and is a Tuscan seafood stew. It is very delicious. To accompany these main dishes you can choose either Risotto Milanese or the Arancini Venesiani. That is one of my specialties, crispy and light Venetian rice fritters. Afterwards I will have served some Sgroppino. This we serve in Italy between courses. It is soft and slushy palate refreshener of vodka, prosecco and sorbet.

Dinner can be followed by one of our many liquors that are imported from Italy. Your waiter will take your orders and answer any questions.

He bowed and slid from the private dining area.

Alfredo was preening himself.

"He is one of the best Italian chefs here in Venezuela. You are fortunate to have the good fortune to indulge in his foods."

As they were enjoying glasses of wine before the dinner, the Admiral turned to Tomasso.

"Where is your friend? That big man. I believe his name was Vincenzio."

Tomasso glanced toward Salvatore who ignored him.

"Vincenzio is not with us. He was sent to a special place. I do not believe he will come back to Venezuela"

"That is unfortunate. I enjoyed his strange conversations. He was a different man."

Tomasso choked and gulped his wine.

Part 4

"A plan is Hatched"

Chapter 55

Malmok, Aruba June 1961.

Jakob felt a renewed vigor in his life. Since he and Solange had retired he missed the action and challenges he faced each day in business. Now he had some real challenges again. He was determined to find out if it was Juan trapped in Colombia and plan to rescue him. In addition he was scheming of ways to stop the criminal influence of the Italian mob and their unscrupulous efforts in obtaining control of certain Aruban businesses.

Though excited and invigorated, Jakob was worried about Solange. Her recent health problems seemed to be getting worse. The Doctors in Aruba were limited in the care and help they could provide. He intended to get Solange to visit a Doctor in Florida during their upcoming trip. He knew she would initially resist but he would seek assistance from her family to have her visit the Doctor.

While Jakob now had his projects, he continued to grapple with his thoughts of the past life in which he had betrayed and used people. His thoughts strayed back to Holland and the life he had shared there with Anke, his former wife and her family. He regretted his impetuous decision to travel around Holland and to Germany in search of ancestral family. He often wondered about the farm near Leiden where he had worked while searching for the Dutch ancestral relatives and the trips he had taken through Holland before the war.

Jakob found that his thoughts were becoming darker and darker as he realized there was no second chance in life. He vowed that before he died he would find those people and try to make amends.

As he sat in his spacious living room looking out at the Caribbean, Solange entered. She looked at Jakob and quickly deduced his mood.

"Jakob I have packed my clothes for the trip to Florida. What will you need there?"

"It will be hot in Miami so I will just take light clothes. We will only be gone for a few days. I will not need much. Come and sit with me. There are things I want to talk about."

Solange sidled over to the long chaise lounge and sat with her legs folded beneath her. The afternoon sun was setting over the Caribbean and the room was bathed in a golden light. She looked at Jakob. Even at the age of 55 he had maintained a youthful appearance.

Before she could speak her body was racked with a deep chesty cough. Jakob went to her and massaged her shoulders and back.

"Solange I am worried about you. You look weak and tired. You now have this persistent cough. You must visit a Doctor."

"I visited my Doctor and she is unable to determine what the problem is. I will visit my family's Doctor while we are in Miami. I feel fine. It is just the cough and the continual weakness."

"Will you be able to travel? We are meant to leave tomorrow afternoon."

"Yes I will be fine. Don't worry. I really want to see my family and nothing is going to stop me."

Jakob knew her determination. After years of marriage he knew she would not be stopped from making the trip, still he was worried. Solange seemed to be getting worse each day.

It was a surprise when Carlita arrived with Hans and Moreno. They joined Solange and Jakob in the living room. No sooner had they sat down when Solange's coughing returned. Carlita was troubled by this.

"Solange can I get you water or something. Your cough sounds serious. Have you any medicine for it?"

"I am fine and don't need of you fussing over me. My cough is from the cold I had weeks ago. It has just stayed and will pass. Now tell me why you are here."

An air of silence fell over the room. Moreno shifted uncomfortably in his chair. Finally Hans spoke.

"We came here with Carlita to discuss an idea, but also to tell you some important news. Moreno has met a young lady here in Aruba. I will let him tell you about this. The other matter is one of importance. Moreno has spent time with one of the Colombians who shared some information with him. We are certain that it is Juan at that drug producing operation in the jungle of Colombia. We are going to plan a trip to Colombia and find him. If we succeed in finding him we will then get him out of there. We need a reason to tell the authorities why we are visiting. I was thinking that we could be representatives for the Klassen business and visiting Solange's relatives to discuss buying coffee for import to the island. We will use that disguise to spread the word that we are looking to buy more than coffee. Moreno will need to be very careful. He is returning to a situation he fled. I am hoping that either you or Jakob can assist us to get some false identity papers for him."

Jakob had sat listening intently.

"I have some ideas and we will meet when Solange and I return from Florida. I believe we can arrange papers for Moreno. Now we want to hear about Moreno and the lady he has met."

Moreno blushed and rubbed his hands together in a circle. He was nervous. Carlita placed her hand on his knee and smiled at him.

"There is nothing to be worried about Moreno. These are your friends and almost your family here in Aruba.

Moreno turned to Solange and Jakob.

Solange watched as Moreno ran his hands through his dark brown and grey flecked hair. She had always thought that he was a handsome man and had always been curious about him. It was unusual to see Colombian men with brown hair.

"I met her while on the beach assisting with the water sports company. She was selling jewelry she had made to tourists on the beach. One day there was a sudden rain storm and she came into the shack for shelter. We started to talk and I was intrigued by her background. She had suffered some bad situations in her past. It seems that many people here in Aruba have come to escape from events. I arranged to meet with her again and it ended up with us seeing each other with increasing frequency. Before long I missed being away from her for any period of time. Initially she insisted on keeping our friendship quiet. I was intrigued by her mysterious behavior. Eventually she told me the story of her life.

Her parents are Italian and royalty. They fled Italy during the war to Argentina. Through contacts they were able to move their fortune with them. Shortly after setting in

Argentina they gave birth to a daughter, Gabriella. By birth she is a Countess. The family invested in vineyards and wineries and prospered. Gabriella was sought after by many men. She had grown up privileged and spoiled. After a succession of affairs she met a man she fell madly in love with. He soon became bored with her. Gabriella was curious when he started to make frequent visits to a nearby church and convent. One evening she followed him. Parked a discreet distance from the convent she observed a light turn on. After a few minutes the light was extinguished. Curious, Gabriella silently entered the convent and proceeded to the room where she had seen the light. Stealthily she opened the door into a sparsely decorated room. In the bed she saw her man completely naked with part of a nun's habit wrapped over his head. After tearing it from him she uncovered the naked nun. It was an old girlfriend of his.

After this encounter she fled to a friend's home and finally made her way to Aruba under an assumed name.

We have spoken in detail of her past. She has fled from that life and has pursued a different one here in Aruba."

Jakob was intrigued.

"Where does she live? What does she do for a job?

"She has her own business. She makes jewelry. One day on the beach she saw a necklace worn by an American woman. It was made of hand-blown glass. Gabriella liked it and decided that she wanted to make necklaces and rings like it and try to sell them to the increasing number of tourists. She has made a workshop in her home in Alto Vista."

Jakob was impressed.

"Why are you telling us of her life story?"

"I am going to marry her."

Carlita beamed. "Isn't that great news? Moreno has found someone and will be part of our little group."

Solange attempted to speak but surrendered to a major coughing attack.

All in the room watched. When she stopped coughing and regained her composure she asked, "When are you going to marry?"

"We will marry very soon. I need to get the necessary papers and make arrangements."

Hans had sat quietly observing them all. "Now we need to speak with Jakob. We have some ideas for getting Juan out of Colombia."

Jakob's interest level arose.

"Let's go into my den and discuss this. We can have a nice drink there as well to celebrate Moreno's announcement."

They excused themselves and followed Jakob to his den.

Chapter 56

In the den the men filled their glasses with Aruba's Palmera Rum and wandered to the chairs that were arranged to look out into Jakob's prized garden.

"Hans tell me what these ideas of rescuing Juan are."

Hans downed his rum and walked back to the table that held the bottle and a collection of glasses. He poured a large glass of rum. He realized this would be a long evening and he wanted to visit his girl.

"Jakob there have been developments that I think can help us with Juan. After we met with those Colombians, Moreno and I had a chance meeting with a former Dutch Marine. I hired him to assist with the boats and diving operations of the water sports company. He is young and strong. He trained in jungle warfare and has experienced action. I am thinking that we offer him a large payment to assist us in freeing Juan and getting him back to Aruba safely. We will have another meeting with the Colombians and get more information on the location of the drug lab."

"I would like to meet this Adrien. I will tell you my thoughts about him. Unfortunately there are many former Marines who have tried to stay here on the Island and are very weak individuals. They think because they were in the Dutch Marines that everyone should worship them. Some are poor quality excuses for men. Their interests are the local women, drinks and the island life.

If he is one of those then he is of no use to us and may put our plans in danger."

There was a brief knock at the door before it opened and Isaac Junior walked in. He looked at the gathering and went to pour a drink for himself.

"Jakob I understand that you and Solange are leaving for Florida tomorrow. I am not sure she is well enough to travel. Are you sure that this is the right time to make this trip?"

"She has arranged appointments with family members and some of the managers in the family's business there. I highly doubt that she can be persuaded not to take the trip. You are welcome to try and convince her otherwise."

"Jakob you know she is unwell. Why are you allowing this?"

"Isaac, calm down. I am allowing it because there is a particular Doctor that has looked after her family for years. Solange has agreed to visit with him."

Isaac quieted and joined in sitting with the others.

"She is my mother and has done so much for Jakob and me. I worry that if she does not receive treatment then her problem will get worse."

"Isaac we all want what is best for Solange. I promise you that she will be well looked after. If she tires we may delay our return trip. Now sit and listen to our ideas on rescuing Juan"

The conversations drifted through different scenarios of finding and rescuing Juan.

It was late when Carlita joined them.

"I have taken Solange to her bed. She is very fatigued. Jakob you must not allow her to do too much in Florida. I know that it is her family and she is excited to see her brothers and their families.

I am relying on you to look after my dearest friend."

Jakob cradled his head in his hands and rested his elbows on his knees.

"In case none of you realize this, she is my wife and lover. She is the most special woman I have ever known. Don't lecture me or worry that I will not ensure she is looked after."

Jakob was angry. The others were embarrassed. Carlita signaled to leave Jakob alone. It was clear he was worried and distressed.

They filed from the den, leaving Jakob alone with his thoughts.

When he was alone he refilled his glass. It was too early to retire to bed. He went to his desk and removed a document from a file folder. It was the deed and ownership of his Canadian farm.

He sat with the deed in his hand and slowly sipped the harsh rum. Tears filled his eyes as he thought of the days he had spent on the farm with his parents, friends and Anke, his next door neighbor. He was filled with regret for his treatment of her and abandoning his faith. He wondered how his life would have been if he had stayed on the farm and not pursued his insatiable appetite for knowledge of past family.

His thoughts wandered and he reminisced on the journey he had undertaken.

The rum was having a morbid effect on his thoughts. He drifted into his past world and recalled the various people he had met, many of who had helped him.

The longer he sat drinking the more depressed he became.

The tears continued to fall. He thought of the many he had betrayed and those who had put their trust and faith in him.

Jakob slumped forward in his chair and fell into a sleep. His glass fell from his hand onto the floor and loudly shattered. Isaac Junior heard the thump and the breaking of the glass. He returned to the den.

"Jakob you cannot sleep here. I will assist you to bed. This is not like you. What is wrong?"

Jakob looked blearily at Isaac and in a slurred speech attempted to tell him of his worries.

"Isaac. When I was young and travelling from Canada to find those relatives I treated some good people very badly. I now regret it. Every day I think about it. I am saddened by what I did. It was long ago and I no longer know where those people are. It is a continual burden in my mind. Those people did not deserve the way I used them. I wish that I could correct the wrong things I have done."

"Jakob you were a good husband to Solange. I could not have ever wanted a better father. You have assisted so many here in Aruba. I think that you are not considering all the good you and Solange have done here. I know there are some here who are critical of you, but they are ones with their own problems.

Now let me take you to your bedroom. You are tired and exhausted from thinking about the need to rescue your good friend Juan."

Isaac bent forward and placed his arms beneath Jakobs. He gently lifted Jakob from his chair and walked him to his room where Solange lay sleeping. Isaac gently lowered Jakob into the large bed.

Chapter 57

It was 7:00am when Solange awakened. She was well and in better spirits. She looked at Jakob. He was in a deep sleep. His complexion was grey. The stubble of a beard grew on his chin.

Solange wondered what the men had discussed in the den the previous evening. These days it was unusual for Jakob to drink excessively.

Her years of life with Jakob convinced her not to pursue such matters. She gently shook him awake.

"Jakob it is time for us to get up. We need to finish packing and prepare to leave for the airport."

Jakob looked at her and grunted some unintelligible sounds.

Solange left the bed and went to the bathroom to bathe and dress for the trip.

Upon returning to the bedroom she found Jakob slouched in his favorite chair looking out the huge window.

She joined him and gently ran her hand across the back of his neck.

"Jakob you are troubled. Is it about Juan? If it is too much for you then you should let the others plan and rescue him. I know he is your friend and you want to help."

"No Solange. When I was young I had serous conflicts with the beliefs that my religion demanded. For years I fought that conflict. It is now returning, but this time it is about how I treated others in Europe and during those war years. I close my eyes and I see their faces. It has become a demon in me. I am not a good person. My life has been one of deceit."

"There is nothing you can do. What happened occurred a long time ago. You were trapped in Germany. There was a war. Horrible things were happening. You could not control those things."

"Solange what I did was unforgivable. I got Hans' mother pregnant and deserted her. I abandoned Anke in Holland and made no real attempt to save her. I used her family. I used the contacts I made in the clubs in Germany to plot my escape. I have never tried to find or thank the person who helped me the most, Jan Zelder. It was Jan who assisted me to flee the ship when we docked in San Nicolaas."

"Jakob I have an idea. For years we have spoken of this. I am feeling well and want to do this. After our trip to Florida I would like you to take me to Canada and show me the farms and the land your parents helped settle. Will you do that for me? I have always wanted that. I am feeling better and a trip like that, to understand your childhood, would be major for me."

Jakob was surprised.

"Yes of course. We will discuss this on our Florida trip. I will plan and make the arrangements. This makes me happy and takes away last night's rum."

Jakob pulled himself from the bed and went to shower. When he returned to the bedroom Solange was gone.

He smelled the aroma of fresh coffee wafting into the bedroom. As he dressed he hummed to the latest tune playing that was playing on the stereo he had recently purchased. The voice of Ben E King singing *'Stand by me'* boomed from the system.

"How appropriate" he thought.

He stood and enraptured by the words as they drifted across the room.

He listened to King sing of the night and darkness and yet the moon provided light and removed any fear he may have. As the song continued and the words expressed that as long as his love stood by him all would be fine.

It seemed to Jakob to capture his life with Solange.

Jakob wondered how music could capture such emotion and life. He sat on the edge of the bed and reflected on his life. The music had brought back more memories and made him aware of the darkness of the recent events that their business and the Klassen family faced. He thought of all that Solange had done for him and the community.

Jakob sat in quite reflection. He was melancholy and wondered whether he would break from his desperate desire to amend his past or carry the burden of guilt for the rest of his life.

A voice called to him from the kitchen. It was Carlita. She had spent the evening at the Klassens concerned with Solange's health and Jakob's state.

"My friends I have made you some nice Dutch coffee and made a breakfast. You have a big day today. Isaac will be here later this morning to take you to the airport.

Solange, my friend. Are you well enough to travel? I worry about you."

"My dear Carlita I am well. This trip will do me well. I will be home in two days. It is a short trip to attend to some family matters. I will enjoy the trip and seeing my family."

Solange and Jakob pulled up chairs and sat at the counter to enjoy a breakfast of Calentado, a Colombian dish of beans, rice, eggs and chorizo.

Jakob chuckled as he spooned into the food. There was little Solange could say. She would not want to offend her friend. He would indulge in this meal and forget his Doctor's advice about different foods and his blood pressure.

Carlita looked across at Jakob. Her feelings for him had never abated. If not for Solange then Jakob would have been her mate.

Solange observed the look that Carlita gave Jakob as she handed him his plate of food. She no longer cared.

With a coffee in his hand, Jakob left the kitchen and went to his garden to relax and consider the day ahead. Solange had been secretive and not told Jakob or Isaac of the business she intended to conduct with her family.

Jakob had dealt with the family previously and was not worried. He knew the brothers of Solange and some of the relatives. Business with the family had always been cordial and honest.

On this trip, Jakob had a hidden agenda. He would seek out companies and individuals who were doing business with Commercial Loan Bank of Aruba. He would also find out those who were dealing with the Italians. He had kept his plans quiet and concealed from Solange.

Jakob's revenge against the Italian mob was about to start. He intended to rid Aruba of the evil influences they had brought to its shores.

Chapter 58

Suitcases were put in Isaac's car for the drive to Reina Beatrix airport.

As they were pulling away from the house, Jakob turned to Isaac.

"Please stop at the beach for a minute. I have something I need to discuss with Hans."

They drove down the small hill to Boca Catalina and along the coast toward Palm Beach. Jakob noticed that many of the palm trees were being cut down and new houses built. He was saddened by this. He loved the sprawling coconut plantations. He wondered whether Aruba needed this progress.

Isaac wheeled off the road and onto the dirt track that wound down to the beach.

He stopped the car and Jakob left to find Hans.

Jakob spied Hans at the water's edge. He called to him and waved Hans to join him.

"Jakob this is a surprise. I thought you and Solange were going to Miami today."

"We are on our way to the airport but I wanted to speak to you before we left. Please contact the Colombians. Ask

289

them for as much information as possible on the activities of Tomasso and his friends. This is very important. Please do not ask me for a reason. It is time that their activities here are stopped. I intend to do just that. I may not succeed but what I have planned will slow them down and create some problems. I am counting on you to obtain that knowledge. It will be critical for my plan to work."

"I will contact Moreno and we will find some way to get it for you. Now go and have a safe trip. Try and take some relaxation while you are there."

Jakob returned to the car. Isaac was curious. Jakob said nothing. They continued to the airport in silence.

Isaac pulled up in front of the new passenger terminal. Travellers arriving in Aruba waited on the concrete sidewalk waiting for taxis or friends to pick them up. The day was hot and a strong wind was blowing. Women held their dresses down and with their other hand clasped at their hair or hats. The air carried the smell of aviation gas. In the distance Jakob could hear the roar of a plane's engines as it revved to pull away from the terminal and onto the runway.

A porter approached the car. Isaac opened the trunk and removed their cases and handed them to him.

He walked to Solange and hugged her.

"Please be careful. Do not spend too much time doing business. I am concerned you will tire and become ill again."

Jakob patted Isaac on the shoulder and after taking Solange by the arm, started toward the Pan American Airlines counter.

A group of passengers were seated and awaiting the instruction to board the plane. Jakob looked through the group hoping to see a friend or former business associate. There were none.

At the counter he was greeted by a friendly agent.

"Welcome Mr. and Mrs. Klassen. It is our pleasure to have you travel with us today. The plane is not full so I can offer you a choice of seating. Do you prefer smoking or non-smoking?"

"We prefer non-smoking."

"There are seats at the front or in the middle. Do you have preference? The plane is one of our new DC6's and while it seats 55 people there are only 27 travelling today."

"My wife and I will take seats at the front."

The agent checked their passports and travel papers and advised them to sit in the waiting area until the flight was ready.

While they were waiting, smartly dressed young ladies in pale blue uniforms and wearing pillbox hats arrived. They were in high spirits and giggling amongst themselves.

They were escorted through a gate at the side of the counter and disappeared behind a door and into a walkway that led out to the tarmac.

Jakob sensed that this would be a casual and enjoyable flight. He looked forward to the four and a half hours they would take to reach Miami. He would read and enjoy the food and drinks. Pan American service was renowned for its quality.

The young lady who had served them at the counter made her way to the front of the waiting passengers.

"We at Pan Am thank you for choosing us today. The plane is ready. Please follow me and I will walk you out to the plane."

The group stood and followed the agent. At the plane a steep set of stairs in front of the wing led up to an open door. Waiting at the door there was an attendant to assist the passengers.

Solange and Jakob slowly climbed the stairs and were quickly guided to their seats. They were no sooner seated when an attendant arrived at their seats with a silver tray upon which a selection of wines and juices were arranged. Jakob loved the attention.

When the passengers were all seated the attendants walked the aisle checking them and ensuring that the seat belts were fastened.

The plane rocked gently and the cabin lights dimmed as the pilots started the giant engines. There was a whine as the starter engaged the engines, followed by a sputtering and a roar as each engine fired into life. Inside the plane there was a loud hum from the four engines.

Jakob sat listening to the process. Engines revved and there was a slight lurch as the brakes were released and the plane started its turn and taxied to the end of the runway.

Within minutes the engines revved and roared as the plane rolled down the runway, gathering momentum before the front inched up into the air. There was a heavy drone as the plane lifted off and the engines pulled its heavy weight aloft.

After thirty minutes the attendant returned with yet another tray of drinks. Jakob requested the attendant to prepare a Rob Roy for him. Solange gave him a look. Jakob laughed.

They talked for a while and Jakob then took a copy of the Miami Sentinel newspaper that was offered to him by the flight attendant. Solange closed her eyes and reclined in her seat.

Jakob thumbed through the paper and stopped when he read the following headline:

'United Nations Convention on Narcotic Drugs, 1961 Concludes. Florida to receive increased help in fighting drug smugglers'

Jakob dove into the article and read it with great interest. It was a long story. He tore it out of the paper and folded it into his breast pocket. He sat back in his seat in almost a trance and considered what he had just read.

His thoughts were running wild. A plan was forming in his head. He would have a busy day in Florida.

He was shaken from his deep thinking by a tap on the shoulder. Two flight attendants were wheeling a trolley up the aisle. They stopped next to Jakob and Solange seats.

"Would you care for our hot meal?"

The attendant removed the large cloche covering a roast hip of beef. Jakob salivated at the aroma. The attendant removed the cover from a second tray and showed the dish to them.

"Madam, would you like the beef or the coq au vin?"

Solange ordered the chicken with a glass of sauterne. Jakob ordered a double serving of the roast beef and vegetables. He was hungry and contemplated that he would not have much time the next day as he intended to find the reporter who wrote that article.

As the roast beef was placed on his tray, Jakob ordered a glass of Pinot Noir.

This trip was starting well.

After he and Solange had finished eating, he fell into a sleep and remained asleep until the plane started its descent into Miami.

Chapter 59

Miami, Florida

The landing was smooth. They taxied to the terminal. Jakob was observing the activity outside with great interest. The plane turned a came to a stop on the apron. The passengers gathered together their possessions while waiting for the cabin door to be cracked open.

A set of stairs was rolled up to the plane and they descended onto the asphalt tarmac. As he was leaving the plane, Jakob looked across at the adjacent area. A huge plane was parked there. He continued down the stairs and stopped to speak with the crew who had gone down first to wish the passengers farewell.

"What is that?" he asked the Captain pointing at the huge silver and white plane.

"That is one of the new jet aircraft that will be entering service early next year. That one is a Douglas DC-8. It can fly to Europe and places like Australia without needing to refuel. Those jets are going to change flying and travel. I believe this one is here on a demonstration flight."

Jakob considered this. He immediately thought of Aruba and what that would mean for tourism.

When they were leaving the baggage area, Solange heard her name called. She looked around and noticed a young man with a cardboard sign with her name scrawled on it. He waved to her and started across in their direction.

The young man was around twenty years of age. He was extremely tall. Slicked back dark black hair, a body builder's physique and a flashing white smile gave him the appearance of a movie star picked from the silver screen.

"Aunt Solange. Welcome back to Florida. I am here to meet you and take you to our family guest house."

He turned and looked at Jakob. "You must be Jakob. It is a pleasure to meet you, sir. I have heard so many things about you."

Jakob wondered what those things could have been.

"Nice to meet you too, son. What is your name?"

"Eric. My family and friends call me Sparky. Here, let me take those cases from you both. My car is parked across the road from the terminal. It is a very short walk."

They crossed over the busy street to where a duck egg blue 1960 convertible was parked. Jakob admired it.

"Dad gave me this when I graduated and was accepted into Medical school."

Sparky opened the trunk and placed their suitcases in it.

"Would you like to stop anywhere for either a drink or food or should we just drive to the house?"

"It has been a long day. Let's just go to the house. Besides I have some things to check and I want to try and set up a meeting tomorrow. It's not too late and I may be able to get that done this evening."

Sparky nodded. "Is it something I can help you with?"

"I want to see the reporter at The Miami Sentinel who wrote an article of extreme interest to me."

"We will be driving past their offices. I can stop there. Reporters have strange hours. He may still be there working."

"Sparky I hate to correct you. It is she I need to meet. The reporter is a young lady."

Solange looked at him with a frown. Now what was he up to?

They pulled away from the curb and into the heavy traffic departing the airport. The road was only a two lane highway and jammed with cars and trucks. Sparky pointed across to where heavy earth moving equipment was tearing into the ground.

"They are working long hours to complete the new freeway. It is opening in December. They still have a lot of work to do."

They wove through traffic and turned into a district of office buildings. The pace was quiet here.

Sparky slowed and stopped at a building with a pink marble façade and huge swinging glass doors. Brass plaques adorned the wall next to the doors. One contained the name and some information for the Miami Sentinel.

Jakob opened the door of the Thunderbird. He turned to Solange. "I won't be long. Just going to see if I can get a meeting scheduled."

Solange frowned. She had no idea of Jakob's plans and knew not to ask. If he wanted her to know he would tell her.

Jakob disappeared into the cavernous entrance. He strode to the elevators and rode up to the seventh floor. He exited the elevator and entered the busy centre of a newsroom. A mousey girl, obviously a receptionist offered to assist him.

Jakob took the article he had torn from the paper and showed her. He asked to meet the reporter.

"Please wait. I will see if she is here. I think she has left already, but let me check."

Minutes passed. The receptionist returned with a young lady dressed in a red suit. She was a beautiful Cuban American. She offered her hand to Jakob.

"I am Benita Flores. How may I help you?"

"I have just arrived here from Aruba. On the flight I read your article on the Narcotics convention. I would like to meet and discuss this and some situations you may find interesting."

Jakob briefly described his interest.

Benita listened intently.

"Wait here. Let me get you a copy of the United Nations report. I think you should read it before we meet. Some is just about procedure but other parts you will find interesting."

She spun and walked back into the office. Moments later she returned and handed a document to Jakob.

It was entitled 'Single Convention on Narcotic Drugs, 1961.'

She smiled and asked Jakob to meet with her at ten in the morning.

Chapter 60

The sun was setting as they drove to the house. Solange was eager to see her sister again. They turned into several streets lined with tall palm trees that were silhouetted against the golden sunset.

Sparky turned onto a cul-de-sac and slowed its end. He swung right and onto a long driveway that lead to the nine bedroom mansion. Manicured lawns and gardens bordered each side of the drive. A decorative fountain in the middle of a circular paved entranceway shot water skyward. Sparky hit the horn. The door burst open and a younger version of Solange ran toward the car.

Jakob looked at her. Even though she looked like Solange she could not match her beauty. Heavy gold jewelry draped around her neck clanged as she bounced across the pavement. As he studied her he was horrified at the layers of makeup she had slapped onto her face and neck. It looked like she had been plastering the bedroom wall. "So this is what people who live on Star Island Drive are like" he thought.

As she approached the car, Jakob recoiled. There was an overpowering blast of perfume. He wouldn't have minded if it was delicate, but this smelled like fly spray.

He was grateful they would only be there for two days and he had arranged business that would take him away from the house.

Sparky jumped from the car and retrieved their cases.

Solange gingerly hugged her sister and introduced Jakob.

"This is my younger sister, Yolanda. We had so much fun growing up together until I was taken ill. I will never forget those days."

Jakob suppressed his breath and stepped forward to shake her hand. She was a walking chemical factory.

"I hope you are all hungry. I have had our kitchen staff prepare your special meal Solange."

Jakob wondered what that could possibly be. He had been married to Solange for years and thought he knew all of her likes and dislikes. He said nothing.

"My husband Henri and his brother will be joining us for dinner. They had a meeting with the City late this afternoon. Some new construction project they want to get approved. Personally I don't know why they bother. They have so many projects now and besides he is so busy with the pharmaceutical company we purchased ten years ago. It prints money. I wish he would stop and just take me on travels around the world. You know, to those exotic places. He can forget the nasty ones. Afghanistan, those barbarians in Africa and the dog eaters in Korea. Give me Tahiti or a nice Caribbean Island or two."

Jakob could not believe what he was seeing or hearing. He scratched his head. Solange had come from this? He remembered the fine deportment and manners of Catherine, the mother of Solange. How could she have produced a daughter like Yolanda?

As they walked up the immense marble stairs, Sparky signaled to a butler to take their cases to the guest house. They walked through the central hallway of the house to enormous glass French doors that opened out onto gardens that extended down to the waterfront.

Yolanda beckoned them and they crossed over a patio and were escorted to a stylish guest house set off from the main house in a growth of trees. It was completely private.

"It has been a long day for us. Will you excuse us while we freshen up?"

Sparky responded first. "Yes of course. Jakob what is your preferred drink? We will meet on the patio for drinks before dinner."

Jakob was becoming tired of the pretentiousness. "Just get me a beer. Any old brand will do."

After showering and changing into casual clothing, Solange and Jakob returned to the patio.

While sipping on his beer and describing Aruba, they were joined by Henri and his brother Chas. Introductions were made and more drinks flowed.

It was dark when a maid arrived to announce that dinner could be served.

Henri boomed how hungry he was. The group moved close together and proceeded into the dining room.

A polished rosewood table was in the center. Louis XV chairs were pulled up at each place setting. A silver candelabrum was placed in the middle of the table and a tall white candle burned brightly.

Henri took immediate control of the conversation.

"Solange tell us why you are making this trip"

"No that will wait until tomorrow. That is business and tonight we all be sociable and enjoy each other's company. I want to hear about Sparky's plans once he completes Medical school. I also want to hear about you Henri. I understand you have become political and are considering running for election."

Jakob's level of curiosity arose at this comment.

Yolanda launched into a speech that only a doting mother could. In her world Sparky was the only one and could do no wrong. Sparky sat unabashedly at the table soaking up every word.

Jakob could not contain himself any longer.

"Henri please tell us all about those political aspirations of yours."

Henri was pleased to have been asked and given a stage on which to perform.

"I have been planning this for some time now. I have spoken on many occasions to the President. As you may know, Chas and I own a construction and road building firm. We were awarded contracts to build the new freeways and Interstate highways that the President nurtured. It was one of his pet projects.

I have discussed with him my possible candidacy and received his support and encouragement. Now we have a new President coming into power. I know the Kennedy family. We have done business in the past. I am hoping that relationship will help. I have personally made significant political contributions and received assurances from his close allies that my efforts will continue to be supported.

I need to find an appropriate platform that will appeal to the large and diverse population we have here in Florida."

Jakob could not believe what he was hearing. Maybe luck was on his side.

Chapter 61

Talk around the table continued until a servant entered to announce dinner would be served.

Another servant dressed in a black suit wheeled a serving trolley to the table. Yolanda indicated to start the service by serving Solange first removing the cover from the large casserole dish. The server took a platter and using tongs served a mixture of calf liver, tripe and sautéed onions in a white sauce. Solange beamed. She had not been served this delicacy since moving to Aruba. Jakob was horrified and remembered the sopi mondongo he had once had in San Nicolaas.

Plates continued to be served and placed in front if the diners.

Jakob looked at his and attempted to hide his disdain of the food. He plunged his fork into the tripe and cut a sliver which he then attempted to swallow.

The slimy tripe was chewy like rubber. As he tried to swallow it became lodged in his esophagus. He coughed and choked. Sparky quickly moved to Jakob and gave him a heavy thump on his back. The creamy colored tripe, which was stained with red wine residue from Jakob's throat dislodged and flew across the table landing in Yolanda's cleavage.

Jakob spluttered an apology.

"I am sorry. I suffer from acid reflux. I will not be able to continue dinner. Nothing I eat will stay in me. Please excuse me. It looks like a delicious meal and I appreciate that you have gone to great effort to provide Solange with her favorite dish."

As he watched the piece of tripe slithered down and disappeared into Yolanda's ample cleavage.

Henri and Chas erupted into uncontrollable laughter.

"Come on Jakob. Let's go to the library. Chas and I were fed at the meeting. We are not really hungry. We will go have some Courvoisier and cigars while enjoying some man talk.

Jakob was relieved. He slid his chair back from the table and joined Henri and Chas.

In the library Henri's laughter boomed out. "Jakob that was a magnificent performance. I think I could get to like you. Now please explain why you have come on this trip."

Jakob filled his snifter with Courvoisier and settled into the massive armchair.

"It is a long story. After I settled in Aruba I worked at several jobs before starting a business of my own. I purchased some real estate and then branched into restaurants and the tourism business. Things went well. I met Solange and we have never looked back. Recently however, life in Aruba is changing."

Jakob spent time discussing the changes. He told them of the influx of different people since Castro has taken control in Cuba. He discussed the strange events with the casinos and clubs. As he continued, Henri leaned forward and listened intently.

"We have been visited by members of the Italian mob from Venezuela. They are buying their way into local businesses. They have taken over the ExImFreight company and bought ships. There are strange shipments through the Free Trade Zone. In addition they have opened a bank. The clients of that bank are coerced to deal with other clients. The Italians make no attempt to disguise their purpose. They want to establish Aruba as a replacement for Cuba. Because of Aruba's location close to Colombia and Venezuela they have established a complex drug operation to ship drugs through to America and Europe.

I have learned of the recent convention that the United Nations sanctioned on controlling narcotics.

Tomorrow I am meeting with the reporter for Miami Sentinel who wrote an article on the convention and the goals set by the participating countries. I have a copy of the report and will be reading it tonight.

It is my plan to expose the activities of the mob and make their life very difficult in Aruba. I do not want to see my country destroyed by them."

Henri sat and stared at Jakob for the longest time.

"You are giving me an idea. The people of Florida are tired of gun battles, drug dealing and other drug related crimes. This could be the ideal platform to rally support for eradication and control of the situation. I am going to speak with my advisors.

I would like to join you tomorrow when you meet that reporter."

The library fell into silence.

"I have contacts at high levels in the Bureau of Narcotics Control. I think we should visit them as well. I think that there are many sources here in Florida that can assist you."

Jakob considered this before speaking.

"Henri, we are a small country. There are only 55,000 people living on the island. It should be easy to create enough of a problem to convince the mob to go elsewhere. Because of our size many people are related or know each other. It will be simple to spread the news of any plan to deal with the Italians and punish anyone who helps them."

"Before that meeting tomorrow morning I will contact some others in policing, customs and local government. My contacts will be at the political level. I will find and determine what is being done here and in the Caribbean, as that is where the drugs come from."

Jakob stood.

"Good night all. I am going to retire and read that report."

In the bedroom of the guest houses Jakob lay on the bed. He took the fifty page report and started to read. He scanned it and bypassed the pages dealing with procedural matters. He stopped at the page listing the participant countries. He noted that Venezuela, Colombia and The Netherlands were all participants. Of particular interest was the appointment of the Dutch representative of the Conference. He found it of particular interest given that Aruba, Curacao and Bon Aire were all Dutch.

Jakob read over the definitions of the narcotic drugs, the responsibility of member countries and the penal penalties. The document was very clear in these matters.

He lay the document aside and reflected on the drug smuggling he was aware of. The convention document stated the responsibility of countries with bonded warehouses in which drugs were stored for trans shipment. He thought of the ExImFreight company in Aruba and the Free Trade Zone. He doubted any effort was made to comply with the provisions stated in the report.

It was late when he finally put the report down and prepared for bed. Solange had not returned. Jakob assumed she was speaking with her sister and family.

He rested on his back and closed his eyes. It hit him hard. Negative thoughts and feelings of guilt overtook his mind. He tried to think of different situations. Everything he envisaged turned into a negative situation. Jakob was experiencing a mental occurrence worse than he had endured as a youth when he was tortured with his conflicted reasoning about his religion. His thoughts were racing. His mind flashed back to Europe and the war. He could not conjure up any positive thought. As he lay on the bed he dropped into a depth of depression and fear.

He had never felt this level of despair in his life. Something had done wrong. He doubted himself. As his mind ran he considered the possibility of ending his life. He had reached a point of hating these sessions.

Solange entered as Jakob lay there. She looked at him and realized he was having an intense period of self doubt and depression. She lowered herself onto the bed and gently brushed his forehead.

"Jakob we need to get you help. You are getting worse. I am sure I can get you an appointment with my family's Doctor. Please let me do this. The treatment you got in Aruba doesn't seem to be helping. I love you too much to see this happening. Please let me get you an appointment."

Jakob looked deeply into her grey eyes. He sensed her concern.

"You can try but I must go to my meeting in the morning."

Solange gave him a smile of encouragement.

"Jakob let me fetch you a strong drink. Maybe that will help expel your demons and help you sleep."

Jakob agreed. Solange went to the room's bar and poured them both a stiff brandy.

Within minutes Jakob was tired. Solange stripped his clothes from him and assisted him into the bed.

Jakob fell into a deep but troubled sleep within minutes. Solange sat on the edge of the bed wondering what was happening to her lover, friend and husband. She had seen him slipping over the past few months and was unable to find him any help in Aruba. She swore that she would find a qualified Doctor while they were in Florida. She didn't care about the cost. She did not want Jakob slipping further into depression and paranoia.

It was almost an hour later when she retired and extinguished the lights.

Chapter 62

Solange arose early. She left the guest house and walked through the garden to the patio. The early morning sun glinted on the water and the reflected rays bounced off the beveled edges of the glass panes of the French doors creating prismatic bursts of color.

She pulled a dark green cushion onto the chair and seated herself at the white wrought iron table. The temperature of the air was pleasant. It was too early for the intense heat of Florida.

"Good morning Solange."

She turned to see Sparky jogging around the side of the mansion. He sprinted up the stairs and joined her. Within minutes an old servant joined them. He was black and in his aging had developed an aura of calmness and humor.

"Missus and my friend Sparky what can I bring you this morning? Our crazy chef has made a breakfast that I don't think anyone will eat. Kippers and eggs. Oh the smell. Just like stale socks. Take my advice. The Eggs Benedict are great. Why I even thought of taking some to the bushes and hiding there with them while I ate."

Sparky dismissed him after he and Solange ordered the Eggs Benedict.

Sparky became serious.

"Is Jakob well? Last night he seemed to be distracted and impatient."

"He has had to adapt to a lot. I think he misses work now he is retired. He gets bored. Life in Aruba is different. It is a small island and does not have many of the attractions or life that you have here. Jakob spent time in Europe at the beginning of the war. I know he does miss certain activities. He was a musician. I have tried to get him to play again but he refuses. I wish I knew why that is the case. He will not talk about it. There is something there that he wishes to keep secret."

"This morning I will be stopping at the College before travelling to the Hospital where I am getting experience as an intern. Jakob has a meeting with the Miami Sentinel people and I will take him there on my way. Is he awake? He should come and eat with us."

The words had no sooner rolled off Sparky's lips when Jakob appeared. He walked down the garden path toward the patio. He skipped up the stairs and kissed Solange on her cheek.

He sat and the older servant reappeared.

"Good morning sir. What can I get you from the kitchen?"

Jakob sniffed the air.

"Are those kippers I smell cooking? If so bring me some. I love them. Ask the chef to put them with some runny eggs."

Minutes later the strong smelling plate of fish and eggs arrived. Jakob ate them without hesitation. His plate was empty within a short time. Solange and Sparky watched in awe as he demolished the dish.'

"Jakob I will be driving downtown in about thirty minutes. I can take you to the Miami Sentinel building. You will be a little early."

"I appreciate your kindness. Yes I will go with you. I may stop in one of those little coffee shops while I wait."

"I will meet you at the front in ten minutes. Sparky wiped his lips and got up and left the table.

"Solange what are you plans for the day?"

"Yolanda has called my brothers and we will have a family meeting here."

Behind them they heard the opening of one of the French doors. Yolanda walked out wearing a fluorescent green jump suit. It took Jakob every ounce of control to contain his laughter. She wore a gaudy purple bead necklace and her arm was heavily populated with a number of multicolored bracelets. Jakob thought to himself that she looked like a bull frog in full armaments.

While Yolanda was wealthy beyond calculation, there was no accounting for her lack of taste. She had developed a special reputation in Florida and was actually invited to parties in South Beach so the social press and others could be shocked at her tackiness.

Underneath the image, Yolanda possessed a heart of gold. She contributed to children's causes and assisted the homeless. Besides her charitable work she also had business acumen that was envied by many.

Jakob stood and excused himself.

"I must go and retrieve some papers from the guest house that I will need at my meeting with the reporter at Miami Sentinel."

Yolanda looked up at him.

"Ask for Kitty Dupree while you are there. Send her my love. I think she is the best social columnist in all Florida."

Jakob smiled and nodded to her and left to fetch his portfolio from the guest house.

He waited for Sparky on the front steps. The Thunderbird arrived and pulled to a halt. The tires squealed on the new asphalt as Sparky braked hard. Minutes later they pulled out and onto the main highway. The morning temperature was rising. They coasted along with the roof down, passing slower cars. Sparky had the radio turned up and strains of

Patsy Cline singing 'I fall to pieces' filled the car and spilled out causing other motorists to stare at them.

Jakob hated that tune and told Sparky who then pressed a button to select another radio station. Within seconds Bobby Darin was blasting out 'You must have been a beautiful Baby.'

Jakob gave up. All he had hoped for was a quiet drive to the meeting so he could collect his thoughts. His head still pounded from last night's mental session. Even though he had slept, he was tired.

They finally arrived at the Miami Sentinel. As Sparky pulled to the curb, he noticed Henri's black Mercedes parked there.

"Jakob are you expecting to meet Henri here? That is his car."

Jakob glanced at the car. A chauffer was waiting in the driver's seat. Jakob thanked Sparky and then walked over to the Mercedes after exiting the Thunderbird.

"Hi I am Jakob. I am Henri's brother in law. Is he here? I hope I can find him and have a coffee with him. I don't see him very often."

"Sir I believe he has business with the Sentinel up on the seventh floor. Good day to you."

Jakob was annoyed. It was obvious that Henri had listened to his plan and was twisting it to suit his political agenda.

Jakob strode across the foyer and punched the elevator button.

Chapter 63

Jakob rode the elevator to the seventh floor. The doors parted and he stepped out. The mousey receptionist recognized him immediately. She reached for her phone and punched in some numbers and spoke in a whisper.

Benita Flores arrived at the desk in minutes. She was dressed in a tight light grey skirt and an expensive white cotton blouse.

"Good morning Jakob. We will be meeting on the tenth floor this morning. My editor and the paper's Managing editor wish to join us and hear your story. We also have Henri Martins joining us. I understand you are related to him by marriage. He is a powerful man here. It seems he will be running as a candidate for the election here. He called to discuss my article and told us of your plan to use the new resolutions against the crime mob in Aruba and the Caribbean."

Jakob was furious. How could he betray Jakob's confidence?

He rode the elevator up to the tenth floor with Benita. Neither spoke. They stepped out of the elevator and into a stylish reception area with plants, soft lighting and some soft background music playing.

The receptionist greeted Benita and told her to go ahead to a conference room where the others were waiting.

They walked along an aisle past cubicles until they reached the conference room.

Framed pages of major news stories that the paper had covered hung on the walls.

The men stood as Benita and Jakob entered. Henri had sat himself at one end of the table where he could observe everyone during the meeting.

A tall insipid man with thinning brown hair, a high forehead and little wireframe glasses introduced himself.

"I am Curt Stoner, Managing Editor and this is the News Editor, Rocco Frati," gesturing to the short plump man beside him.

Jakob shook their hands and was given a seat at the table.

"Benita has told us of your story. We are interested in investigating and reporting on it. Please tell us what you know or suspect. If we decide to follow the story we will be sending investigative reporter to Aruba and Venezuela. It seems there will be a lot to find out about."

Jakob mulled over his response before speaking.

"I am delighted that you find the situation so worthy of your attention. Before I speak though I must have the commitment of the paper that nothing will be disclosed until all the facts are exposed and then the paper can publish. I don't want the parties involved in this to find out. I will help you and introduce your reporters to those who can further assist. Is that an acceptable situation?"

It was Henri who spoke first.

"Jakob I don't see how you can ask these good people to remain quiet. What you are alluding to is huge. It could affect many here in the US as well as in Venezuela and Aruba. The crooks involved in the drug trade here are vicious. This is going to be a very dangerous assignment for this paper."

"That is why it must be kept quiet until the authorities can arrest and detain those responsible."

The Managing Editor addressed Benita.

"You have covered that United Nations Conference. Were you able to detect any irregularities on the part of representatives from certain countries? I personally find it strange that there were representatives sitting in and voting on the control of illicit drug manufacture and trafficking, when they come from the worst drug dealing countries."

"No. There were a lot of passive observers. You must take into account that while it is the United Nations it is not an organization of individuals with pure objectives for the human race. There are rogue nations with representation. The belief is that it is better to have them visible and observe how others view them and their actions, than to keep them in isolation. I am sure the interaction helps somewhat. They are exposed to the opinion of the world."

Curt Stoner stood at the end of the table nestling his chin in the palm of his hand.

"Here is what I am prepared to commit to. During the investigation there will be arrests. We will cover those arrests. That is news. We will not tie them to the larger project nor will we mention the involvement of any authorities associated with the main project. They will look like normal arrests that get made because a crook has slipped up. We will give credit to local police. This will be easy here in the States but what about in Aruba and Venezuela?"

"I do not know. That is something that will be decided by those in control there."

"If you are comfortable with my proposed plan to cover this will you tell us of your findings?"

"Here is what I have seen and believe."

Jakob spent the next hour detailing the events that he was aware of. He described the mysterious disappearance of Juan, the arrival of unknown foreigners on the island, his family's interaction with the Aruba Commercial Loan Bank, the suspicious death of Jose from the import and export company, the investments into local companies and their takeover by the Italians, the control of the clubs and prostitution in San Nicolaas by the mob, the presence of Tomasso, Tony Vitto and Vincenzio on the island. He provided examples of how old family friends had changed and the problems doing business with anyone who allowed the bank to lend money to them or invest in their business.

Throughout his speech, Benita had scribbled notes into a flip pad she had brought to the meeting.

Curt and Rocco Frati sat looking at Jakob without speaking a word. Finally Rocco spoke.

"It seems that there is definitely something happening there and a story."

Curt interrupted.

"Jakob, why do you want to expose this?

Aruba is a very small island. You and your family will probably be in danger. Venezuela is only fourteen miles away and there is a large Italian population there. The criminals have deep ties with the Colombian mob. I think you are heading for serious trouble."

"I do not want any visibility in the investigation. I just want to thwart these criminals and the impact they are having on our society. I realize it is impossible to stop all crime but these individuals can be stopped. There is nothing being done to stop them at present."

Curt turned to Henri Martins.

"Henri I can see how this could assist you in a campaign where you are taking a stand against the criminal element and drugs here in Florida. Again why? You too will be in extreme danger. Unlike Jakob your position will be known publicly and they will probably target you."

"I will get elected by running on a platform against crime and the extreme impact that drugs have had on our kids and community. I will have protection. I have decided upon this."

Curt sat and thought.

"What will you do next?"

Henri spoke. "I have well placed friends in the Federal government here. I intend to spend time with one in particular. I will visit him with Jakob after we leave here. I will inform you after that."

Jakob was astonished. He was not expecting Henri's involvement so soon.

"Let me use a phone to call my close friend and arrange a lunch meeting."

After calling and setting up the lunch, Henri and Jakob stood to leave.

Curt came to shake Jakob's hand. "Please keep Benita informed of every move. We will be investing a lot to bring your story to the public. You have my personal word that there will be maximum discretion until we can run the whole story."

"I certainly hope that is the truth."

Jakob left the meeting happy. He had lit the fuse to start the problems for the mob.

He and Henri left the building and drove in the Mercedes to a restaurant located at a golf club. They were seated at a table with a window affording them a view of the course and a fountain in a manmade lake.

Henri spoke.

"Jakob you are going to need the help of some powerful people here to make this happen. I can help you with this. You must trust me."

Chapter 64

While waiting for his guest, Henri ordered drinks. Time passed. Jakob was concerned that it was possible that Henri's friend had second thoughts and had changed his mind.

They were about to order when Henri heard his name called. Walking toward their table was an athletic looking man accompanied by another in a naval dress uniform and carrying a cap tucked under his arm.

Henri and Jakob stood to greet them.

Henri introduced Jakob first.

"Jakob please meet my friend of many years, Kevin Connelly. Kevin and I attended school, college and university together. Kevin may I ask who the gentleman is with you?"

"Henri and Jakob, please meet Rear Admiral Phillips of the US Coast Guard. I believe he will have some interesting things to tell you both."

Once they were seated back at the table Henri signaled the waiter for more drinks. The Rear Admiral declined and requested a tomato juice.

Henri took control of the situation and spoke quietly.

"Jakob my friend here is in charge of the Bureau of Narcotics Control here in Miami. I gave him brief details of your situation in Aruba. He is the person here who can start an investigation into drug trafficking here in Florida. He is aware of the methods that are used to bring the drugs here from South America.

I am not sure why Rear Admiral Phillips is here with him. Maybe Kevin you can tell us why you brought him."

"He is an integral part of our program to intercept the drug traffickers before they reach our shores. I told him a little of Jakob's situation. He is most interested to learn more and offer assistance if possible."

Jakob was impressed. He had two of the best people to help him with his plan.

Henri turned to Jakob. "Please tell our friends here all that you have told me and the people at Miami Sentinel."

The mention of press involvement caused both Connelly and Phillips to pause.

"This is a sensitive situation. Why is the press involved?"

Jakob assured them of the confidential arrangement they had entered into with the paper. He then described the situation with the Italian mob in Aruba. He spoke for over an hour. Both Connelly and Phillips were entranced by his account of the problems that had arisen since the mob had arrived in Aruba. He told them of the fear that the

Colombians had expressed. He assured them of the accuracy of the information. He described the arrival and circumstances of Moreno in Aruba and how he had recognized some of the Italians as mob members from Venezuela.

When he had finished both Connelly and Phillips said nothing. Henri used the pause to call the waiter to take their lunch orders.

Connelly was grave.

"Jakob what you have just told us confirms what we have recently heard. We are aware of a little of the situation. I have Rear Admiral Phillips with me as he is also a member of a special unit that has been formed to investigate and deal with this. The FBI and a few select officials in Customs are involved as well. Your information is important to us. Rear Admiral please tell us of the role of the Coast Guard in this project?"

The Rear Admiral glanced around at the neighboring tables. Satisfied that their conversation could not be overheard he spoke.

"The Coast Guard has been aware of a recent number of changes the traffickers have made. We have been closely monitoring the situation. While observing them, we have allowed some shipments to proceed and land here. They think that the shipments have passed unknown and they have avoided interception. Once the shipments have been landed they are tracked. This problem is not just here in

America. The Dutch have identified that there are shipments through the Free Trade Zone in Aruba. Once in Rotterdam the drugs are distributed by a well known criminal motor cycle gang. They are organized like military with different ranking of their members, who also draw salaries. It is a professional and deadly organization. The problem has gotten worse over the past year. The demand is now for cocaine.

The Coast Guard is suspicious. We have cutters constantly patrolling the southern Caribbean. The number of intercepts and drug confiscations are erratic. Some of the cutters consistently report the same number of intercepts and the amount confiscated remains about the same.

We have some that we suspect are either not patrolling correctly or possibly shielding the drug traffickers. Last month at a meeting of the Admiral, Vice Admirals and Rear Admirals a strategy was devised and has been implemented. On those cutters that we suspect of irregularities, we have placed undercover officers.

Within weeks we will know if our suspicions are correct. The FBI and the Bureau are fully informed. I am working closely with Kevin here in Miami on this project. That is why he has brought me here today."

Henri and Jakob sat in disbelief.

"This is much bigger than I realized. Is there any surveillance back in my Aruba?"

"We have a Dutch Liaison Officer and an agent stationed there. We also have an informant working for us in Venezuela. It is important that secrecy of this project is maintained. We intend to crack and destroy this criminal gang."

Chapter 65

For the remainder of the lunch their conversation drifted through politics, sports and each telling of family events.

Lunch ended and as Connelly and Phillips were leaving Connelly turned to Henri.

"We will be keeping you informed of developments. Jakob it has been a pleasure and hopefully we will meet up in Aruba one day soon."

Jakob was feeling tired, anxious and discouraged on the drive back to the house.

"I am going to take the rest of this afternoon off and spend it with Solange and you. It is so seldom that we get to see her."

They arrived back at the mansion in the mid afternoon and found Solange and Yolanda on the patio.

Solange was curious.

"Jakob did your meeting go well? I hope that you will tell me what it was all about."

"Solange it is best that you do not know at the moment. I am not feeling well. I think I will go for a rest and maybe a sleep."

Solange looked at him. It was very unusual for Jakob to sleep during the day. She sensed something serious was happening to him.

Jakob excused himself and went to the guest house. His head pounded and wild thoughts ran through his mind. Again he was experiencing demons in his head. He could not dismiss the worry and disturbed images of the past and the people he had betrayed. He had trouble focusing on the present and his situation. Eventually he collapsed onto the bed and fell into a deep sleep.

Early in the evening Solange went to check on Jakob. He was still in a deep sleep. She gently shook him awake. He jumped and looked at her with an expression that scared her.

"Jakob you are not well. Tell me what the trouble is."

"I am having trouble thinking and talking. Where are we?"

This shocked Solange.

"Jakob stay and sleep some more. I will be back soon."

Solange went to find Yolanda and Henri. She described Jakob's condition.

"Solange we have a friend who is a Doctor. I will phone him at his home. His wife and I shop together and attend the same club. I am sure he will help."

It was later in the evening when the Doctor arrived at the house. Solange spent time advising him of Jakob's condition and his past. She mentioned the recent frequent depressions and his constant reminiscing of Europe and the issues he had dealt with there. She talked of their life in Aruba and how Jakob had seemed happy. The Doctor listened in earnest.

"Solange has there been a lot of stress in his life recently?"

"We retired from our business a couple of months ago. He has been filling his time with the grandchildren and some projects. He has been annoyed and pre occupied with some developments that are affecting our business in Aruba. He has had meetings that he will not discuss with me."

"I suspect he is suffering from a situation that needs to be assessed by professionals trained in that discipline. When will you return to Aruba?
"We intended leaving tomorrow afternoon."

"Is it possible to change your schedule? I would like to contact an esteemed colleague and have Jakob evaluated. In the meantime take me to the patient and I will determine if there is any other illness. I take it there has been no vomiting or temperature or other symptoms."

"Until this afternoon he was fine. The only problem I have seen has been his preoccupation with things from the past."

The Doctor arose and accompanied by Solange they went to the guest house. Henri and Yolanda watched from the expansive living room windows.

In the guest house Jakob had awakened and was huddled on the edge of the bed. His hands were shaking.

"Jakob I am Dr. Charles. I am here to see what is wrong and if I can help. Now Solange can you leave us in private while I examine Jakob. I will meet you back in the house when I am finished."

Without a word Solange retreated to the house.

It seemed that hours passed before the Doctor returned.

"Solange your husband is ill and needs help. It is not an area of my specialty. Please change your trip to leave later in the week. I will contact my colleague and arrange a visit with him."

"Is it serious?"

"That question is best directed to those who specialize in that field of medicine. I am a surgeon and not qualified to diagnose or treat Jakob."

Henri interjected. "This is family and I will have the travel plans for Jakob and Solange changed. They are welcome to stay here with us. Thank you for coming to the house. Is there anything we need to do for Jakob?"

"From what I know of the condition I suspect he has it is advisable that he has no alcoholic drinks. Please try to make that happen and keep him from drinking until I get him to see Dr. Steinberg."

Yolanda and Henri were curious.

"Who is Dr. Steinberg? I don't know of him."

"Dr. Steinberg recently arrived in Miami. He is Professor of Psychology at the School of Medicine at the University of Miami. He is also Senior Psychologist at the Hospital. He is world renowned for his research and treatments."

The group looked at him in disbelief.

"Are you saying that Jakob's problem is mental?"

"As I said earlier it is not my field of expertise. I strongly urge you to have Jakob examined by Dr. Steinberg. Now I must bid you all good evening. I have other appointments to attend to."

Chapter 66

The appointment was scheduled for the Friday morning. Solange had contacted Isaac Junior with the news that Jakob was not well and needed to visit with a specialist in Miami. Naturally there was concern in Aruba.

Isaac told Solange that a formal looking letter had been delivered to the Klassen offices from the law firm in Germany. It was marked as 'Personal and Confidential' and addressed to Jakob.

Solange asked Isaac to hold onto the letter and not bother Jakob with that information while he was dealing with the medical situation. Isaac agreed. He asked Solange whether he should open it. She advised against it but wondered what it could be.

At ten in the morning Jakob and Solange arrived for the appointment. The receptionist accompanied them and opened the door to the Doctor's office. They entered and found Dr. Charles standing with a tall bushy haired man and a petite woman.

Dr. Charles spoke. "I would like to introduce Dr. David Steinberg and Dr. Marilyn Stinger. I have informed them of my visit and initial assessment of Jakob."

The Doctors stepped forward and gently shook both Solange and Jakob's hands.

"Jakob please make yourself comfortable. This morning I will be asking you many questions about your past and what has been happening with you recently. It is important I understand what you have experienced in life."

He went to his desk and removed a recorder and sat it on the desk.

"I hope you do not mind that I record this. I will need to review it later should I need to fully appreciate our conversation this morning."

Jakob nodded his agreement and asked the Doctor to start with his questions.

"Tell me about your childhood."

Jakob described growing up on the farm. He spoke of the attack on the farm by the misinformed and drunken soldiers. He described the discrimination he and his father experienced in the town when they were mistaken for being German at the outbreak of the war. He continued and at mention of his father's tragic death started to sob.

They all waited until Jakob composed himself and continued.

He went into detail and told them of the conflict he experienced between the beliefs and teaching of his Old Order Mennonite religion and the modern changes.

The Doctor listened carefully and asked a number of questions.

Jakob detailed his insatiable desire to pursue his ancestral relatives in Europe. The way he had treated people and the situations he created were of particular interest to both Doctors.

After spending considerable time answering questions, Jakob proceeded to tell them of his life in Aruba. He described in detail the recurring thoughts and intensity of his need to go back to Europe and find the people he had badly treated.

The Doctors asked Solange and Jakob to wait in the adjoining office while they spoke.

Thirty minutes went by before they were invited back into Dr. Steinberg's office.

"Jakob we have a preliminary diagnosis of your problem. It is our learned opinion that you are suffering with the illness OCD- Obsessive Compulsion Disorder. If it is not treated it can worsen as you age. There are treatments available. As I am a psychologist I can only work in the area of the mind and mental health. My associate here, Dr. Marilyn Stinger is a psychiatrist and can treat you with medications and a program to assist you.

The medical community has studied OCD for many years and there are many possible reasons why people suffer from it. Some are hereditary, but research has shown that exposure to traumatic events at a young age can trigger the disease. We believe that what you experience growing up on the farm and witnessing the attack on the farm and the destruction of neighboring property along with the accidental death of your father caused your situation. It also accounts for your inability to maintain friendships and your behavior in Europe.

Patients with OCD show different symptoms. Some will become obsessed and perform the same task repeatedly, like continual washing if hands. Others will have dark thoughts regarding sex or things in the past. It is that latter category we have diagnosed as your condition.

We believe that the present anxiety you suffer and the continual and persistent thoughts that you find uncontrollable have been accelerated by the stress of your retirement and matters you are dealing with in Aruba.

There is a research program we are running at the hospital. As part of the program there is treatment included. I encourage you to consider it. We are testing new medicines and procedures.

We will need to see you for detailed assessments every two weeks. Is that possible?'

Solange did not hesitate.

"Yes we can arrange for Jakob to attend. What do we need to do for Jakob to be entered into this program?"

"I will make all the arrangements. I will contact Dr. Charles with the details. Do you have any questions? I am sure you will after thinking about all of this. I am available by phone to answer your questions. "

Jakob was stunned. He wondered how it was only now that this was discovered. He was despondent.

Solange thanked the Doctors and assisted Jakob from his chair and out where Sparky was waiting to drive them back to the mansion.

Upon their arrival Yolanda greeted them and took them to the living room. She was worried. Solange relayed the information and diagnosis of the Doctors.

"I am sorry to hear this. I have been making a lot of enquiries about Dr. Steinberg while you were gone. From the reports I received he is one of the most respected psychologists in America. I will have the guest house made into a home for you for when you come for treatments."

It was too much for the normally strong Solange. She retreated to a bathroom and cried until there was nothing left in her.

When she was able to compose herself, Solange returned to join the others.

"Tomorrow Jakob and I will return to Aruba. We will need to attend to some matters and plan for Jakob's treatments here."

Chapter 67

Malmok, Aruba.

It was late on the Saturday morning when Isaac stopped to see Solange and Jakob. He found Solange alone in her room. Jakob was working in the garden.

"Tomorrow I have arranged a luncheon and a day at Carlita's on the beach in Savaneta. I want Jakob to relax and be distracted with other things rather than the medical news he has just received. It would be good if you could join us with the children. I am going to ask Hans and Moreno to join us as well. I want them to bring their partners. We will have a big family day."

"I will be there and bring the family and some food. I will contact Hans this afternoon. I believe Moreno is with him. I will invite them."

They talked for a while and Isaac handed her the envelope from the law firm in Germany. She looked at it apprehensively.

"This worries me. Each time we have receive mail from Germany it has been bad and troubling news. I will not give this to Jakob now. I will wait until he is a little more settled. He has been difficult since receiving the news. Go and see him in the garden."

Isaac took a couple of cold beers and strode out to see Jakob.

"Jakob it's time for you to take a break. Here I have brought you a drink."

"Isaac. I am glad you are here. There are things I want to tell you about."

For the next thirty minutes Jakob told Isaac of his plan and the involvement of the Narcotics Control and US Coast Guard in Miami. He stressed his intention to expose the mob activity in Aruba and disrupt their activities and hopefully stop their intrusion through the Miami Sentinel paper.

Isaac listened and when Jakob had finished he spoke.

"Jakob I too have been busy these past couple of weeks. I will not tell you what I have done. I can guarantee that it will not hurt the business or our family. I will need to leave at some point and I will be gone from the island for a week or more. I do not want you or Solange to worry."

Jakob was immediately concerned.

"Isaac if you are planning on doing something alone I caution you to consider it carefully. These people have many contacts and long tentacles. You are one man. They are a well organized and powerful group."

They fell silent. Isaac turned to Jakob.

"Solange has told me of the diagnosis you received in Miami. I understand there are treatment programs. Will you agree to be treated? You are still young and the family needs you."

"There are many things on my mind. It seems a lot to ask Solange to keep joining me on trips to Miami and for us to impose on her sister. I will wait until I hear what the treatments entail. I will decide after I hear that. Now let us discuss other matters. Tell me about what is happening at the company. Are you looking at any new construction projects? I was thinking that with Solange having an investment in her family's construction business that maybe we should have them establish here on the island. There isn't enough trained labor here and all I hear from friends is the need to import that from Haiti or the Dominican Republic. We could set up a construction firm here and bring in equipment and labor from Florida. It would be a company with resources superior to anything that exists here now."

Isaac responded. "Jakob, for God's sake stop. You are retired. You have been diagnosed with an illness. Why don't you just find a way to go and enjoy your retirement? I like your idea but without you involved. Between us it makes sense and let me think about it. If it makes sense when I evaluate it then I will ask you to help me develop a proposition to the family. Is that reasonable?"

"I guess that is better than sitting with nothing to do."

"You must stop wanting the past. I mean that. You cannot keep going back to your youth or those days in Europe or the past life and business here in Aruba. Stop and look at what you have. Make the most out of it. You have a family, money and many friends. Enjoy that."

Jakob was about to speak when he was drowned out by a flock of screeching parrots passing overhead. He looked up at the bright blue sky and the green and red birds swooping by.

"Isaac I wish I was free like that."

"You are. It is only in your mind that you do not have that freedom."

"Isaac I have a piece of business in Canada that is unfinished. As I have told you I own the farms there. I need to decide whether to keep them or sell. The Mennonite family that leases from me has expressed a desire to buy the land. I need to know if you and Hans are interested. The farms are located on very desirable land. Are you interested in me transferring the land to you? I will of course ask Hans as well"

"I am not a farmer. I wouldn't know where to start, especially in a strange land like Canada. It is cold there. What do you do in those cold months with all that snow? I have never seen snow. From what I understand I may never want to see it."

"It is very different to live in a cold country. Hans did that during his growing up in Germany after the war."

"It is far away. I think you should sell it. Take the money. Use it to travel and see other places while you are young. Hans and I are making good money and do not need anything. You and Solange deserve to take some time and spoil yourselves."

Jakob was not fooled by Isaac.

"What you are telling me is now that I am diagnosed with an illness that could get worse I should go away."

"No. I did not say go away. I said very clearly for you and Solange go and spend time together and experience new things and places. Solange has never been to Europe. You owe her some luxury in her retirement. It's not all about you. It is time for you to stop being selfish.

I may be your son but that will not stop me from telling you how to behave as a father, husband and human being. Am I clear?"

There was a rustling of the palms and Solange emerged from the dark green growth anxious to know what the raised voices were about.

"I was explaining a thing or two to your husband. Now I will leave you two. I will see you at Carlita's tomorrow."

Solange sensed the remnant of a disagreement. She decided to leave matters alone.

Chapter 68

The Sunday family gathering at the beach was filled with laughter as the kids played in the water. Some stray dogs from the neighborhood joined as they splashed in the water.

The men lit a fire in a pit they had constructed from the rocks that lay scattered on the beach. Hans draped some chicken wire across to make a grilling surface.

Isaac placed chicken and some meat on the fire as the hungry kids ran up from the gentle surf.

Jakob walked away from the gathering and strolled to the end of the beach. He had many fond memories of the time he had lived in the apartment he had rented here from Juan and Carlita. He missed Juan. The memories he had of him differed from those involving the people in Europe.

He returned and joined the rest of the family for the feast of chicken, fire roasted vegetables and meats.

After the meal the kids were tired and Isaac decided it was time to leave. Hans took the signal and along with Moreno they all left.

Carlita faced Solange and Jakob.

"Will you take treatments Jakob? I do not know about the illness. Solange has told me what she knows. I think you should go and try them."

Jakob was silent. He eventually left Carlita and Solange on the porch and walked down to the small incline that bordered the beach. He stood and stared down the beach and past the fofoti tree that grew in the sand. He stared for ages out to sea and watched the clouds as they gathered on the south west horizon over Venezuela.

He thought of the heated exchange he had with Isaac yesterday in his garden. It was unusual for Isaac to get upset with him. The more he considered what Isaac had said, the clearer it became. He was right. He needed to give Solange something back in life.

He continued to look at the sea and the unusual hue of blue that was reflected from the sky in advance of the gathering tropical storm.

On returning to the porch he pulled up an old weathered chair and sat.

"Carlita I have decided. I am going to take those treatments. I am also going to do something for Solange. I am going to take her to see my land in Canada and on to Europe. We will visit The Netherlands and Germany. It is late in summer and we will travel soon before winter arrives in Canada and Europe. I will start planning tomorrow."

Solange could not believe what she was hearing.

"Jakob, do you really mean this? I have wanted to travel and see Europe. We were always too busy."

"Yes. We will speak to the Doctor in Miami on Monday to better understand the treatments. I will then plan our trip."

Solange rushed across the bare weather-beaten wood boards of the porch and threw her arms around Jakob. She looked forward to the change. She wondered if being away from Aruba, the business and the situation with the mob would help him."

"I am so pleased you have decided to do this."

She had no sooner spoken when there were bright flashes of lightning. Thunder roared above them. Huge raindrops the size of grapes crashed down onto the villa. They stood huddled together and watched as the storm raged as it moved out over the Caribbean.

The air smelled of freshly damped soil and all around the neighboring villas and beach were illuminated in an eerie blue glow."

It was dark when Jakob and Solange left Savaneta to return to their home. While they were driving Jakob made a decision.

"Solange it has been a difficult week. Would you like to stop in Oranjestad for dinner? There is a new restaurant I would be interested in trying."

"Jakob there are things we need to speak about and that would be somewhere we can speak and not have any family interruptions."

Twenty minutes later Jakob parked on Main Street and they sauntered to the restaurant. Solange was in no hurry and spent time gazing into store windows along the way.

Upon entering the restaurant, Jakob was surprised to see Alejandro seated and in deep conversation with two men he did not recognize. Jakob chose to ignore him and allowed them to be taken to a table far from Alejandro's. He whispered to Solange who looked over at the three men who had papers on the table. They were so absorbed in the discussion that they did not see Jakob and Solange enter.

Jakob was curious. What was Alejandro involved with.

Time passed and Alejandro stood to leave the table. As he did so he reached into his pocket and handed an envelope to the men. Jakob watched carefully. Alejandro was paying for something. The two men got up and left. Alejandro turned to leave and saw Jakob and Solange sitting and looking at him.

He blushed and became flustered. He crossed over to them.

"Please don't tell Miguel about tonight. Those men are helping me with something very special. I cannot discuss it now. It is nothing bad."

Jakob was intrigued. It seemed to him that everyone had something to keep quiet.

He asked Alejandro to sit with them.

"This afternoon we were at Carlita's villa with our family. We wanted to spend time together. I will be going to Miami for some treatments. Solange will be accompanying me. We have decided to take a trip after the treatments. I will show Solange the place of my birth and where I grew up in Canada. After that we will travel to Europe and tour for a while.

I ask you to please work closely with Isaac and Hans to keep the restaurants operating properly. They will have a lot to handle in the coming weeks."

"You need not ask Miguel and I owe you for many favors and the help you have given us over the years. Now if you will excuse me I need to meet Miguel in San Nicolaas."

He stood. "Good night Solange. Good night Jakob"

He walked to the door quickly without looking back and roughly shoved the restaurant door open and disappeared into the night.

"Jakob I will be going to see Isaac at the office tomorrow morning. There are papers to sign. Before I leave we will phone Dr. Stringer in Miami and make the arrangements to start your treatments."

In the softly lit atmosphere Jakob saw the beauty he had come to know in Solange. He would undergo the treatments. He owed much to Solange. He thought of Anke. He did not want to create a situation and cause her any grief.

"I agree. We will call her early. I am ready."

Chapter 69

The first light of dawn cast a dim grey ambiance in the bedroom. Solange turned and observed Jakob who was still in a deep sleep.

She gently eased from the bed and decided to brew some of the fresh Colombian coffee to take to the back garden and watch the sunrise.

She had plans for the day and needed time alone to think about how she would need to tell the others of her actions. While not deceitful, she had embarked on a plan for rescuing Juan. She had discussed this in detail with Yolanda and Henri. They had kept it private from Jakob. After his diagnosis they did not want to burden him.

Later in the day she expected to receive a call from either Yolanda or Henri. She had asked them to call her at the Klassen office. She did not want Jakob to know of the plans in case arrangements could not be made.

Now she was worried and wondered if the scheme she had devised would work.

In the garden an iguana inched up toward her foot looking for food. She watched the bright green creature as it cocked its head and stared directly into her eyes. Feeling pity for the iguana she returned to the kitchen and took some fruit from a bowl. She poured her strong coffee and returned to the garden. The iguana chewed on the flower of Jakob's prized orchards. She threw the fruit on the ground to distract it. The iguana slithered down the plant and across to the fruit where it gorged itself.

She heard footsteps and turned to see Jakob approaching with a mug in his hand. He looked refreshed. He sat on the chair next to her.

"Bon Dia, Solange. Today we start a new voyage."

Solange reached forward and put her hand on his knee.

"Yes. I think we will learn a lot today. I am hoping all will be well. I have a good feeling this morning."

They sat in thought as the sun climbed slowly into the sky.

"Before we phone Dr. Stinger I am going to take a walk on the beach. Do you care to join me?"

"Yes. We haven't walked together in the early morning for such a long time. Indeed this may well be the start of a new voyage for us."

Still dressed in her gown and Jakob in his pajamas they carried their coffees and walked down to the beach.

At that hour only a few fishermen were casting their rods out into the low surf. Only a few sounds, other than gulls squawking and the loud splash of diving pelicans, could be heard. It was an idyllic and calm scene. They walked for hours past the end of the sandy beach and into the bush that ran beside the rocky coastline.

They talked and laughed. Solange suspected that Jakob had known of the problem but had attempted to keep it private. Now that it was known to her and the family his relief was evident.

"Jakob we should return. It is time for us to phone Dr. Stinger."

They made a strange sight dressed in their sleepwear. Some of the locals knew them and called or whistled to them.

Jakob was in a good mood.

"Has Moreno talked to you about his plans to marry Gabriela? He told me that they plan a small wedding at Mangel Alto. I am not sure when but he made it sound as if it would be soon. And then we have to consider Hans and his young lady."

The mention of Hans caused Solange to go silent. Jakob sensed a change in her.

"What is the problem? Do you not accept that Irma will be a good wife for Hans?"

"No Jakob. Since we met with those Doctors I have done a lot of thinking. You may remember Dr. Steinberg telling us of the reasons that can trigger the illness and that it may be hereditary. I have been wondering if that is why Hans behaved so badly when he was a youth in Germany. Could it be that he has the illness? I now worry if that is the situation it may come back and haunt him later in his life. We should ask the Doctors whether there is any test to determine if Hans shows any signs what treatment he should receive."

"I think you are worrying too much about the wrong things. We will ask. I think that Hans' behavior was because in post war Germany everything was destroyed where he grew up. He was in street gangs and trying to prove to the others that he was a leader. He needed show the other thugs he was in control. He did some really nasty things and committed crimes to prove that point."

"I still think we should ask."

On approaching the house the phone could be heard ringing. Solange ran to answer it. It was Dr. Stringer.

Solange answered and remained quiet as she listened to the Doctor. When the Doctor had finished Solange brought up her concerns about Hans.

She asked the Doctor to wait while she spoke to Jakob.

"Jakob I have a question. Dr. Stringer is about to take her annual holiday. She is asking about visiting Aruba. I would like to offer her to stay with us. Are you agreeable with that?"

Jakob nodded enthusiastically.

Solange extended the invitation for Dr. Stringer to stay in the little apartment off the main house. She assured Dr. Stringer that she would have privacy.

The women continued to talk about the island and vacations. Jakob left to dress and find Hans and Moreno.

He located them on Palm Beach at the restaurant on the pier with Alejandro. As he neared them they stopped talking.

"Bon Dia. What is happening? Why are you here and not at the beach shack?"

"There are no customers this morning. It seems there are only a few tourists staying this week. It is slow so we decided to relax and chat. We are telling Moreno how his life will change after he marries."

Jakob smiled, "And yours will too, Hans."

They all laughed.

"I came here because I want you to know that I have taken action to cause some discomfort for the Italians and the trouble they are creating."

He described the visit to Miami and the meetings with the Miami Sentinel and the Narcotics Control director. He elaborated on the lunch he had and the involvement of the US Coast Guard.

When he was finished the group remained quiet. It was Alejandro that spoke.

"Jakob the men you saw me with last night are from Colombia. I have purchased a boat from them. It is in Colombia. They are old friends of Moreno's. He introduced us.

I purchased the boat as we are going to go to Colombia and find Juan."

"When do you intend to do this? I am not sure this is a good idea."

"Moreno knows some there who will help us. We will select a few and pay them well. It will be dangerous. We will be very careful."

"I demand to hear all the details before you make any move. If you make any mistakes it will be your lives and probably Juan's as well."

It was noon when Jakob left to return home. As he arrived, Solange was preparing to leave.

"I have a lunch with Isaac and then I need to attend to some things at the office. I should return in a few hours."

He escorted her to the car and watched as she drove off in the direction of Oranjestad.

Chapter 70

Late in the afternoon, Solange returned. Jakob greeted her.

"Did everything get resolved at the office? While you were gone I have planned out a nice dinner for us. I have fresh grouper from one of the fishermen who I saw coming to shore. I went down to the beach and bought some."

"That is nice Jakob. We will need to eat early as I have summoned a family meeting here for this evening."

"Why? Is there a problem?"

"No but I think the time has come for everyone to say what they are doing. I am not stupid. I see little signs that can easily be understood by me. I didn't build a successful company by being stupid. I intend to make everyone state what they are doing.

Since Hans and Moreno found out from those Colombians about the possibility of Juan being alive, they and everyone else seem aloof and avoid speaking of what they have been doing.

We saw Alejandro with those men at the restaurant and he was in a big hurry to leave us.

You were acting strange with Henri in Miami.

Isaac is taking a trip but isn't telling me where he is going. That is very strange as we have always had an honest relationship.

It is time for some honest answers.

And now this arrived at the office."

She thrust forward the large envelope from the German law firm.

"I can't imagine what is in that letter Jakob, but every time we received anything from them it lead to some sort of trouble."

"Solange there is nothing more in Germany or any disagreement with Ilsa. When we agreed to help and take Hans, we had an agreement that was signed. Don't panic until I have a chance to open this and see what it contains."

Even though Jakob tried to be outwardly calm, his mind was in turmoil. He was anxious to open the letter but didn't want to appear to Solange to be concerned.

"Solange I am making us cocktails. We will go to the patio and relax. It seems you are agitated after the trip to the office."

"No Jakob. I am not agitated. I don't like the situation with everyone acting strange and keeping secrets. Tonight we will sit down as our family and understand what is happening."

"I will read this letter to you while we have our cocktails."

Jakob inspected the letter. It was postmarked 6 weeks earlier. He waited for Solange to join him before he ripped it open.

There was a folded letter and another envelope inside the main one.

Solange joined him. He opened the letter.

Horst, Horst and Weiner

Solicitors

99 Pannerstrasse, Munich

Dear Jakob Klassen,

We hope this letter finds you healthy and prosperous.

I am writing to you as we have had a gentleman enquiring about your whereabouts. Naturally we do not disclose this type of information. This gentleman has been persistent and visits often. He claims that he became aware that we know of your whereabouts through Ilsa Wolfe.

We advised this man to write to you and we would forward his letter to you. I hope this is more than acceptable.

Enclosed is the sealed letter he provided to us.

We leave this matter in your hands should you wish to respond.

Please advise us if we can offer any services

Herman Horst.

Jakob handed Solange the letter. She read it through and frowned.

Jakob looked at the thin envelope. His name was neatly handwritten in a red ink. While he was fascinated by receiving the letter in this fashion, he was also apprehensive.

"Solange, I am going to make myself a strong drink before I open this. This orange juice cocktail seems inappropriate."

"Then you had better bring one for me as well."

Minutes passed before Jakob returned with two Rob Roy drinks in large tumblers.

His hands shaking, Jakob carefully tore open the envelope.

Chapter 71

Jakob extracted the folded letter and unfolded it. In neat handwritten cursive was letter penned in the same red ink.

June 15th, 1961

124B Kongresstraffe

Munich, Germany

Dear Jakob Klassen,

It has been many years since we last saw each other, but I have never forgotten you. I trust you are well.

Please excuse me for the length of time that has passed. On a number of occasions I tried to find you. I remembered your wife had relatives in Holland but I could not locate them. After the war there were so many displaced people. I checked with the Canadians and there was no record of you but the search did find Klassens in Ontario and an address. I wrote to that address but the letter was returned. I had given up hoping to find you when by strange coincidence I met with a woman Ilsa Wolfe during intermission at the opera. We talked and naturally the war years came into the conversation. I told her of my days on that merchant ship. She seemed interested and I told her of some of my adventures, including that one in Colombia. She asked your name. I told her it was Jakob Klassen. She was shocked. We did not return to the opera. She wanted to talk. We went to the lounge in the opera house where we spoke. She told me that she had worked for Herr Josef Klassen after the war and was certain the person I was looking for could be you.

She declined to provide me an address or your details but sent me to the law firm Horst, Horst and Weiner. I met them several times and they were reluctant to help. I finally met with Herr Henri Horst. He agreed to send this letter on to the address they had in their files. I hope this letter has found its way to you.

My life turned interesting after you left our ship in Aruba. On the return voyage we were sunk by a English Royal Navy destroyer off the Irish coast. Most of the crew died in that attack. I survived and received treatments at a prisoner of war location in England.

I was then sent to a prisoner of war camp located in Ontario, Canada. It immediately made me think of you and the times you spoke of your life there on the farm.

I was sent to a prison camp that was in an area called Lake of Woods in Ontario. It was the best place to spend years during that stupid and horrible war. At the camp the Canadian guards were very caring. We had activities that included swimming in a river, canoeing, fishing and they taught us hockey. I was selected to work on a farm assisting with logging. I was paid a little for this and used the money for some beer and cigarettes.

I must admit to you that I missed Canada when I returned to Germany in its destroyed state. I missed the beauty of the bush, lakes and rivers. In fact I felt homesick for the life I had there. I often thought about returning, but I had started a business here in Munich. Things were changing. BMW had their head office here and Siemens was expanding to handle replacing the many systems that had been knocked out. I started a small machine shop. There was plenty of work. The business grew and recently BMW purchased it. I received a large amount of money from the sale.

I am now retired and looking for more adventures.

I would like you to mail me please. In Fact I would like to invite you to visit me in my little cottage in the town of Au. The cost of your trip will be mine. I have made all this money and now need to spend it with friends. I hope you accept this offer and plan to bring your wife. I am sure you have one.

I await your reply and hopefully your acceptance of my offer.

Very Respectfully,

Jan Zelder.

Jakob handed the letter to Solange. His mind was racing. He remembered the time in Colombia and the violent fight in the cantina. Jan Zelder had rescued him from that situation. Suddenly he felt himself becoming agitated. He thought back to Aaron who he helped on the farm near Leiden and who had helped Jakob travel across the Netherlands in search of his relatives. He recalled the clubs and his time with Ilsa. Over and over his mind raced. He started rubbing his hands and then started walking back and forth across the patio nonstop.

Solange read the letter. She sat it down on the side table beside her chair and watched Jakob. She saw his anxiety. She said nothing. Jakob was disturbed.

After five minutes she went to him and took his arm. He roughly shook her away. She was scared. Jakob had never acted this way before.

"Jakob you are scaring me. Please try to calm down. What can I do?"

Exhausted Jakob sank into a lounger. He was pale and shaking.

Solange helped him from the chair and escorted him into their bedroom.

"Jakob, rest here and I will get us a dinner prepared."

After ten minutes she returned to find Jakob in a deep sleep. She went to her kitchen and phoned Dr. Stinger in Miami for advice.

Chapter 72

Caracas, Venezuela

Tomasso was nervous. The Palermo brothers had called yet another meeting. He had returned to his apartment to change after an active afternoon of tennis and Yulia. He reflected that he must do something about her. She was getting too close and too demanding.

Since returning from Aruba things had not been the same.

Tony Vitto had become distant since they dispatched of Vincenzio and the Palermos were constantly in foul moods.

Tomasso wondered what new event required yet another meeting.

He dressed in light casual clothing as the Caracas heat was stifling, even at this hour.

His Lincoln Continental was parked in the entrance. As he was about to open the door, he looked across the front lawn to the bench seating. There was a man watching him. Tomasso had seen this man before. He wondered if he was being followed.

Tomasso made it appear he had left something behind in his apartment. He turned and went back into the lobby. He hid himself in an alcove off the lobby and looked back at the bench. Another man had joined the watcher. He was gesticulating with his hands and after a few minutes walked off.

Tomasso returned to his apartment and phoned the Palermos.

"Yeah. What do you want?"

It was Salvatore.

"Boss I am being watched and followed. There are two men. I have seen one of them before. He was at a bar I stopped in and also I have seen him when I have gone out to buy wine and groceries. I am definitely being tailed."

"OK. Do not come here. Go to the movies or something else. Call us in a couple of hours. What we have to discuss with you will wait. I will let the others know you were delayed due to trouble with your car. I don't want to discuss this with them and you won't either. I don't want anyone nervous at this point."

Tomasso hung up. He thought about the man and how to proceed.

He picked up the phone and called Yulia.

"Yulia I have decided to go to the movies tonight. Would you like to join me?"

Yulia purred her enthusiasm to accompany him. It would be a relief from another boring night in her shoebox sized room in the sky.

Tomasso looked over to the bench. The man was gone. Relieved he started his car and drove to the working class neighborhood where Yulia had her apartment. As he drove he constantly checked his rear view mirror. He noticed a nondescript grey Fiat had been following him for a few miles. He braked sharply and drove into a one way lane. The Fiat followed.

Tomasso was worried. Were these members of another gang or were they attached to some government.

He drove on until he reached her apartment. She was waiting in the dingy lobby for him.

In the car Tomasso and Yulia bickered in a friendly manner over which film they wanted to see. Yulia was adamant and insisted on 'La Dolce Vita' or 'An Affair to Remember' while Tomasso wanted to see 'Psycho." Tomasso won their little argument. The irony of going to 'An Affair to Remember' was not lost on him. They parked and walked to one of Caracas' oldest theatres The **Teatro Ayacucho.**

Tomasso excused himself during the movie, with the excuse he needed to find the men's room. He crossed the lobby to an enclosed phone box. He called the Palermos.

"Salvatore. I am at the movies. I was followed by the two men. They are driving a grey Fiat."

"Tell me where you are. I will send some men over. If it's a Fiat it sounds like government. The other boys would be driving something a little more elegant. We will find out what this is all about. The timing for this is bad. You will understand when we all meet. Can you come soon? Pay that tramp secretary of yours to take a taxi. Give her some excuse but try to get here soon. Don't leave before the boys arrive. I will send Tony Vitto with them. You will recognize them."

Tomasso hung up. In the theater he complained to Yulia of not feeling well. Fifteen minutes later he left for the men's room again, blaming the food he had eaten."

Yulia was frustrated. She was enjoying the film but not his interruptions.

As Tomasso exited the dark interior he saw Tony Vitto standing and scanning a poster advertising an upcoming film. Neither acknowledged the other.

Tomasso returned to his seat. Yulia looked up at him with a scowl.

"Yulia. Here take this money. Stay until the film is finished. I must go immediately. I have had an accident in my pants. I need to get home. I think I have food poisoning."

At the thought of what was deposited in Tomasso's pants, Yulia screwed her face up in disgust. She took the bills he extended to her.

Tomasso left the theater and walked a leisurely pace to his car. He was aware of the two men following. He deliberately fumbled with his keys to give Tony Vitto and the boys a chance to move in.

He heard a scuffle and turned to witness a street fight. The boys pretended to mug his pursuers.

Tomasso laughed and climbed into his car for the drive to the **Santuario di Formaggio restaurant** and his meeting with the Palermos.

On his drive he turned up the radio and while completely off key sang along with Dean Martin belting out 'Volare'.

When he reached the restaurant he noticed that there more cars parked than normal.

A sign hung at the front door "Closed for private function" and there were a couple of gorilla like men standing at the door to make sure there was ambiguity with the message the sign clearly stated.

Tomasso entered .The security goons recognized him and waved him through.

Alfredo the owner was fussing around ensuring that there was adequate food and drink. Tomasso identified a number of people who worked with the Palermos. He noticed the presence of Admiral Maduro. He sidled up to him.
"Good evening Admiral. I think we are in for an interesting

evening. Did our friends from the US coast Guard leave port yet?"

"Yes they sailed this morning. I believe they will sail north to the Dominican Republic and then return to the southern Caribbean to patrol off Colombia. Lieutenant Slate advised me that they have orders to extend the patrol. They will return for the cheap fuel here and to replenish the food supplies. I believe they will be visited by some of our people during this trip. I am able to contact them through those PYE radios that the Palermos arranged. We have tested them and they work perfectly. I am able to contact Slate or Ramirez without others listening. It is perfect."

While they were chatting, Salvatore joined them.

"Tomasso I need to speak with you. We had those two men 'mugged.' They think it was a street gang. Our boys pulled it off perfectly. They stole their wallets and papers. Those men were from the US Bureau of Narcotics Control in Miami. Do you know why they were following you?"

"No. I wonder if this is one more of the problems the Klassens have created. Since Vincenzio sabotaged the boats and beach hut and the removal of Carlos from the EximFreight Company in Aruba we have had things like this happening."

"You are being watched. Those men were narcos attached to the office in Miami according to their documents. After tonight's meeting you will return to Aruba. It will become clear in the meeting why this is necessary."

Tomasso groaned at the prospect of spending more time on that barren and boring rock. He hated Aruba.

Chapter 73

The restaurant tables had been pulled together to form one long conference table. Jugs of water and pots of strong coffee were strategically placed along the tables with glasses and cups.

Salvatore called the assembled men to sit at the table.

"I am sure that many of you are wondering why I have called this meeting tonight. Before going further let me welcome and introduce some here."

Salvatore stood to perform the introductions and as their name was announced called the person raised their hand.

"We welcome fellow business associates here:

Frankie (Spuds) Spangolli

Enzo (The Blade) Costa

Johnnie (Stumps) Silvestri

They are here with some of their people.

The next two weeks are going to be very important for us all. I want you all to make sure that your guys don't interfere with our business. It has taken years to plan and build this operation and I don't want any problems. I have made 'arrangements' here with the local police and army chiefs. They will stay away from our little venture. There is a possibility that some of those street punks may try something but I have offered a reward to certain officers to see that doesn't happen.

We have a large shipment of goods coming here from Colombia. They will be guarded heavily while in transport from Colombia to our warehouse here. The shipment will be loaded to our boats to be sent to Aruba.

In Aruba we have established relationships. My man there is Tomasso Rossini.

Tomasso identify yourself."

He walked to the front of the table.

Salvatore continued.

"This is the first shipment we are making from our new suppliers. In the future there will be opportunity for your participation and investment. This operation is being monitored closely by our bosses in Chicago. Any attempt by any of you will start a war. It can be prevented.

Now you all know what is planned and I expect you to make sure your troops are controlled."

It was Frankie (Spuds) Spagnolli who spoke.

"Salvatore. You call us here to give a lecture and stupidly tell us what's going on. This going to cause a great temptation. It must be huge for you to take this risk. What's in it for us?"

"Spuds, maybe you get to keep living if you do as I say."

"Sal, why don't you get us in on this?"

"We are working with a new supplier and partners. The Aruba connection is our concern. Tomasso will be there with some of my boys to help.

If this goes well we will be expanding the operation. At that time you will be able to participate. It is in everybody's interest to make sure this succeeds. I don't want any family squabbles over the next few weeks. We all need to keep a low profile.

Tonight we had some unwanted visitors. Narcos from Miami were trailing one of my men. I haven't been able to find out what they know, but I will."

It was Johnnie (Stumps) Silvestri who spoke next.

"Salvatore. This is Venezuela and not Sicily. If you use local labor then that is a risk. It is impossible to control these guys once they smell money. How you gonna control that?"

"For this shipment it will be totally handled by my men. The only exceptions will be the crew on the freighter that we had our company, EximFreight purchase. I will have a couple of my men on it at all times. Our fishing boat here will also have my guys on it."

There was a pall of silence at the table.

Enzo (The Blade) Costa finally spoke.

"I want to know how you intend to sail from here to Aruba without those Dutch or Venezuelans stopping the boats and searching them."

"I have taken good care of that. Let me introduce Admiral Maduro. He controls the naval north coast operations. He is working with us. He will ensure that the boats are safe while travelling to Aruba. He will assure his Dutch counterparts that they are carrying commercial goods and that the fishing boat is taking fish and shrimp to the market in Aruba."

He paused and waited. There was some talk between the mobsters sitting around the table. Salvatore waited for minutes before continuing.

"Does anyone have any comment or questions? This operation has been carefully planned over many months. I suggest that any interference will be fatal and lead to an all out war between our families. Am I clear? Now let us enjoy a fine dinner."

Tomasso seated himself next to the Admiral.

"How will you be sure that the boats will be safe to get to Aruba?"

The Admiral stared at Tomasso for minutes before answering.

"Tomasso, I did not get to be an Admiral by chance. In the Venezuelan Navy it is very political and corrupt. One must know the game and the players. You can be assured that there are others who will be assisting me. They will not know of this operation that Salvatore and Emilio are running for Chicago.

The assistance I will have will be from men I command. They will adhere to the instructions they are given, realizing that to do otherwise will mean the end of a wealthy relationship. I have contacts in Aruba who will advise their patrols to leave the boats alone. I suggest you ask no more questions about Aruba.

During the voyages we will send some decoys for the US coast Guard to intercept. These will be peasant fishermen scrambling for any money and prepared to take the risk of taking small boats loaded with marijuana to Aruba. We will have them captured off Colombia and Venezuela by our patrols and the US Coast Guard. Those fishermen are disposable and not important in our operation. The amount of marijuana we lose will be insignificant when compared to the money involved in the shipment."

Tomasso was in shock. He had not expected to hear words like this from The Admiral. When he first met him he had believed he would be an educated and civil man who was just greedy for money.

Chapter 74

The Klassen Home, Malmok, Aruba

Miguel and Alejandro were the first to arrive at the home. They had been requested to attend by Solange. She had determined that if the family members were planning anything related to Juan, then they should attend. The next to arrive was Isaac Junior. He joined the small group who were in the living room chatting. Time passed. Solange was being a graceful host and offering drinks and hors d'oeuvres. Finally Hans and Moreno arrived along with a stranger.

They entered the home and introduced him to Jakob and Solange.

Hans placed his hand on the strangers shoulder.

"Solange I would like you to meet Adrien. He is from Holland and has been working for me on the boats. I hope you don't mind that I have brought him with us. He is important in my plan to rescue Juan from Colombia."

The group listened and studied Adrien.

"No that is fine. He is welcome to join us. Now please everyone, take a seat where you will be comfortable."

Jakob smiled. The old business woman approach was back in Solange. While it was to be a family get together she had taken on the air of running it like a structured business meeting.

"I have asked you all to come here this evening because it seems to me that there are things being done to get Juan back from Colombia. I am not stupid. I have seen and heard little things and then the behavior of Alejandro the other evening made me even more curious. I have Isaac here telling me he is going away for a while. He won't tell me where or how long he will be gone. Jakob has gone to private meetings and acts suspiciously. He must think I am stupid, but after all these years of marriage and doing business together I can assure you I am far from stupid. I see those indicators that he is up to something. I have also detected strange behavior from you Hans since you and Moreno met those Colombians who told you about a man that might be Juan. I remind you that it might be Juan. We have no proof that it is yet you are all scheming to go rescue someone who may not be him or may possibly be dead. It is shameful for each of you to be plotting and planning individually. We need to consider the possibility that it may not be Juan."

Amongst the family there was an uncomfortable feeling. No one had considered that possibility.

"Now I will start and disclose what I have done. I will be totally honest and I expect nothing less than this from each of you.

After listening to Hans and Moreno and the demands those Colombians had made I thought about their request. I am not prepared to just give them money when we have no proof of the existence of anyone in Colombia that may be Juan. I have therefore come up with my own plan to address this. I caution you all not to try and convince me of any other plan.

I met with other members of my family in Miami as well as my sister and her husband Henri, who some may know is heavily connected in politics. I discussed this situation and how important it was for us to find out if the person is Juan and if it is how we could rescue him. All agreed that this is a very risky situation. Some did not trust the Colombians, so a plan was developed that satisfies everyone's concerns.

Hans and Moreno will meet the Colombians again and present our offer. It is a generous offer and will help them address the fears they expressed about being exposed as informants. There will not be any money paid to start.

My family will contribute funds to help with the costs associate in rescuing Juan if indeed it is him. Here is the plan so far.

Henri has spoken with representatives of various US government departments and all I tell you has been approved. There are written agreements to that effect. What I am about to tell you must remain secret between us.

While the Colombians claim the man is Juan, they need to prove to us he exists. I know they are asking for money and scared of reprisals. We have worked out an arrangement to address that.

We will pay them a small amount now with the promise of more money after Juan is back on Aruba. We will protect them for assisting us in the following way. Henri has negotiated for them to receive papers for entry into the US. Once there, their identities will be changed. They will receive official papers. There will be birth certificates and copies of employment and tax records. In addition they will be offered jobs in my family's construction company. It is a secure deal and will only happen after Juan is here in Aruba. The US government will arrange secure transportation for them in a military plane.

You are all probably wondering why the US government would agree to this. The answer is simple. They have been watching the increase in drug shipments from Colombia through Venezuela. They have undercover agents in the mobs in Chicago and it has leaked that the mob run by those Palermos is the kingpin in the smuggling. They need the intelligence to crack the ring. The Colombians can help as it is difficult for them to penetrate the society there without suspicion.

I have also made some other arrangements. Hans and Moreno will fly to Bogota. They will pose as coffee buyers for one of the companies. They will wait in Bogota until contacted by an undercover agent of the Bureau for Narcotics Control. The US government will send a scout party to the location where it is suspected that Juan is being held.

There is more. This is a sensitive operation. Now I ask Jakob to tell us what he has been doing."

Jakob was flabbergasted. He had no idea that Solange had done so much. He was excited. His adrenaline was pumping.

"Well I am sure you are all surprised by that little lecture.

I have also been busy. I am determined to stop that mob from Venezuela from destroying our lives here in Aruba. I have met with different people to achieve this. It is not possible for us alone to stop them. I have gone to those who can harass and disrupt their activities here and elsewhere.

I met with the senior managers at The Miami Sentinel. I have told them of the situation here and our plan to slow them down. I discussed the situation regarding Juan. They have agreed not to publish any details of this. I had meetings with the Director of The Bureau of Narcotics in Miami. We spoke for a long while. They are aware of the mobs activities here and have agents on the island following developments. I was guest at a lunch with Henri and the Director. He brought a US Coast Guard Officer to the meeting. The Coast Guard suspects that there may be some collusion between some patrols and the drug smuggling the mob runs. There has been a detailed investigation.

It is my intention to have the press involved as the mob is busted and expose them and the crimes.

I used a United Nations Conference which detailed the obligations of signatory countries in my talks with The Miami Sentinel. The paper had covered the conference and created great political awareness of the event.

My brother in law, Henri is politically astute. In Miami the population is weary of the shootings and crime associated with the drug situation. He is going to make his political platform one of fighting this scourge. He has many highly placed contacts and will convince them to support the effort to bring down the mobs activities here and in Venezuela."

The group had listened in silence. No one asked any questions.

Solange smiled and nodded her support for the actions he had taken.

Hans decided it was time to speak.

"Solange I appreciate your efforts and yes, Moreno and I will go to Bogota pretending to be coffee buyers. There is only one problem and that is our friend Adrien. I think it is best he tells you who he is and why he is here on the island."

Adrien arose and positioned himself to face them all.

"My name is Adrien van der Flug. I am a Dutch Marine Captain. I have been in Aruba for the past three months now on a task along with several others. We are operating undercover and independently of the other marines stationed here. The command is concerned there may possibly be some marines here who are involved in drug trafficking. I cannot disclose all the details. We are well aware of the use of Aruba's Free Trade Zone to transit drugs. Our intelligence has uncovered that the majority of drugs that are shipped through Rotterdam originate here in Aruba. We intend to stop that.

I was extensively trained in jungle warfare in Indonesia and have been in action.

Our operations here are in conjunction with the efforts of the Americans. We share our intelligence and mutually plan for the destruction of this drug operation."

Jakob excused himself and headed to the bathroom. When he returned he looked at Isaac. He was uncomfortable. Jakob invited him to tell the group of what he had planned, but Isaac just shrugged and explained he was too busy with business.

Solange was not convinced. "Isaac, why won't you explain your planned absence? Are you hiding something?"

"No, but I need to handle some matters privately. I ask everyone to respect that. Miguel and Alejandro have not spoken, yet you claim they have been acting strangely. I think they should inform us if they have planned anything. After all they are family to Juan."

Alejandro rose to address the extended family.

"Miguel and I have many friends who are from Colombia. We have spoken to them about the possibility of Juan's imprisonment. We have received comments and stories from some. It is possible that what we heard is not true or has been distorted on purpose. The criminal organizations that run the drug business have spies working for them, including here in Aruba.

I have purchased a boat. It is in Colombia. It is capable of crossing from there to Aruba. If we can rescue Juan then we will escape Colombia in the boat and bring him home to Aruba."

When he had finished speaking, Solange spoke.

"There needs to be someone in control of this. Too many individual efforts will not work. Neither Jakob nor I will be able to do this. What should we do? Is there any suggestion on how to coordinate our plans?"

The family spoke amongst themselves for a while. Finally, Hans spoke

"There is only one person with the necessary skills and leadership training. We all think that Adrien should lead our attempt at the rescue. He has been trained in jungle warfare and has experience, he is an active Dutch Marine with contacts that we do not have."

After some discussion it was decided that Adrien would be the leader.

They broke up into small groups. The conversation drifted from local gossip to politics.

Solange took Hans aside and away from the others.

"Hans I am concerned about Isaac. I do not know why he will not tell me about the trip he has planned. It is unlike him. I suspect there is some type of problem he does not wish to share with me. I need you to promise me that you will be extra observant and contact me if there is trouble. I am uncomfortable making this trip and leaving under these circumstances. It is important that Jakob start his treatments or we would stay."

"Do not worry. I will be vigilant. Take Jakob and get him the help he needs."

As they joined the others, Jakob announced he was retiring for the night.

"Goodnight everybody. We need to get sleep as we have that trip to Miami tomorrow."

It was close to midnight when the last guest left the house.

Hans remained.

"I will be here in the morning to drive you to the airport. You must not worry about our business here. Go and enjoy your trip."

Chapter 75

Hans arrived early for the drive to the airport. He gathered their luggage and placed it in the trunk of the car.

Hans took a route to the airport that bypassed Palm Beach and Oranjestad. There was little traffic.

At the airport Hans assisted Solange with her bags. They entered into the small terminal and made their way to the counter. After their papers were checked and the passes issued, they were wished farewell by Hans.

As they sat in the lounge waiting to board the aircraft, Jakob recognized a former business acquaintance and walked over to speak to him.

Solange sat reading magazines scattered on the table in the waiting area. She watched as Jakob laughed and waved his hands around as he spoke to his friend. He seemed very calm. She was happy.

After thirty minutes the attendants called the passengers to board the flight.

Jakob and Solange settled in for the five hour flight to Miami.

After they were aloft, neatly dressed Pan Am flight attendants moved through the cabin offering drinks and sandwiches.

Jakob could not resist. He ordered his favorite Rob Roy for himself and a Martini for Solange. When the drinks arrived Jakob absently stirred the Scotch and Vermouth mixture while he gazed out the window at the deep blue ocean below them.

"Solange, do you think we are doing the right thing? Should we be leaving now? There is so much happening. What if it isn't Juan?"

He sat his drink down on the little tray between them and started wringing his hands. Solange observed that his anxiety was increasing. She reached over and firmly took his wrist.

"Jakob, we have left this in the hands of fine people. I am encouraged to learn of the involvement of the Dutch Marines in our scheme. I am sure that with Hans and that Marine Captain that all will be fine. Please be calm."

Jakob sat back in his seat and slowly sipped his cocktail. He had no sooner finished when the attendant arrived with a fresh drink for him. Solange frowned at him.

"Did you order two drinks or is she just being friendly? There are times when I wonder about you Jakob."

Jakob smiled a disarming smile and closed his eyes.

The flight continued on without incident. It was about two hours after leaving Aruba that a hip of roast beef was wheeled through the cabin. Jakob was ravenous and selected an end cut with a side of roast vegetables and a large serving of the pale horseradish sauce.

After the meal had been served, the flight attendants returned and offered the passengers decks of cards and some copies of People magazine.

They passed the time playing cards until the Captain announced their impending descent into Wilcox Field, Miami.

Jakob looked out at the high rise buildings as the DC-6 swayed from side to side in the strong winds. Solange clasped his hand in fear as the plane continued to seesaw during its descent.

The landing was rough. The heavy aircraft thumped down onto the tarmac and taxied across to the low terminal building.

Jakob and Solange exited down the steep stairway and walked to the entrance into the terminal. At the baggage area they found Sparky waiting for them.

"Welcome back and so soon. Here, let me take those bags for you."

He gathered their cases and waved to a bellhop to bring a cart to transport the luggage to his car.

On the drive to the house Sparky engaged in small talk. He updated them on recent developments with Yolanda and Henri.

The weather was hot and humid. In Jakob's mind the temperature was hotter than Aruba. A fact he found surprising.

During the drive, Jakob wondered about his idea of informing the Miami Sentinel of the upcoming assault on the mob in Aruba and Venezuela. He carefully considered what had been disclosed to the reporter and the editor. He was convinced the press coverage would hurt the criminals and slow down their activities in Aruba.

In no time they wheeled into the expansive driveway of the mansion. Again, Yolanda sprinted down the stairs to greet them.

"I am so happy that you are back so soon and that Jakob can start his treatments. Come in. I am awaiting the arrival of Henri. He has been out visiting others as part of his political campaign and I understand he was at the newspaper this afternoon."

On hearing this Jakob's interest was piqued. What had Henri disclosed?

Sparky leapt from the car and removed their bags and carried them to the guest house.

Yolanda had set up a table on the patio with cheeses, cake and bottles of white wine for their arrival. She guided Solange and Jakob to the patio and poured each of them a glass of California sauterne.

The women sat talking while Jakob relaxed. His thoughts started to run repeatedly in his head. He had visions of the past in The Netherlands. He could clearly see the faces of his former wife, Anke and those of Sabine and Ilsa.

He had been enraptured by Sabine and when she had betrayed him and his uncle, he was deeply hurt. He did not understand how this beautiful woman had been convinced to become an informant in the Nazi war machine. He was thankful that she had allowed his uncle to escape with him before the Gestapo arrived. He had often wondered why she had allowed them to escape. Surely she would have been punished. He decided to find Sabine while visiting Germany on this trip.

His mind flashed to Anke. He could not find any self forgiveness for how he had treated her and finally abandoned her in Holland. He now realized that Anke had been supportive and had assisted him in his quest to find his ancestors. Without her advice he would have failed and been lost into a deviant life.

The thoughts occupied his mind. He was unaware of the conversation that Solange and Yolanda were having. His head started to pound. He stood unsteadily and announced he was leaving to lie down in the guest house.

Yolanda called Sparky to assist Jakob who had become disoriented.

Sparky arrived in minutes and helped Jakob to the house and helped him onto the bed.

Chapter 76

It was early evening when Henri returned. Upon hearing that Jakob was feeling unwell he strode over to the guest house. He knocked and entered to find Jakob in a deep sleep. He quietly left and returned to the patio where he joined the women.

"It seems that the day has worn Jakob out. He is in a deep sleep."

Concerned, Solange stood and excused herself. She hurried to wake Jakob. She wondered if the OCD had progressed rapidly in the past couple of months.

She sat on the edge of his bed and gently shook him awake.

"Jakob it is getting late. We need to dress you and join Henri and Yolanda for dinner. Are you alright? You seem to be exhausted."

"I am just getting some rest. I was tired from the travel today and want to be alert for when I see Dr. Stinger in the morning. Now let us shower and change into some light weight clothing. I cannot believe how hot Florida is at present. It seems hotter than Aruba. Is that possible?"

After showering and changing, Jakob escorted Solange through the garden to the patio where Henri and Yolanda sat enjoying the evening.

Henri enthusiastically greeted Jakob.

"I am pleased you are back so soon and have agreed to be treated by Dr. Stinger. I am sure that it will all work out fine and you will receive excellent care and a cure."

"I am certainly hoping that will be the case."

Henri walked across to the bar which was a small table covered with a white linen table cloth.

"Jakob, would you care for a glass of fine wine or one of your favorite Rob Roy cocktails?"

Solange interjected. "Henri, the Doctors advised us that Jakob's condition can worsen with too much alcohol. You will serve him a wine and not tempt him with other options. I will be watching you both."

Henri laughed. "This is why we marry my friend."

Solange scowled at him. Her icy look convinced Jakob to accept the offer of a glass of wine and not argue.

While they sat talking, one of the kitchen staff appeared.

"Madam would care for us to prepare the outside dining table or will you wish to eat in the formal room?"

"It is very warm and a beautiful night. We will dine outside. I believe everyone is happy with that," she exclaimed as she looked to the others.

Henri boomed, "Yes that will be fine."

Food was brought to the table on large platters. It was a light evening meal in view of the heat. There was fried chicken, beets, smoked salmon rolls, cheeses and an assortment of pickled vegetables.

When they had eaten, Henri invited Jakob to join him in his study.

Henri reached into the draw of his credenza and removed a box of Cuban cigars and offered them to Jakob.

"Here try one of these Cohibas. Finest dam cigar Cuba has ever produced.

Jakob declined. "Thank you but I do not smoke. I tried it when I was young but never enjoyed it."

"In that case let me tempt you with another vice of mine. Here try this aged Napoleon Brandy. To hell with what Solange says. A man must enjoy some things in life."

Jakob took the warm brandy snifter and swirled the contents around while he savoured the aroma from the golden amber liquid.

"There are some things I would like to tell you about. While you were back in Aruba, I had a meeting with that reporter and Curt Stoner, the Managing Editor at the Miami Sentinel. As you know I am running for election and campaigning hard. There are some who, because of my success in business, would like to see me fail. I will not accept that and will fight them with whatever tool will assist me in winning. I discussed with them the plans to attack the mob in both Aruba and Venezuela. I have also spoken to my friends at the Bureau of Narcotics Control and the FBI. The Miami Sentinel is prepared to cover these events and back me in my election attempt."

Henri continued talking for the next hour. Jakob sat in silence not interrupting. He was dismayed that Henri had widely discussed the details of the sensitive operation.

"Henri, I do not appreciate that you have done this. There are lives at stake and we wanted complete secrecy. How could you do this? I told you this. It was to be a confidential matter. Now you have told too many. The secret has probably been leaked. Are you a fool or just so absorbed in yourself and the need to win?"

Henri was surprised at Jakob's sudden outburst.

"I have been assured by Curt that he has only informed the most discreet journalists at the paper. I am sure they will not want to jeopardize or lose a story like this. I think you are worried about things unnecessarily."

Jakob was seething. He decided it was best to leave and retire for the night.

"Henri, we will probably never agree on this or on some of your political views. I need to leave early in the morning for those appointments, so I am going to wish you a good evening and retire."

'I will ask Sparky to drive you."

"That won't be required. I have already ordered a taxi. I have other business in Miami that I wish to attend to so it is best I make my own arrangements."

The two men shook hands and Jakob turned to leave.

"Jakob please relax. I am sure that the authorities will succeed."

Jakob silently thought "You fool. You have no idea what else I planned. I must keep the rescue of Juan quiet."

With a low wave of his hand, Jakob left for the night.

Chapter 77

Before the others in the mansion arose, Jakob slipped away and walked down the expansive driveway lined with laurel oaks and palm trees. The early morning sun shone golden in bushy crowns of the trees. He walked through the imposing gates and took a seat on the antique stone wall. Within minutes the taxi arrived. It was precisely on time.

Jakob pulled open the rear door and sunk into the cool air-conditioned interior. He gave the driver the address and settled back for the ride. Even at this early hour, the traffic was heavy. After thirty minutes they arrived at the low medical building. Jakob thanked the driver and thrust some money into his hand.

He walked up the narrow concrete stairs and through the barren lobby to the bank of two elevators. The lobby looked shabby and in need of paint and cleaning. The windows that looked out to the street were stained and coated with fine dust from the passing traffic.

Jakob punched his thumb against the chipped black button to summon the elevator. A dim light lit below the button. He heard some clicking and a whirr as the elevator car descended. It arrived with a thump and the doors inched open with a squeal.

Jakob was not impressed with Dr. Stinger's professional office building.

He entered the car and pushed the button for the third floor. The doors squealed shut and the car inched its way up to the third floor, where it stopped with a sudden jerk.

Jakob stepped out into a dimly lit hallway. He read the plaque and followed the arrow to Dr. Stinger's office. He knocked on her door and was surprised when she answered the door. She had a pile of files and papers stacked on the reception desk. She had been searching for something in the pile but decided to stop.

"Good morning Mr. Klassen. Welcome. My secretary does not start until ten on Monday and I am useless at finding anything in her filing system.

Would you care for a coffee? That is one thing I can do well." She laughed.

Jakob followed her past some other offices that were obviously occupied by other Doctors.

He looked around. The place was depressing. The walls were painted a light off green and the carpet was a flat worn industrial grey with a variety of stains on it.

Dr. Stinger was bubbling on about the morning and the weather and asking about the flight from Aruba. Jakob politely replied.

She stopped and turned and looked at him.

"Mr. Klassen I think these premises do not meet with your expectations. I should explain. My husband, a neurosurgeon and I bought this building a month ago. We have plans for a full renovation and we are awaiting the approvals from the City. I apologise that it looks so shabby. We have had to evict a number of tenants since the purchase. The former owners were not in the medical profession and allowed some practises to operate here that were very questionable. My husband and I have discussed relocating until after the renovations are done. I am sorry if you consider the office to be scruffy. I assure you that your treatments will be anything but that. You will receive superior help from me and my team."

Jakob was embarrassed. "I think you have made a good purchase. You are right downtown and I am sure that once you fix up the building that you will get some fine tenants."

"We are hoping that will be the case. Now let us start with you. I have the report here. The treatment is going to consist of some exploring your past and there will be a medicinal component. The medicine will be a mild sedative to help you relax and hopefully stop those reoccurring thought patterns you are experiencing. The pills will have some side effects. They will make you a little tired but will otherwise have some pleasant side effects. You need not worry. I want to perform the treatment each morning this week. I understand you are taking a vacation trip next weekend and will not be back for a month. During that time you must take the medicine I prescribe while you are travelling. I will prescribe enough for the month. Now please sit back and let's talk about the past.

The hours passed by. Jakob could hear the arrival of the secretary and other patients. The sound of doors opening and closing banged loudly as they were shown into the other offices.

Jakob spoke at length about the days he spent growing up on the farm. When he described the Mennonite community and the beliefs of the church, she stopped him and delved deeper into what he believed and why he rejected certain aspects of the faith. He described his loneliness as the other members of the church did not share his position. He broke down in tears when he talked of the attack on the family farm by the bigoted soldiers and their misinformed beliefs about the Mennonites.

He was sobbing and deeply affected while telling her of his past.

"Jakob this is a good start. I want to stop now. Tomorrow we will continue. Please come at the same time. Here is the prescription for you. Start those pills this afternoon."

Jakob wiped his face against the sleeve of his shirt.

"I am sorry for this."

"No don't be sorry. It is a good thing and we can confront what it is that is causing you the problems. I am encouraged. Don't be ashamed or discouraged. You are a good patient. Often it takes a number of sessions before the patient experiences those emotions."

He smiled weakly and thanked her. She escorted him to the front door and patted his forearm.

"I look forward to continuing with you tomorrow."

Chapter 78

Jakob checked the time as he left the building. It was shortly after noon. He made a quick decision and hailed a taxi.

The bright yellow Chevrolet taxi screeched to a halt at the curb. The radio was blaring and the windows were down. The inside of the taxi had previously seen a better life. The driver was a huge Hispanic man. Jakob cautiously climbed into the back of the taxi.

"Where you want, mister?"

"Please take me to the Miami Sentinel offices."

"You one of dem dam snotty reporters. They don't know nuthin. Make up bullshit stories and make trouble. Ought to be a law against them. Pieces of shit. All of them."

Jakob decided to play it safe. "No I am not a reporter. I need to see someone there."

He wondered why the hostility from the driver but decided against asking and invoking any kind of heated discussion."

The driver continued mumbling and cursing as they drove.

The day had turned hot again. The traffic crawled. Every once in a while the driver would shout some obscenity from the driver's window. He spared no one. Pedestrians and other drivers were all fair game.

The intensity of the heat mixed with fumes from the cars and trucks were making Jakob nauseous. Finally they arrived at the Miami Sentinel offices. The driver turned to Jakob.

"Sure you aint one of them? I should go in there and fix things for my brother, Rauol. Those bastards say he was a drug king. What the fuck do they know? We good clean Catholic boys. Go to church every fuckin Sunday."

Jakob decided to give him a generous tip so he could safely be away from him.

A few people were leaving the building and coming down the stairs. Jakob walked into the cavernous lobby area and was immediately confronted by a security guard.

"I am here for speak with Benita Flores. We are working together on a story."

"Do you have an appointment?"

"No. I have been in town on another appointment."

The guard motioned to some chairs across the lobby.

"Wait here while I call up to her office."

Jakob sat and listened as the guard called and spoke. He laughed and then waved Jakob to join him.

"Miss Flores will be coming down in a minute. You are lucky as she was just leaving for lunch. She asked you to wait as she is on her way down."

Within minutes, Benita emerged from the elevator and walked directly to Jakob.

"It is a pleasure to see you here again. I understand you wish to see me. I am just leaving for a quick lunch. Would you care to join me? There is a small place nearby that we all use. They know the staff here at the paper and are very generous."

Jakob looked at his watch. The time was one fifteen. He considered returning to Solange at the mansion but decided to stay and join Benita for lunch and then meet with Curt Stoner.

"Jakob is there something important? Has something happened since we met?"

"I have a concern I wish to discuss with you and Curt Stoner. I will wait until we are all together. That will be best."

The server came to their table with a small blackboard on which was written the daily specials.

"I strongly advise you to try the grilled swordfish. We received it early this morning fresh from the boat."

They did not require any further convincing and placed their order.

"I am most curious about why you wish to meet, but I will wait. Please tell me how you came to live on Aruba."

Jakob was pleased that she had diverted the conversation in another direction.

"Yes. That is a long story."

He reminisced and told her the story of his life. He had not completed when the waiter arrived with their plates of steaming swordfish. The waiter placed the plates in front of them and returned with different little containers with sauces and condiments.

The waiter beamed and wide smile. "Enjoy your lunch, Benita."

"Jakob, please continue. I find your story fascinating. Very different to the life and childhood I had in Cuba."

He continued the story up until the loss of Juan. He stopped there.

Benita looked up from eating with a puzzled look.

"Please, go on."

"No. The rest of the story I will tell when we are with Curt Stoner."

Benita was finding Jakob to be a truly intriguing man.

"We should go before too long. Curt often leaves the office early. I am dying to hear the rest of your story and why it is so important for you to meet with Curt."

He looked at her across the table and marvelled at her appearance. She was in some ways similar to the Aruban girls but also very unlike them.

"Let us finish then. I don't want to keep you wondering too long."

He reached into his pocket to take out money to pay their bill.

"No. No. We are on business for the paper. I will put this on my expense account."

As soon the bill was settled they left for the short walk back to the Miami Sentinel offices.

As they entered, Benita called to the security guard to contact Curt Stoner and ask him to meet them in the conference room.

Benita and Jakob rode up to the tenth floor in silence.

Upon entering the conference room they found Curt there awaiting them. He seemed impatient.

"Yes. What is so important to have this immediate meeting?"

Jakob pulled out a chair and sat opposite Curt. Benita had already claimed a seat beside Curt.

"There is a little more than what I have already told you. Before I share that I must discuss another matter."

He had their riveted attention.

"As you both are aware, Henri Martin is my brother-in-law. I found out last evening that he has been here at the paper and has been trying to use the upcoming actions against the mob and drugs to his advantage. He told me he has had conversations with certain reporters here. I am worried that the information will leak. I cannot be convinced that the information will be kept secret and confidential. The authorities are determined to make the raids successful and need to make them surprise raids. It is possible that one or more of your reporters could be bribed and leak the plan.

I want your assurance that you will not disclose anything to Henri. I am sure he will try to force information from you. He is determined to win his election and he will use whatever he can to win.

How can you convince me that the information has not been leaked?"

Curt drummed his fingers on the table top.

"There are only three people who know of this. There are Benita, myself and a photographer who has covered wartime conflicts. I can summon him to join us and then you can make your own decision. I trust him completely. He has been with the paper for ten years."

"Are you sure the information has not leaked?"

"Yes I am sure. This is a huge story for us and I will not allow it to be destroyed by office gossip. I fully understand your worry. Now what is the other matter that you have not shared with us?"

Jakob felt awkward and looked to Benita.

"While I was living in Savaneta, I rented an apartment from a couple. In fact I worked with the husband for a while and assisted him with his daily fishing. We became very good friends. I had taken a job at the oil refinery in Aruba and was no longer working with him. He invited me to go out fishing with him one evening. He never returned. His damaged boat was found by the Dutch Marines. There was a huge piece of the hull missing. It was assumed that a shark had attacked and damaged the boat.

It was years later when we assisted a man who was abandoned on the beach at Savaneta. He was in bad shape. Eventually he became confident that we were not a threat to him and he told us of his life and fleeing Colombia. In Aruba there is a small Colombian community. By accident he found that these young men had been workers at a Colombian drug lab. They told us about a man who claimed to be from Aruba and a fisherman on the island.

The more questions we asked the more it sounded like my dear friend Juan. We are sure it is him. He is imprisoned at a camp in the jungles of Colombia.

We have checked the information and prepared a rescue attempt. There are members of the rescue plan who have training in jungle warfare. It is a small group. We have reason to believe the Venezuela mob is one of the key financiers of the lab. It will be a small rescue group.

It will be a very dangerous mission. I wanted to tell you this. I want you to send a reporter or photographer to record the rescue. They must make their own way to Colombia and operate under some pretense.

We are planning this rescue at the same time as the assault on the mob."

Curt had leaned forward and was totally absorbed by the latest news. Benita stared at Jakob.

Finally, Curt spoke.

"How sure are you?"

"One of those in the party is my son. If I was not sure I would not allow it."

Curt sat back and ran a hand through his thinning hair.

"I think it is time for you to meet our photographer. He is probably the only person with experience in a situation like this."

Benita stood to leave the room and find the photographer.

Chapter 79

Benita returned some fifteen minutes later accompanied by a tall and rugged looking man. His hair was a mass of longish brown hair and a huge thick curly beard adorned his face. His clothes comprised of old faded jeans and a combat vest from which pieces of photographic equipment protruded.

Curt turned to him and pointed at a chair at the end of the table.

"Jurgen, this is Jakob Klassen. He is the man who has provided us the lead and story of the mob and drug running from Venezuela and Colombia and their activities. He has just added more information to what we already know, but first I must review some concerns he has raised."

Curt delivered a firm but accurate recap of the concerns that Jakob had raised. Jurgen listened and nodded.

"Mr. Klassen I respect your concern. I have been in a number of situations where any leak could have had deadly consequences. You can be assured that nothing has been discussed with anyone other than Curt and Benita."

He stared a penetrating look at Jakob.

"Now what is this other information and why have I been asked to join with you here?"

Before he could answer, Curt asked for Jakob's approval to tell Jurgen the story of the rescue. Jakob nodded his approval.

Curt relayed the story. As he did so, Jurgen frowned and cast a look at Jakob from time to time.

When Curt had finished, Jurgen spoke.

"I have some questions. This is indeed a dangerous mission. Those Colombian drug labs are heavily protected by local peasants who know the jungles well. It will be difficult to get to the lab without detection. How do you plan to do this? Who is in charge?"

Jakob took a minute before answering. He told them of the Dutch Marine Captain who would lead the rescue and gave details of the plan.

"I am interested in covering this but I have a lot of questions. I would like to go to Aruba and meet with that captain and the others in the party. Is that possible?"

Both Benita and Curt looked at Jakob.

"I will arrange it for you. I need to be here in the downtown every morning. I will come to the office in the next day or so with the details."

Benita looked at her watch

"Jakob it is getting late in the day. The afternoon is getting late. I am going to be leaving soon. I am happy to give you a ride to your home here."

"That is very kind but I will take a taxi."

"Don't be silly. I drive close to your home on my way home. It would be my pleasure. Plus, I would love to meet that formidable wife of yours, Solange."

Jakob accepted the offer.

"I will come and visit after my morning appointment on Wednesday."

Curt and Jurgen stood and shook Jakob's hand as he and Benita left the conference room.

Benita quickly stopped into her office and picked up some shopping bags and then they left for the elevator.

"I do not want to inconvenience you, but I need to stop at a pharmacy and get this prescription filled."

"That is no problem. There is one on the way that is easy to stop at. There is parking and a bar. We can have a drink while we wait for them to fill the prescription."

"Please let me use your phone. I will call Solange and tell her to expect us."

They left the office and went to the underground parking. Benita headed across to an area marked "Private parking" and stopped beside a red and white 1961 Corvette. She pushed the key into the lock and sprang the door open. She glided onto the seat and pulled open the passenger door lock. Before Jakob could get into the car, Benita released the locked hinges for the convertible roof.

Jakob pulled himself into the car. Benita cranked the engine into life and a roar of the exhausts filled the garage. She slid the car into gear and accelerated out of the garage and into the busy Miami traffic.

Soon they were out of the downtown and Benita swerved into the entrance of a new shopping mall.

"Jakob there is a pharmacy at the end. I will go and wait in the little bar for you. What drink should I order for you?"

Jakob chuckled. "I will have a Rob Roy."

Feeling rejuvenated he opened the door and almost ran to the pharmacy.

Within minutes he returned and entered the bar. The lighting was dim and it took minutes for his eyes to adjust from the bright sunlit day.

He spotted Benita in a booth and went to join her. On the table was one if the biggest Rob Roy drinks he had ever seen.

The air was cool and a soft music was playing. He started to feel relaxed but was worried that his problem may arise at any moment.

"Benita, I thank you for driving me home. I really do appreciate it. I talked to Solange and when we get to the mansion she has invited you in for a cocktail so don't drink too many here. Solange makes quite the drink."

"I am really looking forward to meeting the woman who was able to tame you. From what you have told me you were a wild boy in those days."

"They were different times. There had been two wars. People were scared. Food was rationed. I did what I believed in."

"I wish I could have met your wife Anke. It would have been interesting to write her story of her growing up with you in a strict religious family. It must have been hard for her to accept your challenges to the faith and taking that trip to Europe. Do you ever regret leaving that life?"

Her question hit him like an iron fist to the stomach. He had not expected it.

His mind flashed back to wartime Europe. He envisioned the clubs he had visited and the people. He felt his old enemy creeping up on him. He tried to control the runaway thoughts.

Benita watched as Jakob struggled to compose himself. He reached for the Rob Roy and within several gulps emptied the glass of its contents.

"Benita I am not feeling so well. Let me go and get my prescription and then we should head to my home."

They quickly finished up and left the bar and proceeded to the pharmacy.

The pharmacist approached Jakob and handed him a small vial of pills.

"Mr. Klassen the Doctor has written a note on the prescription. You are to take one immediately and another later this evening. It seems she wants you to have taken these before your next visit with her tomorrow morning. Now I caution you that this medication, Clexstera is strong and you may experience some side effects. The main side effect will be drowsiness. There are others. You may find your sex drive increases. If it gets out of control talk to your Doctor and she may change your dosage."

Jakob couldn't believe his ears. "Finally as I get older they give me something to drive my libido through the roof."

He left to pharmacy and joined Benita in her Corvette. He gave her the address of the mansion. She dropped the Corvette into low gear and screeched the tires as she peeled out of the parking and onto the road.

"Easy Benita. This medicine is to calm me down. If you drive like that I will need to get a stronger prescription."

She threw her head back and laughed. "Come on Jakob. Enjoy some freedom. You need to relax and enjoy the life around you. Don't be so tense."

Jakob thought about those words and settled back for the ride.

Thirty minutes passed until they arrived at the house. Already Jakob was experiencing the effects of the medication. He was feeling slightly tried yet quite euphoric from the effect of the major erection he was experiencing.

He directed Benita to park in a small clearing to the left of the stairway.

They had just parked when Solange came down the stairs to meet them.

"Solange I would like to introduce you to Benita. This is the reporter from the Miami Sentinel who will be covering the story of our little surprise for those Italian boys."

"I am pleased to meet you Benita. I hope Jakob is being a perfect gentleman in his dealings."

Solange had no sooner spoken the words when her eyes fell to Jakob's crotch. She was shocked at the baseball sized bulge in his pants. She immediately wondered what Benita had done. Instinctively she cooled toward her.

"Thank you for driving him home. Now please excuse us. We have been invited to a function and must leave very soon. Jakob will need to freshen up and change into his formal wear. It has been a pleasure to meet you and put a face to the name."

Jakob was bewildered. What function and what formal wear. All he had were his linen trousers and shirts and slightly heavier clothing for the trip in Canada and Europe. He knew better than to challenge Solange. He sensed the anger.

Benita frowned. "I was hoping to spend some time and get to know you. I am intrigued by the story of Jakob's life and wanted to meet with the woman who tamed him."

"There will be another time but now I must say goodbye."

Benita went to kiss Solange on the cheek but stumbled as Solange pulled back. Embarrassed Benita left for her car.

Chapter 80

Jakob was angry with Solange. The evening activities did nothing to remove the chill from the air. Henri had returned home and was holding court describing his latest business success and how his election campaign was strong, since he had exerted pressure and blackmail on a leading opposition politician.

Jakob could not stomach the night. He silently left the room and slunk off to his bed.

Solange apologised for Jakob's mood and departure.

"He started onto a medication today and it has made him tired and intolerant."

Henri was indignant. "That man has been trouble. From his early years until now he has created situations. I doubt he will ever grow up and accept the responsibilities of life."

Solange glared at Henri.

"I should tell you he is one of the most focussed and dedicated men I know. He stood up for the beliefs he had and has never treated me bad. I will not let you malign him like that. How dare you?"

Yolanda sat on her chaise lounge unsure how to intervene in the situation.

"Solange and Henri, we are family. There are pressures on all of you. I ask you to stop and think. Why can't you enjoy the success you have had Henri? You must stop being so self centered. Other people have lives and you don't seem to recognize that. It is not all about you and your political aspirations or your businesses. It is time for you to re-evaluate your life."

Solange was shocked at the outburst.

"But Yolanda this has been my life."

"It is time for you to grow up and recognize the interests and needs of others around you. I cannot believe that you expect to succeed in politics with that attitude. May I remind you that when I first met you things were very different? You were broke and struggling. If it hadn't been for the generosity of our family, and I mean Solange and me, you would never have bought and built the pharmaceutical company or had the money to invest in construction. You need to remember here you came from and how quickly I could put you back there."

"I meant no disrespect. I consider what I have built to be an achievement for the both of us."

Solange slid off the couch and walked up to Yolanda. She bent down and hugged her.

"Thank you. It has been a difficult evening. I need to go and ensure that Jakob is alright and hasn't done anything stupid."

She excused herself and instead of returning to the guesthouse she walked through the garden and down toward the water shore.

An old weathered wooden bench faced the water and Solange went to it and folded her slim body onto it.

Over the water a bright blue-white moon shone its reflection off the water. An occasional boat putted by. The night air cooled and the sound of chirping crickets filled the air.

She sat alone and in deep thought for over an hour.

She wondered why she had been so jealous and nasty to Benita. The girl had done nothing wrong and had graciously brought Jakob home. She didn't understand why she had acted in that manner.

Tired and despondent she returned to the guesthouse. She opened the door and walked in to the darkened rooms to hear Jakob snoring gently in the bedroom.

She turned on the light to the bathroom and prepared for bed. As she did so, Jakob stirred from his sleep and called her.

"Solange, my sweetie. Is that you? I can't wait for you to be here in our bed. I am sorry but I had to leave. I was tired and Henri was annoying. I was about to say some dreadful things."

"Jakob I think those dreadful things were told to Henri by Yolanda tonight. Remember that you made yourself. Henri did it using my family's money. You are a much stronger and better man than he is. Tonight Yolanda told him exactly that."

"I need to have my medical appointments every day. The last one is on Friday. Can we leave for Canada on Saturday? I fear that if we stay longer I will create a bad situation. I am angry. I am not an old man but I am being made to feel like that. Henri boasts and attempts to make me feel insignificant."

"Yes, Jakob. We will leave. I don't want to lose my connection with my sister. It is too important to me. Come now, let's get some sleep."

"Solange I have to ask you a question. Why were you rude to Benita? She is the one who can help us the most. She will get the story of the mob's actions in Aruba into the papers here in America and also in The Netherlands. We need her to help."

"I am sorry but I really don't know what came over me. I saw the two of you get out of the car and from what I saw you were very sexually excited. I assume that the two of you had been doing more than just driving home and enjoying a nice conversation. Your pants were bulging with an exuberant member."

Jakob fell back on the bed and burst into uncontrollable laughter.

"Oh, Solange. No it isn't like that. These pills that Dr. Stinger prescribed have some serious side effects. One of them is an increased level of sexual desire. I cannot help what happens to me. I must say it's not all bad. Now come to bed with me and enjoy a little of that side effect?"

"I am so sorry. I didn't even think of that. I love you so much Jakob that the thought of another woman taking you makes me go a little crazy."

Jakob reached his arm up and gently pulled Solange down to him.

"It is our night to enjoy. I need to awake early again for more treatment and who knows. Maybe Dr. Stinger will give me even better pills."

Solange laughed and together they embraced and after some lengthy moments of passion fell into a deep sleep.

Chapter 81

The taxi arrived at the end of the driveway and Jakob crawled in.

"Same place as yesterday, sir?"

"Yes and it will be until Friday."

The driver turned off the radio and asked Jakob about sports teams and those he preferred. Jakob replied that he was not from mainland America and that on the island of Aruba he had no particular liking for any team.

Conversation then moved to life in the Caribbean.

Jakob spoke at length and the driver was fascinated.

They bantered back and forth until reaching the office building of Dr. Stinger. As he was leaving the taxi, Jakob turned t the driver.

"I will need a ride back at around noon. Do you wish to pick me up or should I hire another cab?"

"No sir. I will meet you here."

Jakob entered the building and took the old creaking elevator up to the Doctor's floor. He pushed open the door and found her sitting on a chair in the waiting area looking at some patient files.

"Mr.Klassen, good morning. I am glad to see you are here on time. We will start immediately. Would you like a coffee?"

"Yes I would. Let me come with you. I know where the machine is."

With coffees in hand they retreated to her office to start the next treatment.

"How do you feel Mr.Klassen after taking that medication? Has it helped you?"

He wanted to smile and tell the truth.

"Yes it has. I woke this morning and feel fresh and I am not thinking about all those dark memories. It is amazing."

"I am pleased to hear you have reacted so well and so quickly to them. Have there been any other effects?"

"Yes and they are enjoyable. I haven't had an erection so big or for so long since I was twenty years old."

Dr. Stinger blushed. "Yes those pills can do that. Now to our session please."

Jakob grinned. He knew he had hit some nerve in the almost humorless Doctor.

She continued on exploring Jakob's earlier life and on occasion stopped and had him provide intricate details. He found himself tiring quickly. Again his member started to awake.

"Doctor I am feeling very tired. Will this take much longer?"

She looked at the thin strapped silver watch on her wrist.

"No we will be finished in thirty minutes. Will you be alright with that?"

"Yes. I am just so tired."

"You will be tired from those pills for the first day. After that you will be back to normal. Certain of the side effects will continue."

The appointment finished early. Jakob considered changing his plans and instead of returning to the mansion taking the taxi to the Miami Sentinel office and Benita. He was deeply embarrassed at Solange's treatment of Benita. She has done nothing to receive such a berating.

He stood outside the building considering this when his trusty taxi driver arrived. He dismissed the idea and asked the drive to take him home.

After arriving at the mansion, Jakob went directly to the guest house. He found Solange packing clothes into the suitcases.

"What are you doing?"

"I have thought about your comments last night. You are right. Henri is not so nice to you. I didn't see it but now you mention it I can. I phoned the airline and changed our

425

flight. We will leave on Thursday morning. I have also changed the hotel in Toronto."

Jakob was both pleased and dismayed to be leaving Miami and Benita.

"How will you explain this to Yolanda?"

"I have already told her we need to be in Canada earlier, as you have to meet with the lawyers for the sale of the farm. I explained that the buyer will not be available on the dates we had originally planned."

Jakob sat on the edge of the bed and considered this.

"It will mean that I cannot complete the full week of treatment with Dr. Stinger."

"Jakob when all this is over we will return to Miami and rent our own house for a vacation and for you to receive the full treatment. I will phone Dr. Stinger and discuss the change in our travel plans."

"Solange let me take you out for a late lunch. I am really uncomfortable here with Yolanda and Henri."

"I will be ready in fifteen minutes."

"I will wait for you in the garden on that old wooden seat."

Together they left to find a local restaurant.

Chapter 82

Jakob and Solange spent a quiet evening alone. Yolanda and Henri attended a political function.

Wednesday morning Jakob awoke feeling fresh and relaxed. He had not felt this way in some years. He was invigorated.

After dressing he drank some fresh orange juice and walked down the driveway to find his taxi already there and waiting.

"Good morning sir, it's a beautiful morning. Today will not be so hot. We have an onshore breeze that has blown away some of that sticky heat."

Jakob could feel the difference

"Yes it certainly seems more pleasant this morning. I will go to my appointment and at around noon I will be going to a meeting at the Miami Sentinel office. Should I take another taxi or are you available?"

"I will be there for you."

They drove on chatting about fishing, Aruba, Florida's baseball team and nothing of any consequence.

Traffic was light and they arrived at the Doctor's offices early. Jakob decided to go in and see if Dr. Stinger had arrived. He opened the door and found the waiting area empty. As he stood there she arrived from the corridor leading to the offices.

"Mr. Klassen, please come on in. How are you feeling? I hope that you are not experiencing any bad side effects of that medicine."

"No I am actually feeling great. As I told you the other day, in some ways I feel as if I was a teenager again. That is an amazing medicine. I have not had the same obsessive thoughts and I am sleeping very well."

"I am pleased to hear that. Now I feel better about the phone call from your wife. I understand you are going to be leaving tomorrow for your trip. I think that in just these past few days we have made good progress and that medicine I prescribed is the correct one for you. There are several different anti anxiety medications and Clexstera is a relatively new one and seems to be the most effective. I am going to increase the prescription so you will have enough to last you for your trip."

She opened his file and made some notations and then continued to ask him questions regarding his past life.

It was noon when Jakob emerged from the building and took his taxi to the Miami Sentinel offices. The security guard recognized him and immediately picked up the phone to call Benita.

The guard indicated that Jakob should take a seat and wait.

After ten minutes the elevator door opened and Benita stepped out. She looked stunning dressed in a casual linen dress of pale green. She carried some papers in her right hand and had a handbag hanging from her left wrist. She crossed to Jakob.

"Good afternoon Jakob. That was quite the cold reception that bitch of a wife of yours gave me. What the hell is wrong with her?"

"I am really sorry about that. She is normally a relaxed and casual person. I think the stay at her sisters and the antics of the husband, Henri, have greatly upset her. I apologize for her behaviour and hope that one day we will all be able to sit as friends."

"What is it you want? I have taken this afternoon off."

"There has been a change in our travel plans. I will be leaving for Toronto via New York tomorrow morning. I wanted to see you and finalize arrangements for the coverage of the stories. Do you have time?"

"I am going out to the coast. If you wish then join me. We can talk there. We do not need to be in the office."

Jakob agreed and they descended into the parking area beneath the building.

Again Benita removed the convertible top and started the Corvette. The roar from its exhausts was deafening. They pulled out of the garage and headed to the freeways that lead to the coast.

The wind rushed through the car and made normal conversation impossible. Benita's Latino temperament was evident in her fast and aggressive driving. Jakob was pleased when they pulled onto Lincoln Road. She slowed the car and cruised through back streets until she reached one that lead to the waterfront area of South Beach.

She drove into the entrance of a tall condominium building with a sign pronouncing it to be The Pelican. Benita stopped the Corvette at the front stairway and a uniformed concierge rushed to open her door.

"Buenas tardes, Benita. ¿Cómo estás? Es un buen día"

"Estoy bien. ¿Cómo estás tú y tu familia?"

"¿Cómo está tu familia, Pepe?"

Jakob watched the interchange with curiosity. It was evident that Benita was known here.

Pepe took the bag and papers that Benita was carrying walked up the stairs before her and pulled open the polished brass and glass doors.

Pepe escorted them through the marble clad lobby. He stopped and pressed the button to summon the elevator.

To Jakob's surprise there was an attendant in the elevator.

Again Benita was greeted.

"Buen tardes. ¿Supongo que vamos al ático?"

"Sí. Estaré en casa esta tarde"

The elevator ascended quickly and the doors opened into a lavishly appointed apartment

Benita stepped out and beckoned Jakob to follow.

Jakob looked around at the interior which was expensively decorated. He turned and looked out through large glass doors that opened onto a balcony overlooking the ocean. The balcony was decorated with potted plants including some miniature palms. Lounge chairs were arranged to face the ocean.

It was pure luxury.

Benita sat down her bag and papers and started toward the kitchen.

"Can I interest you in a mid day drink? Don't tell me you will want one of those Rob Roy drinks."

A blender howled for a few minutes and Benita returned with Jakob's Rob Roy and another tropical cocktail with crushed ice and a slice of lime in it.

Suddenly the truth hit Jakob. He didn't want to believe his thoughts.

Benita put down her drink and looked at Jakob.

"I am going to go and change into something more casual. Then I will make us a Cuban lunch. Why don't you go and wait on the balcony? It is such a nice day."

Jakob walked over to the sliding doors to the balcony. He pulled them open.

A rush of warm wind forced him back inside. He closed the doors and returned to the sofa.

Minutes passed and Benita appeared wearing a revealing blouse and shorts.

Jakob's medication sprang into action. His mind filled with fantasies. Benita positioned herself behind the sofa and caressed Jakob's neck.

"Are you hungry? In Cuba we had a meal we would eat late at night. It is more a sandwich. It is called medianoche. I will make some for us."

She kept massaging his shoulders. Jakob was in heaven. Visions of past affairs flooded his mind. He saw Ilsa, Sabine and some of his other two-timing encounters.

He felt control slipping away from him. As quickly as Benita had started she stopped and moved toward the kitchen. Jakob was bewildered.

He looked around the apartment again. There was no way a reporter could afford the apartment, art and furnishings. He got up and joined Benita in the kitchen.

"Benita you told me this was the apartment of a friend. He must be very wealthy, unless there is some other explanation. A place like this could never be bought on a reporter's wage."

"No Jakob. It does not belong to a friend it is my home. I own this."

Jakob went quiet. He thought of the expensive Corvette, her designer clothing and this lavish apartment. There could only be one answer. He finally decided to ask her.

"Benita, the things you own in your life are all very expensive. You must have another business. Are you running a sex business here?"

She doubled over laughing. "Jakob you make me laugh. No I am not a madam. There are some days I wish I was. My Catholic upbringing can be boring and restricting at times. No in Cuba my father was an owner of a casino. He sold everything before Castro seized control. He moved the money here to America. He died shortly after leaving Cuba and left me a large inheritance. I invested in properties and this apartment. I have been lucky I get to do a job I love and live well."

Jakob shook his head. "I did not mean to offend you. You are indeed lucky. Are there any more surprises?"

"Well, I haven't been totally honest with you. I bought this whole building as an investment and I am a large investor in the Miami Sentinel."

Chapter 83

Jakob was in shock. He did not know what to say.

Benita arrived with a tray of the medianoche and a bottle of Chablis. They sat at a glass and chrome table that looked to the strip and beach. The wind was blowing and beyond the surf there were whitecaps breaking. It seemed a storm was forming.

"Benita what I need to tell you is that I will be leaving tomorrow morning. We will first fly to New York and change planes to continue to Toronto, Canada. I have some business there. I own farmland and wish to sell it. After we are complete in Canada we will travel to Europe. We will be in Germany and Holland. I have an old friend in Germany who has invited us. I look forward to seeing him. I also have some unfinished business there."

Jakob proceeded to tell Benita of his life in Holland and Germany during the war years. He was totally honest. He mentioned the clubs, getting Ilsa pregnant and leaving her to have the child. He continued and told her of Josef Klassen his uncle and their escape just before the Gestapo were to raid Josef's house. He told her of Sabine and how he had loved her. When he completed the story of those years he described how he had really betrayed a lot of people and it now haunted him.

"When we are there I intend to visit some of those people and seek their pardon. I used and hurt people."

Benita had remained quiet throughout Jakob's soliloquy. Now she spoke.

"I think that after all this time it might be best to leave those things alone. You might create problems for yourself."

"Until I try I will never be at peace."

"Jakob there were men worse than you during that horrible time. So you had affairs and broke the rules of your church. At least you didn't murder and steal and commit other crimes."

"This is the reason I am here in Miami. I am receiving special treatments. I was meant to stay longer for more treatment but now we must leave."

"I will miss you Jakob Klassen. Of course we will be in touch about the raids. I am already working on some ideas and making preparations.

When you return to Aruba will you be travelling through Florida? I would hope to see you then and maybe Solange will be more receptive."

Jakob was feeling dejected. He finished his lunch and took the wine to the sofa. Benita followed him and curled her body up next to him. Jakob's medicines worked again to arouse him. He looked into her dark brown eyes and lowered his head towards hers.

She reached up and pulled him down to her. As he reached for her there was a loud and resounding crash on the glass sliding door. A large seagull had crashed into the door and lay flapping its last throes on her balcony.

"That is extremely bad luck. Now I am really worried about what you plan to do on your trip."

"Benita that is just a silly superstiticion. I will be fine. Now I think I should leave before we get ourselves into trouble."Benita pouted.

"Please can I phone for a taxi?"

"Yes and the concierge can call us when it arrives. I will miss you Jakob. What a fascinating man you are."

Chapter 84

It was mid afternoon when Jakob arrived back at the mansion. His mood was sullen. To avoid another confrontation with Henri or Yolanda, he walked around the side of the mansion to the guesthouse where he and Solange were staying. He opened the door and entered into the dim interior. Solange had drawn all the blinds in an effort to reduce the heat from the sun.

Without turning on the lights, Jakob sat down heavily on the couch in the living area. He sat in the darkness and reflected on all the recent events. He realized that something had changed in him. He was experiencing periods of almost uncontrollable sexual arousal and impatience. Now he found himself attracted to another woman. He had never felt this desire in all his years with Solange. He was growing angry when the door opened and Solange walked in.

"Why are you sitting here in the dark? Is something wrong? You have been acting strangely and your behavior toward Yolanda and Henri is terrible. They have gone to great lengths to make us welcome and comfortable here. I demand some answers from you. What is troubling you so much?"

"Solange, I do not know. I was just sitting here and trying to understand. I feel inadequate and betrayed by Henri.

Yolanda is upsetting me with all of the ostentatious display of wealth. I wish we had stayed at a hotel."

"Jakob, she is my sister. Remember that you too have faults."

"I wish we had just stayed in Aruba then we wouldn't be dealing with these people and arguing with each other. Tonight is our last night and I cannot bear the thought of sitting at their table and hearing Henri boast of his business smarts and politics."

"You won't have to my dear. I have made us a reservation at the Mariners Cove. We will have an early dinner and have drinks with Yolanda and Henri when we return. We will need to leave for the airport early in the morning. I have already booked a taxi to take us there."

He looked straight at Solange. She was still as beautiful to him as the day he had met her. A sudden twinge of sadness surged through him. This was another emotion that had just developed. As the feeling of melancholy grew, he started sobbing. A deep sadness crept into his soul.

Solange watched his torment with concern. Jakob's demeanour troubled her. Throughout their years of marriage she had never observed him acting this way.

"Jakob, is there anything you want to tell me? Is something troubling you? Do you want to cancel our trip and return to Aruba? I will understand."

"No. I don't know what is wrong. I think and try to understand what is happening to me. Is it that I am getting old? Is this what old age is about?"

She slowly crossed over the room and took his head in her hands and cradled him in her arms.

"You have done so many good things for people. Please don't be so hard on yourself. I am sure when we arrive in Canada and you return to the farm you will forget the sadness. I am sure you and your old friend Jan Zelder will have a great time in Europe. You have a lot to look forward to. We have plans to try to bring Juan back to Aruba. There is to be the wedding for Moreno and Gabriela. You have Isaac Juniors children who think you are the world's best grandfather. You have wealth, friends and generally good health. Come on now. Be happy.

As much as you are annoyed at Yolanda, let us go and have a cocktail with her before we leave for our dinner."

Jakob sighed. Her words had calmed him.

Within minutes they joined Yolanda and Henri on the garden patio for drinks.

Henri stepped forward and faced Jakob.

"I have done some serious thinking about our last discussion. You are right. I acted selfishly. It was not my intention to interfere with the plans to rescue Juan or jeopardize the drug raids. I saw an opportunity and took it.

440

Here in Florida we have had too many deaths related to the drug dealing. Our citizens are fed up. I thought if I supported the efforts and made it visible then I would get more support in the coming election. I am truly sorry that I didn't think more clearly before I acted. Please accept my apology. I will not continue to make this a key part of my election until the rescue and raids are complete. You have my word."

"I accept your apology. I too should apologize. I certainly did not mean to be rude. I don't know what has happened to me. I have not been the same since we left home in Aruba."

The men moved to the chairs near the railing that overlooked the lush garden. Henri poured a crisp white wine into a glass and handed it to Jakob.

"Here let us toast to a safe trip for you and Solange."

 Henri and Jakob sat talking. Solange and Yolanda disappeared inside the house. A short time later they emerged with trays of canapés. Henri smiled when he recognised one of the servings.

"Jakob you must try this. It is delicious. It is Dungeness crab in a sauce rolled into those little pastry shells. It is my favorite."

The little group ate and drank while making light conversation. The afternoon was getting late.

It was Solange who stood first.

"Yolanda and Henri. I am taking Jakob out for an early dinner. We have a busy day of travel tomorrow. He has not been feeling so well and I want him relaxed and calm before we leave in the morning."

As Jakob stood to join her he was hit with a sudden spell of dizziness and started to stumble toward the railing. Henri jumped from his chair and threw his arms around Jakob to stop him from falling. He guided Jakob back into his chair.

"Jakob, can you hear me. What just happened to you?"

Solange stood motionless watching the scene. Jakob's face was an ashen grey color. Something was very wrong.

Henri turned to Solange. "Please get me the medication that has been prescribed for Jakob. I want to check it. I think the side effects are too strong for him."

Solange hurried away to the guesthouse to fetch the pills and returned to the patio with them.

"I am going to call the chief research chemist at my office. I do not know this drug Clexstera. Our company may produce it but it is not a name I know."

Henri left them to go inside to his office and call the company. It was fifteen minutes later we he rejoined the group.

"I have some bad news for you. This drug is very controversial. It has been responsible for causing behavioral changes in patients and some cases of suicide are attributed to it. It is known to interfere with the neurological functions in patients and cause some nasty side effects. I suggest Jakob stop taking this medicine. He was fine without it so until you return I suggest he stop taking it. That is the opinion of my research doctors."

With a flourish, Solange took the pills and headed back to the guesthouse. She rushed inside and picked up the phone to call the office of Doctor Stringer.

The phone rang at the doctor's office for minutes before it was answered.

"This is Solange Klassen," she announced to the receptionist who answered.

"My husband, Jakob Klassen is in treatment with Doctor Stringer. I am concerned he is suffering some serious side effects from the medication she prescribed. Is she available? I need to speak with her."

The receptionist advised that the doctor had left for a meeting and would be returning shortly. Solange left the telephone number and asked for the doctor to call her. She explained the urgency to the receptionist and the fact that they were travelling in the morning.

During the hour that passed before the doctor called back, Yolanda and Solange settled Jakob into the sofa bed.

The bells of the phone clanged loudly with the doctor's return call.

"Thank you for calling me back Doctor Stringer. I am concerned about Jakob and how he is reacting to the medication."

The doctor asked a series of questions and then offered to call back after checking some matters.

Time dragged. Jakob had lapsed into a deep sleep. Finally the phone rang again.

"Solange, this is Doctor Stringer. I have consulted with my associate. We advise you to stop Jakob's treatment with Clexstera. I will prescribe a sedative that will calm him. Is it possible for you to pick up the script? It is important he take the sedative when stopping Clexstera. I will be in my office for the next two hours."

"I will find a way to get to you."

Solange hung up the phone and turned to Henri.

"I will drive you to the doctor's office. Let us leave now before the traffic becomes bad. I have spoken to Yolanda. Given Jakob's condition we are going to accompany you to dinner tonight. It will be our treat. Don't even think of objecting."

Solange put on a light jacket and walked with Henri to the car for the trip to the doctors.

Chapter 85

The evening passed without any drama.

Henri was gracious and recommended dinner at one of Miami's top restaurants, The Bull and the Marlin. Jakob was relieved and enthusiastic. The restaurant was both a steakhouse and a premier seafood establishment. Jakob missed the selection of meats on Aruba.

They arrived at the restaurant a little after six. The maître'd escorted them to a elaborately set table in the center of the main dining area.

After they were all seated, Henri spoke.

"I am truly sorry if my actions have caused any problems. It was certainly not a deliberate action on my part. I again apologize. Let us enjoy the evening."

Jakob reflected on his apology. He wondered at the sincerity.

"Henri, both Solange and I appreciate all your help here in Miami. It has been a difficult time for all of us. I know that my behaviour changed while I was taking that medication. I already can sense the change since I took this new medication. It is called Zaralax. It has made me feel very calm."

"I think we have all been worried about you and Solange. You have many things happening in your life. There is the rescue attempt of Juan, the plan to disrupt the influence of the mob on the island, the need to protect the businesses you built. We are not surprised that all this has caused you stress Jakob."

Jakob looked at him and silently nodded.

The conversation was interrupted by the arrival of the tuxedo clad waiter.

"Good evening. Can I assist in helping you order? We do have some special items this evening. Is the choice to be from our fine seafood selection or the meats?"

Jakob looked at Solange. In his mind he knew the answer she would make and laughed when she spoke.

"I will enjoy something from the seafood selection."

"Excellent, madam. May I recommend the Chicken Neptune?"

"I do not know that dish."

"Madam it is a startling preparation. A meal fit for a queen. It is a chicken breast stuffed with a Mornay sauce of fresh lobster, crab and shrimp. It is served tonight with fresh white asparagus and baked baby tomatoes that are so sweet."

Solange needed no encouragement.

"That sounds superb. I would like that."

The waiter addressed Yolanda.

"Have you decided upon anything from the menu?"

"No. I do not see anything I would really like."

"I suggest then another fine special for this evening that has received accolades. It is the Lobster Thermidor. The Lobster Thermidor here is a French dish consisting of a creamy mixture of cooked lobster meat, egg yolks, and brandy and it is stuffed into a lobster shell. We serve it with an oven-browned cheese crust of Gruyère cheese. Our special sauce contains fine grained mustard.

This is one of my personal favorites. We have won awards for our adaptation of this dish."

Yolanda's mouth was dribbling at the edges. She could barely proceed to order without saliva running down her jaws.

The waiter turned to Henri.

"What is your preference, sir?"

Henri did not hesitate.

"I will take the twenty-eight ounce Porterhouse steak. Have them prepare it medium. I will take the battered onion rings, the baked potato with chives and sour cream, fresh asparagus, and a little steamed spinach. Before the main course please bring me a French onion soup."

Solange looked at him aghast." How could he eat so much?" she wondered.

The waiter turned to Jakob.

"And what will be your choice, sir?"

"Please tell me about this item on the menu, The Black and Blue rib eye."

"Yes sir. It has to be one of the finest meals available in all of Florida. **It is a** hand-cut rib eye steak prepared in a cast-iron pan and blackened with our own Cajun seasonings and then topped with melted bleu cheese. We offer two serving sizes. There is the eighteen ounce or the twenty-four ounce."

"I will have the twenty-four ounce with a side of Portabella Mushrooms, Caramelized Onions and Béarnaise Sauce. For a starter I would like the pan seared scallops."

Solange and Yolanda sat and looked at Jakob in shock.

Jakob smiled and then spoke.

"I know. I know. It seems that the new medication, the Zaralax makes one very hungry."

Solange shook her head but inside was secretly happy to see the old Jakob back.

The meals were served and Henri ordered fine French Sauternes and Chardonnays for Solange and Yolanda and two aged Chateau Nerf du Pape for himself and Jakob.

It was around nine when Solange announced that they should call it an evening as she and Jakob needed to depart for the airport early next morning.

Henri spoke."We will have a nightcap at the house. Jakob, I have some fine brandy."

They exited the restaurant and waited in the cooling evening air while the valet fetched their car.

They rode back to the mansion in good spirits.

Chapter 86

The morning arrived quickly. As Jakob and Solange were tidying up and packing away their personal items into the suitcases, there was a light knocking at the door.

Jakob went and opened the door to find Yolanda standing there dressed in a long bathrobe.

"I have prepared some coffee and a light breakfast for you. Come and join us. We are out on the patio."

Fifteen minutes later, after they had completed the last of their packing, Solange and Jakob joined Yolanda and Henri on the patio. The sun was rising and cast golden shafts of light across the lawns and through the gardens. Colored orchards shimmered as the light breeze danced across them. The scent from the frangipani blossoms carried through the air and every so often perfumed the patio. It was a tranquil scene.

Jakob was invigorated and relaxed. He realized the impact that the other medications had caused.

They all sat and made small talk as they drank the Colombian coffee and munched on the toast dripping melted butter and coated with Yolanda's fine homemade marmalade that she made from the proliferate orange trees on the property.

While they were finishing their breakfast the front doorbell chimed. Henri went to the door and greeted the limousine driver.

"Mr. and Mrs. Klassen will be ready in a few minutes. Come with me. Their baggage is in our guesthouse."

Henri led the tall Hispanic driver to take the bags and load them into the limousine.

After the bags were loaded, Solange and Jakob thanked Yolanda and Henri and walked to the waiting car.

"Good morning. My name is Ramón and I am pleased to assist you this morning."

Solange eyed the tall dark skinned driver. She was embarrassed at her thoughts so early in the morning. She wondered what was happening with her.

Ramón realized Solange's mannerisms were those of a woman on the prowl. He grinned slightly when he followed her eyes and they dropped to examine his crotch. He turned in order to show his tight buttocks. Solange had a full appreciation of the view.

"Damn. I wonder what Yolanda put in that coffee. I am not like this. Good God. I am not a lusty woman. I haven't felt like this since I was eighteen. What is wrong with me." She silently thought to herself.

Jakob had seen the furtive glances Solange had taken. He smiled. "This trip could be fun," he thought.

The drive to the airport was slow. The early morning traffic of Miami was snarled and they made little progress through the congestion.

Ramón spoke. "I can take you another way. It is longer but it will be faster. I promise you that. It will cost a little more but you will be at the airport with plenty of time to check in for your flight and relax before your flight leaves."

Jakob agreed and instructed Ramón to take the alternative route.

They wound through side roads and passed through fields until they arrived at a road that lead around the perimeter of the airport to the main terminal entrance.

Ramón turned to Jakob. "Which airline are you flying with?"

"We are taking the Eastern Airlines flight to New York and then connecting with Trans-Canada Airlines through to Toronto, Canada."

The airport was not busy and Ramón eased the limousine to the curb in front of the sliding glass doors that opened to the entrance to Eastern Airlines.

Ramón jumped from his seat and went to the trunk to remove their baggage. A skycap arrived at the side of the car and quickly loaded the bags onto a cart and stood waiting for Solange and Jakob.

Jakob exited the limousine and handed Ramón some bills and thanked him. He advised the sky hop of the flight information and they all proceeded to the counter to check in for the flight.

Solange and Jakob were surprised to find a group of smartly dressed Eastern Airlines employees at the counter handing gift bags to the passengers. Jakob approached them and asked what the situation was about.

"Sir welcome. You are one of the lucky passengers to be n our first inaugural jet light to New York. Today we are introducing the advanced Douglas DC-8 jetliner service. You will enjoy a fast and smooth trip to New York.

These gift bags are souvenirs of the occasion."

Jakob was thrilled. He had heard of these jets and had often wondered what it would be like to travel on one.

The staff at the counter checked the tickets and provided boarding passes. With the formalities over Jakob and Solange sat quietly in the lounge with the other passengers. There was an air of excitement amongst those waiting.

Jakob walked across and looked from the glass window out onto the tarmac at the DC-8 which sat parked back from the terminal. A set of stairs were attached to a door at the front of the plane.

The plane was painted in the white and sea green colors of Eastern Airlines. The company logo was prominent on the side of the aircraft fuselage.

As Jakob stood marveling at the craft, he observed who he believed to be the pilot and others walking around the plane and inspecting various areas. The pilot was pointing to certain parts and speaking with others.

Jakob felt excited. Suddenly this trip was becoming a positive adventure.

A loudspeaker crackled and a woman's voice announced that Eastern Airlines flight number six to New York was boarding and asked passengers to proceed to the passageway leading down to the tarmac for the short walk to the plane.

Jakob returned and took Solange by the arm to guide her. They descended the stairs and walked over to the plane. Jakob was amazed at the size of the aircraft.

Upon climbing the stairs and entering the plane, the Captain stood with several other staff handing out replica DC-8 lapel pins as mementos of the inaugural flight.

Jakob and Solange settled into their first class seats and sat drinking champagne served by the stewardesses dressed in their pale blue uniforms and pillbox hats.

When all passengers were aboard and seated, the Captain announced details of the two and a half hour trip to New York.

Jakob listened intently to the sound as the jet turbines were stated. Within minutes the plane started a turn and rolled bouncily from the apron out to the main runway where it turned and stopped. Finally the jets screamed and Jakob felt the immense pressure as the plane accelerated down the runway. There was a thump as the aircraft lifted its nose into the air, followed by a grinding sound as the landing gear was retracted. Jakob watched from the small porthole window as the ground shrunk and the plane punched through a layer of cloud to emerge into a sunny blue sky.

He reached over and squeezed Solange's hand. He was relaxed and happy.

Throughout the flight they received constant service from the stewardesses offering food and drinks.

Half an hour before the flight was due in New York, the Captain announced their arrival information. The drink glasses and plates were removed and the stewardesses handed out candy to help with the pressure the passengers may experience during descent into the airport.

Jakob listened to the different sounds as the aircraft descended. The different whine of the jet turbines as they slowed and the grinding followed by a heavy thump as the wheels were lowered for landing. Eventually a quietness happened as the jet was powered back for the last few moments of glide descent, followed by a bang and a jerk as they touched the surface. The jets screamed as the reverse thrusters were engaged. Jakob and Solange were pulled forward in their seats as the plane braked heavily.

Slowly the plane turned and moved toward the terminal. There was a whine as each turbine was shutdown.

The first class stewardess arrived at Jakob and Solange's seats carrying their lightweight jackets.

Jakob stood and stretched before reaching to assist Solange. Together they gathered the few items they had taken on board with them and walked up the narrow isle to leave the plane. The Captain stood at the cockpit door and thanked each passenger.

In the terminal, Jakob inquired where the Trans-Canada Air Lines flight would leave from. After receiving the information they proceeded to find the counter and presented their papers to the uniformed girls. After checking their papers they were escorted into a private lounge to wait until the departure.

Solange left to visit the private powder room to freshen up.

Jakob was becoming bored. The wait was three hours. He decided to take a walk around inside the airport to pass the time.

He returned after a couple of hours and found Solange engaged in conversation with a group of women. She saw Jakob enter and raised her hand to beckon him to join them.

"Jakob these women are missionaries and are returning from work in the Caribbean. We have been talking about Aruba and the different Islands."

"It is my pleasure to meet you all. Are you all from Canada?"

"Yes. We are from the Montreal area. We are excited to return. We have been gone for over one year and are eager to see friends and families."

As they made small talk an announcement was made to prepare to board the flight.

Again they walked down a passageway and onto the tarmac to cross over to a Lockheed Constellation painted brightly in the colors of Trans-Canada Air Lines.

Jakob felt deflated after having just travelled on the latest passenger jet. He laughed aloud when he realized that the trip to Toronto was short and he would be happy as long as he and Solange arrived safely at their destination.

As he walked by the nose of the Constellation, Jakob was amazed at the difference between the sleek DC-8 and this plane. It seemed old and tired. He and Solange climbed the stairway and were greeted by the friendly cabin crew and taken to their seats.

After some delay, the doors were closed and there was a whine and rumble as the each of the huge engines were fired. As each engine started, clouds of blue-grey smoke flooded from the engine cowls.

The plane sat with all four engines running awaiting clearance to taxi to the runway. A loud and steady drone and hum of the engines filled the cabin.

Jakob sat back into his seat and stared to drift into a sleep, lulled by the constant hum of the engines. When he awoke they were high in the air on well on their 3 hour trip to Toronto, Ontario.

Chapter 87

Florencia, Caquetá Province, Columbia.

The rainy season had arrived in Caquetá, Columbia. Hidden in the jungle not far from Florencia was one of the largest clandestine marijuana and drug labs in Colombia.

Men heavily armed with FN FLA and Galil automatic rifles surrounded the drug lab and acted as guards for the mob who ran the operation. The rifles were old and cheaply available. These men were ruthless. It did not matter to them if punishment was to be inflicted on a brother or other family member. Their allegiance was to the boss who selected them and paid them well to protect the mob's interests from other drug gangs in the jungle.

Sitting hidden and disguised on the banks of the Yari River, the drug lab was a sad, lonely and evil place. Men from the lab would transport drugs down the river in their pirogues, the long narrow wooden boats often carved from the huge fallen trees. Often the weight of the bales of marijuana would perilously sink the small craft down in the water until the sides of the narrow craft were almost level and awash with the surface of the river water.

Many of the men were peasant farmers who had been stripped of their dignity, their farm animals taken and often they had been displaced from their farms. A social class had developed between the peasant farmers. Each would silently protect the other.

When shipments were too large to take by boat, the men were coerced to transport the drugs by mule, an often dangerous task where they were frequently ambushed by rival gangs.

On their return trips the men would often transport barrels of ether, fuel and other chemicals used in processing the cocaine. It was a new and an extremely profitable venture for the mob.

A long, dusty and winding dirt road, the width of a track for donkeys wound out to the road to the town. The locals who lived on farms and in the barrio feared the men from the camp. Unless selling produce or a woman to the men, they stayed away.

The jungle growth was thick and hostile. During the day the temperatures would soar and at night drop to extreme cold. The canopy of the tall trees shielded the camp from the blazing sun.

Near the river there was a structure that was built without any enclosed walls and a rusting corrugated iron roof. Inside some men labored packing the marijuana into the brown hessian sacks. Wisps of smoke drifted from a chimney that had been built over the rough stone fire pit that was used to heat the vats of chemicals used in the production of the cocaine. On the ground outside, exhausted men lay resting in the dirt while smoking and drinking.

Occasionally a fight would break out and all the workers would gather and place bets on the likely winner. It was a place of violence and death. There was no loyalty between anyone. No one asked when someone disappeared without explanation.

Off to the right-hand side of the camp and close to the riverbank a barbed wire enclosure contained several wooden huts built on stilts to protect them from the river when it swelled from flooding during the rainy season and also to keep out unwanted animals and reptiles.

The wooden huts were built of roughly hewn lumber. At night they were cold and dark. During the day they baked. Each hut had an entryway without a door and a window opening through which countless stinging insects and flies would swarm in. The floors were made of wide and filthy wooden boards. Outside each hut there was a barrel that was used to catch rain water which was used for bathing and after boiling for drinking. Mosquito larvae dotted the water and wriggled actively in the water.

Juan hated the place and all the men who either worked or guarded the camp. He had long given up any thoughts of escape. Any attempt would be met with a fierce pursuit by the guards or an encounter with an anaconda, or other jungle beast. He had resigned himself to this pitiful life.

It was here that Juan had found himself after being kidnapped at sea.

The years had not been kind to him. He was still physically strong but his spirit was almost broken.

Juan sprawled on the bed as daylight faded. The bed consisted of boards lashed together and sitting on some large rocks from the riverbed to keep it off the floor. The mattress was two large sacks stitched together and filled with old clothing and rags.

He took the enamel bowel that had been served to him as the evening meal. A plate of nondescript beans and rice with pork fat that had been prepared by the young Columbian girls who lived in the huts at the entrance to the camp. Juan wondered who they were and what relationship they had with the men. He guessed they were no more than eighteen years old.

He ate the sticky and glutinous meal and relaxed back onto the bed. He laid thinking of how he had ended up in this situation.

Chapter 88

Juan lit one of the poor quality cigarettes he had been able to bribe from one of the peasant farmers. His mind drifted back to the events that lead to his capture and enslavement.

He remembered the late afternoon he had left from Savaneta to fish. It had started to darken as the sun started to slip below the horizon in the west. Juan motored further out as the wahoo were running and after a poor week of fishing, his luck had changed. He wished to land a catch large enough to sell to the restaurants. He motored south beyond the refinery in San Nicolaas. The further south he went the higher the ocean swell became. As his small boat crested the waves and dropped down into their valley with a resounding crash, he decided to head back to Savaneta. He had a good catch of fish and was content.

As he continued his trip back, the ocean calmed. The sun had set and it was twilight. Early darkness was arriving. Hoping for more fish in the now calm waters he decided to head out from shore a little.

His little boat rolled with the motion of the waves. Juan was soon disappointed as there was no action. He started to turn toward the direction of Savaneta when he heard the deep pounding throb of heavy diesel engines. He could smell the diesel exhaust fumes drifting over the water. Juan gingerly stood and peered across the undulating sea. There some eight hundred yards away on his port side and in darkness was a US Coast Guard ship. Juan sighed. He had been stopped many times by both the US Coast Guard and the Dutch patrols and challenged for his papers. Juan assumed it would be another routine stop.

Juan was curious. Instead of a small boat being lowered to transport sailors to his fishing boat, there was no activity on deck. Juan watched the US Coast Guard ship in curiosity and within minutes the ship became bathed in lights.

He sat and observed the strange actions of the ship. After a while a powerful searchlight near the bridge shone out onto the water. Juan followed its beam. He noticed a small boat caught in the light that was heading out from Barcadera. Juan had heard rumors of smuggling but did not expect to see a ship from the US Coast Guard involved.

The small craft from the shore was approaching fast and close to him. He decided to immediately start back to shore and dock at the small jetty the local fishermen used. He gunned the motor and spun his boat toward the shore. As he did so, he noticed a long shallow boat tendered to the side of the Coast Guard boat. On the ship, some sailors stood smoking and laughing at the railing. They had a small crane that was off loading bales into the shallow boat from the deck. Suddenly there were shouts. Men were pointing in the direction of Juan. A crew member raised a rifle started firing. Another crew member ran to him and pushed the rifle away. Within minutes the small boat that was heading out from the shore raced to Juan's boat. Juan knew it would be impossible to escape and outrun the high powered craft.

The boat closed in on Juan and soon some men jumped into his boat. He was shocked and confused as he recognized them.

"We should kill you now. You have already seen too much. You know who we are. We cannot let you return to shore. You will betray us."

Juan attempted to object and plead.

"I will say nothing. Let me go. I saw nothing. You have my word."

As he bargained with the men, another man jumped in to join them. Juan was shocked. It was Alejandro.

"Alejandro. You too? Why? You have a good job and money. We have a nice family. I have helped you and Miguel."

"Leave Miguel out of this. That stupid idiot knows nothing. He thinks that the restaurants and that Jakob Klassen will make him rich and save him. He is too stupid to see what money we can make by working with the Venezuelans and the Italians on the island."

The local men watched on in silence.

"Alejandro we cannot let him return. He will tell the authorities. All of our lives will be in danger. The Italians will kill us all. We must kill him and dispose of his body here."

Juan fixed Alejandro with a stare. Alejandro turned away.

"No we will not kill him. I have another idea. You men stay here with him while I go across to the others who are offloading our goods."

Alejandro returned to the boat they had arrived in. The man at the helm increased the speed of the motor and they raced across to the Coast Guard ship.

Juan watched as Alejandro climbed aboard and entered into an animated discussion with the men. His hands waved erratically in the air and Juan heard the occasional shout.

Thirty minutes passed before Alejandro returned.

"We have a plan. The Colombians will take Juan back with them. He will be a prisoner and forced to work in one of the processing operations. They promised me he will never escape or be hurt."

The men gruffly pulled Juan into their boat and sped across to where the unloading was taking place.

Alejandro sat on the stern of Juan's boat and pondered the next move.

"We need to make this seem like an accident. Bring me an axe and lots of blood from the fish. We will hack a hole in the bow of this boat and spread blood around to make it seem like a shark attacked and Juan was lost during the struggle."

The two Colombians returned with an axe and smashed the bow open. Soon the little boat was taking on water and slipped beneath the surface. The jagged edges of the hole imitated the damage that they believed would happen from a shark attack.

"Say good bye to your friend, Alejandro. You will never see him again."

As they approached the US Coast Guard ship, Juan noticed another launch that had been hidden from his view by the hull of the ship. It was a high powered luxury boat. There was no visible registration.

As Juan watched and tried to absorb the action, one of the Colombians crept from behind and clubbed him. Juan lost consciousness and slumped down into the bottom of the boat. The Colombian called his partner and together they off loaded Juan onto the high powered launch for the quick trip back to Colombia.

Hours passed until Juan awoke. He had been drugged and blindfolded. He was tossed and thrown around in the open tray of an old pickup truck.

They drove through the night and finally ended up in a small village of six adobes.

Juan was roughly pulled from the truck and thrown into one of the little houses.

He listened as instructions were loudly shouted to others who were now charged with guarding him.

The Spanish was poor and he did not recognize the dialect. He assumed they must be inland and somewhere south.

Chapter 89

Juan heard the distant rumble of thunder. He eased himself off the bed and went to sit in the open doorway. He knew a storm was coming. After having lived in the desert conditions of Aruba, he loved to watch the magnificence of a storm.

The thunder was weak but distinct. Juan decided he should relieve himself before the storm broke. He called to the guards and a young man approached him. Juan asked permission to be taken to the area where open holes had been dug and boards sunk into the mud to place ones feet on while squatting.

"I take you. No trouble or I will shoot you. I don't care if I have to shoot you in the back. I don't like you. You are strange. You are not one of us. You look old and strange. I hope the bosses let me kill you. I will ask them for that honor."

Juan shrugged. There was no response to the hatred this guard had.

Together they walked the short distance behind the huts. Mounds of dirt were piled in the area where the holes had been dug. As they got closer Juan almost retched at the overpowering foul smell of the raw and rotting feces. The ground was crawling with beetles and huge shiny flies swarmed the open holes. There were so many flies that they sounded like the buzzing of a small motor.

Juan had heard rumors from the other men that those who disobeyed or were deemed no longer useful were buried alive in these pits.

Juan was eager to be done and within minutes they returned to his hut. Tonight was different. For the first time, the guard handcuffed Juan and pushed him through the door. Juan stumbled and fell. The young guard laughed and walked off calling some obscenities out to his mates.

As he lay face down on the muddy floor he heard footsteps coming up the boards that served as stairs. A strong hand reached down and pushed Juan over onto his back. It was one of the bosses.

"I don't know what you have done or said to that guard. His hate of you is enormous. I fear he will kill you given the slightest reason. Here let me take off those cuffs. You are no risk."

Juan thanked him.

The boss stood in silence and stared at Juan for the longest time without saying a word. He finally turned and idled off in the direction of the larger huts where the bosses lived.

Juan returned to his position in the doorway. The thunder was louder and closer. He had not heard such an intense thunder storm in the time he had been at the camp. The thunder clapped with such ferocity that Juan felt the hut shake and vibrate. Intense flashes of lightning danced across the thick foliage of the tall trees casting eerie shadows and creating ghostly images. A wind started to blow and increased in strength. Within minutes huge raindrops pelted down. The rain was so intense that Juan could no longer see the neighboring huts. He had never experienced a storm like this before.

Water puddles formed on the ground and within minutes streams of muddy water flowed on the pathways from the huts.

As Juan watched, there was an immense clap of thunder and the sky was illuminated with lightning for what seemed minutes. There was a roaring crack as the lightning struck a huge tree on the riverbank near the drug processing lab. The tree split and fell. The crown of the tree landed in the river and the huge trunk blocked the path that they had built down to the water.

The rain was constant and Juan found himself being lulled and comforted by its sound hammering down on the tin roof of his hut.

He pulled himself onto his feet and crashed back onto his bed listening to the rain and dreaming of an escape until he fell into a deep sleep.

When morning arrived the ground was soaked. Thick mud covered the paths. The skies remained a dark leaden grey and already the humidity was high.

Juan washed his face and upper body with water from the overflowing rain bucket outside his door. He grinned when he observed that most of the mosquito larva had been washed out with last night's rains. He felt invigorated.

After he washed he dragged an old chair outside and sat waiting for the guard to bring the breakfast meal. On most mornings the meal was white rice, red beans, avocado and sometimes and egg. A tin mug of bitter coffee accompanied the meal.

A voice called to him.

"Buenas dias, Senor Juan. Desayuno"

Juan looked to see one of the older guards walking toward him with an old white enamel plate containing the heaped rice and beans.

The guard handed the plate to Juan and then surreptitiously looked around. Satisfied that no one was watching the guard reached into his pocket and withdrew something small wrapped in brown paper. He slid it onto Juan's plate.

Before leaving the guard again looked around and then gave Juan three roughly rolled cigarettes, before quickly walking off to join the other guards for their breakfast.

Juan went into his hut with his breakfast and sat on the edge of his bed. He then unwrapped the brown paper package. Juan was ecstatic. It contained fried pork belly.

It had been weeks since Juan had eaten meat other than the tough and scrawny chicken dishes.

As he ate his breakfast slowly, he wondered about this guard. He had never spoken to him other than to ask permission for using the toilets or requesting some required item. Juan found it interesting that there appeared to be a rapport between them.

He wondered whether he could develop that into a stronger relationship. Maybe the guard would tell him where he was being kept.

There was something about the man that Juan liked and respected. He was unlike the others.

Chapter 90

Aboard US Coast Guard Clipper USCG Pearl

For the past two weeks strong easterly winds and squalls had lashed the Caribbean Sea during the daylight hours. The *USCG Pearl* had rolled and bounced like a cork. Even the most seasoned of the men experienced some form of seasickness. The men were tired and impatient that their extended patrol would end.

Lt. Slate stood with his confidante, Hector Ramirez on the bridge. For them, the trip had proven to be extremely profitable.

The afternoon was growing late and already the sun was setting.

"Hector I believe we will have more good fortune this evening. I received a radio message from our friends in Venezuela. It seems there is going to be some interesting Colombian activity tonight. I want you to staff the bridge with our friends in this venture. Ensure we have others who are loyal to us on the deck to man the winches."

"Yes Jeremiah. I will hand pick the best men. Do you know when we will encounter the shipments?"

"No. The message stated that they are sailing very near the coast and not out in the open sea. We will need to launch a couple of zodiacs and patrol near the shore. I want you to go on one of the zodiacs. Take Johnson with you. It would not trouble me if he was to have an accident."

Hector laughed.

"You just don't like him. I think he represents the authority and values that you hated at the academy. I suggest you don't let those feelings cloud your judgment."

"He has seen too much. Already he is asking why we are off loading the bales of marijuana and not transporting them to port. He has also challenged my decision to not arrest the men in the boats we apprehend. He is trouble. Find a way to neutralize him, even if that means death. It will either be his fate or possibly ours if he files a report on our return."

"Jeremiah I suggest we request an early return to our home port. Make a claim of a mechanical problem. We can certainly make one happen. To proceed and kill Johnson is madness. You may have suspicions but we do not have any evidence he will report the irregularities of this patrol. Maybe we should try to recruit him to join us. It is amazing what people will say or do for money."

"Hector it took months for us to assemble a crew who would be complicit with our actions during these patrols. I am not prepared to sacrifice the years I have put into developing this business. You must select some men with similar feelings about Johnson and deal with him. I will report the unfortunate incident and request we be granted an immediate return to base."

"I will go and select a crew."

"Hector, after I report the mechanical failure I will also ask approval for a short stop in Venezuela to have the damage assessed. We will meet our friends and handle some financial business. This plan will work out."

Hector left the bridge and descended below deck to assemble the men for the intercept. He stopped at Johnson's cabin and knocked. The door swung open and Johnson stood facing him.

Hector looked past him and noticed papers and books strewn across a table. He observed what appeared to be a map that partially covered a set of headphones, but wasn't sure.

Johnson was impatient.

"What is it you want?"

"I have orders. You are ordered to accompany the small vessel intercept team this evening. We have a report of a large shipment. Lt. Slate requests you be part of tonight's mission. He wants someone experienced and knowledgeable to ensure the process is conducted correctly."

Johnson scowled. "That's very thoughtful of him. What time is the team assembling?"

"We will meet on the stern deck in thirty minutes. With the winds and rougher seas I suggest you dress in heavy clothing. We will be operating very close near the shore. The conditions will be rough."

Johnson's anger at the interruption was apparent.

"Why tonight of all nights? I am deep in study."

"I do not make the decisions or orders. If you have any complaint I recommend you go to the bridge and speak directly with Lt. Slate. He is the one in charge."

Hector backed away from the door but attempted to steal another look into the cabin and the headphones he thought he had seen. Johnson slammed the door shut.

Hector returned to the bridge and relayed to Lt. Slate what had transpired and his suspicion of the headphones.

Slate was furious.

"I told you that I was wary of him. Make sure he does not return tonight. I will have his cabin searched when you are gone."

Hector checked his watch and went about assembling the crew. Thirty minutes passed and they all stood at the fantail of the ship.

Two zodiacs were hoisted over the railings and down to the surface of the choppy sea. The men clambered down the rope ladder and jumped into the craft.

Hector checked his radio and received a crackled response. They motored away from the ship in the direction of the shore.

They were barely a few hundred yards from the ship when the radio crackled again.

"Party one. This is mother hen. Action to your south. A half mile from you. Prepare to fish."

Hector laughed at the message. He always enjoyed the way they coded the messages. He looked across to the other zodiac and waved to them to join in the intercept.

They sped south after nearing the shore. The evening sky was now dark. Hector ordered the zodiacs to stop and idle. He scanned the water for a sign of the boats transporting the drugs. On the horizon, about 1 mile away, he spotted three small open fishing boats. He signaled the other zodiac and together they raced across the rolling water to the fishing boats. As they approached, Hector ordered the powerful searchlights activated and trained on their prey.

One of the fishing boats started to turn and accelerate away. Hector gave the order. One of the men took the automatic rifle and fired a volley into the hull of the fleeing boat. Smoke erupted from the vessel followed by a sheet of yellow flame. The fuel tanks had been hit. There were shouts and panic as men jumped from the burning boat.

Johnson turned and commanded Hector to rescue the men. Hector decided this was his chance. He directed the zodiac to the men in the water near the flaming craft. Johnson lay on his stomach across the side of the zodiac and tried to reach one of the men. It was too late. An immense explosion blew the fishing boat to pieces and the men were engulfed in the flames as the petrol spread across the water.

Hector's zodiac rocked back from the explosion. His mood grew darker. He took control and raced to the remaining boats. He ordered his men to train their weapons on the crews and in Spanish ordered them to take the tow lines for the trip back to the USCG Pearl.

The terrified men on the fishing boats complied.

Hector looked across at Johnson. He was watching and mentally recording every move. Hector wondered how he could complete his task and kill Johnson. It seemed hopeless. He hoped that Slate would understand. Besides, there would be other occasions.

They slowly towed their captives to the ship. Some of Hector's men jumped into the fishing boats and forcibly pushed the crew out and onto the rope ladder for the climb to the deck.

When the men were onboard they were ordered to sit on the deck while Hector questioned them in Spanish. Slate joined them and listened to the questioning and interpretation. He felt sorry for these men. They were poor fishermen who struggled for a daily living. The lure of making quick trip for an amount of money they could never earn in a month was too tempting. These men were uneducated and poor. Many had left wives and family inland on poor farms in an effort to find work and earn enough to protect them.

While he had the authority to arrest them, Slate decided not to. He would make this the final intercept for this trip and deliver the cargo in return for the payoff.

Slate returned to the bridge followed by Hector.

"Hector, we are no better than those men. Find someone Spanish speaking to go to them and get them some food and drink. I will not arrest them. We will load up the bales and let them go."

Hector nodded. He left to find a crew member to help the smugglers and then went to supervise the loading of the bales on to USCG Pearl with the small cranes on the forward deck.

An hour passed and Slate assembled the fishermen. Hector interpreted for him.

"You are free now. Go back to your port. You cannot tell others of this event. We will know and your lives will be in danger. We have many friends in this business."

The men looked dejected and beaten. One turned to Slate and pleaded in broken English.

"We cannot go back. They kill us. We failed. Please, please take us to America."

Slate ordered them removed by force. His thugs stood at the railing and grabbed each fisherman and threw them off the ship and into the dark waters below.

Chapter 91

Slate was pleased with the night's haul. Again they found cocaine amongst the bales. Tonight would yield a healthy profit.

He was worried about Johnson. Hector had been right. The raid on Johnson's cabin revealed a radio transmitter and a book of frequencies. Slate was now convinced he was sent to spy on them.

He made a decision and summoned Hector to his cabin.

"Hector we need to get rid of Johnson. I have a plan I would like to discuss with you."

Hector sat across the desk from Slate. He took a cigar from the box on the desk and settled back to hear the plan.

""I will have the ship's medics declare that we have a deadly virus outbreak that has infected several of the crew. I will report it as an emergency and advise we are going to dock in Venezuela for assistance. I will have the men quarantined and our friends in the medics will play up this 'outbreak' so all on board will believe it. Only you, the medics and I will know the truth. When we dock in Venezuela our business partners can arrange Johnson's disappearance. I will report it. We will then leave Venezuela and proceed over to Aruba. We will wait off shore again in the area out from Barcadera. I will have our friends contact their people in Aruba and again we will offload our cargo onto their boats. We will not dock and we will stay far enough away from the shore so we do not have another situation like the one we did with that Aruban fisherman, Juan."

Hector sat quietly smoking the cigar and thinking about the plan.

"I think that will work. What will we do next?"

"It will be then that I report our mechanical distress and request permission to return."

Hector liked the idea.

"I have talked to our partners in Venezuela. They will assist. They love our method of supplying the drugs. We are stopping and raiding the products of the rival drug gangs in Colombia. They love it that they do not have to pay farmers to grow and pick the stuff and nor do they have to take the risk of shipping it. We are doing it all for them. The Colombian gangs don't know that we are not really acting as the US Coast Guard and seizing the drugs. They are so happy they are increasing the payments to us."

Slate and Hector sat laughing. Slate arose and took a bottle of dark rum from his cabinet. He sat two small glasses and poured the amber nectar into them.

Slate went to the locked cabinet on the wall next to his desk. He slid in the key and unlocked the hinged doors. He removed the radio that they used to contact the mob in Venezuela.

Slate transmitted a coded message and waited. Time passed with no response. He repeated the message several times. Finally a static filled response was received. Slate strained to make out the message. It was hopeless. He decided to try later when they were moving closer toward Venezuela.

Slate called for the radio operator.

An extremely young sailor appeared.

"Yes sir. You called."

"I need you to transmit the following message to the bases in both Puerto Rico and Florida. Advise them that we have an outbreak of what appears to be cholera like virus. Two crew members are in quarantine. We are going to request an emergency docking in Venezuela."

The young sailor took scribbled notes.

"Yes sir. I shall send it now. Are you requesting acknowledgment and approval?"

"Of course you dimwit."

The young sailor blushed and stumbled his way out of Slate's cabin.

Slate looked over to Hector.

"Where do they find them?"

He called for the ships navigator and requested he plot a course back to Caracas, Venezuela. He advised the navigator to calculate a speed that would see them dock in the mid morning.

He poured rum for Hector and himself and sat smiling.

"Now, it's time for me to recruit the cholera patients."

Slate called up to the bridge and provided the names of the men he wished to see immediately in his cabin.

Five minutes passed before there was a knocking at the cabin door. Slate opened the door and admitted two of his closest allies on the ship.

"You two have been selected for an easy trip. It seems you have contacted some evil and contagious disease. I am quarantining you both in the sick bay for the trip to Venezuela. I want you to stay out of sight. The crew will be told of your illness. In the meantime, enjoy yourselves. Here, take these bottles of rum with you. That's probably the only medicine you will need. "

The men laughed and stumbled off toward the sick bay.

Another knock on the cabin door and the young radio operator entered holding some papers.

"Here is your approval to alter course to Venezuela. You are requested to stay in contact and update on the men's illnesses. There is also a copy of the transmission to the Venezuelan authorities advising them of situation and requesting their assistance."

The young sailor stood waiting.

"Will there be anything else, sir?"

"No. That is all. Thank you."

When they were alone, Hector and Slate roared laughing.

Slate opened the cabinet and tried to radio his mob contacts in Venezuela again. This time he received an instant response.

"This is a message for Admiral Maduro. Advise him the US Coast Guard Pearl will be docking in Caracas tomorrow morning. Can you get him to contact us tonight?"

"Is this urgent? We will need to send someone to his home tonight."

"Yes. It is very important I speak with him tonight."

"I will contact Tomasso and tell him."

Slate and Hector stayed in the cabin and for the next hour smoked cigars and drank rum until it felt painless.

Hector plucked up the courage to ask Slate what his plan was.

"Hector, we know that Johnson is a problem. I am going to request a meeting with Admiral Maduro. Johnson will not suspect anything. We will arrange for the Admiral to have Johnson disappear. Afterwards we will search for Johnson before leaving to rendezvous with our Aruba contacts and offload some of this cargo. With that accomplished we will then head for home port. We will still have roughly half of the drugs we intercepted during the trip. No one will be suspicious."

They sat talking and playing a card game when the PYE radio burst into life.

Slate recognized the Admiral's voice.

"Good evening Admiral. Tomorrow we will dock in Caracas. I need your assistance. We have a possible problem here. Can you arrange a dinner meeting? I will attend and bring our problem with me."

Silence ensued.

"Will we need the help of the Palmeros for this?"

"No not for the dinner. Maybe later."

"I will arrange a private dinner at the El Matador. I will meet you at the dock at six tomorrow evening. Tomasso will be my driver. I will see you then. For your sake this had better be very important. I will advise the others immediately of this."

"Trust me Admiral, if you want your balls to be safe you will arrange this."

Slate clicked off the radio and again he and Hector convulsed in laughter.

"Those idiots. They have made us wealthy and have no idea what we have planned for them."

Hector attempted to stand but the effect of the rum and the ship's roll contributed to the massive crash he took on the cabin floor. Slate found this even funnier than their earlier jokes and deceptions.

Slate helped Hector to his feet and clumsily escorted him to his sleeping quarters.

Chapter 92

As daylight broke, the coastline of Venezuela was visible. The officer on the bridge called for Lt. Slate to join him.

After the night of drinking, Slate wearily pulled himself together and ambled up to the bridge where he was apprised of their progress and the estimated time for the docking in La Guaira, the main port for Caracas.

Slate looked at the report. He was annoyed. They were arriving at the port too early.

"Slow the ship. We do not have permission to dock until ten this morning. At this speed we will be there at eight. The pilot boat will not be available to us."

The officer spoke to the navigator and between them they calculated a new cruising speed.

Slate's head thumped from the previous nights session of drinking and smoking. He felt like hell.

"I am going back to my cabin. Call me when we are thirty minutes from docking. I am feeling a little ill."

The officer on watch spun toward him.

"Sir, I hope you have not contracted the illness that has quarantined those fellow sailors. Shall I arrange for the ship's doctor to visit?"

"No. I am just over tired. I will be glad when this mission is over and we return to Florida."

Back in his cabin, Slate threw up the contents of last evenings drinking. His face was flush and his head spinning. He had never had a hangover like this one. He considered that maybe he was sick.

Within minutes he fell back into a deep sleep. Even the bitter acidic taste of the vomit that lingered in his mouth was not enough to prevent him from slipping into that sleep.

Hours passed. There was an urgent knocking at the cabin door. Slate heaved himself off the bed and across to the door. To his surprise he found Johnson standing there.

"Lieutenant, I have been looking for Hector Ramirez. He is nowhere to be found. I was wondering if he was with you."

"No. Last night when we completed our duties he did join me for drinks here in my cabin. He left to return to his quarters. Have you checked the sick bay?"

"Yes. No one has seen him this morning. We are scheduled to dock in forty five minutes. I need him on the bridge."

"I will summon some men to do a complete search. I will join you on the bridge shortly."

Slate cursed. Why had Johnson gone looking for Ramirez? He called the Chief Petty Officer.

"I need a full search of the ship. It seems that Officer Hector Ramirez has not reported to the bridge this morning. Some men have looked for him but it was not an organized search. Please have this done immediately as we are about to be boarded by the pilots in order to proceed through the harbor and dock."

The Chief Petty Officer grinned and nodded.

"Yes sir. The search will start immediately."

Johnson had watched the whole interchange with a passive look on his face.

"There is nothing we can achieve here in my cabin. Let's go to the bridge where we can monitor the situation and our progress into port."

Johnson spoke to several crew members on the bridge. He was asking when Hector Ramirez was last on the bridge and in what condition he had been. He took notes. Slate was concerned. He took some relief knowing what was planned for Johnson that night.

The door to the bridge flew open as the wind caught it and sucked it wide open. Hector Ramirez walked in. He was covered in a grey brown dust.

Slate eyed him.

"Where have you been? There is a party searching for you."

"I was completing a count of the drugs we have confiscated. We will need to advise our base prior to returning to Florida. They will have the appropriate departments to take the drugs."

Johnson was confused. He asked to see the manifest.

"I will relay this information to our home base. There are other matters I need to communicate with them that relate to my next assignment. I don't believe I will be sailing on the *Pearl* again with you. There was a communiqué that arrived last evening. It seems I will be posted to a base in Europe. That will be both interesting and a challenge. I am informed that there will be a promotion involved. I am looking forward to the change and away from the heat and strange patterns of the Caribbean."

Slate thought to himself of the plans that were about to unfold. Little did Johnson know of the events that would unfold that coming evening.

The ship slowly entered into the shipping lane and the buildings that dotted the shore and dock area became visible.

The white and black pilot boat motored toward them. Slate ordered the engines cut and a gangway dropped for the pilot to come aboard. He was surprised to see four men leave the launch and swing themselves onto the dangling ladder for the climb up onto the deck.

Slate requested Johnson to join him in greeting the pilots aboard and descended the metal ladder onto the main deck.

He stood at the railing and watched the four men as they stepped on deck.

"Good morning Lieutenant. You are arriving right on time. We will take control at this point. These other men are observers and in training. I will need to have you with me at all times as we dock. Today we must use extreme caution. There is a ship containing explosives and dangerous materials. We will be docking immediately behind the ship. Until the ship is secured we will take full control. Is that acceptable?"

"It seems we have no choice."

"You do have a choice. If that is unacceptable, we will leave and order you away from the harbor."

Slate bristled. He hated to be spoken to by anyone displaying an authority higher than his.

"I guess we have no alternative."

An uneasy silence enveloped the men who stood grouped together. They climbed to the bridge. Slate issued the order to the helmsman and engineer to take commands from the pilot.

Slowly the ship berthed alongside an old wharf. Slate studied the strange ship docked in front of them. Cranes were busy swinging back and forth unloading the cargo. He was surprised to see military vehicles on cradles being swung from the forward hold and out onto the pier. Soldiers dressed in fatigues surrounded the vehicles as they were released from their sling and poured gasoline from a parked tanker truck. Slate understood they had docked in a secure area behind a munitions ship.

Johnson was also watching intently and noting down information as he observed the crane unloading different trucks, jeeps and a couple of tanks.

The pilot stood back and returned the control of the ship to Slate.

"I ask you to order the engines shutdown. We are docked. You are to request the assistance of the port control before firing up your engines. You are familiar with La Guairá port. Is there anything further we can assist you with? If not we will leave. I will need the following papers completed by you."

Slate took the forms and scanned them. They were the customary customs forms, a declaration of dangerous cargo if any, a description of on board general cargo, whether the ship would require fuelling, a head count of the crew and a listing of names, an estimated date of departure and other standard questions.

As they were standing and completing formalities, Slate noticed the same military attaché from the US Embassy drive down the dock and stop below the side of the ship.

The attaché left the jeep and climbed the gangway. Slate went to greet him.

"Welcome back. I wasn't expecting any visits from the Embassy today. Why have you come?"

"I was dispatched to see what assistance is required with the sick men. A Naval doctor will be joining us shortly."

Slate cursed under his breath. He didn't want or need this intrusion. He needed to think quickly and head off the deception that existed with the quarantined men and their fake illness.

"Let me have the ship's doctor brief us. I have not had the chance to speak with him this morning. I was preoccupied with the formalities of docking here again. We will need refueling and making arrangements to have the men removed from the ship for hospitalization or air transported to a base medical facility.

Would you care for one of our notorious coffee while we wait for the doctor? I will have him meet with us in the mess."

The attaché remembered the previous time he had attempted to drink the sludge that passed for coffee.

"No thank you but if you have a genuine American cola I would enjoy that. We have only been getting local product at the Embassy. It is not the best."

"Come and we will get you some."

They strode off to the mess. The attaché asked about the mission. He was particularly interested to learn about the intercepts and the quantity of drugs they had confiscated.

Slate was careful and did not disclose too much. He deflected the conversation and focused on other issues. He told the attaché of how the smugglers were now heavily armed with more sophisticated weapons and the cautionary steps they needed to take during any action to apprehend them. The attaché became totally engrossed in the stories Slate disclosed.

"I cannot tell you why, but there seems to be particular interest in your ship. There were some secret communications received in code at the Embassy. My security clearance did not permit to read these. It is strange that a regular Coast Guard vessel would be the subject of these bulletins. Do you have any ideas?"

Slate's curiosity was piqued. He shrugged. Beneath his controlled appearance he was starting a mild panic.

"I have no idea. We are just a normal Coast Guard clipper on a standard patrol. We have reported a large number of successful seizures. I am sure HQ is just ensuring we are able to safely return to base without being stopped or hijacked by certain criminal elements. Thanks for letting me know of those bulletins."

"My pleasure. I too found it a little strange."

The ship's doctor arrived. He looked from Slate to the attaché.

"How can I assist? I assume it is about those two cases we suspected as cholera outbreaks. I have had adequate time and testing to convince me those men do not have cholera. They had a watery diarrhea and other common symptoms. I had all the tests repeated. They do not have cholera. I suspect the tests that were performed were contaminated. This morning they have normal temperatures and display no symptoms of any illness. I suspect they were affected by some simple virus. It is not unusual for such viruses to be on our ships and be dormant. This is not the first time I have seen this."

Slate was relieved. He knew the doctor had fabricated the story for the attaché

"I am pleased to hear that. I guess you will be on your way back to base after you refuel here."

"I will request pilot assistance to depart in the morning. I will give the men time ashore tonight. They have been at sea for too long a period and a leave is overdue."

The attaché spoke. "Well then. If there is nothing more I can assist with I will return to the Embassy. You can contact me in the event you require any assistance. Good day gentlemen."

Slate smiled and shook the attaché's hand and watched as he descended to his jeep and drove away.

Chapter 93

Throughout the day, Slate completed mundane reports on the trip. He had phoned Tomasso and made arrangements for the evening. He sent a message to Johnson to join him.Johnson arrived at the cabin

"We have been invited to be guests of Admiral Maduro this evening. The Admiral is responsible for all naval operations here on this part of the coast. It is a real privilege to be invited to dine with him. His invitation is extended to you and Officer Ramirez. He is sending a car for us early in the evening. I suggest we dress in full uniform as it will be an official dinner."

"It will be interesting to meet Admiral Maduro. I have heard of him and his campaign against the drug smuggling from Venezuela to Curacao and Aruba. I look forward to this dinner. At what time are we scheduled to be available for the drive to the restaurant?"

"I suggest we be available at five. In the past we have always been picked up and taken for cocktails before going onto the dinner. I suspect this will be the same this evening."

When Johnson had left his cabin, Slate phoned Tomasso to lay out the evening plans. Tomasso chuckled. He advised

Slate that what he asked would be straight forward. He added a question that Slate had not anticipated.

"Should we off Johnson?"

"No. I suggest he remain talking with the Admiral. Ramirez and I will excuse ourselves on the pretext that we need to make some final arrangements before we sail in the morning. The Admiral must insist that Johnson stay on and will get him involved into deep conversation. Get the Admiral to suggest a visit to the patrol headquarters here. On the way have them kidnapped. Have a ransom demand sent to the Coast Guard offices in Washington. Let a week pass before making this demand. We will need time to get our goods off loaded in Aruba and complete our mission to Fort Myers. Do you see any faults with this plan?"

"No it is brilliant. Are you sure you don't want him to disappear? What will he do once he is released? He may have dangerous information that could jeopardize our operations."

"I will speak to Ramirez about this and let you know."

He hung up and reflected on the wisdom of killing Johnson. He could not decide. He called for Ramirez to join him.

Sitting in the privacy of his cabin, Slate discussed the idea with Ramirez.

"Jeremiah, we need to be very careful. There are a number of men here on this ship and many are aware of the unusual actions we have taken as US Coast Guard. I am concerned they will file reports and there may be investigations. If Johnson is killed then this will only cause the investigators to look deeper into the mission. I say we just allow the kidnapping. Besides we will make it look like it's the mob that was responsible. We will get our friends to start a rumor that it was done in retaliation for the actions of the Coast Guard and the Venezuelan Naval patrols. It will be easy to get that rumor started and into the local paper. We should be able to throw the investigators off the trail for weeks.

Besides, as we have agreed we will both be resigning the Coast Guard upon our return. By the time Johnson is found we will be civilians. I am looking forward to that. I cannot wait to get some enjoyment from the money we have amassed."

"Hector I have warned you before. Do not start to spend that money and draw attention to yourself. Remember that you are a retired officer with a modest pension and few savings. Give it time before you do anything that could alert others to an unusual lifestyle."

"I am going to speak with the Palermos and move to Venezuela. I find my life in America restricts me and I am tired of the people."

They finally decided that Johnson would live for the foreseeable future. Both of them agreed that they would discuss the situation again after the kidnapping and they knew more about the investigation and the likelihood of being implicated.

The afternoon wore on. Ramirez returned to his quarters to sleep. Slate approved shore passes for the crew and rested in advance of the exciting evening.

Just before five, Slate called Johnson and Ramirez to meet him on deck at the gangway. As he waited for them he spotted the large black limo slowly driving down the wharf. It came to a halt at the base of the gangway and Slate watched Tomasso climb from the driver's seat and wait at the bottom stair. Slate waved down to him.

Johnson and Ramirez arrived and all three walked down the steep gangway to meet Tomasso. Introductions were made. Tomasso ushered them into the limousine.

"Gentlemen we will be meeting with Admiral Maduro at around six. I will take you for cocktails at a favorite bar before we go on to dinner."

He drove a zigzag pattern through the backstreets before stopping at the bar. Slate recognized it. He had been here with the Palermos before. It was owned by the mob.

The inside was dark and cool. Tomasso selected a table near the back of the bar. They would be left alone in the quiet corner.

A scantily clothed drink waitress came across to their table. Slate observed a reaction in Johnson. He recognized that Johnson had an urge. He had found Johnson's weakness. For a moment he wondered how he could play this to his advantage, and then gave up remembering that the kidnapping was imminent.

Tomasso kept up the pretense that he had never met Slate or Rameriz previously. They engaged in small talk. Tomasso turned his attention to Johnson and started to question him about his past and his exploits in the Coast Guard.

Time passed until six. Tomasso signaled for the bar bill and the four left the bar.

Slate could not follow the direction in which Tomasso was driving. It seemed to be an area of Caracas that he had never visited before.

After driving down a narrow alley with a cobblestone pavement they arrived at a bold sign announcing the El Matador restaurant.

Tomasso pulled his car up onto the sidewalk and parked.

They walked to the entrance. There was a large oak door with fake antiqued black hinges. Tomasso pulled open the door and they entered another world. The walls were a deep red and all the tables and chairs were black. Posters of matadors and announcements for bullfights lined the walls. Black ornaments adorned the spaces not taken up by the posters.

A waiter attired in a toreador's attire showed them to the table. He offered them a choice of sangria or a wine from the extensive list.

Tomasso chose an aged Tempranillo. While waiting for the Admiral, Tomasso described some of the Spanish foods. He went into raptures when describing his favorite, Chicken Basque.

"I cannot do this meal a favor by describing it. Let me try. It is a delicious combination of chicken and rice, olives and peppers and the Spanish version has spicy chorizo sausage and a hint of paprika. It is a true treat. I have never had it better at any other restaurant."

While they chatted about different items on the menu, the Admiral arrived. He was in full dress uniform. They all stood to greet him. Slate introduced Johnson.

After the formalities they were seated.

After listening to Tomasso extolling the Chicken Basque they all ordered on his recommendation.

Two hours into the meal and after a dessert had been brought to the table, Slate excused himself.

"I have some matters to attend to before we sail in the morning. Excuse me as I must leave. Tomasso please stay with Hector, Johnson and the Admiral. I will take a taxi back to the ship. He rose to leave. As he did so, Hector stood.

"I will join you. I did not sleep well the past few evenings and I am tired. Please excuse me as well."

The Admiral raised his hand.

"If you must leave, I understand. Possibly Johnson will remain with me. I would like to take him to our command headquarters and show him some of the technology we use. He and I have had a fascinating talk this evening. I will arrange a driver from the base to take him back to the ship. Tomasso, we will be fine. Go with these men and drive them. I will have the restaurant call my driver."

Tomasso, Slate and Ramirez took the cue and made their farewell for the night.

Slate was ecstatic. He could not believe things were progressing so well.

In the car Tomasso spoke. "It is going well. Soon he will be of no risk. You will be able to transport the cargo to our men off the shore of Aruba safely."

Ramirez was puzzled. "Why Aruba?"

"There are Free Trade Zones there and many direct shipping links to Europe. One such link is to Rotterdam. We have a special customer there who has a huge distribution operation. The customer is one of Europe's largest motorcycle gangs and nobody in their right mind fools with them."

It was midnight when Tomasso dropped them back at the *Pearl*.

"I wish you all the success tomorrow. The men in Aruba have confirmed they will be awaiting your arrival. They are going to meet you further away from the shore. They do not want a repeat of a local fisherman stumbling upon the unloading process. We will be monitoring the radio carefully. Tomorrow all conversations must be in code."

Ramirez and Slate left Tomasso at the gates of the dock and walked nonchalantly to the ship. No one paid them particular attention.

Slate was relieved to be rid of Johnson. He decided to perform a full search of Johnson's cabin to be certain their mission had not been compromised.

The search proved pointless. They found nothing that indicated That Johnson had been spying or recording their actions during the patrol.

Slate decided to call it a night.

Chapter 94

The pilots came aboard the *Pearl* at ten thirty in the morning. Slate was in a great mood and joked with the others on the bridge. He was glad to be starting the trip home. He envisaged the financial reward that would be awaiting him and looked forward to his retirement from the Coast Guard.

All that remained was the unloading of the drugs off the shore of Aruba. After that they would sail on to Fort Myers, Florida and dock. Slate had calculated the quantity of drugs they would need to return to Florida with and not arouse any suspicion.

He wondered what the mob had done with Johnson. Slate chuckled. "What an arsehole" he thought. "He could have been in on it too."

The pilot questioned Ramirez on the destination and planned course. Ramirez was annoyed and gave the standard answer.

"We are a US Vessel charged with monitoring and policing the oceans. While we will take the route we have provided, we can and will detour from that route if it becomes necessary to take action to intercept suspicious vessels or offer assistance to any craft in distress."

The pilot was uncomfortable and showed it.

"Your ship will be tracked."

It was eleven when Slate ordered the engines fired. The ship vibrated and roared into life. Thick black diesel fumes belched from the exhausts and obscured the dock.

Ten minutes later the mooring lines were released and the *Pearl* slipped back toward the channel, nudged by an old rusted tug boat.

The pilot stayed on board until they were some thirty minutes out from the docks and in the main shipping lane.

The pilot boat came alongside and bobbed against the side of the ship. The pilot climbed down the gangway and jumped into the waiting launch.

Slate was pleased to see the last of him. He did not trust the man.

They started the slow cruise across from Venezuela to Aruba. They sailed toward Maracaibo where the oil tankers ferried oil from the fields to the refinery in Aruba.

Slate decided to use one of the main shipping routes and appear as a ship making a normal crossing over the 14 mile distance. He slowed the ship several times. The winds and ocean currents were pulling him to the destination point too fast.

When he was three miles from the coast of Aruba he ordered the ship to turn north and cut engines to a speed that would hold them stationary against the current.

The *Pearl* stayed in this position until late afternoon. Slate was scanning the waters when he saw the first boat approaching them. It was an old fishing trawler. A larger boat was following.

Slate left the bridge and went down to the forward hold. He addressed the men.

"We have very little time to get this unloading done. Be quick and careful. I want us out of here in the next thirty minutes."

The large bales had already been lifted to the deck in preparation for the off loading.

The fishing trawler bumped the side of the *Pearl.* Men rushed to drop bumper pads over the side to lessen the impact. Ropes were thrown and the boat was tethered to the ship. The forward hold crane ground into gear and lifted the first of the bales.

As the unloading took place, Slate was hailed by one of the men on the second boat. He did not recognize the man who was shouting for permission to come aboard.

Slate gave his approval and ordered a small rope ladder be dropped for the man to use.

A short man with a Latin appearance heaved himself over the railing and onto the deck.

Slate went to meet him.

"Who are you and what business do you have aboard my ship?"

"My name is Alejandro. I am one of the main importers here. I need to be sure that the product you are delivering is correct. We are expecting fifteen bales of marijuana and six packets of cocaine. Do you have all the shipment?"

Slate took an instant dislike to the man.

"Why are you questioning us? Maybe you would like to join me in a radio conversation with the Palermos in Venezuela or Tomasso? That is who we take our instructions from. Now get the hell of this ship before I have you thrown off,"

Alejandro was seething. His Latino temper was flaring. He tried to remind himself of the high stakes involved and managed to calm himself.

"I will be sure to report this to the boys. Remember that our link is with Chicago and Europe. You are just a small time player."

Alejandro turned and headed back to leave the ship. He was no more than ten yards away when Slate smacked the deck axe across the back of his neck. Alejandro dropped to the deck. Slate walked across to him. He reached under his armpits and lifted the body. He dragged it to the side and heaved the inert body over the side.

He looked down at the men on the trawler and in the second boat and called to them.

"If any of you have any ideas let that be a starting lesson for you."

Slate's own crews had watched the attack and were nervous. No one wanted to mess with a riled up Slate.

The unloading was completed in record time and the two craft pulled away for their return trip to Aruba, minus one person.

Slate gave the order to resume the trip to Florida. He assigned an officer to the bridge and went with Ramirez to his cabin.

Ramirez was disturbed.

"Why did you have to kill him? Now it is likely one of those Aruban men will speak. You should have been patient with him. He was nothing. There were other ways to deal with him. I am also worried that our men saw this. Someone may tell the authorities. That was a bad and stupid move."

"Shut up and get out of my cabin. I don't need any comments or review from you. Stay away from me until we reach port. When the time comes to settle the accounts I will let you know."

Ramirez gave Slate a look of death and slunk out of his cabin.

Chapter 95

The navigator plotted a northerly course that took them past the coasts of the Dominican Republic and Puerto Rico until they skirted between Cuba and the Bahamas on their return to Fort Myers, Florida.

The high winds pushed continually against the ship, slowing their progress. Slate was eager to return. This patrol had been long and he was exasperated with shipboard life. His mood darkened each hour. The crew and officers avoided contact unless absolutely necessary.

He stormed to the bridge and ordered the ship's speed be increased to 15knots. At the 10knots the ship was travelling it would take five days or more to reach Fort Myers. Slate wanted to get there in less than three days. He had plans.

A hurricane to the south east was playing havoc with shipping. Slate listened on the marine frequencies to the fishing trawlers and ships calling their positions and requesting assistance. He had no intention of rendering any help. His days as a Coast Guard officer were over as far as he was concerned.

He returned to his cabin and recalled the thoughts he had while in Venezuela. The idea to desert ship had been strong. He thought about asking the Palermo brothers to assist him in settling in Venezuela and working with the mob. He quickly realized that while he occupied his position with the Coast Guard he was an asset and benefited them. Once he left the Coast Guard he was of little or no value.

He vowed that his life after the Coast Guard would be different. He would return to Connecticut and start a real estate career. He had a vision of starting his own real estate company and possibly entering politics one day.

He was dreaming of his new life when his cabin intercom sounded.

"Lieutenant. Please come to the bridge. We have company."

Slate swore up a blue storm.

"What was this interruption he wondered?"

As he crawled up onto the bridge he saw his officers standing with binoculars and looking out to the port side. He crossed over to them.

"What's happening now?

"There is a US Navy vessel off the port bow. They have ordered us to heave to. It seems they wish to board. It is the *USS Randall Jones* out of Puerto Rico."

Slate looked at the sea and weather conditions. They were raw and unforgiving.

"Deny them permission. Advise them the weather conditions prevent a safe transfer of men."

The radio operator scurried away to transmit the message. He returned ashen faced and nervous.

"Sir. Here is their response."

Slate snatched away the sheet of paper from the radio operator.

The following message was scrawled onto the paper:

Our orders are to board you regardless of the weather conditions. We are launching a team and will use whatever means are required to get aboard.

Slate took a pair of the binoculars with the huge magnifying power, known affectionately by the men as "Big Eyes" and trained them on the ship. He could plainly see men in bright yellow all weather gear preparing to descend into an inflatable craft that was tossing violently in the sea.

As the craft started its slow and ominous crossing to the *Pearl*, Slate thought back over the patrol. He could not recall any event that may have tipped off the authorities that anything was amiss. He decided that this was probably just some naval drill and they had not been alerted to make the exercise seem real.

He donned all weather gear and attaching himself to the rescue lines proceeded down onto the deck to meet the boarding crew. The deck was awash as waves broke over the bow and sides of the ship. The winds were whipping up to near gale proportions.

The inflatable hit the side of the Pearl and the men quickly secured the lines dropped by the crew. They clambered up the rope ladder and assembled themselves on deck. Slate saluted them and directed them to the bridge.

On the bridge the commanding officer of the boarding party spoke.

"Lieutenant our orders are to stay on this ship and act as escorts for your return trip to Fort Myers. I cannot give you any further details as I have none. We received orders only three hours ago. I will be assuming control of the ship. The USS Randall Jones will act as escort vessel. You will arrange some quarters for my men immediately."

The men from the boarding party summoned their counterparts. The radio operator was relieved of duty first, followed by the ship's engineer and navigator. Men from the boarding party assumed their positions.

"Lieutenant, you are now relieved of duty. This ship and its crew are now under command and control of the United States Navy."

Slate started to object.

"If you resist or create any problem, I will have you arrested and transported across to the Randall Jones where you will be incarcerated. Am I clear? I suggest you go to your cabin and find something to keep you occupied until we reach Fort Myers."

Slate was confused. He sat in his cabin wondering what could have possibly gone wrong. Had one of the crew reported the intercepts and how the contraband was tallied? He thought about each incident and pulled open his log book with the accounts of each incident.

There was nothing to indicate any problem that would warrant the Coast Guard requesting the Navy to seize the ship. He figured that there was something else. It had to be a Navy exercise. He laughed at the stupidity of the games they played.

Throughout the night, they sailed on toward Florida. The crew from the Navy increased the ship's speed again.

In the morning the winds had dropped and the waves had calmed. A second boarding party from the USS Randall Jones was ferried across.

The Commanding Officer from the Navy called for a full crew meeting in the mess. The men crowded in curious what was happening.

The Commanding Officer spoke. "We have been ordered to take control of this vessel and proceed to your home base of Fort Myers at the fastest possible speed. The reasons for this are unknown to me and my men so it is pointless to ask questions. You will all continue to perform your jobs until we reach port. I have ordered an increase in speed and modifications to the course that will see us dock tomorrow morning at around ten. You are all dismissed."

There was a loud murmur as the crew talked with each other while trying to understand the situation. They drifted away from the mess and back to their assigned roles.

The day passed without any further events. The Navy men kept away from the Coast Guard sailors. Dinner at the mess was broken into shifts to prevent contact between them.

The ship pounded on through the night. Slate had gone on deck and sat trying to fathom out the situation. He knew it was serious. There was nothing he could remember that could implicate him or his crew to any of the seizures on this trip. He thought back to his past trips. Again he was unable to remember any incident. Then he thought of Johnson and his disappearance in Venezuela. Slate decided that was the reason. Until there was an investigation, he and the crew would be suspects in his disappearance or murder. Slate was convinced that was the reason. He stood to go back to his cabin and looked out and noticed lights twinkling from the shore. He assumed that they had reached the southern tip of Florida.

The rising sun streamed across the water creating a sparkling effect. In the distance the shoreline of Florida was distinct. Some dark clouds hung above the land. Lt. Slate stood at the deck rail and took in the morning sights. They had entered into a shipping lane and outbound cargo and container ships passed them. While he watched them pass, he became aware of the ships engines slowing. The grey pilot boat approached. Slate noticed the boat was not from the Port Authority but a Navy pilot. The boat slid to the side of the ship and the waiting gangway.

Instead of just the pilot coming aboard, four uniformed men joined him. The pilot was meet by the Commanding Officer and taken to the bridge. The four men stayed on the deck.

The *Pearl* started a wide turn toward the Coast Guard docks. The speed was reduced and the ship slowly glided toward the wooden pilings. As it neared them the engines were reversed and the ship slowed to a halt. Slate marveled at the accuracy of this particular pilot.

The engines were no sooner cut off when the four men rushed toward him.

"We are with the Coast Guard Intelligence. These other men are Military Police. Lt. Slate you are under arrest. You are charged with acts of piracy, manslaughter, theft of Government property, smuggling, drug and narcotics trafficking, conspiracy and treason against the United States. Other charges are pending."

Slate was not read the Miranda rights as they were onboard the Coast Guard ship.

The four men stepped forward forcibly and grabbed Slate's arms. Handcuffs were tightly locked and they turned him to walk to the exit for the gangway. Slate looked toward the stern of the ship to see Ramirez pacing and shouting wildly.

Slate was escorted off the ship and down to the dock. He was shocked to find Admiral Maduro of the Venezuelan Navy standing with Johnson. Both men were dressed in full uniform. Slate stopped and tried to form a question to ask Admiral Maduro.

"I have always been loyal to my country. Those thugs had no idea of my role as an informer and intelligence source. This is just the beginning. I should like to thank you for allowing me to enjoy a most pleasant evening with Commander Johnson of the US Coast Guard Intelligence Service. He is a fine man and an officer of excellence. You have chosen your enemies dangerously."

Slate spat at him.

Johnson stepped forward and smacked the back of his hand across Slate's face.

"I can assure you that no one will report or have seen this. Now move on. The press is waiting inside the building for your photograph and to break this story."

Part 5

Lives unravel

Chapter 96

Ontario, Canada.

The Lockheed Constellation circled over upstate New York and Southern Ontario before starting its descent into the airport. Solange was thrilled as they crossed over Niagara Falls. She had heard so much about the Falls and had wondered if they really were as large as many claimed.

As the plane banked and turned she looked down at the curved outline of the Falls. A white mist arose and she could see the water cascading over the lip and crashing to the river below.

"Jakob, will we be able to visit this? Is it close to where we will be staying?"

Solange was excited in the same manner as a young schoolgirl.

"Yes. I have planned to take you to visit some areas I know will interest you. We will stay at an Inn at Niagara-On-the-Lake. It is a small town and close to the Falls. There are many stores there. The town is typical of the many little villages throughout Ontario."

Suddenly the engines roared and the plane accelerated toward the airport for the landing.

Jakob looked from the window at the farmland passing below. He was amazed to see new developments under construction and highways being built. Ontario had changed since he left. He wondered what had happened near his farmland.

The engines fell quiet and they started to glide across the runway. A jolt and a bounce accompanied their arrival into Toronto.

The engines revved again and the plane turned and taxied to the terminal building. It stopped short of the terminal.

"Ladies and Gentlemen. Welcome to Toronto and Malton airport. We will be leaving the plane by the front exit door. Please gather your possessions and come to the front. Should anyone need assistance please let us know and we will be pleased to assist you."

The door of the plane was opened and Jakob smelled the humid air as it filled the plane. It was late summer and the humidity was still high.

Jakob and Solange descended the stairs from the plane and walked across the tarmac to the door where they were directed to claim their baggage and proceed through Canada Customs.

The Customs Officer greeted them and after a brief chat regarding their trip to Canada, they left the terminal to hire a taxi for the ride into downtown Toronto.

A skycap wheeled their bags out to the curb and hailed a taxi. Jakob handed him a tip. The bags were placed into the trunk. They settled into the taxi.

"Where are we going?"

""Please drive us to The Royal York Hotel. We are not in a hurry. Please drive us by the lake."

The driver was only too happy to be asked to take the long way downtown. His fare just doubled.

As they drove, Jakob pointed out various points of interest to Solange. She was amazed at the difference between an American city and Toronto.

The taxi pulled into the entrance way to the hotel. A uniformed bellhop ran to the car and opened the door. His greetings were profuse.

The bellhop accompanied them to the counter. Jakob presented the reservation confirmation form. Within minutes they were registered and were leaving the front reception desk when the clerk called out.

"Mr. Klassen. We have an urgent message for you. Please wait and I will fetch it for you."

The clerk disappeared behind a dark stained door and emerged a few minutes later holding an envelope.

Jakob took the envelope and ripped it open.

He removed a cream colored sheet with a telephone message written on it. He showed the message to Solange.

It read:

Please call me immediately upon your arrival. Things are starting with the plans we made. You have been receiving calls at home and at the office from a Kevin Connelly and a Rear Admiral Phillips in Florida. There are more calls from a Benita Flores of the Miami Sentinel. Henri has also called.. They all say it is urgent they speak with you. Isaac

Jakob folded the paper and tucked it into his shirt pocket. Solange observed his clenched jaw as they walked through the lobby to the bank of elevators.

The elevator attendant greeted them and inquired which floor they required. He moved the lever across the highly polished brass controls. The door quietly closed. With a slight jerk and humming sound the elevator commenced its ascent to their floor.

When they reached the twenty eighth floor the attendant stopped the elevator and assisted the bellhop to unload the baggage. The bellhop opened the door and Jakob and Solange walked into the room.

Solange gasped. The view was panoramic. It looked out over the Toronto Islands and Lake Ontario. She turned to Jakob and beamed.

"You certainly know how to make me happy."

The bellhop stood back waiting.

"Will you require anything further sir?"

"No thank you. This is excellent."

Jakob took a five dollar note and handed it to the man. The bellhop's eyes widened at the size of the tip.

"My name is Alfred. If there is anything you need, call the front desk and ask for me. I am at your service."

Jakob walked across to Solange and took her in his arms.

"It has been too long since we were alone and in a strange place. I have that certain feeling."

Solange knew what he meant as she could feel that certain feeling pressing against her thigh.

Chapter 97

Jakob was relaxed when he picked up the phone to return the calls to Isaac Junior. The phone at his home rang unanswered. Jakob called the office. It was late. The phone was answered on the third ring. It was Isaac.

"Jakob thank God you got the message. There have been developments here. Things have happened that we did not plan on. You need to contact Kevin Connelly. He will fill you in on everything. The Americans have apprehended a Coast Guard officer and his crew in Florida. It was part of an operation that raided the boats attempting to smuggle drugs from Colombia and Venezuela to Curacao and Aruba. The Coast Guard ship was supplying the local mob here and they were using the Free Trade Zone to ship the drugs to Rotterdam. Things are developing fast. If we are going to rescue Juan we must move sooner than we had planned.

I am angry and concerned. That pompous arse brother-in-law, Henri Martins is making this a huge political matter. He has photos in newspapers and is claiming a victory in the assault on drugs from Colombia and Venezuela. He has gone so far as to announce there are further plans for more raids.

We must move now."

"I will return and be there with you."

"No. You cannot assist here. We have our plan. Moreno, Adrien and Hans are all ready. We have all discussed the latest events. Moreno and Hans will leave in the morning for Colombia as agreed. They will pose as coffee buyers and visit at Solange's business there. Adrien has been working with some contacts he has in Colombia. He is keeping matters very quiet and private."

"I must return."

"As I have said there is nothing you can do here. You will be a problem. Besides, it is better you are not here on Aruba in case that James Mastronardi and the crooks at the Commercial Loan Bank of Aruba discover your involvement. We need to surprise these people. Your being away on a trip will confuse them."

"I am not happy to be away and not involved."

"It is best for all of us that you stay away."

"Isaac I need you to do two things. I want you to fly to Miami and get Henri Martins to stop. While you are in Miami I need you to visit the Miami Sentinel and explain to Benita Flores the situation. She is friendly and working with us. She is aware of our plan and is ready to provide immense press coverage that should cripple anyone involved with the mob in Aruba or in Venezuela. You can trust her."

"Tonight I will meet with Hans and Moreno. There are some last minute details we need to address."

"I will check with you in the morning. Tomorrow I am taking Solange on a tour to the Muskoka area that is north of Toronto. It is a beautiful place with lakes and summer cottages. There are steam boats that travel the lakes. We will hire a car and drive there. We will be gone all day and return the next day. I will stay in contact with you."

Jakob hung up and sat reflecting on the conversation. He wondered if Isaac was right. Maybe it was better that he was not on Aruba during the action.

As he completed dressing, Solange joined him. She was dressed in a fashionable gown. Jakob was proud of her. Even though years had gone by she still possessed a radiant beauty.

"Let us go on down to the Imperial Room. We will dine like royalty and enjoy the show that the nightclub has this evening. We are lucky to be here now. The Royal York suffered a strike and for the past year the famous Moxie Whitney was not playing. Tonight all is back to normal and I am advised the entertainment is beyond comparison.

First, let me call our man Alfred and arrange for a hire car for tomorrow and contact Isaac Junior."

Jakob called the switchboard operator and provided the numbers. In Aruba the phone at Isaac's house and office rang unanswered.

Jakob made arrangements for the hire car. When he was finished he escorted Solange to the elevator and down to the Imperial Room for a night of fine dining and relaxation.

They walked into the Imperial Room and were greeted at the door.

"Good evening Mr. and Mrs. Klassen. Welcome to the Imperial Room. We have a special table reserved for you."

The maitre de led them to a table next to the stage area and pulled back the gold chair for Solange.

Solange looked around at the opulent interior of the room with the crystal chandeliers and fancy wall sconces.

Within minutes a waiter arrived at their table with the wine sommelier. He handed them the voluminous menu and wine list. The sommelier offered to answer any questions regarding the wines. Jakob was impressed and happy with the service they were receiving.

The waiter returned. "May I take your order? I recommend the chef's special menu this evening. It is some of the finest Ontario produce and wines served as a four course dinner."

"Please tell us more."

"We start the dinner with a Caviar and served with a Blanc de Blanc white

The first course is a Consommé à la Royale of Chicken Dumplings and Brunoise of Mire Poixe .

The second course is a Pork Terrine with house mustard and served with a Sauvignon Blanc from the Niagara region.

The third course is a Coquille Saint Jacques with Gruyere cheese, mushrooms and fine herbs. This is served with a Chenin Blanc, again from the Niagara Peninsula.

The fourth course is the piece de resistance.   Duck à l'Orange. A roast breast of duck and a confit leg served with Pommes Salardaise. The course is accompanied with a Gaia Merlot.

We complete the menu with a dessert of a Chocolate Éclair or Crème Bavaroise."

The waiter stepped back and bowed ever so slightly.

"Well that is a really full and interesting menu. It sounds like a huge meal. I worry that we would be unable to complete the meal. I hate to think of the waste."

"No sir. On the contrary our chef carefully proportions the dishes. You will be fine."

"Solange, would you wish to try this? "

"Yes. It sounds intriguing."

"Please bring us an order for two. I would also like to order a Dom Perignon for us to enjoy before the meal."

"Yes sir. Excellent sir."

The waiter scurried away to place the order and advise the wine waiter to take the champagne to their table.

A silver ice bucket was brought to the table and the Dom Perignon placed in it to chill. The wine waiter returned minutes later and opened the bottle with a flourish.

Jakob and Solange toasted to a good trip and sat sipping the champagne.

The waiters returned with huge tray containing the small silver dishes of caviar with crusty bread **and surrounded with small bowls of chopped egg yolks and egg whites, lemon wedges, red onion, chives, creme fraiche, and Toast Points.**

Solange was starving. She scooped some caviar onto a toast point and ate the small serving hungrily. She sipped more champagne.

Jakob looked around the room at the other diners. It was obvious most were business men entertaining clients or partners. Most were dressed in drab grey or navy suits. Jakob and Solange stood out in their expensive, colorful and casual clothing.

"Solange, we stick out in here like the testicles on a dog."

She was unable to contain herself and attempted to choke back a laugh. Champagne flew from her mouth in a fine spray across the table and coated the men sitting at the adjacent table. Jakob looked at her in horror. The caviar had been sucked back into her nasal passage and was oozing from her nose like a trail of ants climbing down yellow strips.

He stood and quickly moved to her side and placed the crisp white starched napkin over her face. She coughed and more caviar flew.

The head waiter sprinted to their table.

"Sir. Is everything alright? Does your wife need help?"

"It has been a long day of travel. As a result of the plane trips she has experienced some severe sinus problems. I think it best we return to our room and take a light meal there. We need to travel very early in the morning."

With her head bowed and embarrassed, Solange walked with Jakob through the dining room to the elevator. Inside the elevator they both collapsed laughing. Their new friend, the elevator attendant, joined in the merriment when they told him what had happened.

Back in the room, Jakob again tried to contact Isaac. Again there was no answer.

Chapter 98

Disturbed by his inability to contact Isaac, Jakob sat on the edge of the bed in deep thought.

"I am concerned. I cannot reach Isaac. I have tried the office, his home and our home. None of the phones get answered."

"Try and call Miguel and Alejandro at the restaurant. Maybe they know where Isaac has gone."

Jakob took the phone and gave the operator the number. Through the static of the bad connection he heard the phone ringing in Aruba. It rang for a long while until a female voice came on the line.

"This is Jakob Klassen. I am looking for Miguel or Alejandro. Are they there?"

There was silence on the line.

"This is Millicent. I work here as a waitress. You must not have heard the news. This morning near the refinery they found the body of Alejandro washed onto the beach. The police say he was murdered. Miguel has gone to Carlita's in Savaneta."

In shock he handed the phone to Solange. She introduced herself and listened as Millicent told her the news of Alejandro.

Solange asked for more details and then hung up the phone.

"I think we need to return to Aruba, Solange. I am getting a bad feeling about this. Why was Alejandro killed? I wonder if it has to do with the mob."

"I have Carlita's telephone number with me. Let me call her."

The phone at Carlita's was answered by a man. Solange announced herself and within a minute Carlita was on the phone.

"What has happened? We heard from the waitress at the restaurant that Alejandro has been killed. Is that true?"

"Yes. This morning a family of one of the refinery workers went to the beach. Their son was rushing into the water and found Alejandro's partially sunk body at the shore. The refinery called the authorities. They took the body to the hospital for examination. They have told us that Alejandro was murdered. His head was smashed at the back and barely attached. Miguel is here. He is in shock. The doctors have given him injections to calm him. He went crazy and started smashing things, screaming and lost all control."

"Would you like Jakob and me to return? Can we help there?"

"No I don't think so. Isaac Junior is here and helping with details. I will get him for you."

When Isaac was on the phone, Solange launched a barrage of questions.

"Are you alright? What is happening there? Why was Alejandro found in the water? Where are Hans and Moreno? Has our Marine friend left for Colombia yet? Should we come home?"

"Please, please. Let me tell you what I know. It seems Alejandro was washed onto the beach by the strong current that flows in at the end of the island. The authorities claim he must have been miles offshore to be swept into that current. There is evidence he was in the water for some time. He has bites all over him. It seems some fish attacked him. He had water in his lungs according to the doctor at the hospital. He was probably not dead when he ended up in the water. The police are definite in stating that he was murdered. There is a huge gash on his back and his head is barely attached. The police do not think this was done by the mob. He was killed from behind and pushed into the water. We think he was on a boat from here. The locals are all talking about the situation.

Carlita is handling things well. I am not sure about Miguel. The doctors are considering putting him into the hospital. They are concerned he may try to kill himself.

Hans and Moreno left for Bogota this afternoon. Adrien the Marine left a few days ago.

I am assisting Carlita with Miguel and Alejandro's family and relatives. There is no need for you to return. There is nothing you can do.

I have spoken with Florida. Kevin Connelly and Admiral Phillips want Jakob to call them. The Admiral has given me his home telephone number. He asked that Jakob call as soon as he can."

"I will have him call when we are done speaking. Now tell me what Hans and Moreno are doing."

Isaac shared his knowledge of the plans for the Colombia rescue and explained that Adrien had requested a large sum of money to purchase some equipment there.

"Adrien has had papers forged and will present himself in Colombia as an oil exploration surveyor for Royal Imperial Oil. Part of the funds he requested will be used to buy 2 Jeeps and some official looking equipment. He is going to meet with Hans and Moreno in a day or so. They will take the other jeep and pretend to be assisting with the survey. Adrien chose that cover in order to get into the jungle and close to the drug camp. He has advised me that there are a couple of former Dutch Marines living outside of Bogota who could possibly help with the rescue. He wasn't sure if he would ask them yet. He wants to determine how difficult a recue will be."

"I will call you tomorrow evening. Where will you be?"

"I will be staying close to my home as that is the number that Hans and Moreno have, as well as Adrien. It is the central point for communications."

Jakob had sat listening to the conversation without speaking.

After Solange ended the conversation, he took the phone to call the Admiral in Florida.

Chapter 99

The phone at the Admiral's residence was answered on the third ring.

"This is Phillips speaking."

"Good evening, this is Jakob Klassen. Sorry to call you this late. I am in Canada with my wife. We have only now received your message. I hope this is a convenient time to call you."

"Yes. Indeed. I was hoping you would call. There have been a number of developments that seem to be tied into your situation with the mob in Aruba. We had an undercover officer onboard the US Coast Guard clipper *Pearl.* For some time we had our suspicions about what was happening with this ship and the crew. Our concerns were borne out as our officer was able to document many illegal practices performed by the crew. We were able to establish that the ship was transporting contraband and drugs to a drop point off the coast of Aruba. The drugs were seized from other smugglers attempting to run them through to Florida or other locations. The *Pearl* operated as a legitimate US patrol and would seize the drugs but release the smugglers. Those drugs were then off loaded onto small craft that came out to meet the *Pearl* from the areas of Barcadera and Savaneta.

On the last drop something went terribly wrong. The senior officer attacked and killed one of the men who had come out for the drugs. He attacked him from behind with an axe and threw his body overboard. Our man Johnson witnessed this. We have an added bonus. One of the junior officers on the ship, a Hector Ramirez, is singing like a canary. He is trying to make a deal by providing critical information. We will be taking him to a safe location. He is providing essential information."

Jakob felt ill. He wondered if the murdered man was Alejandro. It seemed to fit based on what he had been told.

"I think I may know who that man was."

Rear Admiral Phillips listened as Jakob updated him on the news he had been given by Isaac Junior.

"There is more that I must tell you. For years, we have worked with Admiral Maduro from Venezuela Naval Operations. He has been a source of information and has the evidence that confirms the Aruba mob is connected to the Palermo Brothers in Caracas. Now that the ship has been arrested, he will no longer be safe in Venezuela or America. He will be assisting us in documenting events that we will use in trial. He has also provided us with significant information regarding the Commercial Loan Bank of Aruba and the players involved. The Treasury Department is investigating the bank's business dealing here in the States. There are huge sums of money involved. The bank has transferred tens of millions of dollars each month from Aruba. They have traced the money back to some shady companies and the mob businesses in Venezuela.

Until we make further arrests and seizures, I plead with you to stay away from Aruba. It will not be safe for you to return. It seems that James Mastronardi, the Manager of the bank had suspicions about you and Isaac Junior. It would be wise for Isaac Junior to take a trip as well. Maybe he could join you?"

"That is not possible. No he will stay in Aruba. Isaac is smart and knows how to look after himself."

"What are your plans?"

"We will spend the rest of the week in Canada before travelling on to Europe to visit some friends and people who helped me during the war years. For months I have had so many recurring thoughts of these people. I need to see them."

Solange listened to the conversation without interrupting. She was watching Jakob closely. The signs of his illness were starting to show. She realized that when he was stressed that the symptoms started. She crossed the room to where he was standing and took the phone from him and gestured to him to sit down.

"Admiral Phillips, this is Solange Klassen. I am concerned that all of this is having a negative effect on Jakob. You do not know but Jakob was receiving treatment in Florida for advanced OCD-Obsessive Compulsive Disorder. Discussing this situation will not help him. If there is anything more that we can assist you with, please let us know when we call you again within the next few days."

Solange hung up the phone. Her anger was clearly visible.

"I will not allow the criminal actions of others to tear at you. Let the appropriate authorities deal with these people. They are dangerous. If you continue you will put all of our family and close friends in danger."

"I am determined to stop the infiltration of these criminals into Aruba."

"The US Government has far more capability then you. Let them do their job. Now, let's plan for tomorrow. I am hungry. That dinner fiasco has left me starving."

Jakob picked up the phone and called the front desk to request room service. He asked if his new found friend, Alfred was still working at that late hour.

Fifteen minutes passed until there was a soft knocking at the door. Upon opening it, they found Alfred with a cart containing food and a large bottle of Champagne.

"Good evening Mr. Klassen. I understand you will be leaving us tomorrow to continue your travels. I wished to see you before you left and wish you and Mrs. Klassen farewell."

Jakob had developed an instant liking to the little man.

"Yes tomorrow we will drive north to the Muskokas. I am looking forward to that. I have never been but have heard many reports of the lakes and the beauty of the area."

"At what time will you be leaving, sir?"

"We will leave around six in the morning. It is a long drive and I want to be at Windermere House before late afternoon.

"You are staying at Windermere House? That is an extremely beautiful hotel and location. The view over Lake Rosseau is amazing. I think you will enjoy your stay there.

Since you are leaving so early would you care for me to have the kitchen prepare some food for you to take with you?"

"That would be very nice. Thank you."

Jakob reached across the bed and picked up his jacket. He pulled out his wallet and removed some bills which he handed to Alfred.

"Oh no, sir. That is not necessary. It has been my pleasure to meet you both and I hope to see you again."

Jakob pushed the money into Alfred's jacket pocket as he shook his hand.

"Thank you for all your help."

Alfred smiled and turned to leave.

"I will inform the desk to remind you of the food for your trip tomorrow. Good night."

Chapter 100

The morning arrived quickly. Fall was approaching and it was still dark outside. Solange opened the heavy drapes and looked out to Lake Ontario. In the east, the first early light of dawn was breaking. A few clouds dotted the sky and reflected a light pink light. The waters of the lake seemed deep blue.

She shook Jakob awake.

"You wanted to leave early this morning. I am ready and have already packed our cases."

"I will dress and call the desk for assistance with the baggage and ask them to get our car."

Fifteen minutes passed until Jakob could check them out of the hotel. Even at that early hour of the morning the lobby was busy with people starting their day.

Jakob and Solange exited the lobby through the larger door onto Front Street and their awaiting car. Jakob asked the valet for directions to the recently opened Don Valley Parkway and then drove to start the trip north.

As they drove northward, the houses thinned and soon they travelled through farmlands that were familiar in layout to Jakob. He thought of the days ahead and his planned return to the childhood farm.

Hours went by and they continued further north. Solange was intrigued by the change in landscape and commented to Jakob about the dense forests of trees. She had never experienced such a concentration of tress and greenery.

It was late afternoon when Jakob pulled off into the sweeping driveway of the Windermere House. He had no sooner stopped that an eager boy was holding open the door for Solange.

"Jakob this is a magnificent place. It seems like I am in a fairy tale here."

With the formalities of registering completed, they were taken to their room on the second floor. From the bedroom there was a panoramic view of the lake. The windows opened onto a small deck.

After settling themselves in, they went to enjoy drinks on the lawn that sloped down to the lake and a jetty with pleasure boats moored to it. A gentle cool breeze blew from the lake. The early fall sun was warm and Jakob drifted off into a light sleep. Solange watched as his head slumped forward. She knew he was tired from the travel. She decided to leave him to rest and returned to their room.

In the room she placed a call to Isaac Junior at his home.

"Isaac we had a conversation last evening with Admiral Phillips. I am concerned with what he told us. I am worried for your safety. It seems that the activities of the mob are more widespread than we realized. The Admiral advised us that James Mastronardi at the bank is wary of you and the Klassen business. Please be very careful. He explained that there is going to be some major action taken. Have you heard from Hans or Moreno? The timing of the attempt to rescue Juan is bad. I fear that the mob's businesses are about to be raided."

"Please do not worry about me. I told you that I have plans and will be travelling soon. I think that it is excellent timing should they raid the Venezuelan mob. It will surely be a distraction at the drug lab in Colombia. They think the operation is hidden and safe. Their concern will be selling the drugs and getting them out of Colombia. I believe that Adrien has planned things well. I am not concerned. In fact I think this will make things easier for them to snatch Juan."

"Isaac I am asking you again. Where are you going and when? I am your mother and business partner. You owe it to me to share that information."

"I will not. How is Jakob? I hope the stress of travelling is not too much. He seemed very tired before you left."

"He is fine. He is sleeping outside in a chair by the lake. It is so beautiful and calm here. He needs the rest. Now again I ask. Where are you going to?"

"Again I must tell you that I will not tell you. Now I must go and get the children. Goodbye."

She returned to find Jakob awake and sipping on a mint julep. She smiled and gently rubbed her hand over his shoulder.

"You look relaxed. Do you want to stay here longer than we planned?"

"I don't think that is possible. We need to travel to the farm and I want to show you Niagara Falls and Niagara-on-the-lake. After that we must return to Toronto for the flight to Amsterdam."

Solange nodded and sat to join him. A drink waiter arrived and took her order. Soon she was sipping on a cool Chenin Blanc while gazing off into the distance at the lake and surrounding vegetation. She found a peace and relaxation at this place.

The sun started to slip below the tree line and a slightly cooler breeze blew.

"Let us go in now. We will dress for dinner. I looked in the dining room earlier. It is magnificent. I am looking forward to a nice dinner and not another disaster like last evening."

At the mention of the previous evening's aborted meal, Jakob laughed.

They dressed and left for the first sitting in the dining room.

The menu was seasonal and reflected the local foods available at the start of autumn.

Jakob read through the menu and was delighted to see that some of the favorite foods he had known when growing up in Ontario were available.

He offered to order for Solange.

The waiter stood quietly and scribbled the order on a white pad.

Jakob placed his order for the following:

Two Waldorf salads.

Smoked trout appetizers.

Prime rib with horse radish, field tomatoes, baby carrots, roasted potatoes, freshly picked spinach and butternut.

Flaming baked Alaska.

The dining room was quiet with the buzz of low conversation. They finished their dinner and retired to the verandah. Jakob watched two older men sitting in cane rocking chairs and enjoying huge cigars whose smoke drifted toward him.

They pulled up chairs and sat watching the setting sun while drinking Courvoisier. Darkness fell and soon they were alone. Jakob stood and extended his hand to Solange.

"Let's go for a walk around the edge of the lake. It is a beautiful evening."

They walked down to the edge of the lake and along a narrow path. They were totally alone. In the darkness they watched as the occasional firefly flashed and disappeared into the shrubbery.

As they walked further away from the hotel the feel of the surrounding vegetation closed in on them. The sound of frogs croaking and crickets chirping added to the atmosphere. After thirty minutes of walking, Jakob motioned to sit on the grassy area near the shore.

Solange rested her head against Jakob's arm. There was a tranquility here that she had never really experienced before.

Suddenly, Jakob stood up quickly. He reached down and pulled off his shirt. After kicking off his sandals he fumbled with his belt and removed his pants. Totally naked he ran and leapt into the lake.

Solange watched in disbelief.

"Solange. Come and join me. Everyone in Canada has gone skinny dipping at some point."

"No. I cannot. What will happen of someone comes by here?"

"We will wave to them and wish them a good evening," he laughed.

Bashfully Solange stripped and sprinted into the lake. She was surprised at the warmth of the water. Together they floated and laughed.

An hour passed and they finally pulled themselves from the lake. Jakob gave Solange his shirt to use as a towel and dry off. They dressed and sat back down.

Solange looked across the lake at the line of huge dark pine trees silhouetted against the pale white light of the rising moon. On the surface of the lake the moon's reflection was disturbed by ripples created by the breezes.

They finally made their way back to the resort and collapsed into bed. After the lake swim their bodies felt cool and their minds tired.

Solange thought about how it seemed the troubles they had left in Aruba were far removed.

Chapter 101

Breakfast was served on the garden patio. Solange absently stared at the sun's rays reflecting off the surface of the lake. Every now and then a mild breeze would blow causing a ripple effect on the lake. She was totally relaxed.

They sipped on mimosas and picked at the fresh fruit platter. Neither spoke a word but quietly took in the calm surrounds.

"Jakob what will we do today?"

"This will be our day to do nothing except enjoy ourselves."

A waiter dressed in a light white uniform approached them carrying a silver coffee pot and a smaller jug of fresh cream. He reached to the center of the table and took two cups and poured the thick aromatic coffee.

"Would madam care for cream and sugar? The cream is from the neighboring farm."

"Yes I would like that."

Jakob held his hand over his cup. He preferred the coffee to be black and heavily sugared.

"Let us finish. I have a Canadian activity for you to try, but first we will go to our room and change into some casual shorts and shirts."

Solange looked at him with curiosity.

After they changed, Jakob led her down to the narrow wooden dock that jutted out into the lake from the shore. He signaled the boy attending to the various boats toward them.

"I would like to take out one of the canoes with my wife. We will need it for about three hours. I want to spend time on the lake and show my wife the beauty of the nature here."

The boy asked them to wait on the shore and left to bring one of the larger canoes to them.

He assisted Solange into the canoe. She was unsteady at first and the canoe rocked violently. Jakob laughed.

"You will get a feel for the balance soon."

He wasn't sure, but thought he heard some quietly muttered swearing.

The boy pushed them away from the shore. The canoe glided gracefully out from the bay. Solange sat in the front and Jakob paddled from the rear. They slid out onto the lake and moved toward the opposite shore. Upon reaching it, Jakob turned the canoe and followed along the water's edge. As the morning grew older and warmer, the sound of different insects in the lily pads, grasses and reeds broke the otherwise silent surrounds.

"Jakob, why did you ever leave this country? It is beautiful. Surely you could have had a good life here."

"Solange things were a lot different then. Remember I was part of a strict Mennonite community. We worked long hard hours and relaxation and pleasures were frowned upon. In addition, the winters here are vicious. When I was young people died from sicknesses and starvation. We did not have the opportunity to stay in luxurious hotels like this or take leisurely days."

She lay back and basked in the early autumn sun. The canoe slipped through the water in silence. Jakob maneuvered the canoe back to the hotel. The boy greeted them at the sandy beach and held the canoe to balance it while they climbed from it to the shore.

After freshening up in their room, they went to the outside restaurant on the deck. Summer was ending and there were very few people staying at the hotel. School had resumed and there were no children.

They were offered a table of their choice given that there were so few people.

Solange ordered them both a light lunch.

"This afternoon I will drive you to see the other main lakes here. We will visit Lake Muskoka and Lake Joseph. The assistant at the reception desk told me of a trail we can walk from the road down to Lake Muskoka. I would like to do this. It will be good exercise for us. We will need it before our long drive tomorrow to Niagara-on-the-Lake."

With lunch completed Jakob went to the car and drove to the entranceway to get Solange for the drive.

Slowly they drove through the little villages of Port Sandfield and Port Carling. Jakob stopped at certain locations and they would leave the car to walk around and explore. While driving around Lake Muskoka they stumbled upon yet another stately old resort, The Clevelands House. Jakob stopped the car.

"Come on Solange. Let's check this resort. Maybe we can stay here on a future trip."

Upon entering the resort they were greeted by staff that with great courtesy answered questions and showed them the resort's rooms and facilities. Jakob was impressed.

"Next time this is where we will stay."

He engaged the staff in conversation and asked for directions to the location of the walking trail.

Solange reclined back in the front passenger seat and marveled at the heavy forestation. She had grown up in Florida but had never seen such a dense growth of trees and shrubbery.

Jakob slowed as they reached a clearing that lead to the walking trail. They left the car and prepared for the long walk down to the lake.

As they pushed their way through the small branches that hung over the sides of the trail, Jakob looked down at the thick carpet of yellowing leaves from the oak and maple trees that lay on the ground.

"A sign an early fall is arriving," he thought.

For the next hour they marched on until the trail opened onto a huge opening with a sandy beach. Small waves from the lake lapped at the shore.

Jakob escorted Solange over to a large tree trunk lying on the beach. They sat in silence and absorbed the view.

The afternoon was dwindling and Jakob wanted to return to the Windermere House before dark.

"I think we should start back. It will take us a bit longer to climb up some of those small inclines."

Solange agreed and shuddered. A sudden cool breeze blew strongly off the lake. She removed the sweater she had draped around her waist and pulled it on over her head.

It was almost two hours before they reached the car and started the drive back to the resort.

Jakob looked up at the cloudless skies. He felt a distinct chill in the air.

Chapter 102

After settling their account with the resort the next morning, Jakob and Solange requested assistance to take their baggage to the car.

Upon leaving the hotel they stepped into cold crisp air. Jakob looked around the grounds and observed the dusting of minute ice crystals of a hoar frost on the grass and low plants.

"It won't be long now before the heavy frosts and early snows come to this slightly northern part of Ontario. A frost like this and sunny days are going to create a spectacular display of red leaves and fall colors across the forests."

"Will it be warmer where we are going?" Solange was cold and shivering. After years in the warmth of Aruba, she had forgotten what colder weather felt like.

Jakob laughed. "Only a little bit. Now let's start the long drive to Niagara-on-the-Lake."

The drive took them back toward Toronto and then westward.

Solange dozed as they travelled the miles. Jakob woke her as they approached the area of Hamilton. He pointed to the steel manufacturing companies. Mountainous piles of coal stood in the foreground of the giant stacks that belched open flames and heavy brown smoke into the sky. Rusted and worn looking ships were moored in docks close to the roadway.

"Solange, this is Hamilton, also known as steel town. It produces steel for the car manufacturers and other businesses."

She looked from the car's window at the scene.

"I would never want to live here or near this. I do not like it."

"Soon we will be travelling in the Niagara area and the scenery will be very different. Are you hungry? I will find somewhere for us to stop."

"I could use a break. Yes. Let's stop somewhere soon for a while. How long before we reach Niagara-on-the-Lake?"

"I think we will reach our hotel in the next two hours."

"Now let me see what I can find for us."

They continued to drive on until Jakob noticed a sign advertising food and ice-cream. He turned off and slowly drove into a town with a gas station and a few stores. He looked at the car's gas gauge and decided to buy gas. While the attendant was filling the tank with gas, Jakob asked for directions to the store that sold food.

"Sir that aint no store. Up them roads there is a farmhouse that makes sandwiches and cooks things for travelers. Old Mrs. Smith makes things every morning. You get what she makes. Not much choice but its good."

Jakob thanked the man. Solange returned from the restroom and slid back onto the front seat.

"Jakob, promise me we will have a better toilet during our travels. I swear that God punished me in there."

Jakob laughed.

He drove them up a small incline to an old farmhouse with a sign pronouncing it to be 'Betty's Kitchen.'

Solange looked at Jakob nervously.

"Don't worry. Some of these home kitchens have the best food."

Solange was not convinced.

As they pulled to a halt outside the front gate, a matronly woman emerged.

"Greetings, you youngsters. I am Betty. I will make you food from heaven. Come in, come in."

Betty was a large and formidable woman. Solange tried hard to suppress her laugh. She found it funny that Jakob had been called a young one. They followed her up the path and into the front entrance of an old farmhouse. As they entered the aroma of rich foods filled their nostrils.

"Now you both come in here and take a seat at the guest table. I have a real special meal cooked today. It's a roast leg of lamb. I serve it with roasted vegetables. There are potatoes, carrots, onion and I serve it with fresh minted peas. Lots of gravy for your man there as well, miss, or is it Missus?"

Solange was finding the situation quite unreal. She couldn't believe they were in a country farmhouse with this bubbly and charming woman. She tried to recall an experience like this from her earlier years growing up.

"Yes Mrs. Smith he is my husband for many years."

"I don't think so dearie. You are too young and pretty to have been married long to that old guy."

Solange could no longer contain herself. She looked at Jakob who stood with a look of total astonishment on his face. She doubled over in laughter.

"Mrs. Smith you are funny. I have needed to laugh all day and you are the breath of fresh air to bring that about."

"Now dear I have some advice for you. Just keep an eye on him. When I was young I had boys like that. They want one thing and it's not what you would find at a Sunday school or at ballet lessons. That man of yours has a look about him. I suspect he has had a bit of a naughty life. I would be sure and get yourself a replacement just in case. To me it doesn't look like he will last much longer."

Solange could not believe what they had stepped into. She did not feel threatened in anyway and was enjoying the strange humor of Mrs. Smith.

"My husband has been a little ill. He has worked hard all his life and we are now taking some time to visit places from the past and old friends.

"Hmmph! Don't go expecting too much then. People, including old friends, change over time. Never understood that meself. It's a pity but that is part of life I guess. Now stop all this stupid talk. What are you going to eat?"

"You made that lamb roast sound delicious. We will both order that please."

They spent the next two hours sitting and laughing with the interminable talk of Mrs. Betty Smith before returning to the car and continuing their journey.

Chapter 103

The afternoon wore on as they continued the drive westwards. Solange was intrigued by the vineyards and orchards they passed as they skirted around the edge of Lake Ontario.

They arrived at Niagara-on-the-Lake as the sun was setting. The town appeared to be under construction. Many of the stores had scaffolding or construction materials around them. This did not distract from the quaint atmosphere. Large planters of flowers lined the center median of the street and decorative ornaments hung from the lamp posts that lined the street.

Jakob continued through town until he reached the Prince of Wales Hotel. The old hotel had been built in 1864 and still remained a magnificent structure.

He slowed and finally pulled to a halt in front.

"Solange, I think you will enjoy staying here at this grand old dame. It has been home to royalty and many other distinguished guests over the years."

As he opened the door a tuxedo clad bellboy arrived to assist them.

"Welcome to The Prince of Wales. Will you be staying with us for long?"

"We will stay for just a couple of days. I have some business to attend to in Kitchener. We will stay here and I will take the short drive to Kitchener to complete my business."

"Very good then sir."

They walked in through the grand entrance and into a plush lobby. The lobby was ornate. There were intricate hardwood floors, plush Victorian furniture, a stained glass mural, beautiful sculptures and plenty of fresh roses. Solange absorbed it all as she followed Jakob and the bellboy.

The perfume of the roses filled the air. After registering, Jakob and Solange were taken to their room on the third floor.

Solange gasped. The room was decorated beautifully and each piece of furniture seemed to have been precisely arranged.

"Jakob I had been wondering why you chose to stay at these old hotels. Now I understand why. Each one has its own character and exudes a charm. I have come to like them much better than those modern characterless ones we stayed at in Florida."

"These older hotels have history. They remind me a lot of Europe and bring back memories."

Jakob looked at Solange. She appeared tired.

"Do you wish to take a rest? I am thinking that after we freshen up we can go down to the lake and maybe find a nice Bistro type place for an early dinner."

"Yes. I am tired. I need to sleep a little."

"I am going to the bar and then for a little walk. I will come back and awake you in about an hour."

Jakob started on the short walk down to the shores of Lake Ontario. As he reached the street corner he heard some muted music of a live band. He strained to listen. His memories of Germany during the war years flooded back when he heard the sounds of the wailing saxophone. He drew in a deep breath of the now cooling evening air and proceeded to the door of the tiny restaurant from which the music was emanating.

He opened the door and walked in to be greeted by the strong smell of fresh coffee. The place was filled with the buzz of low conversations. The music cut across the room with a piercing clarity.

Jakob froze to the spot on which he was standing. He had not experienced feelings or emotion like this since he had played at the clubs in Germany.

As he stood there his old nemisis struck. Thoughts flooded back. He recalled the fights in the bars, the confrontation with the Nazi SS Officer, his betrayal of the women who had helped him. He felt himself spin and reached for the back of the closest chair.

A waitress ran to assist him.

"Are you alright? Here sit down. Can I get you some water? Do you need a doctor?"

Jakob looked at the sweet young girl and smiled. "No thank you. I have been travelling for the last week and today I drove for hours. I think I just experienced fatigue. Now who are those men playing?"

She looked at him for a while before answering.

"Those are our local boys. They are becoming famous. They use the stage name The Sultry Notes. Aren't they good?"

"Yes indeed they are. I played saxophone in Europe during the period of the Second World War. Do you think they would let me join them and play a tune?"

She smiled. "Well, since my husband leads the group let me ask him."

She left and Jakob watched as she proceeded to the low stage in the back corner of the restaurant. She reached up and the tallest member of the group leaned forward and down to her. They engaged in conversation until the man raised his head and look over in Jakob's direction.

She moved back from the group and returned to the bar area. The band continued to play. After several more tunes, the group stopped for a break.

As Jakob sat watching, the taller member approached him.

"My wife tells me you used to play saxophone in Europe and would like to join us to play a number. What do you have in mind?"

"My name is Jakob. I have always had a favorite since I first heard it and that is what I would love to play. It is Gershwin's *Summertime*. It seems fitting now that summer here is drawing to a close."

"That is a really fine choice. Do you remember your instrument?"

"Yes, but I will need to ask you to borrow one as I am traveling and do not have one with me."

"I will ask my band members and let you know."

Jakob watched as the tall man sauntered back to the stage. Before he got there he turned back toward Jakob and smiled.

The band struck up some melodic and soft music. Jakob ordered a glass of wine and sat taking in the atmosphere.

The young waitress returned. "My husband says they will be delighted to have you play but they will be stopping for dinner soon. Can you return in an hour or so?"

"Jakob thought. "Yes. In fact I will bring my wife here for dinner.

Chapter 104

Jakob returned to the hotel to find Solange waiting in the lobby.

"Did you have a nice walk?"

"Yes I did. Are you ready to go for dinner? I may have a surprise for you. I found a nice little restaurant only a few minutes from here."

Arm in arm they left the hotel and walked to the restaurant.

Upon entering the waitress recognized Jakob and waved him over to a table near the stage.

"Solange this may be a special night for us."

Solange frowned. She had no idea what he was speaking about. She decided not to probe.

The waitress returned with a simple but full menu which she handed to them.

Jakob ordered them some wine and they took time to read the menu before deciding on a selection.

The waitress returned to take their order and answer any questions.

"There is one thing on the menu for tonight that we cannot resist. I would like to order it for both of us. It is the roast pork tenderloin. Please tell us about this dish.

"An excellent choice if I may say so. It is moist pork tenderloin with thyme, apples and onion served with seasonal vegetables of your choice."

The waitress took the order and left for the kitchen

When she had left, Solange turned to Jakob.

"Jakob are you alright. Have you taken your medications? You seem to be agitated again. Are you experiencing the problem?"

"Not really. I had some memories but I have been able to control them. Please relax. We will have a nice dinner and then tomorrow I will drive you to my family's farm in Kitchener and complete my business with the Friesen family who leased my land."

Solange looked at him suspiciously. After all the years she knew when Jakob was concealing something.

They ate their dinners and chatted. Jakob was sipping his wine when the band returned. The tall player took the microphone to make an announcement.

"Ladies and Gentlemen. Tonight we have a special treat for you all. A guest here who played in Europe has requested to play with us. Please extend a warm welcome to Jakob Klassen who is formerly from Kitchener."

Solange gasped.

"Jakob. How could you? We have only been here a few hours." Did you plan this?"

Jakob just smiled and arose to make his way onto the stage.

He turned and made a slight bow before accepting the saxophone that was handed to him.

Solange was terrified for him. He hadn't played in years. She was worried this would go terribly wrong.

The band started the opening soft notes of *Summertime* and Jakob gradually eased into the tune. Soon the saxophone was domineering the performance. The notes were long, and with a certain sensuous feeling they hung in the air. The diners were in rapt silence.

Solange was proud and emotional. Tears streamed down her cheeks. She knew the music was bringing back many memories for Jakob and some were not good.

As the tune ended, the restaurant was deadly quiet. Suddenly the patrons burst into spontaneous applause. The tall band leader looked on in astonishment. Jakob took off the strap of the saxophone from around his neck and handed back the instrument. He then walked from the stage to their table and bent to kiss Solange in front of everyone.

"That, my dear, was just for you. I played from my heart and my heart is yours."

It was too much for Solange. The silent tears were usurped by sobs as she realized Jakob's immense love of her.

They arose from their table. Jakob went to the counter to settle his account. The restaurant manager came to the counter.

"We will not accept any money from you. That was a rendition that exceeded anything I have ever heard before. Will you come back and play for us again?"

"It would be my pleasure when we are next visiting."

Jakob and Solange returned to the Prince of Wales. She had a night of love reserved for him in her soul.

Chapter 105

It was early morning when they left the hotel to take the short drive to Niagara Falls. Jakob pulled the car into an area near a viewing point and they crossed the road to stand at the wire safety fence.

Solange was impressed by the size of the falls and the massive amounts of water cascading over them. Mist arose below where the water crashed down. She recalled the view she had from the plane during its descent and approach into Toronto. The sound of the water crashing down was much louder than she had anticipated.

She turned to Jakob with a look of panic.

"Jakob all this water is making me have to pee. I am desperate. What should I do?"

Jakob roared laughing. He turned and noticed a small coffee shop.

"I will come with you. I am sure they have had this request more than once. I will order us some drinks and croissants. We need to eat something before we start our drive up to Kitchener. It is not a long drive but I think we should have something to eat before we leave."

Solange agreed and they started toward the little café. Solange was barely able to walk. She was really desperate.

The café was owned by a French Canadian family from Quebec City. Jakob struck up a conversation with the owners while Solange contributed to the areas water supply.

Jakob looked up at the blackboard on the wall behind the bar and was thrilled to see the vast selection of Quebec inspired pastries and breakfast items available. He was reading the menu when Solange returned looking very composed. She smiled at the owner and graciously sat at one of the wooden pine tables that had obviously been brought from Quebec.

Jakob sat across from her and had barely seated himself before the owner arrived at their table.

"Bonjour, Madam. My name is Gaston. I can assist you to order a nice breakfast. Welcome to our petit café. Where are you visiting from?"

Dressed in a long white apron that was lightly stained with sauces, wine and other food, he stood awaiting her answer.

"That is a difficult question to answer. My husband was born in Kitchener and has travelled and finally selected the Caribbean island of Aruba as his home. I am originally from Florida but also moved to live on Aruba."

"Ah, oui. I have never been to the Caribbean, but yes I have visited Florida. Can I assist you as we have a selection of our French Canadian breakfast items? I assure you that you will enjoy them."

"Gaston, I have never been to Canada before. I must say that I am both intrigued and impressed by how different it is to the United States. I always thought of Canada as being a very cold place and just like the States. I was wrong. I have met kind and different people here. The land is so distinctly unlike anything I experienced when I lived in the States.

Please tell me about the foods. I am so interested to learn and experience new things."

Gaston took this as his cue to deliver an animated rendition of the foods he was obviously so proud of.

"Maam, May I suggest you start with our Cretons. You will like them. I am sure that you have probably never had them before. They are a cold meat spread similar to rillettes and are made with ground pork and seasoned with spices such as cinnamon, savory, and cloves. This is a Québec classic and popular. We spread it on toasted corners at breakfast.

We make Feves au lard here in our kitchen. There are no French or English words to describe them."

"I do not know what they are. Please describe them for me."

"They are slow cooked beans and made with pork back, molasses, mustard, cassonade, ketchup and onion. It takes us eight hours to bake and simmer them. The result is a tasted from heaven. We serve them drizzled with maple syrup."

"Gaston, while they sound delicious and tempting, Solange and I will be driving for some hours today. I fear we would gas each other should we have those. We will be coming back here for another day so maybe we can order then."

"Monsieur, I fully understand. They are a meal for those in outside activity."

Jakob continued to look at the menu.

"What are French Canadian Breakfast Crepes?"

"They are similar to pancakes but much thinner and with very crisp edges. We serve them with maple syrup, eggs and homemade sausage."

Solange was fascinated by the selection that Gaston had recommended.

"I will try the Cretons and yes I will take the Feves au lard. Jakob can open the car window."

Gaston laughed. "A good choice and if I may continue please try our Tart au Sucre to complete your breakfast. My wife prepared them early this morning."

Again Solange was confused by the name and asked for a description.

"It is the world's best Sugar Tart."

Gaston turned to Jakob.

"I will take some Cretons and the French Canadian Crepes, please."

"Should I bring you two coffee presses?"

"Yes please."

"Jakob, what is a coffee press?"

Her question was quickly answered as Gaston returned with the two glass presses with silver plungers.

Solange shook her head.

"I had no idea how things here are not the same as in the States."

The breakfasts were served with a great flourish.

Solange and Jakob ate silently. When they finished Solange looked across to Jakob and spoke.

"That was an unusual but most satisfying breakfast. I am so content. Can we come back here before we go back to Toronto to catch the flight to Holland?"

"Of course we will. Now let's proceed onto Kitchener. I have to meet the Friesen family who are leasing my farm."

As they prepared to leave, Gaston quickly walked to their table accompanied by a petit red haired lady.

"This is my wife Sylvie. She makes all our foods here."

Again Solange was in awe. She thanked them. As they turned to leave Gaston gave each of them a huge hug.

They walked hand in hand from the restaurant to the car for the trip to Kitchener.

Chapter 106

Within minutes of leaving the area of the falls, they were on a country highway that cut through extensive farmlands. The road wound gently through low hills and crossed over many streams. Solange rested in the front seat while looking at the landscape with the growth of trees and the little white farmhouses.

"Jakob what are those bright yellow fields we pass?"

Jakob looked across the open farm field to see what Solange was asking about.

"That is Canola being grown. It is before the harvest. It is late for it to still be in the ground. Maybe that is because it has been raining. The harvesting of Canola requires the crop to be dry."

"It is beautiful to see those patches of bright golden yellow."

They continued to drive by fields of high green stalks of corn. Every so often they would come upon a small roadside stand with produce displayed. There were baskets of tomatoes, containers of blueberries or strawberries, trays of sweet corn and other produce.

Again Solange was confused.

"Jakob. They are selling their produce by the side of the road but there is no one at the stand. Who do you pay?"

"Solange it is done by trust. You will find a jar or box to put money in. There will be a card with the price of the items."

"Does that work? Are people here that honest?"

"On occasion there is theft but very seldom."

They drove on in silence until Solange's breakfast of baked beans announced itself. Jakob guffawed and Solange blushed.

As they approached Kitchener there were more houses and the farmland thinned out.

Jakob slowed as the traffic became more frequent. He drove slowly through the town and recognized some of the stores that he and his father had traded with. Others were gone. Some were converted to completely different stores offering products that had not been available when Jakob had visited as a boy. There were stores selling televisions, electrical goods, fashionable clothing, medical supplies, books and other merchandise. It was in stark contrast to the Kitchener that Jakob had left those many years earlier.

He exited the town and started the drive westward towards his farm. Along the way he was shocked to see the number of houses that had been built on what had been neighboring farmland. He wondered where the Mennonite families had gone.

Thirty minutes from the town he turned onto a dirt road and continued for a couple of miles. On the left a wide wooden farm gate came into view. He slowed.

"Solange I will need to go and open that gate. This is the track that leads into my farm."

He left the car and walked slowly toward the gate. Before opening it Jakob stood and looked at the land for the longest time. Childhood memories flooded back in. He continued to stand and take it all in.

Solange had been watching from the car. She became concerned and decided to leave the car and join him.

She quietly walked up and joined him. She took his hand and gave a slight squeeze. He turned to face her. There were rivulets of tears running down his face. They left light marks where the dirt from travelling washed off.

"Jakob what is going on with you?"

"I had forgotten so much. I am recalling many things. In my mind I am unable to think. All my memories are crashing together. I am not feeling well. I will sit in the car for a few minutes before we go in to meet with the Friesens."

Solange escorted him back to the car and they sat together on the running board of the car looking across at some cattle grazing in the nearby paddock.

Finally Jakob spoke.

"Solange, I do not want to sell the farm any longer. I will need to explain this to the Friesens. I cannot sell it. My father, Isaac Senior and my mother Inge built this from nothing. It was just wild shrub land and rocks when they arrived here. In addition, my parents are both buried here on the farm. I cannot sell it. I hope that maybe either Hans or Isaac Junior may want to take it and farm."

She understood the depth of his feelings. For the first time on the trip she sensed a deep sadness on his part.

"Come on Jakob. Let's go and meet them. They will be waiting."

They crawled back into the car and rocked along the narrow dirt track to the farmhouse.

They had barely stopped when Friesen senior arrived at the picket gate. He was dressed in traditional clothing which was a blue shirt, suspenders and black trousers. He had a wide brimmed straw hat pulled down firmly on his head.

"Welcome Klassen. We have been waiting so long to meet you. I invite you into your house. I wish I could say my house but it isn't."

Jakob and Solange followed him up the path to the front door of the house. Jakob looked affectionately at the house and the barns. Before reaching the house he called out.

"Stop. There is a duty I must perform before I enter the house. He spun and turned to walk in the direction of the barn. Before reaching the barn he turned again to the right and climbed a low incline for a short distance. At the top there was a rectangular railing and fence. Two headstones marked the ground where Isaac Senior and Inge Klassen were buried. Jakob bowed his head and in a low voice recited a psalm he remembered. When he was finished he spoke to them and thanked them for the life he had enjoyed.

Solange and Julius Friesen had stood silently while Jakob had visited his deceased parents.

Solange was worried. The emotional toll that Jakob was experiencing was not good. She addressed Julius.

"We must return to Niagara-on-the-Lake this evening. Our visit will be short. Tomorrow we travel to Toronto for a plane trip to Holland."

Julius rubbed his calloused hand across his chin.

"I understand. I am sure that Jakob Klassen and I can complete our business quickly. We shall go with him now into the house. I have had a lawyer review the papers. Nothing was changed. They are exactly as Jakob sent them to me. Once the documents are signed and witnessed, the transaction will be complete. I have the monies here for the purchase."

Solange sensed the problem that was to surface.

Chapter 107

Bogota, Colombia

At the airport Hans and Moreno surrendered their documents to the Immigration and Customs officials. At the booth they were stopped by a rotund and sly looking individual. He was fat and his skin exuded a greasy film.

After questioning them for a few minutes, the fat official took the passports and walked back to an office with a closed door. He disappeared inside.

They were both tired and felt annoyed. It had been an arduous flight from Aruba to Bogota. The two and a quarter hour flight had not been relaxing. Kids had screamed and kicked at the back of their seats. The old women sitting across the aisle had vomited onto the floor and it had splashed up onto Moreno's trousers. It stank.

They wanted nothing more than to get out of the airport and to the hotel to shower and change clothes.

Hans was trying not to sweat. He was worried the official had detected some anomaly with their forged documents. Fifteen minutes passed before the official reappeared. He was accompanied by a smartly uniformed military officer wearing a large sidearm.

"We need more information. You tell me you are here on a coffee buying trip. Where will you be traveling? What company will you be visiting and purchasing the coffee from?"

Moreno responded.

"We will be visiting in the area of Quindío. We will stay at the Las Ruinas in Medellin during our visit. We represent the Klassen Import Group from Florida."

The official lent toward the military officer and attempted to speak to him in a low tone, not realizing that Moreno understood his Spanish and could hear the comments.

"I think we should take these hombres to our game room."

Moreno immediately knew that things were about to get rough and decided to speak before it was too late.

"Caballeros. My partner and I are going to need some supplies for the trip. Maybe you both can assist us. Of course we will pay the correct amount for the supplies."

The military officer looked at him directly in the eye.

"You speak with an accent. You are Colombian!"

"No you are mistaken. I am from outside Guadalajara in Mexico. I was taught at the school there by a Colombian teacher. We played games with words and accents. You are not the first person to mistake me for a Colombian."

The military officer took Moreno's passport from the official. He looked at it closely and then turned to leave. I will check this further. Your friend Hans will accompany Jose to an office and wait until I return. You will come with me."

Moreno instinctively knew they were in problems.

The officer held Moreno's arm firmly as he marched him down a long narrow corridor. Moreno noticed cells with outer locks on each side of the corridor. He wondered what had given them away. Had somebody betrayed them? If so who would that be?

The officer pushed open a door into one of the cells. Inside was an old wooden table with three chairs around it. A glaring light hung above the table.

"Sit down my friend. We need to talk. I am holding your Mexican passport. You say your name is Ricardo Lopez. I think that is not your name, Moreno Cruz."

Moreno felt as if a jolt of lightning had hit him. He said nothing.

The officer stood back and lent against the dirty wall. Blood and other indescribable stains marked the walls. He reached into his breast pocket and withdrew a pack of cigarettes. He shook the packet and two cigarettes slipped out of the pack. He offered them to Moreno.

"Moreno, you do not remember me do you? We grew up in the same village. Do you remember Padre Ignatius?"

Moreno studied the man's face. Flickers of memories of his wretched life in **La Hormiga** floated in his mind.

"I was his favorite altar boy. Do you remember me now?"

"No I am sorry. That was a long time ago."

"Let me see if I can help your memory. Do you recall what happened to your sister Marcia? I was the one who stopped those thugs who wanted to rape her."

"Yes, I do remember but I have forgotten your name."

"Antonio de la Mar. Now please tell me why you tried to come to Colombia with false papers. Your friend has a passport from Brazil under the name of Hans Krueger. He is German and I am not surprised. So many old Nazis went to Brazil toward the end of the war. I guess he has family who were Nazis. Tell me now. That is not his real name is it?"

Moreno realized that their cover was no longer effective. To lie and dig in deeper would surely mean a horrible imprisonment or death.

"Why have you brought me back here? Why are you asking these questions? You could have handed me over to a lesser ranked soldier or police. I do not trust you or this situation."

Antonio continued to slouch against the wall.

Again he reached into his breast pocket and took out the battered pack of cigarettes. He reached across and offered one to Moreno. This time Moreno accepted the cigarette.

Antonio finally pulled back one of the rickety chairs and heavily sat himself down on it.

"Moreno life here is not good. I wish that one day soon I can leave this country and make a new life for me and my family. I have two daughters and a son. My son is brilliant. His life will be wasted here. I hope we can find a way to America or Canada.

I know that you are a fugitive. The drug lords paid a lot of money after you escaped from Colombia to have men find you. It must be something very large that would cause you to come back here and sacrifice your life. Now would be a good time to tell me the whole story."

"I cannot."

"You make it difficult. Maybe there are ways I can help."

"Why would you help? You will get money and a promotion if you arrest us and hand us over to the authorities."

"I have told you that I want out of this country. I believe you might be able to help me achieve this."

"When we are finished here how will you explain all of this to that Immigration man you called Jose?"

"He is so corrupt. He would sell his mother for a peso. Don't worry about him. I have enough to send him away to a prison for many years. As a government official he will probably be killed in days of being jailed."

"What is it you want?"

"I want you to use your business friends to assist you and get me and my family out of here."

Chapter 108

Antonio remained calm. He watched as Moreno digested the situation.

"Moreno please don't make this anymore difficult than it is. I am asking a simple favor."

"Antonio I don't know how to help you at the moment. As you know I fled with the help of others to escape the powerful Palermo Brothers in Venezuela. It is their mob that owns those drug labs here. I cannot ask others I know here to help you. I don't even know what happened to the boys who helped me escape through Venezuela and to Aruba. I hope they were not caught."

"Moreno. For an intelligent man you are stupid. The two boys were caught. They are now helping the marijuana crops to grow. I understand they made excellent fertilizer. If you don't help me then I suspect you too will be helping the plants to grow."

"There is little I can do. We came here to negotiate the supply of coffee for the Klassen Corporation."

"That my friend is mierda. You know it. Why lie to me when I can help you in many ways?"

"Tell me why I should trust you"

"You are speaking to me. I could have called the police and had you taken away. You know how things work here. Why are you being so stupid?"

"You are one of them. When I was trying to escape from the mob, no one would help me. All of you are corrupt. Go to hell."

"What is so wrong that I ask you to help me and my family? I have offered to help you. I am a senior officer. I have rank and many privileges. Think carefully. I can assist you in many ways."

"How can I possibly trust you?"

"Let me bring your traveling partner here to join in this conversation. That may help."

Antonio clicked open the locked cell door. Moreno heard the lock reset as Antonio left.

Some time passed until Moreno heard muffled shouts and curses. The door into the cell flew open and two guards shoved Hans into the cell.

Hans landed spread eagled on the cell floor. He looked up at Moreno in a confused state.

"I expected to see you beaten and bruised. You look like you just dressed for a gala. What the hell is happening?"

Moreno motioned to Hans to sit on the low bunk of the old iron bed in the cell. Moreno continued to sit at the table.

He told Hans of the situation. As was finishing, Antonio entered the cell.

"Herr Hans Krueger, your passport is rubbish. You too are trying to enter Colombia with forged documents. Now I advise you to listen to your friend Moreno and carefully decide what you will both want to do. I am going to leave you both. I will return before the end of my day. I hope for your sakes you make the right decision. In four hours we have a shift change. I will be forced to leave you to the mercy of the new officers. I don't think you will find them as friendly or accommodating as I am."

Antonio barked a command and a pimply young guard hastily pulled open the cell door. The young guard stared an evil look at Hans and Moreno.

After Antonio and the guard left and they were left alone Hans spoke.

"What do we do know? How could we ever have prevented a situation like this? I am concerned that we have put the whole rescue attempt at risk."

"I grew up in the same village as Antonio. The people there are peasants. They are simple but honest people. I am sure that those attributes are still with Antonio. I understand why he wants to escape to a better life. I think we can use him in our mission and make him an ally."

"You are too trusting. I am sure our Dutch Marine friend would not be happy and have a solution for this."

"Hans what are our options? We are literally in a jail here now. I can bargain with Antonio for our release."

"I don't like it but I will agree."

Together they sat in silence or discussed the alternatives until four hours later the cell door opened. Antonio stood in the entrance staring at them both.

"Antonio I think we can offer you some interesting possibilities. They will not come cheap or without your commitment. Are you sure you want to come with us?"

"Yes. I am the senior officer here. I thought things would change when they promoted me to this position. I thought I would have money and be able to care for my family. It is no better. They tell you that you are a high level officer but give you no more money. If you want more money you must become corrupt and do the dirty work for them. If you don't, then all you get is more work and the other men hate you. I want to get away from all of this."

"You start now. Tell us what you can do."

"I will advise them that I am taking you to the main prison for questioning and detention. You will escape. I will take you to a safe place to hide. I will help you. You must trust me. If you share your real plans with me I am sure there is a lot I can do. You know my price. I want me and my family out of Colombia."

"We cannot guarantee that. We will need others to agree first."

"For days there have been rumors here. It seems that some friends of the Palermo Brothers encountered problems. I understand the American sailors were caught."

Neither Hans nor Moreno knew what Antonio was talking about.

"We don't understand. What American sailors?"

"I do not know the details. It seems that the Venezuelan gang had recruited some help from the Americans who patrol the waters here. There has been a lot of talk. Much of the talk is bravado and lies."

"Can you get us a secure way to communicate back to our office in the States?"

"Why?"

"You are asking us for help and we must speak to others."

Antonio took some time before answering.

"It can be arranged. I advise you to be careful. In this country there is another faction growing that is opposed to this government. They are rebels and violent. Their operations are financed by the drugs. The Palermos assist them in many ways. They have had others who fled killed in Florida and on other islands. Moreno, there is a lot of money being offered to either kill you or for your capture and delivery to Venezuela. I could have done that. The amount of money is huge and I would no longer need to work in this shitty job. The fact that I did not turn you in should demonstrate that I do want to help you and can be trusted."

Hans spat on the floor. "You Colombians are all the same. You say nice things to a person yet think nothing of stabbing the person from behind when their backs are turned away. You might fool Moreno because he is one of you. Don't expect me to believe every word that comes out of your mouth."

"Herr Kruger. How would you like me to arrange an interrogation now about that passport that is a forgery?"

Hans glared at him.

"You want to help us but have an attitude like that? "

"I can have photos taken and soon we will have your real identity. I think now is a good time for you to be quiet and show me some respect. I do not care if you decide to be a problem. The goons here will be happy to make you calm."

Moreno recognized the temper streak that he had observed with Hans earlier in Aruba.

"Antonio may you and I speak alone? I ask you to assist Hans to a location where he will be safe and can have a drink while we talk about things."

"I will have you both handcuffed and on the pretense that I am transporting you to the prison for interrogation, I will drive you personally. I will explain that you are disguised but the government has been looking for you. It will be only appropriate if a ranking officer handles the arrest and delivery of the prisoners. These morons will accept that."

Antonio shouted for the guards. Within minutes Hans and Moreno were handcuffed and lead through a passageway to a compound at the rear of the building. A small army transport truck stood parked by the entrance. Hans and Moreno were pushed into the back and handcuffed to the metal dividing barrier.

The guards stepped back from the vehicle laughing. One lit a cigarette and deliberately blew smoke into the back of the truck through the open window.

Antonio jumped into the cabin and jerkily the truck pulled out of the yard and onto the cobble stoned street.

Chapter 109

Antonio accelerated away from the administration building at the airport. He was unsure where to take his captives. He had decided to treat them well. They were his ticket to escape the life he lived in Colombia.

As he turned out of the gate, two police on motorcycles pulled alongside his truck. They pointed to the curb and signaled him to pull over. He immediately complied.

A stocky police officer walked up to the driver's window. Antonio lowered the window and the intense heat of the day flooded into the truck's cab. Antonio recognized the cop. They gambled together at a friend's adobe each week during the evening.

"Antonio. I am surprised to see you driving this truck. What is the problem? Can we help?"

"No. I have to take these men for questioning at headquarters. Everything is under control."

The cop stuck his head in through the windows to examine Hans and Moreno. Antonio flinched at the smell of the cop's rancid breath. The truck stunk with the smell of the vomit from Moreno's trousers where the old lady on the flight had deposited her breakfast.

Antonio looked at the cop and wondered about the life he lived. He knew he had mistresses as he would boast of his conquests during the card games. Antonio had never really liked the man but had always been cordial and polite.

Antonio suspected he was one of the most corrupt cops in his division.

"Yes everything is fine. I decided to take these men myself as I want to finish early today and visit some relatives who live near the Presidio. They have a new baby and I have yet to go and congratulate the family."

"Do you want us to escort you? We can have the sirens on and get you through the traffic. You can pay me on Thursday night when we get together at our friend's for the card games. I will let you lose."

The cop laughed, but Antonio detected the underlying message.

"Yes please escort us to the area. I do not want to create great curiosity about these men. Please turn away just before we reach there."

"I understand. So you have a little private mission planned with these two men. All the time I thought you were straight and never did these things. I am pleased to know that you too are able to make a little money from things."

The cop turned and slowly walked back to his bike. He mounted it and kicked it into life. The motor roared and he and his partner flanked each side of the truck.

Antonio drove the truck with the escorts at speed. Cars parted and pulled to the side as the wail of the sirens penetrated the air. After thirty minutes of weaving through traffic, they arrived within a half mile of La Modelo jail and military barracks. The cops slowed and silenced the sirens. They waved to Antonio as they peeled away.

Antonio was bathed in sweat. He had been unsure whether they would honor the agreement or double cross him. There was no one to trust.

With the accompanying cops gone, Antonio pulled the truck to the curb a distance from the gates that opened into the large parking lot. There were sentries stationed at the gate which was equipped with a heavy metal arm. Each vehicle was stopped and papers checked. A sentry would walk around the vehicle and inspect the contents.

Antonio watched the cars and trucks entering and leaving. He saw his chance. A group of jeeps were moving toward the exit. After clearing the inspection they turned out onto the street and proceeded to approach where he was parked. He watched carefully and seized the opportunity to pull from the curb and into the procession when a large gap had presented itself. The truck did not look out of place as it blended in with the other military vehicles.

Antonio stayed with them for a couple of miles and then turned off to head to a quiet area in the south of the city. He waved to the drivers of the jeeps as he did so as a friendly gesture as he left the convoy.

Hans and Moreno had watched the whole incident without saying a word.

Antonio drove down a narrow lane and stopped at an old house built of blocks and rotting timbers. He jumped down from the cab and swung open the rear door of the truck. He reached in and released the handcuffs.

"Now we will have that serious talk."

He pointed to the house and motioned Hans and Moreno to leave the truck and go into the house. It seemed all very casual but Hans remained alert and did not trust Antonio or the situation.

Antonio opened a weather beaten old wooden door and waved them in. Their eyes ceased working in the dark interior. It took a few minutes before they adjusted to the darkness.

They looked around. Some old chairs, a table, a bunk and a bookshelf stuffed with magazines and some leather bound books. A narrow doorway led off to another room.

Antonio asked them to sit. They pulled up chairs and when they were seated he left to go into the other room. He returned with a bottle and three glasses. He set then down on the table.

"Now let's have a drink. If we are to be partners then we need to establish some trust."

Hans spoke. "I told you before. I do not trust you. I think that if you don't get what you want then you will betray us."

"I already had the opportunity to betray you with those cops. They knew you weren't both Colombians. I could have let them take you. It would have been simple for me. Your lives would not have meant much. Their interest is money and they could have bargained with your families."

Moreno knew this to be true.

"Hans what he says is true. We don't have many other options. We need to trust him and bring him into our plan."

Hans continued to glare at Antonio.

"If you do anything that is suspicious I will kill you with my bare hands."

Chapter 110

Antonio pulled up his chair and poured each a glass of Antioqueno Aguardiente.

Hans watched with apprehension as Antonio poured.

Moreno was smiling.

"Moreno, what is that shit he is serving us?"

"That 'shit' is a traditional drink here in Colombia. It is pure nectar. It is made of molasses, virgin honey, sugar and anise. When you drink it will remind you of anise. It is expensive and treasured. Many here only drink it on special occasions. You should apologize to Antonio. I am sure this cost him a lot of money."

Hans apologized and reached for the glass. He gulped it down and immediately started coughing.

"I meant to tell you it is very dry and extremely strong. Be careful or you will soon be kissing the floor."

Antonio refilled Hans' glass.

"Here. We will sit while Moreno goes and removes that disgusting vomit from his trousers."

Moreno arose and made his way into a little room that served as a bathroom. There was a putrid bucket on the floor for urinating. Feces floated on the surface. The stench filled Moreno's nostrils. He recalled these rooms from his days growing up in the rural village.

He took a container of water and poured it over the legs of his trousers. The water ran across the rough stone floor. He returned and joined Hans and Antonio. He looked at the bottle of Antioqueno Aguardiente. It was almost empty. Hans was leaned back in his chair and had obviously enjoyed a large amount of the liquor.

Antonio spoke.

"I have brought you to this place so we can speak without prying eyes and ears around. As I said earlier I know that it must be something most important for you to return here Moreno. You know I could have had you jailed and you would disappear into one of Colombia's infamous prisons. It would take years for anyone to find you. I think this demonstrates that I want to help you in order to get out of Colombia."

"I believe you. My friend here has had a most interesting life. You must excuse him. He lived in a bad situation in Germany at the end of the war. His life was not easy. It is hard for him to accept people. When he makes friends he is fiercely loyal to those friends. He is just being careful with you."

Hans looked across at Moreno. His eyes were bloodshot and his speech slurred. The drink had hit him hard.

Moreno sat and thought for a long time before he decided to inform Antonio of their plans.

"Antonio I will share some information with you as I do trust you. I cannot tell you everything.

We are not here to do anything to offend the government or create problems. We are here to try and help a friend of the Hans' family. He was kidnapped and imprisoned by a drug group who are operating in the south in the area of Florencia. We have information that he is enslaved there and forced to work in a drug lab. We are going to attempt to break into the camp and rescue our friend."

"Those camps are well disguised and heavily guarded. You are either very brave or very stupid. You will be killed. You are just two men with no training or skills in the jungle. If the guards don't get you the wild jaguars or other wild creatures of the jungle will. We send men into the jungle to train and almost every time there is a death. Remember Moreno when we were growing up? We would catch the poisonous spiders and snakes. The area of Florencia is surrounded with heavy jungle and it is so close to the Andes. There is a lot to be concerned about. I think you should abandon your plan. There may be other ways to get him. Do you think you could buy him back? Is he old? If he is old they will agree to sell him I am sure."

"No we will not try to do that. If we failed to negotiate they will surely kill us and our friend."

"There is a huge military base near Florencia. It is for army and air force. There is also a police presence there. I have an idea. I will get posted there. Not many want to go there. With my rank I can transfer on a days notice. I will be able to help you from there. I will have access to the information. I suspect that some of the soldiers there are involved with the drug camps. I will be careful and listen carefully. I will try to find out where the camps are exactly. Maybe I will volunteer to guard one when I am not on duty. No one will suspect anything."

Moreno considered all that Antonio had said.

"There is more you should know. We have another member. He is here in Colombia. He is a jungle warfare trained marine. He is heading the effort. I will need to convince him to allow you to participate in any way."

There was a resounding thud. Moreno and Hans looked across the room to see Hans had fallen from his chair onto the dirt floor.

"We will let him sleep it off. He seems to be a troubled man."

"Where will you meet this other member of your party?"

"He is staying in Cali. He is trying to purchase equipment there. It was too dangerous in Bogota and impossible near Florencia."

"I can help with that. With my military rank I can get equipment. Do you know what he is trying to purchase?"

"No but I suggest we travel to Cali tomorrow."

"People will be suspicious."

"No. We have disguised business credentials. We are assistants involved in an exploration for mineral and oil. We are employees of Royal Imperial Oil."

"That is excellent. I will be able to assist. I will 'get orders' that I am to provide you protection in that area. I will also be able to get you certain items."

"Antonio I cannot ask you to do this. We may all be killed during the operation."

"It may be better to be dead than caught or for me to continue living in Colombia."

"I need to speak with others in Aruba. How can I do this?"

"You are here to negotiate coffee. I will set it up for you. I understand you will need to speak to your company there. That shouldn't arouse any suspicion."

"Where will I use the phone?"

"There is a police post. I will arrange it."

"Don't you think that will be dangerous?"

"No. The commanding officer is my uncle."

Moreno laughed. Nothing much had changed in Colombia since his departure from the country."

Chapter 111

It was late afternoon before Hans regained control. Moreno told him of the agreement with Antonio.

"I suggest we get some food. It is getting late in the afternoon. We have a lot to accomplish tonight and tomorrow."

Antonio spoke. "I will come with you now to be sure you get food and will be safe. I will go onto the base and request a reassignment to Florencia region. The officer who assigns the men is a close friend. He will make sure I have all the papers. Tomorrow we will take the drive to Cali. It will be a long day. I suggest you both eat and then sleep. I wish to leave early in the morning while it is still dark. There will be less curious eyes."

The three left the little adobe and walked to a cantina that served a variety of local foods.

"I recommend you eat well now. It will be a long trip tomorrow and it is unlikely we will stop for any food. I will get us some from the base. The trip to Cali will take us over fourteen hours."

After they entered the cantina and were seated, Antonio ordered a number of dishes. He ate with them for a while before leaving to arrange for their trip.

"I will see you both back at the house. Please do not make any trouble. Eat your food and go directly back there. I will pay now."

Hans and Moreno sat alone as Antonio departed the cantina.

"Moreno you are a Colombian. Are we making a big mistake? Do you really trust him?"

"Yes I trust him. He is taking a huge risk to help us. I understand why he wants to leave Colombia. It is a hard country. For hundreds of years Colombia has been involved in upheaval and wars. Most recently the La Violencia just ended. The people were angry with the military dictatorship. There was a civil war in the countryside. People are still angry with the status of the civilian elite who own and control the farms. It is a situation of a powerful few controlling the lives of many. Colombia has had many wars with our neighboring countries. Our unrest and turmoil goes back many hundreds of years to when the Spanish ruled. I doubt there will ever be peace in this country. In this situation I understand why Antonio is eager to help us if we can arrange to get him away from here and to a place he can live safely and make money to support his family."

For minutes Hans said nothing. He finally spoke.

"I can understand what you say. I saw what war does to people. I remember the streets and the broken people in them after that madman Hitler destroyed Germany. I remember the destruction of the cathedrals and buildings that had been the pride of the German people. I now understand why Antonio will help us."

They finished eating and returned to the house to find Antonio already there and waiting for them.

"I filed papers for the trip. I have requisitioned a Willys Jeep for the trip with fuel and supplies. All was approved. Let us sleep and we leave at four in the morning."

Antonio dragged three shabby mattresses from the back room and set them on the floor.

"This is best. We cannot go and stay somewhere else. There are many here who will lie and report you for just a peso. It will not be comfortable but you will be safe."

"Antonio when can I make that phone call to Aruba? It is important."

"I will take you now. Hans you must stay here. We will return immediately after making the call."

Moreno and Antonio were about to leave when Hans asked, "What do I do if someone comes in here?"

"Nobody has business here. You will be left alone."

They exited. Hans pulled his mattress across the room so he had a full view of the entrance door.

He lay on top of the mattress and started to drift into a sleep that was assisted by the liquor still circulating in his system. His thoughts drifted back to his days on the streets in post war Germany and then to happier days in Aruba.

He was almost asleep when he heard a click at the door. He sat upright expecting to see Moreno and Antonio returning. Instead it was a menacing looking man with rough features. Hans stayed silent. He pretended to sleep. Through a squinted shut eye he watched as the man went to the pile of clothes and started searching the pockets. The man then went to the table and looked at the books and papers. Nor content he went into the room at the back of the little house. Hans took this opportunity and sprang from the mattress. He ran up behind the man and delivered a fierce punch to the back of the man's neck. He crumpled to the floor. Hans turned him over and examined him. Hans soon realized that the man was no peasant or hobo. He was disguised to look the part. He pulled off his belt and strapped it tightly around the unconscious man. Hans looked for other materials to tie him down. There were none. Hans cursed.

As he stood wondering what he should do next, the door opened and Antonio and Moreno entered. They saw the man on the floor. Antonio rushed forward. He lifted the man's face and stared at him.

"We must leave immediately. This is one of the Palermo Brothers henchmen. Your disguises are known. I have the jeep. Come on let's get out now."

Hans and Moreno grabbed the few possessions they had and ran to the jeep with Antonio.

"This is a bad start for you. I hope that the Palermos only know about your plan to buy coffee. If they know more than this it will be a major problem. They may arrange for your friend to be killed rather than allow you to attempt a rescue."

Hans and Moreno threw their gear into the back of the jeep. Antonio jumped into the front seat and cranked it to life. They sped from the side streets onto a major street that led to the roads to Cali.

"When I was arranging for my 'transfer' I spoke with several commanders and they advised me that there are small groups of rebels on the highway. They have been stopping cars and creating problems. If that happens do not say anything. I will speak with them and handle your credentials. Do you understand?"

They drove on into the night. Both Hans and Moreno fell into a deep sleep. Antonio remained alert and sped southward toward Cali. He prayed that they would not be stopped by bandits.

The sky was starting to lighten when they approached the outskirts of Cali. Antonio pulled the jeep off the road.

"Where is your friend staying? We will need to establish contact with him."

Moreno placed a firm hand on Hans arm.

"I know Cali. I know where to find him. You will drive me into the town and I will contact him. There is a church off the town square. You will wait there for me to come back to you."

Antonio nodded and slowly inched the jeep back onto the road for the short drive into the town. As they entered and passed some stores, Moreno asked Antonio to stop. He then jumped from the jeep and quickly disappeared.

Chapter 112

Moreno walked to the address in Cali that he had been given during last evening's telephone call to Isaac Junior in Aruba. He was to rendezvous with the former Dutch Marine, Adrien.

He arrived at a low multi apartment building in the working class, crime ridden barrio of Siloe which was located on a hill in South Western Cali. Moreno was wary of the groups of young men standing around the open air bars. Siloe was renowned for murder, beatings and other gun obsessed criminal activities. Moreno tried to blend in with the mix of locals. He walked on avoiding eye contact or doing anything to attract attention.

It had taken forty five minutes before he arrived at the address. He banged on the door. There was no answer. He continued knocking. He heard a noise behind him and turned to see an old woman shuffling toward him. She was wearing a black widow lace mourning veil and was dressed in a somber black dress. She approached Moreno and passed him. She withdrew a key and opened the apartment door. She beckoned Moreno to enter. Inside was squalor. Dirty food containers littered the table and old newspapers lay on the floor.

As soon as Moreno was inside, she ripped off the veil to reveal it was Adrien, The Dutch Marine.

"You cannot be too careful around here. Where is Hans?"

Moreno sat on the edge of an old collapsing chair. Adrien took a position on an old wooden fruit crate that served as a chair for the kitchen table.

Moreno told Adrien of the recent events and the situation with Antonio.

"I don't like it. I have concerns. It will be difficult enough to get into the camp and break out with Juan should he be there. Neither you nor Hans have the jungle and assault training needed for a mission like this. Now we have a third person. This is a complication."

"I have arranged for us all to meet at the San Pedro Cathedral here in Cali. At that time you will have the opportunity to speak with Antonio and decide whether he will be of value to us and capable of assisting. Remember he grew up here and has trained with the Colombian Army. He has a lot of contacts. I see many benefits for us if he can deliver. If not then I will arrange for an unfortunate accident. I will leave now and meet you at the cathedral in about an hour. The others will be waiting."

Moreno set off to the cathedral. The day was hot and he was parched. He stopped at a colorful street drink stand and ordered a fresh fruit juice. As he sipped it he took in the surrounds and in particular looked for anyone who may be following him. He detected that there was no risk was being followed.

When he reached San Pedro Cathedral he walked up the narrow stairs leading into the Cathedral. Inside there was a center aisle with pews made of dark wood on each side. He spied Antonio and Hans. Antonio was kneeling as if praying and Hans sat on the edge of the seat of the pew with his head bowed into his hands as if reflecting.

Moreno took a position on a pew three behind them. There was a scattering of people in the church. Moreno glanced around quickly. He did not detect any concerns. At the altar, candles burned brightly. A statue of the Virgin Mary was set into an alcove and lit by a small light directed upwards to give the maximum effect of beauty and serenity.

While they all waited for the arrival of Adrien, a priest arrived and opened the door to the confessional. Minutes passed and then the parishioners started entering the doors either side of the one entered by the priest to make their confessions. Moreno chuckled. He could only imagine the sins they told. "Bless me father for I have sinned. I stole my neighbor's marijuana packages and then killed him."

 He imagined the response. "OK my son. Say three Hail Marys, two Our Fathers and remember to contribute to the priests' Christmas Fund"

The church emptied of the sinners who had come to be forgiven. Antonio, Hans and Moreno stayed. As the priest exited the confessional he stared at them but continued on his way. It was obvious he did not want to be delayed from going to participate in whatever heavenly delights he had planned. Again Moreno's imagination ran wild. Did the priest have a prostitute or maybe some strongly fortified altar wine....or possibly a little boy?

Moreno laughed gently. He did not want to draw attention.

They were getting concerned when Adrien did not arrive.

Moreno was about to leave in search of Adrien when another priest arrived. Dressed in a long black cassock and wearing a huge crucifix with a highly polished Jesus on the cross. The priest walked with a stoop and a limp. He headed into the opposite confessional and on his way in pointed to Moreno to enter one of the side confessionals. It was Adrien. Moreno loved the disguises and wondered how he had got the clothing.

He waited a couple of minutes and entered the confessional. Adrien slid open the panel and Moreno could see him through the wire mesh screen.

"I want you to send in that Dutch Marine. After he comes in make sure Hans occupies the other side. We do not want anyone overhearing the conversation. Now go."

Moreno exited and signaled Antonio to the confessional. He walked over to Hans and whispered to go in and occupy the other confessional to stop anyone else from entering. Hans obliged.

Moreno sat in the pew waiting. Several people had arrived in the church for the services which were to be held. Moreno could hear low murmuring coming from the confessional. Ten minutes passed before Antonio emerged looking very contrite. Only a couple more minutes later Hans exited and walked to the rear of the Cathedral.

Moreno got up and walked down the aisle before joining Hans outside in the shade from the cathedrals huge shadow.

"Adrien grilled Antonio. He asked some detailed questions and made Antonio aware of what fate would await him if Adrien was to uncover any peculiarity. He decided to accept Antonio into our party."

"What do we do now?"

"Adrien has rented another house and we will meet there. It is in La Flora, a secluded part of Cali. He wishes to lay out the plans for the rescue. We will meet him there late this afternoon. I have directions and the address."

Chapter 113

Dusk was forming when they arrived at Adrien's. He admitted them and they gathered in a room devoid of any art or furniture except for six chairs.

Hans was uncomfortable. "What is this place?"

"We have locations in different countries where we operate. They are what others call safe houses. Only certain personnel of rank and secrecy clearance get to use them or even know of their existence. This house was deemed to have outlived its usefulness by the forces. Some accomplices who run a security firm bought it. I have arranged for us to use it during the mission."

Antonio paced the floor. He turned to Adrien and asked, "How do you intend to get your friend out of Colombia. Most of those drug labs have police and military officers working for them. Once you snatch your man the word will be sent out quickly. Escape will be virtually impossible. Do you know if your man is still healthy? Will he have the stamina to escape through the jungle and be alert and fast enough to avoid the patrols?"

"We know little about his condition. We are operating on information provided by some Colombians who have fled to Aruba. The information they shared with us is credible. This man is connected to some very powerful people and they have had some facts checked. Now let us discuss the plan."

Antonio was eager to demonstrate his education and military training to Adrien. They discussed methods of approach and how to assimilate with the locals ahead of the rescue.

The conversation carried on for hours. Finally Adrien fell silent.

"Antonio there are critical things I need to purchase. Can you help?"

"It depends, but I am sure I will be able to assist."

"I need to buy rifles. I need a rugged jeep, four walkie-talkie radios, plastic explosives, grenades, binoculars and clothing for our man. He will not be dressed for an escape through the jungle."

"None of those items will be a problem. What type of rifles do you want? I can easily get you some older FN rifles or some newer Galil."

"My preference is the Belgian made FN. In the marines we used these and received extensive training on use and repair of malfunctions. How old are these rifles?"

"Most will be ten years old."

"What about the jeep?"

"I have a contact with the company who buys the old jeeps from the army. I am sure I can arrange to get a good one. As for the other items I will ask some not so honest soldiers here that I know to help. When do you need this stuff?"

"Tomorrow."

"I am not sure that is possible. Why the rush?"

"I want to perform the rescue while the rainy season is still here and strong. I wish to use the elements to my advantage."

Hans and Moreno had sat in fascination listening to the two military men strategizing.

"I will go on base tomorrow and see what I can do. I recommend you plan to be here an extra day."

"There is one thing you can assist with. I have maps of the Caqueta but they are old and not too accurate. If you can get me the military topographical maps they would be of great value."

"I will attend at the base tomorrow with my orders to escort the survey party south. I will requisition the goods you ask for. What I cannot get from the base I will have my contacts on the black-market provide. I will need American money for this."

"You will have it. We will give it to you tonight. Remember my little friend, if you dare make problems we have a deal.

My bare hands around your throat until you choke no more."

Once again Hans decided to confront Antonio.

The hour grew late. Adrien spoke. "You cannot stay here. No one is allowed. You must return to your place. It is unsafe to take a taxi here. Even during the day it is not advised. I will drive you back."

As they were about to pull up to the house that Antonio had arranged, they noticed the cars parked nearby. The house was being watched by the police.

Antonio was angry. "Shit. I paid good money for a private place. Let me think."

Adrien was annoyed. "This is why I did not want anyone else in our group."

"I have an idea. Take Hans and Moreno back into the town. There is a hotel before we reach the main connecting road. It is owned by a friend of my family. I will explain that they are businessmen who drank too much with us and have nowhere to stay. After we leave them there you can take me back to the house. The only thing that those cops will see is my returning from a late night."

"I like that idea. Now guide me to your friend's hotel."

As Hans and Moreno were about to leave the car, Adrien spoke.

"Tomorrow morning I will be here for you. Do not go to the bar tonight. Please go to your room and stay there. We are being watched. Someone has told them something. I heard of the capture of those US Coast Guard men. I think that the drug lords in Venezuela have made everyone here scared. They are watching any American or foreigner they suspect may be an agent for the United States. I will be here seven in the morning. Please be ready. There is a long day ahead of us."

"It seems there is too much to gather before we start the trip to Florencia. I am concerned if we get stopped and searched. How will we explain the equipment?"

Hans was perplexed.

Adrien shot him a look of defiance and an expression of looking at a fool's stupidity.

"Hans. We are a survey party. We need our own protection and that's why the rifles. The plastic explosives are for us to explode in the mineral veins in the areas we think have potential and take samples. The walkie-talkies we need for communicating while we walk individually into the jungle. The grenades are for our personal protection. Hans you should think about how you will transport your cargo. Let me worry about these other matters."

Chapter 114

The next day Adrien and Antonio set about obtaining the necessary items. Things went surprisingly well. Adrien was amazed at the ease at which he could get the rifles and explosives.

"Antonio we haven't been able to get hand grenades. Can you get some from the base?"

"I will be there this afternoon. I will speak to the quartermaster. He is a family member from my mother's relatives. He hates the government here. I am surprised he has not been arrested and thrown in prison. His views are widely known. He will provide us some supplies and requisition the grenades."

The value of having Antonio as part of the mission was evident. Adrien hoped that he was not deceiving them. He would hate to kill the young man to whom he had developed a liking.

It was late in the day when they all met. Hans and Moreno had spent the day getting some food items and some medical supplies. They were unsure whether Juan was healthy or in need of any medications or bandages. They bribed a pharmacist and in return received a large supply of painkillers and other narcotics.

The group decided they would eat a meal at the local cantina. The next day would be hot and long. They did not want to stop and find food during the drive to Caquetá.

"We leave at early dawn. I obtained the papers from the base that authorize me to obtain any items required to protect us on the trip or during the 'survey'.

I am required to report to the base outside Florencia after our arrival."

"Today Hans and I found a store that painted and made signs. I had one made for the jeep."

Moreno produced a glaring yellow sign with bright green lettering pronouncing **"Royal Imperial Oil and Minerals and Exploration Survey."**

Adrien laughed. "That is perfect. Where do we put it?"

"It attaches by magnets to the side of the jeep."

Adrien nodded.

"That is good. We want the locals to know who we are and what we are doing. I expect some will come and ask for jobs to assist us. We must be careful. I intend to use this ruse to try and find out about the camp. You will see how there is no loyalty when the peasants are shown money or food."

"Where will we stay in Florencia?" asked Hans.

"We will do what all survey crews do. We will sleep in our tents. At night we will need to have someone on guard duty. I am sure we will have uninvited guests during the night."

They piled out of the house into the still hot evening air and strolled at a casual pace to the little cantina. It was bustling with people. Upon entering Antonio nudged Adrien and whispered to him to observe the presence of the soldiers at the bar. They were not in uniform.

"I will go and start a conversation with them. It is not normal for soldiers to be in a place like this. There are better facilities on the base and they do not pay for food or drinks. This is strange. I suspect they are trying to find out information on strangers in the area or unusual events. It is better I go and tell them I am the officer to escort the exploration team to Florencia. If they decide to come to the table I want you to stay quiet Moreno. Your accent will give it away. Pretend you do not speak Spanish....any of you."

Adrien watched as Antonio reached the bar and slapped one of the men on the shoulder. They were soon embroiled in what appeared to be a heavy conversation. Antonio reached into his pocket and withdrew some papers. The men at the bar scanned them. When they had finished, Antonio pointed across at Hans, Moreno and Adrien.

Hans immediately assumed that he had betrayed them and trouble was about to happen. He clenched his fists ready for the confrontation.

Antonio started back from the bar toward their table.

"Senors, welcome. My fellow officer tells me you are here to help with discovering our oil and gold. That is good. We need more than just farms here. We need industry. I hope you succeed with your survey."

Hans relaxed and in heavily accented English thanked the officer.

"Where are you from? You sound strange."

"I was born in Germany but grew up in Brazil."

"I have family who live in Brazil. Where do you live?"

Hans stammered. "I live in Rio"

"Well that is a coincidence. My family live in Rio de Janeiro as well. Maybe you know them. They are the Hoffmans. We left Germany. I was born in Berlin. We are Jewish and we left before the Nazi party made it impossible. Where were you born?"

Hans replied in German.

"I was born and lived in Munich."

"Do you have your passport? I would like to see this."

Hans looked at Adrien and then focused on Antonio. He was sure they had been discovered and Antonio had exposed them.

Adrien gave Hans an imperceptible nod. Hans reached into his breast pocket and removed his passport. The officer snatched it and opened the identity page. After reading the details he thumbed through the passport looking for visa stamps.

"I am curious. For a member of a exploration team I would expect to see stamps from the countries you have visited. I do not even see a stamp here for Colombia."

"On our last survey trip into Mexico, we were rained out. The camp was completely flooded. My passport was damaged. I needed to obtain a new one."

The officer opened the identity section again and looked at the place of issue. It was Rio de Janeiro.

"That doesn't explain why there is no entry stamp for Colombia. Maybe you should come with us now to speak with the Immigration officers."

Antonio sensed the danger. "That won't be necessary. It was already checked at my base in Bogota. It seems that as typical the lazy immigration officer was half asleep and didn't process his passport correctly. I have made an appointment for his passport to be entered when we return to Bogota. Both his entry and exit from Colombia will be recorded.

Chapter 115

The officer shrugged and handed the passport back to Hans. They made small talk around exploring and the excitement of a major find. Eventually, the soldiers became bored and drifted back to the bar and attempted to attract the attention of the senoritas at a nearby table.

Adrien was not happy.

"After that exchange we leave tonight. Meet me back at the house. I hope you are all packed. What isn't packed will be left behind. I sense real danger if we delay."

He backed away from the table and quietly slipped out the door.

"We have not eaten yet. Will we be able to get food during the drive?"

"Yes. I think we should leave. Adrien was emphatic that we leave soon."

At the house, Adrien had changed into fatigues and was wearing a peaked cap. He looked like a construction worker. He ordered the others to dress similarly.

Approximately thirty minutes passed before the two jeeps wheeled out onto the highway to start the drive south. In one jeep Adrien travelled with Hans. In the other Moreno was joined by Antonio.

The lights of Cali quickly faded as they drove away. An hour had passed and they had started the climb into the mountains.

After nine hours of winding through the mountains the village of Popayan appeared. Adrien slowed his jeep and Moreno followed. They crawled slowly through the town until Moreno noticed a restaurant with some local men standing around outside drinking beers from open bottles.

He signaled Adrien to stop. They pulled into the curb. Antonio called out to the men. They returned shouts of greetings. The atmosphere seemed friendly.

 One of the older men wearing a beaten straw hat headed toward them as they stopped.

Antonio and Moreno broke into a rapidly spoken conversation with the man. They explained they were travelling with their fellow workers to assist in a survey to find oil. They asked him about getting food at that late hour.

The man frowned and then told them of the foods the restaurant was known for. He explained it was a meeting place for the local farmers and the food had to be good or they would deal with the cook. He laughed at his own joke.

With the jeeps parked, the group pushed through the assembled men into the restaurant. The walls were painted in a faded sickly green. A wire hung from the ceiling and powered two bare light bulbs. It was not luxurious.

The dark skinned woman behind the counter looked at them suspiciously.

Moreno asked for the available foods. She responded quickly. Hans and Adrien were confused.

"Let me tell you what it is possible to have. There are arepas, empanadas and Mazorca desgrandas.

I recommend the Mazorca desgrandas. It is a filling meal. It is a meal made of a bed of griddled corn kernels with sausage slices, pulled pork, pulled chicken, a lot of wilted lettuce and covered in fried cheese. Potato chip sticks are placed on top and it is drenched in hot sauce.

That is what I am having."

Orders for four servings were requested and they moved outside to join the men. Introductions were made. The men were a happy lot. The effects of their hard lives were evident in their features. Faces with weather beaten, cracked and wrinkled skin, calloused hands, missing teeth.

Antonio asked about the road on to Florencia. A couple of the men exchanged looks.

Antonio pressed them. Reluctantly and in halting Spanish they spoke, but in a low voice.

When they had finished Antonio translated for the others.

"They tell me it is dangerous. There have been roadblocks by some who are unhappy with the military dictatorship. They tell me of travelers getting beaten and robbed. They also tell me that with the rainy season parts of the road are washed away or impassable."

Adrien listened and digested the information before he spoke.

"Ask them if there is another road we can take."

Antonio asked the question. The laughter and talk stopped. There was dead silence. The old man with the straw hat shook his finger at Adrien and spoke loudly in Spanish.

Antonio held up his hand to stop the man from continuing.

"He says do not try it. That road is not safe. There are many bandits. Even the farmers will not use it. They get robbed of their chickens or money. There have been bodies found by the side of the road. He says not to go that way. That it is better to take the main road even with the problems."

"Ask him how long before we reach Florencia with those conditions."

Again Antonio asked the question. The men spoke with each other and finally an answer was delivered.

"The guess is about seven hours."

The men started to drift away. It was clear that the talk of travelling to Florencia had created some unease. Moreno and the others went back into the restaurant and sat as heaped plates of Mazorca desgrandas were served.

They ate in silence. All had thoughts of the trip ahead running through their minds.

Chapter 116

After dinner, Antonio gestured to Moreno to join him. Adrien watched the animated conversation with interest. Antonio was particularly animated. He threw his hands into the air and gesticulated. If Adrien had not known better he would have assumed that they were having a major argument. Hans was dozing in a chair near the entrance.

Suddenly Antonio spun and walked directly to Adrien.

"We need to speak. All of us. Wake up that one." He pointed to Hans.

"What is going on with you two? I have been watching you both for some time. Is there a problem?"

"Yes there is. I was born and raised in Colombia in a village not very different to this one. I know when something is wrong. You must believe me in what I am about to tell you. Those friendly men are not to be trusted. I think they are the ones who barricade the roads and rob the travelers. I suspect they made the other road to Florencia sound bad because they want to force us to drive the main road. They will be waiting for us. I am sure of this. I did not like the reaction when we asked about going another way. I do not believe the road is washed out. I would have been told when I picked up my papers and instructions. There is something wrong. Unfortunately Moreno has another opinion. Those men left to take up positions. They expect us to be leaving soon."

Moreno spoke. "They are old men. They are not young radical men. They will be too scared of the military and police to do the things that Antonio suggests."

"How can you be so stupid? You grew up in a village with poverty. Those men are desperate for money and their lives. I know. I had family like that. Please listen to me. If you do not then I will be staying here."

Adrien had listened and considered the differing beliefs before he spoke.

"I am in command here. That was the agreement from the beginning. Here is what I propose. We will leave here but drive to a location in the village that is secluded. We will load the rifles and prepare the grenades in case of an attack. I will lead as my jeep was modified for action in the jungle and is more rugged. If we are attacked do not hesitate to shoot. If they try to block us in we will use the hand grenades. No one is to try and get out of the jeeps. If they do attack we can expect a second attack a little further on. They will have planned that in case the first attack is unsuccessful. Antonio will go with you Hans. Moreno will come with me. Is everyone in agreement? It is possible that Antonio is wrong but we need to be cautious. Those roads in the middle of night are not safe."

Hans was beginning to miss Aruba and the life he had developed there. He could not wait to return and celebrate his marriage to Gabriela.

"I will go and pay for our meals. The rest of you get in the jeeps."

They slowly drove off in the darkened jeeps. Adrien advised not to use any lights and to keep noise to a minimum.

An old church loomed ahead in the distance. Adrien pointed to it and waved Antonio to drive to the back. When the jeeps were parked, Antonio and Adrien took the FN rifles and loaded them. Extra magazines were also loaded. A strap of hand grenades was tied along the inside of the passenger door. Antonio took the jerry cans and ensured both jeeps were fully fuelled.

When they were done Adrien decided to drive back past the restaurant and to make some noise to signal their leaving the village.

They bounced along the uneven surface of the road until they turned onto the road to Florencia. About three miles from the village they encountered the first sign of trouble. An old car was on its side, partially blocking the road. Adrien accelerated. As they sped past a volley of gunfire erupted from the dense jungle vegetation that lined the road. Antonio had been right.

On the wet road the jeeps slid and came dangerously close to crashing off the road. Adrien fought with the steering. He swore when he saw the smashed windshield where the bullets had hit.

He continued to drive fast while looking back to see Antonio had made it through. He was relieved. They had not had to fire a single shot. It was too soon to consider it safe. He slowed slightly. Antonio drove up alongside.
"Is everyone alright?"

"Yes. No casualties here we just have a broken front windshield."

"Stay close. I suspect there is more ahead."

He had barely spoken when they turned a corner that sloped up a hill. A line of men stood on the highway to block them.

"Shit. There is nothing we can do but hit them."

Adrien accelerated again. The jeep picked up speed and plowed into the men. Bodies flew into the air. Rifle shots rang out. More men ran from the bush. This was a serious attack. Adrien reached across and grabbed a grenade. With his teeth he removed the locking pin and hurled it in the direction of where the men were emerging. A huge explosion followed. Adrien observed that Antonio had also lobbied a grenade.

Without slowing they continued to drive south. As they continued their climb into the mountains a steady rain fell.

After an hour had passed, Adrien pulled off the road in front of an old wooden shack that in reality was a farmer's house. There were no lights visible.

"We will stop here until morning. It will be uncomfortable but we need rest and I need to gather information. At daybreak I will go to see this farmer. We are much closer to Florencia than I had calculated. I will take some special items from our supplies. I hope this farmer has children. I have brought with us a supply of chocolate. I will take it with me to offer to his family. This is the start of gathering information about the location of the drug camp. I ask you all to stay here. Please do not leave the jeeps and wander. It is possible there will be patrols and we will need to be together with our papers and Antonio."

They remained in the jeeps sprawled out in awkward positions to try to reach comfortable sleeping positions. The first light arrived two hours after they had stopped.

Adrien pulled himself from the front seat and started the walk down the narrow bullock track to the shack. Already there were signs of life. A young girl was near a shed that was near collapse was throwing some scraps to the chickens and roosters.

Adrien walked toward her. He called a greeting. The girl turned and looked at him before sprinting to the house. She crashed through the door and Adrien could hear her screaming.

The door burst open and an older man stood at the entrance with an old shotgun. Adrien raised his hands and pointed back to the road.

I halting Spanish he told the man they were lost and asked if he would go with him to the jeeps. He told them he had Colombian friends who could speak better Spanish and tell him what they were looking for.

Reluctantly the farmer started to agree. Adrien called the daughter and when she shyly approached he handed her the chocolate bars. It helped. The farmer smiled and a row of missing front teeth was evident. Together they walked back to the jeep.

Chapter 117

Conversation was easy for Moreno and Antonio. The farmer relaxed and pointed his old gun to the ground as he stood talking. Adrien watched closely. Antonio asked the farmer about his life and the farm. As was to be expected he received a tirade of complaints about the government, money and the other criminals.

Adrien's antenna picked up on the mention of criminals. He decided to push the farmer. He took Antonio aside.

"Try to find out what he means by criminals."

Antonio went to the farmer and put his hand on his shoulders. He expressed how difficult it was to farm. He told the farmer of his days growing up in poverty.

When the farmer seemed relaxed, Antonio asked the question.

"We are here to assist in searching for oil and minerals. We were warned about drug camps. We want to avoid them. Can you tell us where they are located?"

The farmer became uneasy. He looked around and finally went to Antonio.

"I have not been there. There are strange things happening south of the town in an area where the rivers flow together. Now I must return to my farm. It is time for me to milk my cow."

Adrien watched as the farmer slowly walked back to his farm house. Unknown to the others he had a pistol under his loose shirt and ready to fire at the farmer.

Adrien decided it was all safe and ordered them all back into the jeeps. They drove slowly until they entered the town of Florencia.

Hans looked at the magnificent buildings and thought back to his days in Germany. He wondered how such a troubled country could have such beautiful buildings. He recognized the style of old Spanish architecture. Deep inside of him he felt a loss and missed the stately old buildings he had known in Germany. It was then that he promised to return with his new bride to show her that part of his life. He knew his mother, Ilsa, would accept his choice of Irma.

The town was waking up. Shuttered windows and doors were opened. Old women emerged from doorways and fruitlessly swept at the constant dust that gathered at the doors.

Adrien took the map he had packed in his canvas bag and studied it. He was looking for the adobe he had arranged to rent. He found it and they proceeded to wind through the tight streets until the adobe was found.

Adrien decided that they would spend the day in the town. Moreno and Hans would shop and try to find items that could be used in any exploration. He and Antonio would use their Colombian backgrounds to ask knowledge and seek out answers. It seemed a perfect plan.

The day was hot and long. Moreno and Hans found themselves in a local store that was also a bar. They sat outside drinking their beers and exchanging greetings with some of the men. They had spread the word that they were in the area exploring and needed some local men to help. It seemed as if the whole village wanted to help.

Moreno was impressed by a young man who had pleaded for the chance to work and earn some good money. There was something about him. Moreno couldn't dismiss him from his mind.

Adrien and Hans had visited several stores and spread the word of their purpose in the village. There was a constant procession of men and women offering their services at the jeeps. Hans had hung the Royal Imperial Oil sign on the jeep's door.

That evening Adrien sat with the rest of them and put together all they had learned that day. No one had spoken of the drug operations. Adrien decided they needed to be a little bolder and ask some direct questions.

In the morning Antonio stood in front of the jeeps. He announced to the men who had gathered around that they were starting the exploration and needed men. He told them that only men with knowledge or experience working at the river would be hired.

A number of men peeled away. Those who remained looked like a desperate bunch.

Antonio felt guilty misinforming his fellow countrymen. In his mind he knew it was false, but he had a mission to complete.

Once he had selected the men he wanted, he set about equipping them with the various items, such as marker points. He stressed the need to mark off the area along the river.

The young man who had impressed Moreno came to Adrien.

"I need work please. I have sickness in my family. I need money. I can do whatever you ask. I will work all day without sleep. Can you please help me?"

"What is you do now to make money?"

"I am a guard at the camp you are asking about. They treat me badly and I am often not paid."

Adrien quickly realized he had scored a major win. This was the source he had hoped to find.

Part 6

Days of reckoning

Chapter 118

Ontario, Canada.

Solange sensed the tension. After years of discussions with the Friesen family, Jakob had decided not to sell his farm. His return trip to Canada had brought memories back to him of his childhood and life on the farm. He became emotional when he had visited the graves of Isaac and Inge Klassen. It seemed wrong to him to leave them with others when he was capable of keeping the farm.

Jakob returned from his visit to the graves. He saw Solange and Julius Friesen standing in front of the humble house. He had decided. He walked to them.

"Jakob let us go in the house. We have prepared some traditional foods for you. I am sure you will remember them and enjoy."

"Julius I need to be honest with you. Until I arrived here it was my intention to sell the farm. After considering it and visiting I have decided I no longer wish to sell."

Julius face showed the shock.

"Jakob we had an agreement. I have taken all your letters to the lawyers and the papers have been prepared. You cannot do this."

"Julius you need not worry. You have had good years here and can live and enjoy more. I am not going to sell to anyone else. I see how much you have done to improve the farm. I want you to stay. I propose that we sit and work out a lease that will assure you and your family for continued life here."

Julius looked down at the ground for the longest time. When he looked up he had a look of relief on his face.

"Jakob please come in. There are many things to discuss."

Jakob and Solange were shown into the house and offered food and drinks. While they were seated, Julius called his children to join them.

"Jakob I am relieved that you have decided not to sell. While I wanted to buy the farm it would have been a burden for us. We have not had luck with money this year. I had to borrow heavily from the community. We were worried that if we told you that we could not buy the farm then we would be required to leave if you sold it to someone else. What will you do now? What are your plans? Will you or any of your family come back here? Will we need to move?"

"Please be calm. No I am not moving back here. None of my family want to be farmers. What I wish to do is arrange a lease that will be for many years. Are you interested in such an arrangement?"

"This is the only home our children have known. They have friends here. I work with others here in the Mennonite community. I would be happy to agree to such an arrangement. We do not want to leave this farm."

"I will send you a lease agreement when we return from Europe. Now we can stay for a little while as we need to return to Niagara-on-the-Lake tonight.

Tell me about how the farm has produced. Has the crop yield been good this year? I see you have more cattle now than we had. Did you open up those fields down by the river?"

Jakob was eager to hear of life on the farm. Solange watched and noticed that he had calmness about him. She wondered whether it would be possible to have a small farm back in Aruba. It would be a challenge with the desert like conditions and lack of water. Still, the idea intrigued her.

After an hour Jakob stood and thanked the Friesens for their hospitality.

On their return trip Jakob chatted about his memories of childhood pranks and adventures. He had immersed himself back and into another time. Solange did not interrupt him. She listened and was amused at some of Jakob's juvenile escapades.

Darkness had fallen by the time they reached the Prince of Wales Hotel. As they pulled up, the valet quickly crossed the sidewalk to the car and opened the door for Solange.

"I hope you had a good trip today. Where did you go? Did you see some of our attractions?"

Solange described her day at the falls, the amazing breakfast and the trip to Kitchener.

"I am exhausted. I will have a light dinner with Jakob. Tomorrow we take the plane to Holland. That will be an adventure for me. I have never been there."

Jakob took her by the arm and escorted her up the stairway. They walked through the lobby and took the elevator up to their room. Jakob poured them drinks from the bar in the room.

"Let's rest a little before we go for dinner."

"Jakob I have a favor to ask you."

"Yes, my dear. What is it?"

"Would you agree to take me for dinner at that little restaurant where we had breakfast?"

"That means we will need to drive back to the falls. Yes that is fine. Let me freshen up. I am sure you will want to dress for dinner. Take your time. I will have another drink while waiting."

He was stunned at her transformation from a tired traveler to a fresh and debonair femme ready for the night.

Jakob considered himself to be one of the luckiest men alive. He had a beautiful wife, a successful business, a smart and loving family, good friends and a life in paradise.

As Jakob was feeling tired they decided to take a taxi. During the drive Jakob was able to sit back and observe sights he had missed when driving.

The drive went by quickly. When they arrived at the falls They were delighted to see them lit up. Solange was impressed.

Upon entering the restaurant Gaston bounced to the door to greet them. The restaurant was busy with a loud hum of conversations. Gaston looked around for a nice table for them. He ushered them to an alcove with a table for four people.

"You are my special guests. This table is especially for you. I will tell Sylvie you are here."

Moments later, Sylvie arrived at their table wearing a huge navy and white striped apron. She was accompanied by a tall dark haired young man.

"This is my son, Charles. He is studying in Paris at chefs' school."

It was clear how proud she was of Charles and his chosen profession.

Charles took Solange's hand and while bowing slightly kissed it. Solange blushed.

"Well Sylvie. You have certainly raised a charmer. I am sure many hearts will be broken along the way."

Sylvie could barely suppress her pleasure.

"I must go back to the kitchen. We have a moron working with us tonight. I am surprised he doesn't burn boiling water."

She ambled off to the kitchen.

Charles lingered.

"If there is anything you need or anything I can do for you my lovely let me know."

Jakob was aghast at the open flirting of a younger man with his wife. He was slightly annoyed but also immensely proud that she could still draw attention."

Gaston arrived back at the table and shooed Charles away.

"I would like to select your dinners this evening. There is no need for a menu. I will bring you one of our best wines. It is a gift from us to you."

"Gaston that is kind of you. This evening we wish to eat lightly as we have a long flight tomorrow."

"That will not be a problem."

The evening was magical. The foods were exotic and matched the ambiance of the evening.

Chapter 119

The morning was crisp and clear. Jakob settled his account with the hotel and thanked the staff who had looked after them.

At the curb his rental car was waiting. Their cases had been loaded into the car for the drive back to Malton airport.

During the drive Solange was surprisingly quiet. Jakob wondered what was bothering her. He dared not ask. He had seen moods of this type before.

At the airport, Jakob drove to the terminal and unloaded their luggage. He left Solange and drove back to the office to return the rental car.

When he returned to the airport he found Solange sitting alone. Other passengers were waiting and talking amongst themselves. Jakob went to her.

"Solange it seems there is something worrying you. Do you want to talk to me about it?"

"No. It is a woman thing. I will be alright. Now just leave me alone please. We will have a nice trip. Are you looking forward to seeing your friends and those whom you met during the years you were there?"

Before he could answer her, the counter staff called for the passengers to assemble for the walk through the terminal and down a ramp onto the tarmac to board the plane to Amsterdam.

Jakob took Solange by the hand and guided her toward the doorway through which the other passengers were moving.

At the end of the ramp there were stairs that led down to the tarmac. Solange and Jakob slowly made their way down. After they reached the ground an attendant held a door open. Jakob was amazed as they exited. There in front of him was a new Douglas DC-8 jetliner. He was ecstatic. A tall set of stairs led up to the entrance into the plane. When he had booked the flight was operated by a propeller driven DC-6 aircraft. Jakob could barely contain himself. He was eager to get on the silver bird and enjoy the trip.

The flight was an evening flight. Their arrival at Schipol in The Netherlands would be late in the next morning, Amsterdam time.

The crossing was tedious. Throughout the flight, Jakob slept fitfully. He was filled with the thoughts of what awaited him and the friends and acquaintances he had betrayed.

Solange was withdrawn. She was unlike the woman he had shared times with in Niagara-on-the-Lake and in Toronto. He worried.

Jakob was intrigued as they flew east and he observed the changes from night to dawn. The skies were illuminated with differing shades ranging from light blues and orange sunrise in the east through to the dark purple of night in the western sky.

The attendants were courteous and offered a breakfast. Jakob shook Solange awake.

She lazily looked at him and then smiled at the young Dutch girl serving them.

"I would love a mimosa."

The flight attendant was confused. "What is that Madam?"

"It is a simple drink of orange juice and champagne."

Before the attendant could return with the drink, the breakfast was being served from a dolly being pulled through the cabin by a huge woman. She was over six feet and resembled a wrestler. She turned to Jakob.

"Sir, what would you like? There is either Lox on a bagel or an omelet of spinach and cheese."

"I will take the lox please."

Solange was surprised. Jakob generally ate a heavier meal at breakfast.

The flight continued in boring monotony. Finally the pilots announced their projected arrival time in Amsterdam and requested the passengers to comply with the flight attendants requests ahead of the landing.

Jakob looked out of the window and to the miles of ocean below.

As he stared down, the coastline appeared. The plane banked and turned for its approach into Schipol.

Jakob watched the farmlands below him as they flew lower and lower on their descent into Holland.

A strange quietness enveloped the cabin as the pilots decreased the engines for the landing. The plane appeared to be gliding. Outside the windows Jakob watched as they passed over lines of trees. He could see the airport spread out to the side of the aircraft. There was a grinding and thump as the landing gear was lowered and locked into place.

The plane gently touched down. The engines whined loudly as the pilots applied the reverse thrusters and Jakob felt himself pulled forward in his seat as they braked sharply.

He was restless and eager to exit. Solange placed her hand on his wrist.

"Jakob be calm. We are here and soon you will be back in a country you know."

Chapter 120

The Netherlands.

The Customs and airport formalities were quick. Jakob retrieved their luggage and headed to a desk to arrange a rental car. He settled on a Renault as he thought it would be easy to maneuver through the streets of Amsterdam.

They left the airport and drove amongst the traffic till they reached the hotel Jakob had selected. He pulled into the front of the recently expanded Apollo Hotel in Amsterdam South. He had chosen this location in order for him to easily travel to Leiden and visit the farm of Henk and Aaron Schmidt, his former wife's relatives. He had worked on the farm when he and his wife Anke had first arrived in The Netherlands in 1939.

He planned to visit the farm after a few days of showing Solange around Amsterdam and The Hague. He would immediately send them a letter to inform of his arrival and intent to visit. First he intended to show Solange some of the famous places for which the area was known.

Jakob said nothing to Solange, but on the drive from the airport and into Amsterdam South he was amazed at the changes to The Netherlands since the war. It seemed so unfamiliar yet in some other ways it did not.

A boy from the hotel came to the little blue Renault to assist them with their baggage.

In perfect English he addressed them.

"Welcome to the Apollo. Is this your first time visiting The Netherlands?"

"No. I was here just before the war started. It is the first trip for my wife though."

"I am sure you will take back pleasant memories. I hope the Dutch weather at this time of year remains nice. It can get very cold and dull at this time of year. You have certainly arrived in such nice weather."

He escorted Jakob and Solange to a stately antique reception desk.

Jakob tipped the boy who immediately left them.

After completing the registration, Jakob and Solange were taken to their room. Again Solange was overcome with the ornate beauty of the older décor. She crossed over the room and looked out of the window over the canal and its harbor and boats below.

"Jakob. How do you know to pick these hotels?"

He just smiled.

"Solange it is still early here. It would be even earlier back at home. Are you tired? If not then I would like to walk for a while."

"I would like to shower and change out of these clothes that I travelled in all day. Then I will join you for a walk. Maybe we can find somewhere for lunch."

When Solange was changed, they returned to the lobby. Jakob went to speak with one of the men at the desk. He asked about restaurants in the area and received a number of recommendations.

On leaving the hotel, Jakob waved down a taxi to take them the short distance to the entrance into Vondelpark. He had read about the park and wanted to see it himself.

Within ten minutes they were walking through the stately entrance into the park. The grounds were magnificent. Huge trees lined the waterways of the park. In the autumn weather the leaves had started to turn. All around them was a kaleidoscope of color. The trees profusely displayed their autumn foliage of ambers and orange, with some showing the early vestiges of red leaves.

Arm in arm, Jakob and Solange walked the grounds. Children ran laughing and calling. A steady stream of riders on bikes passed them on the narrow walkway. Solange breathed in the cool air and felt a degree of satisfaction she had not enjoyed in years. In some ways she regretted her life as a domineering businesswoman. She now wished she had spent more time travelling and enjoying what the world had to offer.

After an hour they decided to start back toward the hotel. As they walked they came upon a café. It had a window with a gold painted name that read "The Artists Canvas". Solange stopped and raised her hand to shield her eyes as she looked through the window. The interior was long and narrow.

"Jakob lets go in here and order a lunch."

Inside they were greeted by a tall and portly Dutchman wearing a long white apron. He showed them to a table. The place was alive with people of all ages chatting and laughing.

"What is it about this trip that is making me feel so different?"

"Solange for too long you have only concentrated on business. You forgot life. This is life."

The heavy aroma of cigarettes and pipe smoke drifted through the café. The waiter returned with two small espresso coffees for them.

"Will you wish to order a lunch?"

"Yes. When I lived in Holland there was a pannekoeken that we enjoyed greatly. It was made with bacon and Gouda cheese. Do you make these?"

"Are we not Dutch? Of course. And then I will tempt you with some delicious Dutch Pastries."

"I think we will have some Stroopwafels afterwards. I would also like you to bring is a bottle of Bols."

"It seems as if you have been with us Dutch before."

The food was served and as they ate, a slight man wearing a beret went to the back corner and picked up a guitar and played the most soothing Spanish Guitar tunes.

For Solange it was the winding down of another perfect day.

After the lunch and as they left the café Solange asked Jakob if they could walk back to the hotel.

Jakob agreed and they started the walk back. They crossed over the canal that ran in front of their hotel and climbed the steep stairs to return to their home for the next few days.

In their room Jakob called to Solange, "I am going to take a sleep. I am tired from the trip and that lunch."

"Go ahead and rest. I am going to stay here and read. There are some nice books here that are about Amsterdam. I wish to read. I find it fascinating here. It is so different to other cities I have seen."

Jakob retired to sleep. Solange removed her clothing and wore a bathrobe. She sat for a while reading until she was sure that Jakob had fallen asleep.

Chapter 121

She checked on Jakob. He was gently snoring in the bed of the adjacent bedroom. She quietly pulled the door closed and returned to the living area. Convinced that Jakob was in a deep sleep she picked up the phone and asked the hotel operator to place a call to Isaac Junior. The phone rang and rang unanswered. Concerned she requested the call be placed again to Isaac's number at the office. Again the phone rang unanswered. Solange was concerned as she hung up. She wondered whether Isaac had already left on his mystery trip. She didn't understand why Isaac's wife did not answer.

The door to the bedroom opened and Jakob joined her.

"Is there something wrong? I heard you talking to someone."

"No. I was speaking to the hotel operator. I was trying to call Isaac. There is no answer. I am worried. Why is his wife not answering?"

"I am sure everything is fine. Try and call Carlita. I am sure she will know what is happening."

Solange had not thought of this. She picked up the phone and provided the operator with the information to call Carlita.

The phone was answered by Carlita on the third ring.

"Carlita it is Solange. How are you? How is everything in Aruba? I am trying to find Isaac. He does not answer his phone."

"Everything here is good. How are you and Jakob? Please be calm. Isaac is here with his family. The children have been playing on the beach and Isaac has been outside sitting with Miguel. They have been in deep conversation for hours."

"Jakob and I are fine. We are having a nice trip. I am enjoying seeing many new places and things. Please let me speak to Isaac."

"I will go and get him."

There was a long wait before Isaac came on the line.

"Hello mother. Are you well? Is Jakob handling the travelling well? I was hoping you would call. I have important news for you both. It would be best we speak later when I am at home. I don't want to discuss things here. What time is it in Amsterdam?"

"Isaac it is good to hear your voice. There is a time difference of six hours. Now you have me worried. Should I be concerned?"

"No I will explain when we speak. I will be home in an hour. We will speak then."

Solange replaced the phone's receiver in its cradle.

She pondered the conversation. Jakob had stood watching her.

"What is going on?"

"I do not know. Isaac asked that we speak in an hour. It sounds serious."

"I suggest you rest. I am going to mail this letter to Henk and Aaron at the farm to advise them I am here and would like to visit them. I will return within the hour and then we can end the mystery of what is happening in Aruba."

He pulled on a sweater and light coat. The weather in Amsterdam was cooling. He left the room and stopped in the bar off the hotel lobby. He did not want to admit or show his anxiety to Solange, but he was nervous about the way Isaac had handled the call. If he wouldn't speak openly in front of Carlita it had to be serious.

He ordered a whiskey and downed it in seconds. He ordered several more and drank each one rapidly. The barman watched him anxiously. He had seen others drink like this and start trouble. After ten minutes, Jakob threw some money down on the bar and pushed his stool back. He walked over to the reception desk and asked how he could mail the letter. The concierge advised him that the hotel would handle it for him. Jakob gave him the letter and then returned to the bar and ordered more whiskey.

Over an hour passed before Jakob staggered from the bar to the elevator. He was in the elevator when he realized he could not remember the room number or where he was. Jakob started to panic. He hit all the elevator buttons. The elevator started going floor to floor and stopping at each before starting to descend and again stopping at each floor. Jakob unsteadily left the elevator at the lobby level and went to the desk.

"Can I assist you?"

"Where am I? I am Jakob Klassen. Am I staying here?"

The clerk behind the desk became disturbed by Jakob's condition.

He called an associate and together they assisted Jakob across to a large lounge chair. After he was seated the clerk hurried back to the desk and started checking the guest registrations. His associate remained with Jakob to prevent him leaving the hotel or causing any further disturbance.

The clerk found the reservation information for the Klassens. He phoned up to the room. Solange answered. The clerk explained the situation and within minutes Solange was in the lobby.

Jakob was murmuring incoherently. Solange recognized the signs. The alcohol had interacted with his medications.

"Please bring me some water. He is having a reaction to his medication. He will be fine."

The hotel employee scurried away to get the water.

Solange was annoyed. The smell of alcohol emanating from Jakob was strong. It was clear that he had drunk a lot.

The employee returned with a large glass of ice cold water. She took the water and forced Jakob to drink. He gulped a couple of mouthfuls before regurgitating the water and other contents. Water and a stream of vomit violently burst from his mouth. Lumps of greenish colored bile dribbled down his chin and fell onto his coat. Solange was now angry.

"Why didn't that barman stop serving him? How much did he drink? I am expecting the hotel to pay for cleaning and to cover the drinks. I am not happy that this happened. Does the hotel have a doctor? He is having a severe reaction to the drugs and alcohol."

"I will call our duty manager to assist you. We will help you take him to your room. We do have a doctor. I will call him now. He should be here in ten minutes or so."

Two large men arrived to help support Jakob and take him to their room.

They settled him on the bed and as Jakob started to shout nonsensical things there was a loud rap on the door.

Solange opened it to find the hotel doctor standing there. He introduced himself. Solange gave him a quick description of the treatment Jakob had received and the medications he had taken. The doctor looked at the bottles and continually nodded his head.

"Mrs. Klassen he is suffering from a poisoning that occurs when alcohol is mixed with these medications. Had he drunk wine or a beer then it would not be severe. The alcohol he has consumed was strong. We have a couple of options and I suggest both. We need to get everything out of him. First I will pump his stomach. I will need to send for my nurse to bring equipment. The second procedure will be an enema. I will ask the nurse to bring a special solution that we use. He will not be in any condition to leave this room tonight. I suggest you ask the hotel to bring lots of toilet paper and towels. He is in for a rough night."

Chapter 122

The doctor and his nurse performed their procedures and prior to leaving they gave Jakob an injection to calm him and assist him sleep.

He was drained.

Solange was angry. She had planned an evening of fun and dining. She called the front desk and was about to order food for the room when there was a loud knock at the door. Cautiously she went to the door and opened it. Standing at the door and dressed in an impeccable manner was the hotel manager.

"Madam, I am personally here to apologize for all that has happened this evening. "

He handed Solange a huge arrangement of flowers.

"The hotel is responsible to our guests. The incident at the bar is most regrettable. I would like to ensure we look after matters and that the rest of your stay is without problems. Is there anything I can do at this time?"

"I need to eat. It has been an exhausting day. I expect the hotel to accept the responsibility for what has happened."

"Of course. I will ask a chef to come to your room. You can tell him what you desire. It will be a meal that is compliments of the Apollo."

"I am worried about Jakob. I know it wasn't the barman's fault. Jakob is on a strong medication. I feel that if he was drinking a lot the barman should have tried to slow him."

"It is almost impossible to know or understand what the situation is with each customer."

"Thank you for coming and expressing regrets for this unfortunate incident. I appreciate it."

"I will go and have a chef visit in minutes. Please order what you wish. I hate to say this, but wine and drink are also compliments of the hotel."

Solange smiled. She felt somewhat sorry for the man. He was trying to handle a situation over which they had little control.

"Thank you. You have been most kind. I will be fine and I am sure Jakob will sleep soundly until morning."

The manager excused himself and left. Solange sat on the couch and awaited the arrival of the chef.

Ten minutes passed before the chef arrived. He was dressed in a full chef's uniform and carried a menu under his arm. He was a tall and good looking man. He flashed a smile that Solange found charming.

She wondered what would have happened if she had been alone and tempted by such a sexually attractive and strong looking man. It took her a few minutes to compose herself.

She looked through the bedroom door at her depleted husband. "Choices," she thought.

"I understand you had a full day of travel and are probably stressed and tired. I do not recommend a heavy meal in this circumstance. My thought is to prepare you a light meal of a shrimp noodle soup and a cheese vegetable grilled rosti. In the morning I will arrange a special breakfast for you and Mr. Klassen in our restaurant. I am sure he will be hungry by then."

He smiled an enchanting smile at Solange. "Are you sure that's all you want then Madam?"

She was tempted. She looked at his tall framed body, his long dark hair and enchanting smile. She imagined a lot more.

"No thank you. I am sure you will look after me."

He smiled again, knowing she desired him. The manager knew he would charm her. He was a master at diffusing situations.

Solange went to Jakob. The procedures had left him empty. She decided to use the time and call Isaac.

The operator took the number for Isaac's home. Minutes later the room phone rang.

"Mrs. Klassen I have Isaac Klassen on the phone now. Thank you. You are connected."

"Isaac, what is going on? I am having an exasperating evening. I ask you not to make it worse. Tell me what is happening."

"No mother. I need to know what is wrong. You sound frustrated and angry."

Solange told Isaac of the events of the night. Isaac was quiet for a couple of minutes before responding.

"I fear that as Jakob gets older these problems will get worse. I will go with him next time. I will meet these doctors. I wonder if the medication and dosages are correct. I too have noticed changes in him that are strange."

"My dear Isaac, I was having such a nice time with Jakob. He has shown me things that I have only dreamed about. I know that this evening he drank heavily. I wish he would tell me the reason. I have been wondering if he is hiding something from us. Is he really ill? Is he dying?"

"I don't think so. He is still too energetic and full of new ideas. I think his health condition has a lot to do with his recent behavior. Now let us talk. You called me. Is there something you want to tell me?"

"I need to know what is happening."

"I received a message from Colombia. The boys have started the rescue attempt. It seems that they have been able to improve upon the original plan. I do not have all the details but Adrien was enthusiastic about the development. They have been able to enter the country using the identities we gave them. They are now on their way to the area where the drug camp is located. I don't expect to hear from them until they perform the raid. They are going into a remote area. It will be hard to communicate with them."

"I will let Jakob know in the morning. Now I am pleading with you to please tell me where it is you are going. Nothing can be that secret to keep it from your parents."

"I have told you before that I will not tell you. Please stop asking. You will know soon."

Their conversation was interrupted by Jakob running from the bed in a confused state looking for the bathroom. The last impact of the enema had hit.

Chapter 123

It was early in the morning when Jakob awoke. His head pounded and he was starving. He turned over on his side and observed Solange sleeping quietly. With great care he eased himself from the bed and went to the bathroom. He was feeling strange. He tried to remember last evening but his memory was blank. He tried to think back to the previous day. He remembered the time in Vondelpark but after that his memory was blank. He tried to understand what could have caused his headache.

"Good morning, Jakob. That was a real performance last night. I am disgusted with you."

Jakob frowned. "I don't remember anything. What happened?"

Solange described the events of the evening. Jakob was shocked and horrified.

"I did that? I honestly have no recollection of any of those things. I feel terrible. I went to the bar? I cannot believe this."

She watched him as he grappled with information.

"I am truly sorry. Why am I unable to remember this?"

"According to the hotel doctor you poisoned yourself by mixing a strong alcohol with the medications. When they escorted you back here it seemed you were in some sort of trance. I am wondering if this trip is too much for us."

"We only have another week and a few days left before we return to Aruba. Is it possible for me to contact that doctor? Something started that caused that reaction. I need to know what caused it. Why did I go to a bar? If I wanted to go for a drink I would have asked you to come with me. Something is wrong."

"I will contact the hotel manager. He came here last evening. He was most concerned for you and annoyed that the barman had served you so much liquor. I will ask him to contact the doctor."

Solange crawled from her bed and went to the phone. She picked up the card the manager had left and dialed his direct number.

After a few short minutes arrangements were made for the doctor to visit at the hotel.

"I am absolutely starved. Let's dress quickly and get some breakfast."

"I am not surprised you are so hungry. Between your vomiting, the stomach pump and the enema I am sure there is nothing in you."

Jakob looked away, ashamed that his actions had resulted in such a fiasco.

They showered and dressed and made their way down for breakfast. Jakob was self-conscious and shyly entered the dining room. It was early and only a few guests were seated. Jakob was relieved. He wanted to get away from the hotel before too many spotted him and knew of the disastrous evening performance.

Solange ordered pastries, Dutch cheese and strong black coffee. Jakob decided upon a juice, toast, poached eggs with smoked trout and cubed roast potato.

When the waiter had taken the orders and left, Solange turned to Jakob and asked,

 "Are you being truthful with me? Are you unable to recall any of last night?"

"I honestly have no recollection. My mind is blank. I am concerned. I will ask the doctor about those drugs. I do not like them. They help me with my thoughts and anxiety but other things happen. Could they have caused me to go stupid like that and then forget everything?"

They sat discussing the situation until their food was delivered, which they ate quickly.

"There is a matter I need to discuss with you. After the doctor has been we will go back to Vondelpark and walk. While there I will tell you. It is not a bad thing. I just don't want to have you get excited before the doctor sees you. Now, if you have finished we should go back to the room. He will be here shortly."

With his head bowed, Jakob walked with Solange past the reception desk and to the elevators. He was extremely embarrassed.

They had no sooner entered the room when the phone rang. It was the desk to advise them the doctor had arrived and was on the way up to the room.

A sharp knock at the door announced the arrival of the doctor. Solange opened the door and welcomed him into the room.

"I am pleased to see you are up and about Mr. Klassen. Last night you were very close to requiring admission to one of our fine hospitals. You must have a very strong metabolism. Now you wanted to see me. What is it I can do for you?"

"Doctor what happened last evening has never happened before. I do not understand it. I never go and drink. I have no memory of the night. We are a long way from our home and I am concerned. I don't want this to repeat itself. I am wondering if it is related to the medicines I am taking?"

"I have only seen you once and that was as an emergency call. I am not your doctor. I have no records or dossier on your past medical history. I am unable to give you an accurate assessment. The medication that your wife showed me is new and the side effects are not totally known yet. I do know that you cannot mix alcohol with them. The consequences can be tragic."

"Doctor I did not drink when I took them. I cannot explain what caused me to go into the bar and start drinking like that."

"I need to ask. Have you had any stressful situations in the past week?"

"We were in Canada. I visited the farm and home where I grew up. I have not been back there in many years. I was going to sell the farm but my emotions stopped me. I visited the graves of my parents and I recalled the life I had lived there with the girl I finally married. I loved her so much. The thoughts all came back to the days we spent playing together. I remembered swinging with her on the old farm gate and trying to impress her when we gathered the livestock from the fields before winter."

The doctor listened attentively.

"I suggest you take a quiet day. The medication you are taking does affect the nervous system. It is possible that even though you were awake and functioning, you may have experienced a type of seizure where it is possible to function but will later have no knowledge of the time, place or things you did. I suspect that the condition you are being treated for with this medicine produced a dissociative disorder. I strongly recommend that you obtain professional assistance and contact the doctors who treated you and prescribed this medication. Now let me examine you. Mrs. Klassen I would like some privacy with your husband please."

Chapter 124

When the doctor had left, Solange and Jakob dressed warmly to walk to the Vondelpark. It was a brilliant sunny day but the autumn temperatures defied the warm look of the day.

Together they strolled slowly along. It was a long walk. In the canal barges moved slowly carrying produce and goods to destinations unknown. Bicycles passed by them ridden by both men and women. Greetings were called as the cyclists rode by them. There were carts set up and selling papers and foods.

It took Jakob and Solange an hour to walk from their hotel to the immense grounds. Before they entered the park, Jakob went to one of the vendors and bought some treats. Solange had waited patiently on one of the wooden seats at the entrance to the park. She watched as Jakob returned carrying a brown paper bag. She noticed oil stains on the bag.

"Jakob what have you done?"

"I found us a real Dutch treat. They normally make these for Christmas. They are called olliebollen. They are like a doughnut with raisins and covered in a confectioners' sugar. I have not had one since I lived in Holland. You will enjoy them."

Solange was happy to see that Jakob had regained some of his younger exuberance.

They continued their walk into the park and arrived at a wide bench overlooking an expanse of water. They sat to enjoy the olliebollen and talk.

Jakob removed his coat and stretched his body back to soak in the sun's warm rays. He was relaxed and wondered how last night could possibly have happened.

"You said there are things you want to tell me, Solange. Is this a good place and time?"

The autumn breezes blew a collection of withered brown leaves past their feet. The leaves swirled and rustled. Solange watched them as she measured her response in her mind. She did not want to cause a situation that could cause a bad reaction in Jakob.

"While you were sleeping last night, I called Isaac Junior. Everything in Aruba is fine. He told me that the efforts to rescue Juan in Colombia have started with Hans, Moreno and Adrien. Isaac said there have been some developments but did not have all the details. I understood that they now have some Colombians assisting them. I told him that we will call him back later today. He seemed busy and distracted. Jakob, do you know where he is going? He will not tell me. I have asked him several times and each time he gets angrier and refuses. I worry that he will do something stupid. It is unlike him to keep a secret like this."

At the news of the mission to rescue Juan having started, Jakob jumped to his feet.

"Come on now Solange. I must go and call people. I must speak to Isaac. We will take a taxi back. Hurry up."

"Jakob by running around here you will achieve nothing. We are not in Colombia. Yes, when we return to the hotel you can call Isaac. There is nothing you can do from here. Hans and Moreno are there and working with Adrien. They will take care and work to find the best way to infiltrate the drug operation and rescue Juan. Your getting excited here in The Netherlands will do nothing. You must calm down."

"No Solange. There are things I can and must do from here. I had setup an arrangement with my friends at The Sentinel newspaper in Miami that they would be included when the action started. They are important and will be of great assistance in helping us expose and collapse the mob's interference in businesses of our associates in Aruba. I made a promise which I intend to keep."

"You are being foolish. It is not your responsibility to take on the mob. Why are you so insistent in doing this?"

"I built a life and businesses based on the integrity and help of many there. It is not right that the community get corrupted by these criminals."

"Please think carefully. You are taking on some powerful enemies."

"Yes but I have also spoken with and met some equally powerful men who want to see this end. It is more than just Aruba. "

"I understand your feelings. I would now like to go back to the hotel and, no, we will walk. No taxi."

As they walked back, Solange noted the growing impatience in Jakob. He was eager to call Isaac and receive an update.

Chapter 125

In their room Jakob sat with a list of phone numbers. He called the hotel operator and asked for a call to be placed to Isaac's office.

The call rang and rang. The operator was about to disconnect when it was answered. Jakob recognized the women's voice who answered.

"Ramona, where is Isaac. This is Jakob. We are travelling and I need to speak with him. It is urgent."

"He is in a meeting with some people from the bank. Should I interrupt him?"

"Yes"

Moments later Isaac came onto the phone.

"Jakob. How are you? Solange told me you had a bad time last night. Are you well?"

"Yes. I am fine. I need you to tell me what's happening in Colombia."

"I spoke with them. As I told Solange they have started the rescue attempt. It seems that fortune has smiled on them. I talked to Adrien and he told me that they have a Colombian military officer helping them. It is a deal and we will need to pay him and get him out of Colombia. I am OK with that. I should also tell you that things are happening here in Aruba. There have been a number of Americans here from the U.S. government. They are asking lots of questions and visiting banks and businesses.

It is best that you and Solange are not here."

"Isaac I made a promise to The Sentinel in Miami that when the action started I would inform them. I need you to assist them. I will contact Benita Flores who is one of the owners of the paper. I will ask her to contact you. Please help her and keep her informed. She is going to cover the rescue of Juan and also the involvement of the mob in Venezuela. She has a journalistic photographer who will be assisting her. I have met him and trust him. He has covered wars and other unpleasant matters. Please be sure they get help. They are the ones who will try to show the impact that the mob have recently had on Aruban politics and business."

"I will be available to her. Ask her to call me."

"I will call her next."

"If I need to contact you where will you be?"

"We will be here at the Apollo hotel in Amsterdam for the next few days. I have people I wish to visit. We will leave for Germany in three or four days from now. I will keep you informed. It is important that you know where to contact us."

Solange took the phone and they engaged in small talk about the family and the grandchildren.

Jakob placed a call to Benita Flores at the Sentinel.

"Benita. It is Jakob Klassen. I am calling you from The Netherlands. How are you? I promised to tell you when the action plan to rescue Juan from Aruba and disrupt the drug operations there and in Venezuela started. They have started. A group has gone to Colombia to start the search for Juan. They are in a small southern Colombian village called Florencia. They are disguised as an oil and mineral survey and exploration party. My son is with them. They have some local help. I suggest you send your man to Colombia now. I am about to leave for Germany in a few days. I am staying at the Apollo hotel in Amsterdam. You can contact me here for the next day or so. I will advise you when we arrive in Germany."

"No Jakob. I am not just sending the photographer. I will be going to cover the story. This is an enormous story. It affects not only the islands, but also Florida and other cities where they distribute the drugs."

"Benita, do not take that risk."

"I am a professional journalist. This is what I trained for. I am no innocent when it comes to matters like this. Remember that I grew up in Cuba during its most turbulent times. You cannot talk me out of this. If I am not here at the paper when you call back with your new contact information please ask for Maria. I will be checking with her for messages while I am gone from the office."

"Benita this isn't what we agreed on. I appreciate that you want to help but this is too much."

"It is the way I will handle it. I want this story. The other newspapers will not get an inside contact."

"Please be careful. I wanted to tell you that I still remember that magical afternoon we spent together. I hope we will meet again and enjoy more times like that."

"I too wish for that. Now I must go."

Solange had listened to the conversation with curiosity. She wondered at the intimacy of the way they had spoken. She shrugged and walked away and back to the bedroom. After all the years she had spent with Jakob she realized that she would never really know him.

Jakob placed a conference call to Admiral Phillips and Kevin Connelly in Miami. He apprised them of the developments.

There was silence from them both. Finally the Admiral spoke.

"I will inform our CIA agents in both Colombia and Venezuela. We have men in both Bogota and Cartagena who can assist if they rescue your friend. Of course the United States cannot be visible in your operation. Your people are operating by themselves. If they are caught we will disavow any knowledge of the matter."

"I understand that but don't think you will hear from them. We have a leader who is well trained. I will not say anything further."

When he had completed his calls he went to find Solange. She was sitting at the desk in the bedroom.

"Jakob you will never change, will you?"

"It is my son and friend who are at risk as well and there are criminals who seek to destroy our way of life in Aruba. I am not prepared to allow that."

"I am sure that if it possible to get Juan out of there they will. They are all intelligent men."

"That is enough of this drama for today. I thought we should visit the Van Gogh and Rijksmuseums today. Afterwards we will find somewhere interesting to relax and have a leisurely late lunch."

"I would like that."

Chapter 126

They spent the day admiring the works of the masters at the museums and found a café with an outside patio that was sheltered from the wind and overlooked a canal.

For Solange the morning faded from her mind. She was totally immersed in the culture and surrounds of Amsterdam.

While they both understood the seriousness of the operation in Colombia, neither spoke of it. They laughed and chatted about funny events that had happened during their life together.

As the sun started to set, the couple commenced the walk back to the hotel. It had been a day of relaxation.

Upon entering the hotel, one of the men on the desk recognized them.

"Mr. Klassen, this was delivered here this afternoon by a man. He was not with the Post office or a courier. I think it is a personal communication."

Jakob took the envelope and placed it in his pocket. He wondered who knew where he was staying and would try to contact him.

They rode the elevator up to their room. In the room Jakob sat on the couch and looked at the envelope. His named was written on it in a hand that obviously did little writing. He opened the envelope. Inside was a neatly folded note on blue paper.

Jakob read it and then handed it to Solange.

"It is from Aaron Schmidt. I had sent a letter to Henk and Aaron to tell them I was here and wanted to visit. Instead, Aaron wants to come here in the morning to meet me. That is all it says."

They were both tired from the day's activity and elected to eat early and retire.

Jakob was first to wake in the morning. He laid thinking about Aaron's note. Why did he decide to come to the hotel to meet him? Jakob had been looking forward to seeing Henk and the farm again. While he was entranced in thought, Solange stirred. She opened her eyes and looked at Jakob and then frowned. She sat up.

"Jakob you seem puzzled and deep in thought. Are you all right?"

"Yes but I don't understand the actions of Aaron. Why is he coming here?"

"We will need to wait to find that out. Now come and dress. We will go down to breakfast."

"What would you like to do today? This will be our last day here."

"I would like to spend time and visit in The Hague."

"We can do that but there is not a lot to see there that is different to here and some other places. If that is what you wish then we will do it."

While eating their breakfasts, a waiter approached the table.

"Mr. Klassen there is a man at reception asking for you. Shall I ask him to join you?"

"No we are almost finished. I will go and see who this person is."

Jakob pushed himself back from the table and left the restaurant and headed to the reception desk. He looked around and did not see anyone. A voice called his name.

"Jakob. Jakob Klassen."

He turned to see Aaron standing near the stairs that lead down to the doors out to the street.

Jakob hurried over to greet him. He looked at Aaron's features. He was no longer the young and strong man that Jakob had known. His face was etched with lines from days spent in the fields and his hair had greyed and thinned. His back was slightly stooped.

"Aaron I am so pleased to see you. How have you been after all these many years?"

"I am doing well."

Jakob detected that there was a hint of unfriendliness in the response.

"I had hoped to visit you and Henk at the farm. I have many fond memories of my days working with you there."

Aaron's face remained expressionless as if cast in stone.

"Jakob you should have remained in Amsterdam. It was foolish of you to go to Germany in those years. You caused a lot of people anguish. I have thought about our trips many times. It made no sense to me why you wanted to travel and pursue the search for those old ancestral relatives. Your parents ran away from here to escape the problems they had created. Why did you have to come back and bring problems for your wife's relatives and my family? You have now come back here and expect us to welcome you. You are not welcome."

"It was the war. I was unable to flee from Germany. My papers were stolen. I had no money. I stayed with my uncle Josef for a while until he needed to flee from the Nazis. We were betrayed by his house keeper Sabine to the Gestapo. We barely escaped. Those were bad times. I wrote to my wife Anke. I explained all that was happening."

Aaron looked at him with skepticism.

"Jakob it is easy for you to say this now. You should never have gone to Germany and left Anke here. The house was raided. Her Aunt and Uncle were killed by an SS invasion into their home. Anke had concealed herself and managed to hide until she was rescued. Why didn't you come back for her?"

"I was unable to leave Germany."

"I wish I could believe you. I drove here this morning to prevent you visiting the farm. It is best you leave here and not visit."

"I wanted to see Henk. I know he will be an old man now, but I would still like to see him."

"You will see him in another life then. He went to find and help your wife after the Schmidt home in Amsterdam was invaded. He never made it. He was killed when the Nazis bombed and destroyed Rotterdam. You have his blood on your hands. You deserted us all and went to build a new carefree life for yourself."

"That is not true. I was told of Anke's death by the Dutch Marines in Aruba. I had escaped there by ship and was trying to get a message to her to join me. I had arranged and sent money through the underground to pay for her trip to the Caribbean. I was told she was in a party that was ambushed as they tried to cross the border."

Aaron looked at Jakob while digesting the story he had just been told. He was not a highly educated man, but a trusting and honest person.

"I am here in Holland with my wife Solange. I would like to introduce her to you. If you wait here I will go and escort her from the restaurant where she has had breakfast."

"I would like to meet her. She must be a strong woman to have lived a life with you."

Chapter 127

Jakob left to go back to Solange and tell her of Aaron's arrival at the hotel and how he wanted to introduce her.

He omitted to tell her about Aaron's comments and his wish that Jakob leave The Netherlands.

"I do not understand this. Why did he come here? You wanted to visit him and his family members. It is strange. Of course I will be courteous to him, but I have my reservations."

Together they left the restaurant and walked back through the lobby. Aaron was seated on a large couch looking at the day's newspapers.

Jakob stopped in front of him.

"Aaron, this is my wife Solange. We have often spoken of the fine times I spent at the farm with you and Henk."

Aaron stood and acknowledged her.

"I am most pleased to meet you Mrs. Klassen. I am correct? You did marry this man, Jakob?"

Solange was confused by his comment.

"Yes, we married many years ago. We have a grown son, Isaac, who is smart and growing to be an excellent businessman."

She was developing an instant dislike for Aaron.

"I came to the hotel this morning as I wish to take Jakob to meet someone special."

"Should I change or is it alright for me to come with you dressed as I am?"

"Mrs. Klassen it is not a visit I think you should make. It is a matter for Jakob only. It goes a long way back to those years of the wars and the invasion of The Netherlands. Please understand this."

Jakob was at a loss. He tried to remember the years he had stayed with Anke's relatives. He recalled the clubs he played his saxophone in. He vividly remembered his sharp criticism from Anke's uncle over his ways and violation of his Mennonite beliefs.

"Aaron, I think we should include Solange in what you have planned. She is my wife. It is only correct she be included."

"No."

"I should refuse to hear more from you and not go with you. My wife is the most important thing in my life. And I want her to be involved."

"Jakob, for your sake and hers it is best that you and I go alone."

"Tell me why it is so important that I accompany you to visit this mystery person."

"If you don't, and then later you find out who that person is, you will regret it until death."

Aaron stood in front of them. He was statuesque. His years working on the farm had resulted in a strong and able body.

"Jakob, I cannot force you to come with me. It is your decision."

Finally Solange spoke. "Jakob, I will be fine here today. I will go and continue visiting some of the local historic buildings and places. I will be fine alone here. Go with Aaron. It seems he feels it is important you do so."

Aaron looked at Jakob and then back at Solange.

"This could be a day that will change your lives," he scowled.

The dislike that Solange had felt for Aaron was growing by the minute.

"It was nice to meet you Aaron. Now I must go to my room. Excuse me."

Jakob stammered and quickly followed her.

"I will be back in a few minutes. I will go with you."

He followed Solange to the elevator. She glared at him.

"Jakob there is something sinister in his behavior. Go with him but be very careful. I fear he hates you so much that he may do things that will hurt us both."

"I have no idea why he is so hostile. It was a long time ago. We were young. The war was just starting. We were friends. I am sorry his father was killed in the war. He told me that after Anke's relative's house was attacked that his father, Henk went to try and save Anke. I did not ask him to do that. I am sorry he was in Rotterdam when the Germans bombed it and he was killed."

"In business and with my dealings with people through the years, I know when there is deep anger. Aaron is hurt and angry. I think it is best you go with him and find out what that reason is. It will not go away. He is an angry man."

Jakob returned to the lobby.

"Aaron before we leave let me buy you one of the fine coffees they serve here. There is a small shop off the lobby that has a most excellent selection of fine coffees."

Aaron nodded and together they ambled to the coffee shop.

After they had ordered Jakob asked Aaron, "Why are you so angry? I was in a horrible situation in Germany. I needed to escape and hide. The Gestapo and SS were investigating my uncle and because I was there I was a suspect. There was a woman who helped in my Uncle's house. Her name was Sabine. She was a traitor. She betrayed us to the authorities. There is still something I do not understand. On the last day I spent at his home she came to warn us that the Gestapo was coming to arrest us. She was one of them. Why did she tell us? I have never understood. I wish I could forget all those days. All that suffering. The death. The destruction. What was it all for? Nobody won. I have never forgotten those days.

I fondly remember the days that you and I rode through Holland and near Germany while I searched for those relatives. I remember our encounter with that Nazi motorbike patrol. You really helped me."

Jakob looked at Aaron and detected the slightest softening in his demeanor.

They sat at the counter of the coffee shop on the stools and slowly finished drinking the strong beverages.

"I drove here this morning. My car is outside. We will take my car. The drive is not long. We should be driving for no more than an hour. Are you ready?"

Chapter 128

Rain fell steadily as they drove north in the old mud splattered black Peugeot. It was no luxury car but rather a farm utility. Tools littered the rear seat and on the floor in front of the passenger seat there were catalogues and empty fertilizer boxes.

Aaron wove his way through the early morning traffic to the local roads that lead north to Uitgeest and then onto the Rijksweg.

It did not take long before they were in the country. Jakob remembered the flat lands and the characteristics of the farms. It brought back many memories for him.

The rain continued to fall, whipped by a strong wind. The sky was grey and the temperature had fallen during the morning. Jakob recalled the Dutch winter. He had forgotten how miserable the winter could be.

During the drive he had attempted to start conversations with Aaron who ignored him.

Jakob sensed seriousness about Aaron. He was not relaxed.

Almost an hour had gone by before Aaron turned off the highway onto a narrow road. Jakob glanced at the road sign which proclaimed "Alkmaar 5Km"

Old houses lined the road and became more frequent as they wound their way into Alkmaar. Jakob tried to remember whether he had met anyone from Alkmaar. Who was the mystery person that Aaron was insisting they visit?

Warehouse type buildings were mixed amongst regular office type buildings. They were ancient.

"Aaron what are those buildings?"

"Alkmaar has a long history of being the main market for Dutch cheeses. Those buildings were specially constructed for storage and ventilation. There used to be an open cheese market here but now it is mainly a show for tourists. It is a pity that so many of our old customs are dying."

The rain had stopped and a fine mist hung in the air.

Aaron continued driving northward for another five minutes and then abruptly turned into a laneway that led back from the canal and into a small cluster of cottages. He slowed and finally stopped in front of old grey wooden cottage with a high pointed tile roof. The grounds were large. A garden of shrubs and late autumn flowers bordered the groomed hedges which offered privacy from the road.

Aaron parked and got out of the car.

"We are here. Now we will go in and meet the owner."

Jakob was both curious and nervous. He wondered why all the intrigue.

Together they walked up the cobble stone pathway to the front door. On the way Jakob looked around at the impeccably kept gardens. He could see past the side of the cottage to the rear and saw the huge vegetable garden. It had been prepared for the winter ahead.

Aaron rang an old style doorbell. They stood and listened to the jangle of the bell as it diminished.

From inside the cottage there was the sound of footsteps approaching. The door opened inwards.

Jakob gasped. He felt his heart burn and stop. A feeling of a tingling sensation rushed through his chest.

Standing in the doorway was a short older lady with white grey hair pulled back in a bun. There was no mistaking the twinkling bright blue eyes. Jakob was standing and facing Anke after twenty one years. He started to weep. Anke remained calm and reached out her hand to him.

Aaron retreated back to his car.

"Anke. Anke is it really you? I was told you were shot while escaping with an underground group. A Nazi patrol had intercepted your group and all had been shot and killed. I had tried to send you money to escape back to Canada. I was caught in Germany and could not get out. I stayed with my uncle Josef Klassen. The German's were watching us closely. It was impossible for me to escape and get back to Holland."

"Jakob. I looked for you for years. Yes I was shot. I was hit near my stomach. I fell with the others. I pretended to be dead. The German patrol had dogs and they came along sniffing us. A SS office kicked me in the ribs and rolled me over. I thought I would die there. He either felt sorry for me or really believed I was dead. I lay there the rest of the night. At dawn a farmer and his son discovered the massacre and went for help to remove the bodies."

"I tried to find you. I managed to escape to the Caribbean aboard a merchant ship. I had friends there who were Dutch Marines. They made inquiries and advised me that you had been killed. Had I known you were still alive I would have done everything to return and take you to the island."

"I tried to find you. After the war I searched through the lists of missing, displaced and known killed people. Europe was in a shambles. No one had accurate records. I went to the Americans. They searched and sent me to the British who tried valiantly. I also spent time with the Canadians. I spent months looking. I slept on streets and in destroyed buildings. I had no money and lived on meal assistance from the Americans. It was a horrible time. My relatives in Amsterdam had been killed in that raid. I had no one to help me. I tried to contact Henk and Aaron. After months I heard from Aaron. He told me that Henk had been killed in the bombing of Rotterdam. I felt guilty because he had been coming to take me back to the farm in Leiden.

That is all old history now."

Jakob stood not knowing what to say.

"Anke it had been many years. I am sorry that we were thrown apart by that war."

"Jakob you will never change, will you? We were not thrown apart. You were a selfish and headstrong fool on a dangerous mission. You didn't care who you hurt or the damage you did. It pains me to see you here today. In some ways I wish you had died a horrible death in Germany. Now I ask you to leave me in my retirement and peace. I do not want you and the troubles you bring to be back in my life. I thought you were dead and as far as I am concerned you are dead."

She reached for the edge of the door and slammed it firmly shut.

Jakob remained at her door for another few minutes. He pondered knocking and trying to apologize for his desertion of her and his betrayals. As he thought about asking her to forgive him he realized that she would never waver. He remembered her strong spirit from their life together those years ago.

He turned and walked back to the car and a sullen Aaron who started the car and turned for the drive back to

Amsterdam. They drove back the whole way in total silence. At the hotel, Aaron called through the open passenger window to Jakob as he was leaving the car.

"Please Jakob. You have no friends here. You are not welcome. Please go. Leave us alone. We have all suffered enough. Now we must live with what we have."

Chapter 129

Florencia, Colombia

Local interest in the Oil and Mineral exploration group from Royal Imperial Oil was high. Many of the village residents were curious and saw opportunities to sell their meager produce and arts to the group.

Adrien had advised Hans and Moreno to show them respect but not to encourage them.

During the day, they would drive the jeeps into jungle areas and familiarize themselves with the paths and tracks that led into the area where they suspected the drug lab was located. The days were getting hotter. At night, Adrien observed that the rains were starting later and were less frequent. The storms did not last as long. He was concerned as he wished to use the rains for cover and take advantage of the confusion the bad weather created.

That night he confided in Hans and Moreno.

"It is time for us to start the rescue. Here is what I propose for an action plan."

Adrien outlined his plan.

"Tomorrow I will go with the young man who is a guard at the camp. It will be risky. I will ask him to take me to the camp alone. I want you two to follow with Antonio. He has provided me a military map of the area. I will take it and while on the way into the drug lab I will mark reference points. As far as the young guard is concerned they are points of interest for our survey. I will ask him to take me into the camp and to the 'boss' on the pretense that we will be working close to the camp and don't want to cause trouble. I want you three to watch carefully and stay behind me during the trip. Look for any guards that may be hiding out in the jungle. If you do detect them do not do anything to arouse their suspicions. Do not try to enter the camp."

A buzzing sound caused them to move outside and look up. The droning sound they heard was from a small single engine military plane that was circling Florencia.

"Antonio, do you know why that plane is circling? It seems to be seeking something out."

"There is a base not far from here. There are planes that are stationed there. I would not worry. It is probably a training flight."

Adrien was not convinced. He watched the plane's maneuvers. It dipped and turned at aggressive angles. No trainee pilot could fly in that manner. He said nothing to Antonio.

After fifteen minutes of low passes, Adrien was convinced. They were either performing surveillance or looking for something specific.

Inside the villa, Adrien took the military map out. He laid it on the old table and called Antonio.

"Look at this map and show me where that plane was circling."

"I think it was in this area here." He placed his finger on a river shown on the map.

Adrien bent and squinted to read the name of the river. It was the Orteguaza River. It flowed into the Caqueta which flowed toward the Andes. He sat back and pondered the situation.

"Antonio, how possible is it that the local military are involved with the drug operations?"

"There is no doubt. They are paid poorly. Most hate the government and will do anything to make more money. They will use their positions and uniforms to disguise what they are really doing. I have access to that base. Let me visit in the morning. I will try to find out what it is like and what the men are like. I will know some. My rank allows me access and to requisition materials if we need anything."

"You are officially assigned to assist us with our survey. Try to get some rafts. Preferably get us three that can each hold three men. Tell them that we need to explore along the riverbank."

"I will take a couple of the local men with me. That way they will be less suspicious."

"Please go early. I want to leave for the drug camp in the morning." While Adrien had been talking, Hans and Moreno had watched. Moreno was uncomfortable.

When Antonio left the room, Moreno spoke.

"I will go with Antonio in the morning. I speak their language and will look for any signs of trouble. I feel that we are about to step into a trap."

"It does seem too easy. I agree. Yes you will go with them. I have some revolvers that I have kept hidden. I suggest you take one. Do you know how to use one?"

"I learned to shoot with my father's old pistol. Yes I will be fine with one."

"Hans please take Antonio outside. Ask him to help you inspect the jeeps. I will open my kit and get Moreno the firearm."

Antonio and Hans agreed to go and check the jeeps for the morning trip.

As Hans stepped off the low stone stair at the front of the Villa he stumbled into the young guard from the camp who had been sitting on the step.

"What are you doing here?"

"I am wanting work. My mother is worse. I do not have money to pay the doctor for help and medicine. Do you have work?"

Hans looked at the guard. He could not have been more that sixteen or seventeen. Hans was impressed that the young man cared so deeply for his mother.

"Wait here. I will go in and speak with the others."

"Antonio please stay with this young man. I will speak with our friends."

Inside, Hans told Adrien of the development. They all fell silent. Finally Moreno spoke.

"In our culture it is very important to care for the parents and especially the mother. I have an idea. I think we can turn the young guard to assist us. If we can offer him enough money he will be ours."

Chapter 130

Adrien considered the situation.

"Bring the boy in. We will find out a few things. I will lead this discussion."

Chairs were pulled up to the table and Antonio held the boy's arm as he escorted him into the villa. He marched him to the table and ordered him to sit.

"What is your name boy?"

"It is Ramon, sir."

"Ramon we may have some work for you. Let us talk first so I can learn more about you and your family. Tell me what is wrong with your mother's health? How many are in your family?"

"My mother has cancer. The doctor says she may not live without the medications. They are expensive. We cannot get them from the government programs. I am the oldest of four sisters in our family. I work at the camp because I need the money. I do not like it there or the work I am made to do. I pay for our food. My father was killed during the period of 'La Violencia." He was a brave man and fought against the politics. I miss him. He was a good man.

He helped the church and would assist some of the poor people."

Adrien listened and asked Ramon to return and wait outside.

"Moreno, he is one of your people. Is he telling the truth? Do you think we should try to buy him? He can either be a huge help to us or a traitor who could ruin any of our attempts to save Juan."

"I am not sure. I think he tells the truth. Let me walk him home. I will see for myself his situation."

"That is a good idea. Do you want Hans to go with you?"

"No, that would not be appropriate. I will find a way to do this and try to get his confidence."

"If you trust him and what he says is all true, then bring him back here tonight."

Antonio had watched the conversation between Adrien and Moreno in silence.

With a smile, Moreno headed to the door. He looked back at Adrien and patted the deep pocket in which he had concealed the firearm.

During the walk to Ramon's home, they talked about all things that interested young men. Ramon was particularly engrossed in baseball. He knew all the major American players and scores of games. He told Moreno that it was his dream to go to a baseball game in America one day and sit and eat a real baseball hotdog with mustard and ketchup.

Moreno smiled and thought of the innocence of such a dream in the midst of the horrible conditions in which Ramon lived and worked.

Along the way they passed by the occasional men standing outside cantinas drinking and laughing. Many seemed to know Ramon and called a greeting to him.

"They know me because of my brave father. He was a friend to many."

A laneway leading to a group of adobes emerged from the dimly lit street. The houses were old and cheap. They were built the traditional way with dried mud brick. As they approached, Moreno could see light coming from the interiors. All of the houses had window openings. There was no glassed window. From the inside the flickering of candles and oil lamps projected onto the street.

Moreno remembered his past and the squalor of the barrio. He had no desire to return to that life. He understood Ramon's desire to help his family and wondered if he had a dream of taking them to a better place to live.

"This is my home."

Ramon stood in front of a rundown adobe. The mud surface of the front wall had started to crumble. Sheets of rusted corrugated iron roofing had been attached to the wall to try and prevent further deterioration. The front door was missing.

Moreno's heart sank when he saw the conditions.

"I will go in first. I will tell my mother that we have a visitor. She will want time to prepare herself for you. I will also need to wake my sisters. It is important for you to meet all my family."

Ramon sprinted off through the open doorway. Moreno heard him calling to his family. The level of light increased as more candles and lamps were lit.

Moreno waited patiently outside. He heard the shrill laughter of the girls as they scampered to dress and receive a late night visitor.

"Mr. Moreno, please come in to meet my family."

As he entered the adobe, Moreno was impressed at the cleanliness inside. It was betrayed by the look of the exterior.

The four sisters stood in line smiling. Each gave a slight bow as Moreno walked in. Sitting on a bright red chair in the center of the room was the mother.

"This is my Madre. Please meet her. Her name is Luciana."

Moreno moved forward to see her better in the poor light. He saw the ravages of the cancer. She was slim and being eaten away by the disease. He was struck by the radiating beauty that emanated from her face and smile. There was no doubt she had been a beautiful woman.

Under his breath Moreno cursed the existence of cancer.

"I am pleased to meet you and your beautiful family. My name is Moreno. Your fine son Ramon wishes to do some work for us. I am sure we can find a job for him while we are here for the exploration."

Luciana replied. "That would make me very happy. That place he works now is wrong. I am a catholic. I do not like him being there. It is an evil place. When he comes home from there I see the demons in him. He is a good boy but when he goes there he changes. I do not like it. I am old and sick. I hope he will find a better life."

Moreno felt pangs of guilt, knowing how they wanted to use Ramon.

The oldest of the daughter offered to make coffee for them. Moreno politely refused. It was time to return to the villa and Adrien.

Chapter 131

Walking back to the villa with Ramon, he decided to ask some questions. He asked about the camp in general terms. He asked how long it had been there and other simple questions. Ramon seemed only too happy to answer and show his knowledge of the camp.

They were nearing the villa when Moreno asked the major question. Who is in charge? Is there a man there doing forced labor?

Ramon looked at him for minutes before answering.

"I do not know the name of the man in charge. He is from Venezuela. He is a very cruel man. There is a man I guard. He is old and works packing the marijuana and that new drug, cocaine. He is not from Colombia. He does not like me because I have to guard him. He seems nice but if I am seen being soft with him I will be punished."

"Do you know his name?"

"Yes. It is the name Juan. He says he comes from some island. I do not know that island."

"Tell me where he is kept in the camp."

Ramon described the layout of the camp and the cabin that Juan was imprisoned in.

At the villa Moreno entered and before anyone could speak he addressed them.

"I met with Ramon's family. They are nice people. I support our hiring Ramon. He has shared some critical information with me. He has confirmed Juan is a prisoner in the camp. He has also told me the exact cabin where he is kept chained."

Ramon was confused. He didn't understand why these men were so interested in an old prisoner.

"Why is this old man so important?'

The rescue team stood uncertain how to answer him.

Antonio stepped forward to answer him.

"We can help you. We will pay you if you help us. That man is an important friend of a powerful man in Aruba. If you want us to help you with money, then you will need to assist us."

"I am scared. If I help you and they find out they will kill me and my family."

"They will never know. It is time for you to know the truth. We are here to rescue Juan."

It was as if the sounds of all around and the jungle went quiet.

"How will you do that? They have guards hiding in the growth outside the fence."

"We will tell you when we are coming. That will give you time to leave the camp. You will take a message to Juan and tell him we are here to rescue him. To assist us you will make sure his chains are removed and he is not locked in. I will give you some socks and another item to take to him. You must not be caught with these. Do not try to open the package either."

"They do not search us going into the camp but do check when we leave. Even if you do not have anything they will still beat us."

"Is Juan's health good?"

"Yes. He is a really strong man. I am surprised that someone his age can do the work they make him do."

"I wish to be clear with you. If you attempt to betray us it will not work. You will be killed."

"When will I get money?"

"I will make the arrangements with others here so it does not seem unusual for you to have money to spend. The medications your mother needs will be paid by us. Later we will get more money to you and your family."

As they talked amongst themselves there was a noise outside. Antonio drew a gun from his belt and stood behind the door.

A rapid knock on the door was answered by Hans. A tall man and a Latino woman stood at the door.

"We are looking for Hans Klassen."

Antonio lowered the pistol and replaced it in his trouser belt. There was confusion.

"Who the hell are you? Why are you looking for Hans Klassen, whoever he is?"

The woman stepped forward.

"I am Benita Flores. I am a friend of Jakob. I am with the Miami Sentinel. We have a deal with Jakob and certain US authorities to cover the raid of the lab. This is my photographer Jurgen."

Antonio was not amused,

"It will be hard enough to rescue Juan from that armed camp and escape without you holding us up. We will be trying to get through the jungle quickly. You are not trained and will be a problem."

"I resent your comment. My photographer has covered wars and had assignments in the jungle before. He is well trained and I do not suggest you try him. He is stronger than any of you. I will be able to accompany you all without causing any delay."

Antonio glared at her.

"Your presence here could give us away."

"No. We are here to do a photo story on the efforts of Royal Imperial Oil to find oil and minerals and bring wealth to the local people. We will be interviewing some families. We will make it pleasant for the local people. They will accept us more easily than you."

Hans and Moreno watched the interchange with some amusement. It was obvious that Antonio had a problem with taking any comment or advice from a woman.

"How did you know where to find us?"

"It was simple. We asked some of the people here. They all know about the exploration men. They knew where you lived and how to find you."

"How did you get here?"

"Before we left Miami our public relations department contacted the Colombian government and explained that we wished to prepare an article on Colombia and we had chosen Florencia. They were excited and arranged for us to be flown here in a small plane. So far, everyone has been helpful."

Adrien stepped to the middle of the floor.

"I don't care about your article. I am in command here and our mission is very well defined. We are here to take Juan back to Aruba. I am not interested, nor will I accept any problems between you, Antonio or you, Benita. If I detect any problem, you are both out. I will not repeat myself on this."

Chapter 132

"There are now six of us. That is too many. I will take Moreno and Hans with me. Antonio I want you to stay and watch for any signs that the raid has been discovered. You will stay in radio contact if you see anything strange."

Antonio started to object. He was quickly quietened by Adrien.

"Benita, what arrangements have you made for sleeping while you are here?"

"We have none yet. We were hoping to stay with you tonight and find somewhere in the morning."

"I will agree to you staying for one night."

The group settled into an understanding of their respective roles and the structure that Adrien had developed. Soon the talk changed from the mission to more general topics.

Adrien and Moreno took Ramon aside for a detailed talk.

"Ramon, you need to realize that what we plan is important and dangerous. We will be taking a huge risk to get into the camp. In the morning I want to enter the camp. I will drive to the camp with you and wait while you ask the commandant to let me visit. I need you to suggest a way for us to get into the camp after darkness."

"There has never been a problem at night. The guards have become lazy at night. They sit and play dominoes and drink. Often they will fall asleep while resting against the back walls of the barracks. They cannot be seen from the main area of the compound. Most of them are drunk by the middle of the night."

"Do you have any ideas how we can get into the camp undetected and reach the hut where Juan is being held?"

Ramon thought for a long while before answering.

"There is one possible way. There will still be a risk that you will be seen. The guards are instructed to shoot to kill. I am thinking that the area where the bano is would be the best."

Adrien did not understand the word bano and asked Ramon to explain.

"It is the area where they dug the big holes for toilets. They are just inside the wire fence that surrounds the whole camp. At night nobody watches or goes there. You could cut a hole in the fence and enter there. If you leave that way you will run into the jungle growth very quickly. The jungle there is dense and dangerous."

"How far is it from the fence to Juan's hut?"

"I think about seventy yards."

Adrien sat and thought through the information that Ramon had given them. He addressed Moreno.

"Tomorrow you will go with Antonio and Hans and check this information. I need you to make sure the information that Ramon has given us is correct and check if we can get the jeeps close to the perimeter fence without them being seen. You will stop and disguise your actions as performing survey work. Take some local men with you. Have them drive in stakes and mark their locations on the maps. It has to look real. We are going to be close to the camp and we must not risk someone giving the criminals any information that would make them suspicious. Tomorrow night there should be a storm with heavy rains. When it is dark during those rains we will cut through the fence and rescue Juan."

While they talked about the rescue attempt, Benita had been listening intently.

"How will we observe your action tomorrow? Can we come during the day? I want to be there when you perform the raid tomorrow."

"You can find someone local to take you to where we are working. You must not appear to be too friendly or involved with us. These people will react to anything they find strange. You must seem to be here alone and trying to learn what we are doing."

Ramon had watched and listened to the exchange.

"There is a man I know in the village. He is one you can trust. He has lived in America and other countries. He has a Ford pickup truck. He takes supplies into the camp. They trust him. He is connected to the military and the bosses at the camp. He deceives them. He is not their friend but has them believing that he supports them. I will take you and Jurgen to meet him tomorrow. I am sure that for a small amount of money he will take you close to watch the 'survey' crew at work. I know you can trust him. He is my uncle."

Adrien agreed and asked Ramon to go outside with him and Moreno.

"Ramon we need to get details to arrange payment to you and your doctor. I have been thinking. If we pay you and you then go spending a large amount of money it will make others wonder where the money came from. It will make it dangerous for you after we raid the camp. I will arrange to pay the doctor directly. We will make the arrangement for him to treat your mother. Please tell him of the details. We will find him tomorrow. I will ask Antonio to pay him when he goes to visit the military base. Can you get the message to him before early tomorrow?"

"Yes, I will get a note to him tonight. I will give Antonio the address for him."

Throughout the next hour, Adrien and Antonio checked the weapons for the raid. In addition, they wrapped a pistol and ammunition in an oilcloth for Ramon to smuggle into the camp for Juan.

When they were finished, Adrien double checked everything with both Moreno and Hans.

"We will only get one attempt at getting into the camp and getting Juan. Make sure you know your weapon and how to use it. If you have questions it is now the time to ask. Tomorrow will come soon and the day will pass quickly. It will be tomorrow night before we know it. Benita, please tell me how you and Jurgen intend to observe our action."

"I will stay outside the camp. Jurgen will go in with you and photograph you taking Juan. He will take pictures of the camp from outside during the day. Our story will be about the existence of the camp and how it is part of the Venezuelan mob. Jurgen will be part of your raid. He has had jungle training. I will stay outside the camp to observe and record the action. We will have the story of the rescue of Juan. Jurgen will not leave with you. He will stay behind and find his way back to the village. He and I will meet and leave for Caracas to be there when the authorities raid the mob headquarters and warehouses. If you succeed in rescuing Juan and make it out alive, you will be able to find where we are staying by contacting Hans's brother in Aruba, as we are in contact with him through our Miami office."

Chapter 133

Early morning, Antonio took his jeep and drove to the military base. He was admitted without any challenge. After introducing himself he asked whether certain of his colleagues were stationed at the base. He found he had some friends there who he had known at other bases.

He spent the morning with some officers and described the assignment he had to assist the survey crew from Royal Imperial Oil. He requested the rafts that Adrien had mentioned they needed. Some junior soldiers were ordered to go to the quartermaster and requisition the rafts and then load them into Antonio's jeep.

At the villa, Adrien was getting impatient. He wanted to reach the camp early in the day. He bounded from the jeep and ran into the villa and paced the floor.

To add to his frustration, the door opened and Ramon walked in.

"I thought we would go together to the camp. It is a long walk for me. Sometimes I can ride the bus that goes near the track that leads into it. I slept in this morning. Don't worry I will tell them a good story. You will get into the camp I am sure. I will go and see the boss immediately and tell them that you want to meet."

"This is not what we agreed upon. You were to go early. I was to arrive at the camp while you were outside patrolling. I was to ask you to let me see the man in charge. Now we have you late and Antonio out visiting his mates."

As they spoke, Antonio's jeep screeched to a halt outside.

"I am pleased. I met with the officers responsible for the base. They are eager to assist us. They believe you are truly a survey and exploration crew. I asked for certain supplies and they provided them. I have two inflatable rafts. At present they are deflated. I have the compressed gas canisters to quickly fill them. I was also able to get a medical supply kit with bandages and some drugs used for common problems here. They also gave me a gift...a bottle of whiskey."

"You did well. I must tell you that there will be no drinking until we finish this mission, so keep your bottle safe. Now it is time for us to leave and drive to the camp. Moreno and Hans you will stay back and let me have at least ten minutes lead time. Remember your job is to tail me and when I take the track down to where we believe the camp is you will turn off the track and then leave the jeep and follow through the bush looking for hidden guards. They should be visible after I pass through several of their checkpoints. Stay hidden. Do not let yourselves get caught.

I will drive into the camp very slowly. This should give you time to hide your jeep and walk through the jungle to the hills that overlook the camp. I will not be in any hurry. Anyone watching me will not understand why I am travelling so slowly. I will stop and take out the map and pretend I am looking at some geological point of interest. Now is your jeep ready? Are the rifles stored safely?"

Hans and Moreno sensed the excitement. Finally they were starting the rescue attempt.

As they were leaving the villa, Adrien looked at Antonio who was dressed in his military uniform.

"That is a nice touch Antonio. It will make it all seem real if you get stopped. Now let's move on."

They pulled away from the villa and started the one hour drive south west toward the river. As they drove through the village, Moreno spotted the old Ford F-150 pickup truck turning out to follow them.

"Damm. It is Ramon's uncle with those newspaper people. We do not want them with us today. Our surveillance must be done carefully and in secret. We cannot take the risk to have them with us at this time."

Antonio pulled the jeep to a halt. Moreno jumped from it and went back to the pickup.

"You do not join us today. We are planning and getting critical information. Your presence today could destroy the mission if you were caught or you get investigated. Please do not follow or go near the camp today."

Benita struck back.

"I was given permission by Jakob Klassen to be a part of this. I will not be told by some nobody that I cannot observe and record all the events leading up to his rescue and the link to the mob in Venezuela."

"Benita, I think you are not thinking clearly. We are performing a surveillance today that will be critical to our plan to raid the camp. Please be reasonable. We will make sure you will be involved at the time of our action. Now is not that time. We need to use every ounce of caution and rely on the training of Adrien and Antonio to get us this information. Please do not try to follow. It would be too easy for the mission to fail. These men in the camp are criminals. They will think nothing of killing all of us. I am sure that Jakob would agree with us."

"You win this time. Promise me that when it is time we will be told in advance."

Moreno returned to the jeep. Exasperated he asked Antonio to drive on.

They passed by a thinning number of houses as they departed Florencia. After an hour, Antonio slowed the jeep and finally stopped. He took the map and studied their location.

"We are close to the track that leads into the camp. It is about a mile in from this track. We will leave the jeep here and walk in the rest of the way."

They trudged through wild tall long grasses until they came to the edge of the huge trees that filled the jungle.

As they walked into the cover of the trees the light dimmed. The heavy canopy of the overhead branches and vines created a curtain that filtered out the sun. In the dimmed light they walked on. As they continued the growth surrounding them grew thicker.

Antonio stopped and addressed them.

"We must be very careful. The jungle has many creatures that will attack us. We must be aware of these as well as the possibility of guards from the camp."

Hans was frustrated and annoyed.

"What type of creatures are you talking about? I don't think there is anything that will attack us that we cannot defend ourselves against."

"Hans, I am Colombian as is Moreno. I grew up here and know the jungle. There are real threats here. We are on the edge of a deep jungle. You must understand that we are bordering the Amazon. There are many things to be cautious about."

"I am mainly scared of the human kind of threat."

"No, my friend. You must look out for the Equis. It is a snake that thrives here. It is deadly. It is one of the only snakes that will make an unprovoked attack on humans. Almost anyone who is bitten on the leg or arm will need to have that limb amputated. The other creature I ask you to look for is the Yellow Striped frog. It is a small creature that rests on tree branches and at the top of the spike of the long grass. It is deadly. Do not touch it. If it should jump or contact you, do not touch the area on your clothing. The Yellow Stripe has a venomous slime on its back. It will kill you. The amount of venom is so strong it is capable of killing ten people."

Hans cursed.

"What a horrible country. It has these creatures that kill, bandits, a corrupt government, drugs and crime that are supported by the people, poverty, and poverty."

Moreno bristled.

"Hans, this is the country I was born in. It is my homeland. Yes there are many problems here but there are also good people trying to make a change. Was it any better in Germany after the war?"

"Stop with this. You two can debate after our mission. Now let us continue. Stop talking. We must proceed in silence. They may have sentries hidden here in the bush."

Antonio gave them stare that was icy and meant business.

They continued their trek through the jungle. Often fallen trees blocked their path or massive clusters of vines fell from overhead that blocked their path.

As they continued, the interior of the jungle grew darker. Clouds were rolling in and blocking the sun. Monkeys screeched and there was the cry of the multi colored parrots that deafened them at times.

Their walk ended as they reached an opening where the trees receded back to the grasses and low bush.

Antonio motioned to them to stop and fell on his stomach to the ground. He waved the others to follow. He took the pair of binoculars and scanned the area. He saw Adrien's jeep sitting on the track. Adrien was standing at the front and speaking with a small band of armed men. He was pointing and their conversation seemed friendly. As he watched, Adrien offered the men cigarettes. They were eagerly accepted. Antonio remembered the status and luxury associated with having real American cigarettes.

He lay on the ground and continued to scan the area. He looked back up the track that Adrien had driven down. There was a fence constructed from old tree trunks that was bound with some type of twine and wire. It had been pulled back to prevent anyone from driving back to the larger track.

As he scanned the area he noticed a white flash near the gate. He focused on the gate and the adjacent foliage. There was nothing.

He returned his scan to Adrien. It seemed that he was not experiencing any problem.

As they watched, a low hum was heard in the distance. They waited and continued to watch Adrien.

Minutes passed and finally an army truck appeared at the gate. It slowed to a halt and waited. Some men ran from the bushes and pulled the gate back to allow the truck to pass.

Antonio swung back and looked for Adrien. He was nowhere to be seen. The truck lumbered across the uneven track and stopped at a low wooden building. A group of men jumped from inside the covered back of the truck. They stood and stretched.

He was curious. He focused the binoculars back on the truck and examined it closely. The insignia above the license plate identified it as a vehicle from the local base. They were soldiers who were somehow involved with this camp and its operations. Antonio realized he had been lied to.

Chapter 134

That night they plotted and schemed in order to devise the best way to get Juan from the camp. Adrien told them of his talk with the camp boss. He described him as a particularly unpleasant individual. Adrien had asked for his permission to undertake field work behind the camp near the riverbank. It was part of their plan to get close to the fence and establish an escape route once they had Juan.

Adrien was worried.

"I have a concern. If we do get Juan I am unsure of the best way to get him out of Colombia."

They sat and discussed various ideas.

"I had originally decided to take him to the coast and take him back to Aruba by boat. I am now worried because there are too many fishing boats and smugglers in those waters. We could be stopped by the Colombian government forces or by some unsavory types looking to stop other vessels and pirate their cargo. Now I am no longer convinced that this would be the best way."

For hours they talked about the different ideas.

It was late when Antonio stumbled upon an idea they all liked.

"I am a ranking officer. I will go back to the base early in the morning. I met the quartermaster on my last visit. I will get an officer uniform for Juan to wear. He will accompany me in my jeep. I will use my influence and some cash to get him the uniform and papers. We will travel without interference. The papers for Juan and I will be signed by our highest ranking officials.

Let us get Ramon. I need him to assist me in selecting the correct size of uniform. He will be able to help. He has been guarding Juan and should know his size."

After some discussion, Moreno left to fetch Ramon.

An hour passed before he returned with Ramon.

Adrien sat with Ramon and told him of the plan. He omitted certain details that could stop the rescue if Ramon was working for both parties.

"I have an idea. Can Antonio take me to the base? I am almost the same size as Juan. I had to take a jacket, shoes and coat to him a month ago when the rains started. I know his size. If I go with Antonio I can try the uniform. I will act as a servant to Antonio and his officer."

Adrien looked to Antonio.

"We did trust you to deliver that item to Juan so I guess we can trust you to help us with this."

Adrien turned to Ramon. "This needs to be done early in the morning. You will sleep here for the rest of the night."

At dawn they woke to the smell of fresh coffee that Moreno had made. After drinking several cups, Antonio summoned Ramon to go to the jeep with him. They departed in the military jeep for the base.

"Tonight we will perform the rescue. Today we will all go to the area I had discussed with the camp boss yesterday. We will hide the tools that we will need to cut through the fence and break open the back of Juan's cabin. I saw an ideal hiding place while I was there. We must also honor our commitment to Jakob and do what he asked. I will go and visit with Benita and Jurgen. I will tell them of the plan for tonight. I wish they were not here but it is what Jakob wants. I am going to tell them to go to the area where you were able to watch me and view the camp. They should stay there until the afternoon. I will send Hans to meet them back on the track. I told the camp boss that there is a journalist covering the exploration for the government. He was not happy and was concerned about them taking pictures of the camp. I promised him that we would prevent them from taking pictures there."

Adrien departed and Moreno and Hans checked the equipment again. They were just finishing when Antonio returned with Ramon. Ramon was laughing and wearing the uniform of a Sergeant. Hans and Moreno saw the spectacle and roared with laughter.

"I doubt any patrol who may stop us will want to argue with Sergeant Major Juan."

It was the first light hearted moment they had shared in days.

Ramon ran inside and changed his clothing back to street clothes.

"I must hurry and return to the camp. I am on a shift for this afternoon. It is possible I will be asked to continue into tonight. If that happens I will find a way to signal you."

"If you do work tonight do not make any attempt to follow us. Stay in the camp. If the escape is discovered provide confusing details. Tell them incorrect things. Show them a direction that is not the correct one. It is going to be extremely dangerous."

They heard a crunch on the stones outside as the jeep stopped. The engine was turned off and Adrien came through the door with Benita and Jurgen behind him. From his facial expression it was clear he was unhappy.

"Last night these fools left their possessions at their villa and went out to a cantina. When they returned their papers had been stolen. Now they will need to get the police involved. They will need their documents in order to leave the country and return to America. The police will ask too many questions. Antonio, can you assist? Will you take them to the police? You are here with your military orders. They won't resist you."

"This will change our plans. The police here are slow. There will not be time for them to observe the camp from the hill. The police will want to go and look at their villa. I suspect they will go to some of the little bars and ask the ones they know are thieves about this. I have another idea. Let me go with Moreno to a couple of those bars and start asking questions. I will also make sure everyone knows that we will pay well for the return of everything and will not ask questions or report the theft. I will tell them that the papers are useless to a Colombian and have no value."

Antonio went to change from his uniform to some less official and threatening clothes.

It was shortly after noon hour when a boy arrived with a scruffy leather bag. He stood at the door and waited. Moreno went to him and questioned him. The boy asked for the money before he would hand over the bag. Moreno contemplated grabbing the bag from the boy but realized that the boy stood in a position to sprint away at the sign of trouble. Moreno left him standing at the door while he went to the back of the villa and into another room. He returned with money in his hand. In Spanish he told the boy to start to hand the bag to him. Moreno moved his hand forward a little so the boy could see the money. Instinctively the boy tried to snatch it. Moreno caught his wrist and spun him to the ground. He picked up the bag and opened it. There were pieces of torn up newspaper in the bag. Moreno placed a firm kick in the boy's rear end.

"That is so typical here."

They had given up hope of getting the papers back when an elderly lady arrived. Her head was covered in a headscarf. She held out a thin cardboard box. Moreno took the box and opened it. Inside were the papers for Benita and Jurgen.

He smiled and thanked her. She continued to stand at the door. She said nothing. Moreno went and placed some coins in her hand. She looked at them and then back at Moreno and remained at the door. She was demanding more. He called for Antonio to bring more pesos.

She grinned a toothless grin and nodded her thanks before ambling off and down the narrow cobblestone street.

Chapter 135

The two jeeps travelled the distance to the camp. They stopped at the gate that blocked the track leading into the camp.

Adrien stepped out of the jeep and walked across to where to men stood. There were rifles trained on him.

"I spoke to the boss yesterday. He has approved our working near the rear of the camp."

The guards were unsure. They dispatched one on a bike to go into the camp and verify Adrien's claim. He returned fifteen minutes later and told the others of the approval.

They wound their way down toward the buildings of the camp and then turned off on a track that led to the rear area of the camp. They could see the river as it flowed past the lower embankment of the camp. It was swollen from the rains and flowed fast. Adrien estimated that it was no more than one hundred yards from Juan's cabin.

They stopped the jeeps and everyone gathered together. Benita was furiously making notes. Moreno and Hans were ostensibly setting up pieces of equipment and Jurgen was examining the area. He was trying to frame pictures in his mind and decide which would be the most dramatic when published.

Throughout the afternoon they went about moving equipment. For anyone watching it all seemed legitimate, except for certain things. Antonio and Moreno moved the inflatable rafts to a gravelly area on the river bank and concealed them.

Every so often, Adrien would glance up towards Juan's cabin. It was late afternoon when he got his first glimpse of Juan. He was being pushed forward by a young guard. It was Ramon.

Ramon looked over at them and aggressively nodded his head. Before entering the cabin, he cast a nervous look behind him back in the direction of the workers barracks.

He had signaled that he would be there that night.

As time passed, the afternoon darkened. The humidity was high and ominous black clouds slowly crossed the sky. Moreno had lived in Colombia to know that this was the sign of an impending major storm. He advised Adrien who smiled. It was what he wanted.

Early nightfall descended. Antonio and Moreno cautiously moved close to the fence and started to cut away the wire. With the gaping hole large enough for two men to crawl through they then slid on their stomachs up to the rear of the cabin. Antonio produced a huge knife. He scrapped at the moss covered boards and was delighted when his knife penetrated one. The wood was rotten. He drew the knife across the boards and formed a rectangle. When complete they slid back down the embankment to the river where the others were waiting. Antonio excitedly told Adrien of the condition of the timber on the hut.

"It will be easy to push it in. The wood was crumbling as I carved into it."

Darkness had fallen and the camp was now lit with a few lights. In the distance they could hear a radio. The announcer was speaking fast. Moreno strained to listen. It was more political propaganda.

Adrien called them together as a group.

"It is time. You will all go back to the jeeps. Antonio and I will enter the cabin and get Juan. Jurgen stay out of our way. Benita, you will leave with the others. Once we have Juan, we will leave in the rafts. The river flows east and with the rains it is flowing fast. Follow Moreno. He will drive to a location east of here where we will beach the rafts and start the fast drive away from Florencia. Does anyone have questions?"

The group was silent.

"Now start to pack the jeeps as if you are finished for the day and getting ready to leave."

Antonio and Adrien climbed back up to the cabin. They crouched behind it and together pushed the center of the rectangular space. The wood crumbled and gave way. Adrien flashed a low beam light into the cabin. In the corner Juan was sitting on the bed with his legs tucked up in front of him. His face was one of terror.

"Relax, Juan. We are here compliments of Jakob Klassen. We have come to rescue you."

Juan did not move. His senses had been nulled by the length of his stay at the camp and the depravation of food and company. He was unsure. The mention of Jakob's name caused some spark of life.

"Come Juan we do not have long to get you out of here."

"I must put on my shoes. First I must inspect them. There might be banana spiders in them. They are poisonous you know. They hide in shoes and in beds at night. Nasty spiders."

Adrien recognized the loss of reality and senses that prolonged captivity can have on a person.

"Juan I will put my arm around you and help you out through that hole we made."

While talking a heavy roll of thunder announced the arrival of the storm. Lightning flashed and cast an eerie image of the camp and the forest beyond.

Antonio slid back through the opening first and waited to guide Adrien and Juan to the ground. The rain deluged and was whipped by a fierce wind.

They gently pulled Juan down to the fence. The rain had reduced the visibility. They found the cut in the fence. Antonio went through first and as he was guiding Juan's head through the opening Jurgen took a picture. The flash from the camera illuminated the fence, cabin and most of the riverbank. Shouts arose from the barracks. Flashlights were pointed in the direction of the cabin. There were more shouts and the barking of guard dogs.

Thunder continued to crash and lightning lit the sky for long periods. During one of those periods, Adrien saw men running toward them. He grabbed Juan and threw him over his shoulder. He ran to the raft and half threw Juan into the raft. Antonio cast them off before jumping into the other raft. The current swiftly pulled them out into the middle of the river and they sped quickly downstream.

Rifle shots rang out. They heard more shots in the distance. The others were trapped in a gunfight.

The young guard, Ramon had hidden between the cabin and the barracks during the rescue. He ran from his hiding place and pretended to be in pursuit of the escapees. He misjudged badly. From behind him, volleys of bullets were flying in the direction of the cabin and the river.

He did not make it to the fence. Several bullets passed through him and sliced his body in half. He was dead before he hit the ground.

In the jeeps there was panic. A vehicle was pursuing them at speed. Rifles were being fired at them.

Moreno pulled the jeep off the road and into the edge of the jungle. Hans followed in the second jeep. They all jumped from the jeep and ran into the jungle. For minutes all was quiet. No gunshots were heard.

"I think we are safe at the minute. They will discover that we do not have Juan and then they will leave us alone."

Hans had no sooner spoken when more shots rang out. There location had been found. Bullets flew by distinctly clipping the branches of the undergrowth. They decided to run to shelter behind the trunk of one of the giant trees. As Hans ran in a crouched manner, a bullet found him. He stumbled forward. The back of his head and the whole front of his skull were missing. Moreno tried to hold him and upon seeing Hans brains hanging on his chest immediately vomited.

The remainder of the group stayed quiet and waited. Shadowy figures emerged from the mist of the jungle and walked toward them. A man wearing a bandana shouted at them in Spanish. Moreno called back.

"Why are you shooting at us? We are just the survey crew returning to Florencia."

"You have one of our men."

"No we don't. Come and search. You have killed one of our men."

The leader shone a bright flashlight on each of their faces and then went to search the jeep. When he was satisfied, he barked an order at one of the others.

"Take them to the gate. Let them go. Get rid of them."

Moreno raised his hand.

"We need to take our fellow worker with us."

The leader spun and looked at Hans' corpse lying in the undergrowth.

"You will leave him here. The jungle will look after his disposal. Now go before I have you all killed."

They were surrounded by men and taken back to the jeeps. The armed men ordered them to drive slowly to the gate.

"Benita, can you drive that jeep?"

"Yes."

"Let us get away from here quickly. We will drive to the location where Antonio and Adrien should be waiting."

They drove back through the village and to the narrowed curve in the river where a pier extended out into the river. The pier was used by local fisherman and boats plying cargo on the river.

At this time of the evening it was deserted.

Moreno made out the shape of the rafts hiding beneath the planking of the deck. He parked and ran down to assist Adrien and Antonio with Juan. He briefed Adrien on the encounter after leaving the camp area.

"This is bad. We leave here tonight. Benita you and Jurgen will come with us. It is for your safety. I should leave that stupid Jurgen here to fend for himself. Did he not think before taking that photo? He gave us away. We would have performed a perfect rescue except for him. We will go and get our things from the villa and start the drive tonight. Antonio you will dress in uniform. Juan will be in his as well and will travel with you. I will be close behind you. Do not do anything to attract attention.

He turned to Jurgen. "Do you understand me you dipshit?"

Chapter 136

Germany

Since his return from the trip with Aaron, Solange had been confused by Jakob's actions and mood. Before he had been eager to stay and visit people in the Netherlands. Now he was in a hurry to leave. He had called for information on the trains to Munich and arranged for the return of the rental car.

He called his old friend Jan Zelder in Germany at the number he had been given by Jan.

In the outskirts of Munich, the phone rang. It was finally answered by Jan.

"Jan it is Jakob. I am in Amsterdam at present. We are leaving sooner than planned. I am booking a train to Munich and will arrive tomorrow night. Can you recommend a hotel for Solange and I that is close to your house?"

"Yes I certainly can. You will stay at the Hotel Zelder. I have lots of room. It's a big house and I am here alone in it. I think that I should sell it. It really is too big for me. Now, what time are you arriving? I will meet you at the station. I think I remember what you look like."

"There is a train at eight tomorrow morning. The trip takes around thirteen hours. We will arrive around nine tomorrow evening. Is that convenient? I am looking forward to seeing you again."

"I will be at the station. Yes it will be good to sit and talk about our lives adventures."

After they hung up, Jakob called the station and reserved his tickets.

"Solange we will need to leave early. We need to go to the station and pick up our tickets. I will arrange with the hotel to pay the account tonight. We will go to one of the bistros for an early dinner. I will help you pack the few things we have used when we return."

Light snow was falling as they left the hotel for the short walk to the bistro.

The atmosphere inside the bistro was warm and welcoming. Once they were seated and served with drinks, Solange decided to try and understand the sudden change of plans.

"Solange, I want to see Jan Zelder and get back to Aruba sooner. That is all."

"Jakob after all this time with you I know when you are stretching the truth. Something happened and you won't tell me. It must be something terrible or you are ashamed of."

"Holland is not what I expected. There is nothing here for me. Now please stop asking questions."

The waiter arrived at the table to take their orders. Solange ordered Sole Almondine and Jakob settled for a beef bourguignon crepe. He ordered a bottle of Sancerre and they settled into a relaxed evening. Solange was quietly fuming beneath her calm exterior.

They hardly spoke over dinner. Instead of staying for a desert and an after dinner drink, Solange stood and demanded they return to the hotel.

At the hotel her mood was crisp. She pulled clothes from drawers and the armoire and threw them on the bed to pack them into their cases. Jakob shrugged and headed down to the desk to settle the account.

He returned to find Solange already in bed.

At five in the morning Jakob arose to prepare for the trip. After they dressed he called down to the desk for assistance with the baggage and to arrange for a taxi to the station.

The mood was still cool. Solange was barely patient with him.

They rode in silence to the station. The taxi pulled up and a porter came for their bags.

"Which platform will you be going to?"

"I am getting our tickets to Munich."

"That will be platform six."

"I am going to get our tickets Solange."

"Don't rush. I will be in the ladies powder room. At least there I don't need to look at the face of deception."

From his years with Solange he knew that this problem was growing into a crisis. She did not like to lose an argument or be detracted from things she wished to know.

He walked off to buy the tickets wondering when, and if, he should tell her of the trip to Alkmaar and the meeting with Anke. If he told her the situation could possibly explode. If he didn't then the mood would remain sullen but calm.

He purchased the tickets and wandered back to platform six still pondering the situation. He finally decided.

Solange was sitting next to their bags. He walked up to her.

"Solange we have about forty five minutes before the train leaves. There is a café here. Please come with me and I will explain it all to you."

He saw the indication of a smile at the corner of her lips. She had used her guiles again to get her way.

In the café, Jakob poured out the story. Solange sat stone faced. When Jakob had finished she reached over the table and took his hand.

"Jakob, that happened a long time ago. There were so many obstacles then. If she had really wanted to find you I believe she could have. Twenty years have gone by. There is something that is not right with her story. I am not upset. I believe you thought she was dead. Now we will speak no more of this. Let us go onto Germany and your friend."

Chapter 137

Other than the stop at the German border, the train trip was boring. They went to the dining car several times and had drinks delivered to them at their seat. Jakob read an English paper he had found at a kiosk at the station. Solange dozed on and off.

The train arrived ahead of schedule. Passengers flooded from the cars and headed toward the exit. Jakob summoned a porter to assist them.

Standing next to the exit was a distinguished looking man.

"Jakob. Jakob Klassen?"

Jakob stared at him. It was Jan Zelder. He had aged but taken on an aura of success and money. He looked aristocratic.

"Yes. Is that really you Jan?"

"It is all me I promise you. I assume this beautiful princess with you is the lovely Solange Klassen. It is indeed my pleasure to meet you."

Solange blushed profusely. Her normal ivory complexion was now in two tones with the flushed red cheeks.

"Let us make our way up to my car. The driver is waiting. "

He turned and instructed the porter where to find the car.

They climbed the ramp to street level and waiting for them was a large black Mercedes. Jan held the door open while ushering Solange into the rear seat.

The car was pure luxury. Real leather seats, muted music and soft interior lights.

When they were seated the driver pulled away from the curb and gently merged with the train station traffic. He eased the car through streets and intersections until he reached a ramp onto the Autobahn. They sped to an exclusive enclave of homes where the driver turned off and slowed to a halt in the driveway of a large stone manor.

The neighboring properties were just as grand.

"My dear, let me escort you up the stairs."

Jan extended his hand to Solange and as she climbed from the car. He placed his arm over hers to ensure she had a firm grip.

They ascended the huge grand stairway to the ornate front door. It was immediately opened by a youthful man with a huge smile.

"I am sure you are both tired and feeling somewhat in need of freshening up after that long train ride. It can be that way. I know. I have taken it on many occasions."

Jakob was astounded by the décor of the mansion as he walked in. There were antiques and artwork everywhere.

"I will have your bags taken up to the guest room. Let me go with you and show you your room. I want to be sure that it is acceptable to you."

"I am sure it will be fine. I assume it is far better than the accommodation we had on the ship."

Jan laughed. He nodded and again laughed.

"I will never forget you my friend. You were scared. Just like a puppy that is taken away from the litter. I remember the talks we had. I liked you. I was never a Nazi nor could I believe in their propaganda. When you were trying to flee Germany I found that you were like a breath of fresh air. Your view of the world was naive."

"I was trapped. My papers had been stolen. I had no money. I was unable to return to Holland and my wife. I could not get messages to her. I was desperate. I needed help. You were the one who did help. I will never forget that."

Jakob was becoming sentimental. Tears started to run down his cheeks.

"Jakob. I knew that you were basically a good person and would create a great life for you and others. This happened didn't it? I am aware of things you did for that son Hans. I am in contact with the law firm who arranged the deal with you. It was I who suggested they contact you. Hans was in serious trouble in post war Germany. If we couldn't convince you to help him he would have been killed. He was involved with the black market and the theft and brutality of the gangs. I admire what you did to help him. Ilsa will always appreciate the efforts of you and Solange in helping him."

The mention of the name Ilsa brought back sad memories to Jakob. He recalled the afternoon in that cold winter when she had come to him and told her she was pregnant with his child. He was ashamed that after guaranteeing to help her and look after her he fled on the ship from Germany. He despised himself for lying to her about his intentions to help her.

Solange had watched the whole interchange between them.

"Jan if it is fine with you I would like to go to our room. I need to shower and remove the dirt of all that travel. It has been such a long day."

"I will take you both up to the room."

Jan opened the door into a room of splendor. It was light and airy. Vases of flowers and roses adorned the bedside tables.

"Please take your time. I will be in the parlor downstairs. Freshen up and then come and join me. I will have chef prepare a nice meal for us. I am so happy you are here."

Once Jan had left, Solange turned to Jakob.

"Were you aware of this wealth and lifestyle?"

"No. We were crew members on a merchant ship trying hard to avoid the war and atrocities of Nazi Germany."

Solange popped open her suitcase and removed a black gown.

"I am going to take a shower in that opulent bathroom. I will be relaxed and then we will go and join your friend Jan for dinner."

Jakob looked at his disheveled image in the bedroom mirror. He decided that he also needed to cleanup for dinner. He went to the smaller bathroom off the main bedroom and stripped naked. He jumped into the hot shower. A melancholy feeling was coming over him.

When they had both dressed, they went down to join Jan in the parlor. He sat with papers strewn around his feet.

"Jakob I am old and have had enough of all this insanity. I have enough money. I don't want the companies anymore. I want to live now. I worked hard. I helped to rebuild Germany after that fool Hitler tried to destroy us and the world. I have rebuilt businesses that were closed by Hitler's regime. I have donated to help with the construction of hospitals. I want to stop now. I am too old. I want to go and live somewhere without all the needs for me to impress other business leaders. It is nice to have this big expensive house but it doesn't make me happier. I envy you. You were able to escape to a world you liked and created. Now I have said enough let us go and see what Chef has created for us."

Solange reached for Jakob's arm to escort her into the elaborate dining room.

They dined on pheasant and roasted autumn vegetables. A traditional German Black Forest cake dripping kirsch and topped with fresh whipped cream and cherries was served for desert.

Solange was in heaven.

A silver urn of coffee was brought to the table along with three small cups for the coffee.

"Jan it is getting late. I want to make a phone call to Aruba. We have been trying to contact Isaac for the past two days. We need to speak to him as we have a project happening there. There is a five hour difference between Munich and Aruba. Is it possible for me to use a phone to call him?"

Yes. There is a phone in your room. It is in the writing desk. Please call him and anyone else you need to contact."

"I will call him when we go back to our room."

"Now we will go for brandy and a talk in the parlor. That will help you sleep soundly tonight."

For the next thirty minutes, they made small talk, and then Jakob and Solange excused themselves and retreated to their room.

As Solange prepared for bed, Jakob tried phoning Isaac. The phone rang without an answer.

"Solange I fear that something is not right."

Jakob went to his case and took out a small book containing the telephone numbers of friends. He started calling. He tried Carlita, the restaurant, Miguel's home number. No one was answering. He was frustrated.

"Jakob come to bed. They will be there in the morning. Besides we have nothing to do but relax. Your friend Jan is charming. I am surprised some woman hasn't swept him off his feet and claimed him."

Chapter 138

A ringing bell awakened them. Jakob sat up in the bed and then put on his bathrobe. He opened the door. There was nothing unusual. He decided to walk downstairs and determine what the ringing bell meant. As he reached the bottom of the stairs, Jan greeted him.

"I see our breakfast wake up bell has worked. Take your time to dress and then join me. I take my breakfast in the sunroom at the rear of the house."

Jakob wearily crawled back up the stairs and explained the ringing bell to Solange. He crashed back onto the bed. He wanted to sleep more hours.

Solange shook him.

"Jakob he is our host and we are his guests. We should dress and join him. You can always take a nap later this morning."

Jakob agreed. They showered and dressed and went to join Jan.

The breakfast was a simple affair of boiled eggs, toast and juices. A pot of coffee sat on a burner that was fired by some type of liquid fuel.

Even though the previous day had been one of travel and disruption, they were not hungry.

"Jan, if you will excuse my rudeness. I am tired. I have been taking this medication since we were in Florida. It does strange things to me. I need to go back to the room and sleep."

"Please go. You are not a prisoner here. Do what you wish."

"I will stay with Jan. I am not tired. It will give me a chance to know him better without you interrupting."

They all laughed and Jakob left the table to return to the room.

He slept for hours.

Solange sat with Jan and they engaged in a heavy discussion about Jakob and his health. Jan also spoke freely of his time in Germany after the war.

It was one in the afternoon when Solange shook Jakob to awaken him.

"Jakob are you really that tired? You have been sleeping for hours. Do you feel alright? I am worried about you."

"I am alright. The travel has made me tired. Go back to Jan. I will join you in minutes. First I am going to try and reach Isaac."

Reluctantly Solange left him. When she had left the room, Jakob picked up the phone and tried to reach Isaac. There was no answer at his home. This worried Jakob and he hung up.

He decided to call the office of the Klassen businesses. A cheery receptionist answered.

"It is Jakob Klassen. I am looking for Isaac Klassen. Is he there?"

"Yes, sir but we have instructions not to interrupt him at this time."

"Go and get him. Tell him it is his father."

The receptionist was flustered.

"I will go and tell him you are calling. I cannot transfer the call. Please wait as I must go to his office and tell him."

Minutes dragged by before a tired sounding Isaac came onto the line.

"Jakob I am pleased you have called. I did not know where to contact you."

"I have been trying to reach you at home. Please tell me what is going on there. What is happening in Colombia? Have you heard anything?"

"Jakob they rescued Juan. He was taken to Bogota and is now on his way back to Aruba. There is bad news. They were stopped by a patrol from the drug camp. A gunfight happened. Hans was killed."

Jakob dropped the phone and emitted a long and loud cry.

Jan and Solange heard the cry and rushed to the room. Jakob was pale white and gasping for air.

Solange picked up the phone.

"Is this Isaac? What is going on?"

Isaac repeated the news of Hans' death. Solange thanked him and told him they would be calling back after attending to Jakob.

"I will send for my doctor. I do not like the way that Jakob looks or how he is reacting. He has me worried. Let's put him back on the bed. I will ask one of the maids to sit and watch him until the doctor arrives. We will make a plan while we wait."

"I do not have relatives here or in Aruba. I was born in the States. My family is there. Not many met Hans or know his history."

"He was born here in Germany. As you know, Jakob was his father. I have always had contact with the law firm who sent him the letters asking for his help. I know where the mother, Ilsa lives. We will need to tell her of this tragedy."

Chapter 139

A somber mood settled in. Jan Zelder contacted the law firm to advise them of the situation. He told them of Jakob's visit and that they wished to arrange a visit with Ilsa Wolfe.

Jakob was distraught. More than ever he wished to return to his beloved Aruba. He called Isaac Junior again.

"Isaac do you know what is happening with the Narcotics office in Florida? Have you heard anything from Henri? Is the US Coast Guard acting on the situation with that crooked crew of the *Pearl*?"

"I have not heard from anyone. I will call today. Give me your contact information. I will call you back. I wanted to tell you that Moreno has been very active. He is trying to arrange for Hans remains to be sent from Colombia. He needs to know where they should be sent. Should they go to Germany or Aruba?"

"I will discuss this with his mother, Ilsa when we meet later today. I will advise you."

He had just hung up the phone when Jan arrived back in the room.

"I have just had a call from the lawyers. They have scheduled a meeting with Ilsa. We will meet at their offices. There was concern that it will be an emotional meeting and better conducted in a neutral place. Since Solange will be with you and it will be the first time that Ilsa will meet her they are concerned. As you know, Ilsa can be aggressive. Her former days as a wartime prostitute have never left her."

"That is probably best. Will you join us at the meeting? I would like that. Remember I am his father. It was Solange, Isaac and I that helped him to grow into the person he became. I hope Ilsa agrees that Hans be laid to rest in Aruba."

While sitting in the den, Jakob recalled the early years after Hans had arrived in Aruba. It had seemed impossible that Hans would change. He had arrived with attitude and a tendency for crime and violence. It had been a difficult time but in the end it had been worth it. As he sat there the grief of the loss hit him. His eyes welled up and tears continually streamed down his face.

With the loss of Hans, the death and treachery of Alejandro, and his failing health, this had him believing he was being punished for his earlier rebellious life.

It was late afternoon. A servant entered carrying a tray with drinks.

"Mr. Jakob the scotch is for you and Mrs. Solange we took the liberty to make you a Pimms. Please try it. If it is not to your liking we will replace it with a drink of your choosing."

Solange sipped the cool drink from the tall glass. She nodded her appreciation.

"I really like this drink. Thank you."

The servant bowed and left. As he did so, Jan arrived.

"I have heard from the lawyers. We are to meet there in two hours. It is not far. I will arrange for my driver to take us and wait while we meet."

They were sitting and talking about Hans and life when the phone rang. Jan answered and then handed to receiver to Jakob.
"It is Isaac."

"Isaac. What have you learned?"

"I have found out a lot. Do you have the time to speak now? This will take some time."

"Yes. I have the time."

"I spoke with Connelly at the Narcotics office in Florida. Things have been moving quickly. Jeremiah Slate and Hector Rodriguez are cooperating fully with the FBI and other authorities. They have provided evidence of the piracy aboard the *Pearl*. The authorities have dates, details of the theft of contraband from the intercepts, details on the murder of Alejandro, dates and places of the meetings in Venezuela with the Palermo brothers. There is much more. Your suspicions about the Commercial Loan were correct. They were able to monitor and trace deposits that were large and unexplainable. Mr. Jim Mastronardi was arrested while he was in Florida. He is in isolation and has no contact with either the Palermos or the mob in Chicago. The FBI and Narcotics people have been able to identify the businesses in Aruba that were infiltrated and coerced to cooperate. Our friend Henri is chomping at the bit to get his name in the paper as a key force in cracking the drug running. The FBI got a court order stopping him from disclosing any information. He is livid.

Moreno has the situation in Colombia under control. He has been working with a military officer named Antonio who was able to convince some Colombian officials to act on the drug lab and to help in retrieving Hans' body.

Jakob, it is time for you and Solange to return to Aruba. Remember I have that trip I need to make. I need to leave soon."

"Isaac, you must tell us where you are going."

"I cannot Jakob. It is for all of us, but mainly for you."

"What is taking place to stop the Palermos?"

"They told me a raid in conjunction with the Venezuelan police is planned. It may happen in the next few days. "

"I need you to contact Benita. She promised to be there when the raid occurs. She will write about the drugs labs in Colombia, the financing of them and the corruption of officials through the Palermos. She will emphasize how

Aruba was compromised and used as a drug trafficking point. It is important for you to get her involved now."

Isaac agreed and after some light conversation about his family he hung up.

Jakob sat thinking of how everything was inter connected and wondered if this strike would end the infiltration of the organized crime into Aruba,

As he pondered this, Jan arrive back dressed in a long warm coat.

"Jakob it is time for us to go."

Chapter 140

It was just getting dark as they pulled up the law offices. Jan again jumped from the car and held the door open for Solange. After Jakob exited they walked across the street level pathway and knocked at the door. It was opened by an efficient assistant.

"You must be the Klassen and Zelder party. Please follow me."

She accompanied them to a conference room that resembled more of a hotel suite than an office in a law firm.

Five minutes passed until she returned with an older woman.

Jakob was shocked. The years had not been kind to Ilsa. Her skin was pale and not an inch had been spared from the wrinkling. He noted that there were large black hairs growing beneath her chin.

Ilsa walked briskly into the room. She stopped in front of Solange.

"So you must be the Mrs. Klassen. Good luck to you. Is he still a liar and an impossible man?"

Solange smiled. She was unsure how to respond. Jakob spoke up.

"And it's nice to see you again after all these years. Yes this is Solange. She has been eager to meet you."

"She must be stupid then."

"No not at all. She wanted to meet the mother of the fine man that Hans turned out to be."

"Hans was nothing but a problem for me. I suppose I must thank the two of you for the help you gave him. His life here in Germany after the war was too hard."

"I am sure you know why we are here. Hans was killed while assisting in the rescue of a kidnapped friend in Colombia."

"Yes I am aware of that. It is tragic. What are the plans for a service?"

"We are trying to have his body sent from Colombia. Do you want to have him here in Germany?"

"No. Germany was not good to him. Please take him to Aruba. He loved it there. He did write to me occasionally. In those letters he would describe his life. He sounded really happy."

"I will be returning to Aruba in the next couple of days. Would you like to join us and attend the service there?"

"I will think about it. I can't just run off like that. I am an important woman with real responsibilities."

Jakob thought how lucky he was to have run away from her when he found out she was pregnant with Hans. His life would have been hell. He wondered what his uncle Josef had seen in her.

"We are staying at the Zelder home. Please let us know of your decision. You are welcome to travel with us and stay in our home in Aruba."

"As I said, I will think about it. Jakob, do you remember that assistant the Josef had. The one named Sabine. She is in a female monastery here. I speak to her from time to time. She always asks about you. I think you should visit her. The monastery is quite close to the Zelder home."

"I never understood her. She was a loyal member of the Nazi party. She knew the SS were on their way to Josef's house and could have stopped us. She had a gun but instead she let us escape."

"She spared your life. I suggest you see her and thank her for what she did."

Ilsa stood and turned to the door. The meeting was over.

"Jakob, that explains a lot of why Hans was such a hard character to help. He had a streak in him from her and the stubborn streak from you."

Jan Zelder had sat and observed the meeting. He was disturbed by her mannerisms. He had known Ilsa for years and never experienced such meanness.

"I doubt she will go to Aruba with you two. I suspect she is hurting and seeing you again did not help her, Jakob. I found her comment about the nun Sabine interesting. I think you should go and see her. The monastery where she resides is less than ten minutes from the house."

"I will go to thank her. I will take Solange with me to meet the woman who spared my life."

"I would like that Jakob. I wonder if there is anything we can do for her? Jan, can you think of anything?"

"No. Those nuns are self sufficient. To try and do anything would be seen as an insult. I suggest we phone and ask to see her. We can do that this evening from home."

On the way back to the house, Jan suggested they stop at his club for dinner. He instructed the driver to take them there.

The club was located in an old castle. It had been spared the destruction that had been so common due to the Allies constant bombardment during the war. It was a grand building.

When they entered it soon became clear to Jakob and Solange that Jan was a well respected member of the club. He was greeted by everyone. Offers were made to take their coats and Jan was asked if he wanted any special table or meal prepared.

When they were seated, Jan ordered a round of dry martinis.

After the drinks arrived they sat chatting about the meeting with Ilsa.

"Jakob I was embarrassed for you. There was no need for her to speak to Solange or you in that manner. She may have inherited Josef's businesses and fortune, but she has no right to carry on like that."

"Do not worry about it. We have more urgent matters to deal with back in Aruba."

Jakob launched into the story of the drugs, crime and mob activity that seemed to be spreading in Aruba. Jan listened intently.

"I think you should visit with the nun and return soon. You will need to be there to arrange a service for Hans and it seems that you have been an important part of the effort to stop the problems that are happening there. I will not be offended by you leaving. In fact I may come with you. I loved the Caribbean when we sailed there. I would like to visit it again. Besides the cold bleak winter months are arriving here."

"You are welcome to stay at our home. I'm not sure it will compare to the grandiose of your mansion."

Chapter 141

Plates of pork schnitzel with spaetzle were delivered to the table.

"I thought it appropriate to order a real Bavarian food while you are here. Enjoy."

Dinner conversation was comprised of small talk. Jan recalled some of the troubles that he had found himself in with Jakob when they had sailed together. He told the story of the fight they were in Colombia. He took particular delight in ensuring that Solange knew that it was Jakob who caused it by paying too much attention to a pretty girl and then openly flirting with her in front of her hot tempered Latino boyfriend. He laughed as he told her of the destruction and the subsequent visit from the corrupt police who tried to benefit themselves from the chaos.

Solange pretended to be shocked that Jakob could have done such a thing.

With dinner finished, they left the club to return to Jan's house.

Jan went to find the telephone number for the nun's monastery. He called the number and explained that they wanted to visit Sabine, but did not know the religious name she had adopted. The elderly nun who answered advised him that she was known as Sister Angelica.

Jan asked to speak with her.

"I am sorry she is in evening prayers. You will need to phone again in an hour. They will be done then and that is when they have their leisure time."

Jan politely thanked her and hung up.

An hour later, Jakob called the monastery and asked for Sister Angelica. She came to the phone. With her thick German accent she inquired who was calling.

"It is Jakob Klassen. Do you remember me from Josef's house? I would like to come and visit you. Is that possible?"

There was a long silence before she replied.

"Yes of course. Can you come tomorrow morning? I have chores early in the morning so please come after ten. I look forward to seeing you again."

"Can I bring my wife to introduce her? I have told her a lot about you."

"Yes. She must wear a head covering though."

"We will see you tomorrow. Goodnight."

Jakob hung up and told Jan and Solange of the arrangement.

"It will be interesting to meet this woman. I wonder why she allowed you and Josef to escape. That could have cost her life or other punishment."

Jakob decided to excuse himself and retire for the night. Solange agreed and joined him.

They slept heavily and in the morning rose to find that Jan was downstairs already and a breakfast had been prepared.

"Good morning sleepy heads. Join me for breakfast and then we must prepare to leave for the monastery. Should I join you or do you just want my driver to take you?"

"I think it best if just Solange and I go. She sounded hesitant on the phone. I detected a little reluctance when I mentioned that I would like to take Solange to meet her."

"That is no problem. I understand. I will ask Günter to drive you and wait for you until you are ready to return. Have a nice time. This afternoon I have a special treat for you Solange. I will keep it a secret for now. I look forward to watching your reaction."

Solange asked Jan why he was teasing her.

Jakob and Solange were dressed conservatively for the visit. Solange had selected a light grey skirt and jacket. She wore a string of pearls around her neck. Jakob was dressed in casual dark grey trousers and wore a navy sports jacket. They put on their coats and walked out to the waiting car.

Günter greeted them and carefully drove them toward a rural area. There were cliffs that seemed to rise directly from pastures.

They turned a sharp corner and arrived at a property with a high hedge shielding it from view. In the middle was a narrow entrance. Günter pulled in and they slowly drove up to the monastery. He parked off to the side of the main entrance.

At the top of the stairs there was a huge heavy wooden door. A bell was mounted on the side. Jakob rang the bell and waited. The door was opened by a young fresh faced nun.

"We are here to visit Sister Angelica."

"Yes. She is expecting you. Please come in and I will take you to our visiting room."

They followed her down a passageway and were ushered into a sunlit waiting room. There were two other nuns in the room who were speaking quietly. From the difference in the habits they were wearing, Jakob guessed one was visiting.

The door opened and Sabine walked in. She was dressed in the old style habit. Her head was covered with a head dress and she wore the traditional long brown tunic. She smiled and headed toward them. Introductions were made. Suddenly in rage and out of jealousy Sabine flew at

Solange. From inside her scapular she pulled a knife. She lunged at Solange. At the same time she was shouting.

"Jakob you fool. It was you I wanted all the time. You ignored me. We had sex at Josef's. You liked me then. I saved your lives and you just went away and ignored me. Then you married this thing. How could you?"

The knife found the critical point on Solange's throat. It slashed into her jugular vein. Blood spurted from the wound. Solange crumpled to her knees. Jakob rushed to her and dropped onto his knees. He tried to compress her vein to slow the bleeding but was all in vain. Solange's head rolled and she ceased breathing.

The two nuns who had been talking rushed and grabbed Sabine. Jakob rushed to them and took Sabine in a tight hold.

"Go and get help. Please hurry. I think Solange is dead."

Sabine struggled and fought with him. He decided to calm her. He raised his hand and with a swift chop to the back of her neck hit her hard. She passed out. He pulled her across the floor and pushed her onto a chair. He removed his leather belt and tied her firmly to a chair.

He returned to Solange. It was too late. She was dead. There was no pulse. Jakob was devastated.

The room filled with nuns. There were gasps and cries. In the distance Jakob heard the wail of a siren as the police sped toward the monastery. He sat and buried his face in his hands. It was going to be a long and painful day.

Chapter 142

The police drove Jakob back to Jan's house. Before they reached the door Jan was on the front steps rushing to assist Jakob. He escorted him into the den and motioned to the policemen to come in.

For the next three hours the police took details. Jakob told them in detail of the time at Josef's house and his brief affair with her. He told them of her association with the Nazis.

The police took pages of notes from Jakob. They were baffled.

As the interviews were ending, Jakob asked the police if he would be able to travel back to Aruba for the funeral service for Hans.

Jan observed that Jakob was at a breaking point. He stepped in and asked the police for private time. They agreed and packed their notebooks and cases and left.

"Jakob are you alright? I am worried about you. What do you want to do?"

"I want to take Solange home to Aruba. She belongs there. This trip to Europe has not worked out the way I hoped. I want to go home and be with the fine son that Solange and I created. I am tired. I have no more fight left in me.

What is the point of living now? I have lost a son and a wife."

"Tomorrow morning I will contact the police and others whom I know. We will make arrangements to transport Solange home."

"I must make some phone calls. I need to tell Isaac Junior of this situation. I will need to contact her sister in Florida."

"If you want privacy, please use my office."

"I would like that."

Jan showed Jakob into the office. Jakob sat at the desk and took the phone to start the calls.

He first dialed Isaac.

"Isaac it is me, Jakob."

"I am pleased you called I have more to tell you about the planned raids."

Jakob cut him off.
"Isaac, stop. What I have to tell you is not good. Solange was murdered this afternoon."

There was silence.

"How? Why? What happened?"

Jakob told Isaac the details. He heard the sobs and a click as Isaac disconnected the line.

The next call was to the sister in Florida. He called on the private number. The phone was answered by Henri.

"Jakob it is great to hear from you. Isn't it good news about the investigation? I am so happy you pushed so hard. I am sure this news will help get me elected."

"Henri, please stop. We have a serious matter to discuss. Solange was murdered this morning."

Jakob listened as Henri placed his hand over the receiver and relayed the news to his wife and Solange's sister, Yolanda. Jakob heard the loud scream.

"Jakob where are you? We can come to you."

"No. I am in Germany. I will be making arrangements to take Solange's body home to Aruba. I will leave here in the next couple of days. Things have been bad. My son Hans was killed in Colombia during the rescue of Juan from that drug lab. We will have a service for him in Aruba."

"Jakob, please hold as Yolanda wishes to speak with you."

"I am so sorry. I am heartbroken. Solange was my favorite in the family. I am so upset. What can we do?"

Jakob repeated the information he had told Henri.

"No Jakob. She will not be buried in Aruba. She was born in America and that is where she will be buried. I will not have it any other way. She is my sister and I insist you honor our wishes. We have many family members here who will want to attend her service."

"I am sorry you feel that way. She is my wife and she will be buried in Aruba. She has many friends there. She helped many in the community. She hardly knew any of your family. I will tell you when arrangements have been made. I told Henri there will also be another service. My son Hans was killed attempting a rescue of a man imprisoned into forced labor in Colombia. Yolanda I have had enough right now. We will speak later."

Jakob hung up the phone. He was about to leave Jan's office when he stopped. He returned and dialed the number. The phone at the other end rang and a happy female voice greeted him.

Jakob sobbed as he told Carlita the horrible news. She too started crying. The news would affect many in Aruba. It would be a sad day when the news was published.

Jakob returned to the den to find Jan sitting and working through some papers. He lay them down.

"I have made a decision. Since I sold my machine shops and made all this money I was busy and enjoyed life. I am a little bored now. I have decided that I am going to go with you to Aruba. I will accompany you and Solange back. I want to be there for the service for Hans. "

He could not believe the dedication of his old friend Jan. They had not seen each other in years but the bond was so strong it was like they were together just yesterday.

"I would like that very much. You are a true friend."

"I told you that when I sold the companies we made a lot of money. It is more than I will use before I die. I intend to use some for us. I am going to hire a private jet to fly us all back to Aruba. Solange needs to go in style."

"That is generous. Are you sure?"

"Yes. I have no desire to be the wealthy one under the headstone."

"What do we need to do to get Solange released to us? What papers need to be prepared?"

"I have contacts that will assist with all the necessary documents and ensure the correct procedures are followed."

Jakob told Jan of the phone call with Henri and Yolanda. He shook his head.

"This is not the time for that type of thing. You are right. You are her husband and the two of you spent years together bringing up a family, building a business and helping others. I doubt her family did much. Don't worry about it."

Chapter 143

All the arrangements were handled by the professionals that Jan hired. The police were satisfied with Jakob's statements. Sabine was taken and admitted to a high security mental facility.

With everything satisfactorily completed, Jakob and Jan left Munich for the long flight to Aruba. The pilots had told Jan of the necessity to stop for refueling. They had selected Gander, Newfoundland. It was a refueling stop for airlines, private charters and military planes. They were advised of the requirement to clear with Canadian Customs.

Jan and Jakob settled in for the flight to Newfoundland.

The events of the last few days crept over Jakob and he fell into a deep sleep. He slept for hours. Shortly before their descent into Gander, Jan shook him awake.

"We are about to land. Did you sleep well? We will need to get off the plane here while they refuel. The pilots tell me that there has been a snowstorm here and the temperatures are cold enough to require them to deice the plane. When we leave Gander it is a short flight of less than five hours. We will be in Aruba for breakfast."

"If we can get a time, I will phone Isaac from the airport to tell him when to expect us."

The pilot opened the cockpit door and looked back.

"Gentlemen we are starting our approach. We should be on the ground within two to three minutes. There is no other traffic. We are the only aircraft landing and refueling. We should be out of here in thirty minutes."

The landing was smooth. The pilots taxied the plane across to an austere looking building and shut down the engines. They waited until a representative of the Canada Customs came aboard.

"Welcome to Canada. Have you any goods to declare? Are there any firearms on board? Will you be leaving any items in Canada? How long will you be here? Will any of you leave the aircraft?"

The pilot had left his seat and joined Jan and Jakob in the cabin.

"No. It is a simple refuel and go situation. During the refuel we will need to deplane and wait."

"There is an area for you to wait. It is secure and since you will not be leaving it there is no further requirement for clearance. Have a nice evening and continued flight."

As they were leaving the plane, a tanker rolled up to perform the refuel. They entered the sparse waiting area and stood around waiting for the job to be completed. The pilot was approached and signed forms related to the refuel and customs declarations.

They were cleared to return to the plane and rolled across the tarmac to an area where large yellow trucks with booms waited. They stopped and waited as the trucks moved slowly along the side of the aircraft spraying deicing fluid. The process was over in ten minutes and the engines whined as the pilots increased the thrust to taxi for the takeoff.

Jakob heard the radio crackling in the cockpit. He watched as the pilot spoke to air traffic control.

"We have been cleared for a fast flight path to Aruba. We will be heading over the ocean the whole way as we fly south. The estimated arrival time will be four hours and thirty minutes from now."

Both Jakob and Jan relaxed and drifted to sleep.

They started their descent into Aruba at ten in the morning. Jakob looked out the planes window at the sights he loved. He watched as they flew over Malmok and the white sands of Palm Beach. He loved the color of the turquoise ocean below them. He watched as the winds bent and tossed the tall palm trees. He saw the red dirt of the land along tracks and edges of the road they crossed. He was finally home.

The engines ceased their whine and the plane smoothly drifted into the airport.

They taxied across to the small white building that served as a terminal. The plane stopped and the pilots cut the engines. The copilot came back from the cockpit and opened the door. A rush of warm humid air flowed into the plane.

They sat and waited. After ten minutes Jakob decided they needed to take action. He stood and walked down a set of rickety stairs to the tarmac. He was surprised to see a uniformed group of men approaching the plane.

Jakob, Jan and the pilots stood and waited beside the plane.

The group of men stopped in a precise line. It was the Chief of Police and some of the governing politicians. The Chief stood to attention and the men behind him saluted.

"It is with great sorrow that we accept back a loyal and true Aruban. Solange Klassen will never be forgotten for the contributions she made to us here in Aruba. My men are here to escort Solange from the plane to the vehicle that will take her for burial."

Jakob was humbled. He turned away so that the others could not see the depth of his agony and despair. He started to walk around to the cargo area of the plane to be there when the coffin containing Solange was released. The Chief joined him.

"Jakob this is the wrong time to discuss things, but I thank you. Please read the newspapers. The United States raided the Venezuelan mafia. They got them all. They have given us all the names of the men they put into our Aruban businesses. You have achieved so much. I cannot thank you enough. Now I will have two of my men take you to your home."

On the way to the Malmok house, Jakob asked the driver to stop. He ran into a Chinese grocery store and snatched up a number of newspapers. He dropped some American dollars on the counter. The owner grinned and burst forth in the Chinese language. Jakob didn't understand a word.

Back in the police car, Jakob looked at the papers. In Papiamento, Spanish and Dutch the headlines screamed the arrests and raids on mafia in Venezuela and Aruba. The photos were graphic. There were pictures of men dragged from offices, photos of piles of money and drugs and one of the Commercial Loan Bank of Aruba. Jakob tried to read the stories but his Papiamento was inadequate. He thumbed through the papers and found a picture of Juan being pulled through the fence as they escaped the drug lab in Colombia. He looked at the story written below the pictures and read the name of Benita Flores. He smiled to himself. She had delivered on her promise.

He showed the papers to Jan and explained what had happened and his role in the whole affair. Jan looked at him in disbelief. He had problems reconciling that the Jakob he knew then was the same one involved in this situation. Jan remembered the serious talk that he had with Jakob on the deck of the ship when Jakob was drifting and unable to find himself. He was proud of how Jakob had left the turmoil of the war and established a life.

Thirty minutes later they stopped at the bottom of the driveway into Jakob's house. He stepped from the police car and stood looking at the house he had built for Solange.

It would never be the same.

He slowly stared up to the house. Before he entered he dropped to his knees and prayed. Jan watched from a discreet distance behind.

He walked up to Jakob and placed a hand on his shoulder.

"Jakob, the pain will pass. You will find a new life. I know. I have been there."

Chapter 144

Days passed into weeks. Things had changed in Jakob's absence.

Moreno and Isaac had introduced Antonio to Jakob. They told him that he was the person who had saved their mission to rescue Juan.

They described how Antonio had assisted Adrien and obtained the materials they needed to succeed.

Finally Isaac spoke.

"He is a quality man. I want him on our team here"

Jakob accepted their recommendation. He was too preoccupied with other matters.

 The services for Hans and Solange were held. Jakob was celebrated as a man who wished to save and help Aruba develop.

Each day he and Jan would walk the beach and swim. He was happy again. Jan had decided to sell his home in Germany and live in the paradise of Aruba.

Isaac had changed. He visited with Jakob often. It was on one of these visits that Jakob asked.

"Where were you going? You were secretive and both Solange and I were worried. Can you tell me?"

"It really is unimportant. Now that Hans and Solange are gone there is no point. I was negotiating with a group of Swiss investors. I was to go there. It was all confidential and secret. We had planned to establish a mental health facility here to treat not only our people but to have an international reputation with some of the best doctors, equipment and medicines available. I was trying to have something in Aruba that made us a force in the world. I have failed."

Jakob and Jan looked at each other and then back to Isaac.

"If you believe in this dream you must follow it."

The day was growing old. Jakob turned to Jan.

"It's time for us. Let's go. He will be waiting."

With the sun setting over the Caribbean they walked down to the white sand beach.

Off to the west, the sun was slide down toward the horizon. For some reason the sun seemed huge this day. It was a large shimmering orange ball throwing its heat and rays across the Caribbean Sea.

Gentle pale blue-green waves lapped at the white sand shore and a warm breeze blew from the land.

Jakob walked over to the old log that had washed ashore on the beach many years earlier. He recalled sitting there with his friends.

He kicked at the sand with his bare feet and then gradually eased himself down onto the log.

They sat there in silence. All three of them looked out at the sea. Nobody spoke.

Jakob felt her hand rub across his back and shoulders. It was a gentle caress. He reached up and slid his hand around her waist. As he did so she responded. He looked up and into the soft brown eyes of Benita. He had fallen completely in love.

The three old men sat on the log.

Jan Zelder, Juan and Jakob Klassen.

Each had lived a different life.

Each had a different story to tell.

Epilogue

Throughout history, the Caribbean has been the region that has seen pirates, bloodshed, wars and smuggling.

The climate in the surrounding countries and islands provides excellent conditions for the cultivation of marijuana, coca and other drugs. Additionally, many of the countries have dense vegetation which makes it easy to conceal these activities.

Given Aruba's proximity to Venezuela and Colombia, it became an ideal location to trans- ship drugs to North America and Europe. Aruba's relationship with the Netherlands and frequent air and sea links provided drug traffickers with an ideal base to operate from.

In 1959, after Fidel Castro kicked the Mafia and the casinos out of Cuba, efforts were made by them to find alternative islands upon which to establish. Aruba was one such island. At the time the political system was loose and corrupt. Gambling and other vices came to the island and criminal activities grew throughout the sixties. It wasn't until in the late 1996 when then President Bill Clinton took action and placed Aruba on the list of Major Illicit Drug-transfer countries that the government took steps to control the situation. An excellent article was published The Trans National Institute regarding the Mafia involvement in Aruba. It is available on the Internet at https://www.tni.org/en/paper/rothschilds-mafia-aruba

Another article published in the New York Times also details the use of Aruba as a transit point for drug smuggling.

https://www.nytimes.com/1985/04/03/world/sunny-aruba-draws-the-drug-smuggling-crowd.html

Significant steps have been taken to intercept and confiscate the shipments of drugs and smuggled items; however shipments are still seized today. Strict money laundering controls have been implemented, but it is rumored that they are somewhat ineffective for the powerful organized crime syndicates.

Aruba has evolved into a formidable tourist destination with many flights from the US, Canada, Europe and South America on a daily basis. Cruise ships have included Aruba as a destination and bring over a million passengers a year to visit Aruba.

CPSIA information can be obtained
at www.ICGtesting.com
Printed in the USA
LVHW031442030419
612835LV00001B/123/P